HIT LIST

Chris Ryan was born near Newcastle in 1961. He joined the SAS in 1984. During his ten years there he was involved in overt and covert operations and was also Sniper team commander of the anti-terrorist team. During the Gulf War, Chris was the only member of an eight-man team to escape from Iraq, of which three colleagues were killed and four captured. It was the longest escape and evasion in the history of the SAS. For his last two years he has been selecting and training potential recruits for the SAS.

He wrote about his experiences in the bestseller *The One That Got Away* which was also adapted for screen. He is also the author of the bestsellers *Stand By, Stand By, Zero Option, The Kremlin Device, Tenth Man Down, The Hit List, The Watchman, Land of Fire, Greed, The Increment, Blackout, Ultimate Weapon, Strike Back, Firefight* and *Who Dares Wins. Chris Ryan's SAS Fitness Book, Chris Ryan's Ultimate Survival Guide* and *Fight to Win* are also published by Century.

He lectures in business motivation and security and is currently working as a bodyguard in America.

CHRIS RYAN

HIT LIST

arrow books

Reissued in the United Kingdom by Arrow Books in 2008

11

Copyright © Chris Ryan, 2000

First published in the United Kingdom in 2000 by Century
First published in paperback in 2001 by Arrow Books

Arrow Books
The Random House Group Limited
20 Vauxhall Bridge Road, London, SW1V 2SA

Addresses for companies within The Random House Group Limited can be
found at: www.randomhouse.co.uk/offices.htm

The Random House Group Limited Reg. No. 954009

www.rbooks.co.uk

A CIP catalogue record for this book
is available from the British Library

ISBN 9780099460145

The Random House Group Limited supports The Forest Stewardship
Council (FSC), the leading international forest certification organisation. All
our titles that are printed on Greenpeace approved FSC certified paper carry
the FSC logo. Our paper procurement policy can be found at
www.rbooks.co.uk/environment

Typeset by MATS, Southend-on-Sea, Essex
Printed and bound in Great Britain by
CPI Bookmarque Ltd, Croydon, CR0 4TD

ACKNOWLEDGEMENTS

All the usual suspects, Barbara, Mark, Luke, Hannah and all the rest of the team at Century.

To Sarah

If you believe in the light, it's because of the darkness
If you believe in the truth, it's because of their lies
If you believe in God, then you must believe in the **DEVIL**

PROLOGUE

Tuesday 5 November 1991
Eastern Atlantic, due South of Gran Canaria

The two men surfaced noiselessly. Raising their diving masks they scanned the area around them. Nothing, only the pale bulk of the *Lady Ghislaine* and the soft slap of the sea against her hull. It was 4.30am, and although no hint of dawn showed at the horizon both men knew that time was limited.

As they watched, a dark figure showed for a moment against the dimly illuminated windows of the stateroom. Moments later a man appeared from the stern door, a white dressing gown belted around his considerable waist. Clearly restless, he stood at the rail for several minutes. The night air appeared to offer him no relief, however, for after a brief circuit of the stern deck he turned abruptly on his heel and went back inside.

In the water the men glanced at each other. The older of the two, his features streaked and obscured by camouflage cream, raised a hand above the surface and tapped the armoured glass face of his watch. The younger man nodded. As one, they moved towards the yacht's stern. Below them, motionless and invisible, waited the two-man Odyssea submarine in which, four hours earlier, they had commenced their silent journey.

It had been a long stalk, but not a difficult one. The word 'yacht' as applied to the *Lady Ghislaine* was a serious understatement – if she had been in commercial ownership she would have been called a cruise liner. She had five gleaming decks, weighed 430 tons, and was over 150 feet in length. Her swimming pool could quite comfortably have accommodated six topless models dressed as mermaids, and indeed – to the raucous delight of an invited party of *Daily Mirror* executives – had once done just that. She was, to say the least, a visible target. And an unsuspecting one. No one was manning her radar that night.

The *Lady Ghislaine* had set sail from Gibraltar on the Thursday. It had taken her crew two days to sail to Madeira, where the yacht had made anchor at Funchal. There, operatives from London were already in place and working on their tans. They had tailed the target to Desertas beach, where he swam without apparent pleasure, and later to the Central Casino, where he lost a little over £9000 sterling at blackjack.

On Sunday, the yacht had sailed towards Tenerife, reaching Darcene Pesquera at 10.00am the following day. Within the hour it had set off again southwards –

the target remaining aboard throughout. His non-appearence was hardly surprising — by then the international press corps had learned what the target himself had known for some time: that his business empire was on the verge of meltdown. The Swiss bank he used was threatening to call in the fraud squad. His creditors were beginning to panic.

That was the point at which London had put the two-man diving team on stand-by, when they'd flown the miniature submarine into Layounne on the Moroccan coast.

By Monday evening the *Lady Ghislaine* was back in Santa Cruz. The target himself was ashore, eating *pil-pil* in the dining room at the Hotel Mencey. There had been a suggestion that the hit might be carried out right there and then — the concern being that he might take a car down to Los Christianos where the Gulf-stream jet was fuelled and ready to fly him back to London. In the event, however, the hit team held back, and to their relief the target returned to the yacht after his meal and ordered the crew to set sail. By then a concealed transmitting device was on board, and from the moment they left port the *Lady Ghislaine*'s course was relayed via geo-positioning satellites to the mission's command vessel five miles to the north.

The final go-ahead came from London at 11.55. It was a calm moonless night, and the Odyssea submarine slipped away from the command vessel around midnight. The wet-sub was a customised craft, built in Florida and refitted at a secret base on the East Anglian coast. It carried 500 cubic feet of onboard oxygen and its powerful batteries enabled it to cover up to twelve miles at a rate of two knots per hour. The wet-sub wouldn't have won any races, but it was perfectly adapted to its primary function of covert naval approach. Twelve miles was well outside the target's detection range.

Using a suction device, the younger of the two divers tethered the Odyssea's tow-line to the yacht. None of the crew seemed to be on watch, he noticed – perhaps the target had insisted that the decks be cleared for his own use. Shrugging off his oxygen-tanks and regulator, moving with the silence and fluency of long practice, he locked it into the specially adapted housing behind the Odyssea's left-hand seat. Beside him, his partner lowered his own gear to the right-hand housing.

From a pouch round his waist the older man removed two magnetic clamps. A cord ran between these clamps and from this he suspended a heavy equipment bag and his fins. Watching as his partner rid himself of his own fins, positioned a collapsible caving ladder against the stern rail and silently shinned up it, the older man opened the equipment bag. Taking care to avoid the percussion of steel on steel, he withdrew two MP5 sub-machine guns, extended their folding stocks, and passed them up to his waiting colleague. Crouching on the varnished teak deck the men prepared their weapons, wincing at the oily clicks as the twenty-round magazines snapped home. Ears straining for the slightest sound – a footfall, an opening door – they drew back and locked the cocking levers.

The target shivered and pulled the towelling dressing gown more tightly around himself. He'd just phoned the bridge to ask for the air-conditioning to be adjusted by a couple of degrees. It was still warm outside, despite the time, but here in the stateroom the air had become uncomfortably cold. It was too cold to sleep, and sleep was what he craved most. A few hours' escape from the pressure – from the desperate worry of his debts, from the inexorable progress of the fraud investigation, from the certainty that the coming share sell-offs would leave his empire in ruins.

He was still one of the most powerful men in the world, but tonight he knew that the end was close. Part of him wished that this journey could go on for ever – just the sea and the sky and the soft thrum of the engines. But he knew that all of that would end within hours. Instead he would be flying back to London for one desperate last stand. Like Custer, he thought wryly – and look what happened to Custer.

Approaching his dressing-table, Maxwell bowed and examined his hair. The roots were growing out again – a centimetre of iron-grey now showed beneath the black dye. Would the law courts have his scalp as well as his dignity? There was little chance he could salvage anything now. If he was lucky, he might escape with a couple of million. And the house, perhaps. And maybe a couple of cars. Living expenses? He shrugged. He was bored with restaurant cooking, and he had all the Savile Row suits he'd need to see him out. But there would be no more helicopters, no more chummy Pall Mall lunches with ministers, no more Fleet Street boardrooms falling silent as he entered. Face it, he told himself, there was a better than even chance he'd have to stand trial, and maybe even go to jail. He'd done things that no lawyer – not even the most urbane of silks – could possibly defend. Face it, he repeated, it was over. This was the endgame, the king brought down by a battalion of pawns. Checkmate.

Or was it? Was his last desperate gambit going to pay off? Was the wildest card he'd ever played going to win the trick for him?

There was a light knock on the door. Some problem with the air-conditioning, he supposed. And he'd told the captain – ordered him, dammit – that he wasn't to be disturbed. Wearily he made his way to the door.

It crashed against him as he turned the handle. Next moment it had been closed behind him and he was being dragged back into the room. He tried to struggle, but his arms were pinned in an iron grip behind his back. There was a crackling sound, and an excruciating pain jolted through his kidneys. He doubled up, retching, and as he tried feebly to straighten lost control of his bladder, warm urine coursed down his leg.

Dizzy with pain and shame, his throat stinging with

bile, he sank to a sitting position on the bed. The dressing gown had fallen open, but he was too shocked to cover himself.

The two figures withdrew to the centre of the pale blue Isphahan carpet. Wiping his smarting eyes and running nose with his sleeve, Maxwell saw to his astonishment that both wore black neoprene wetsuits and carried automatic weapons slung in chest harnesses. Their faces were tiger-striped with camouflage cream. The younger man carried some sort of electric prod.

'Mr Maxwell,' said the older man, his eyes expressionless. 'Please sit still. This is your last warning. If you call for help or or try to escape, we will hurt you very badly indeed. To avoid that, just sit still and answer my questions. Do you understand?'

Robert Maxwell nodded. Anger was slowly beginning to replace humiliation. He drew the dressing gown closed around himself. Who the hell were these people? He had any amount of corporate enemies, but none of them would try a stunt like this. Were they Romanians? Mossad? He spoke quickly in Hebrew: '*Ma perush hadaver haze?*'

The two men looked at him blankly. The older man stepped forward. 'Mr Maxwell, we don't have much time. We need answers to our questions, and we need them right away. I think you know who we are.'

'I haven't the first idea who you are – and nor, for that matter, have I got any cash in this room. You're welcome to my credit cards, though – my wallet's in the pocket of that—'

'Mr Maxwell, you know who we are.'

The voice was anonymous, but unmistakably that of a born English speaker. A faint burr – West Country? Bristol? – but overlaid by the flatter vowels of the Thames estuary. Could they be MI6? Surely not. If those people wanted information from him they just had to pick up the phone, and they knew it.

'Mr Maxwell, I am instructed to tell you that Dietrich Wegner wants his property back.'

That name. After all these years, that name. The jolt of understanding which slammed through Robert Maxwell at that moment was worse than the electronic prod. He was as good as dead. He looked at them. Saw they knew that he knew.

Seeing Maxwell's shoulders slump, confident that the last vestiges of fight had departed him, the younger man returned the prod to his belt. Beside him the older man unzipped a waterproof pouch that he was carrying round his neck. The silence between the stateroom's three occupants was intimate, almost conspiratorial.

How would they do it? Maxwell wondered. Surely they wouldn't use their weapons? It would make a godawful racket and they'd have to kill the entire crew. But a glance at the tiger-striped faces above him told him that, if necessary, they would do just that. By nightfall they'd be the other side of the Channel, probably watching *Match of the Day* over a couple of Special Brews. My God, he thought. If there was ever a lethal race put on this Earth it was the English.

He knew what they wanted, of course. He knew

what they were looking for. He considered stalling and playing for time, but realised that the longer the whole charade lasted, the greater the danger to the rest of those aboard. Any crew members up and about when the men left the ship would be gunned down. And if one died, the rest would have to go too; there could be no witnesses. No, better to go quietly, hope it was fast, and limit the deaths to his own. The fear had gone now – all that was left was a quiet surprise that it could all end like this.

The older man glanced at his watch and out of the curtained window.

So that was how it was to be, thought Maxwell. The sea. No thumb to the jugular, no punch of silenced bullets, just the cold waters of dawn. And these two anonymous soldiers of his adopted country drawing him down to the darkness and the end of all worry.

'Mr Maxwell,' the older man said, 'before we bring this to a close, I'd like you to open your safe and give me the photographs you keep inside.'

Maxwell didn't move.

Seeing his hesitation the younger man's hand wandered towards the electric prod.

Maxwell walked heavily across the pale blue carpet, lifted down a framed *Private Eye* cartoon of himself as 'Cap'n Bob', and spun the dial of a small wall-safe. Taking out a sheaf of fragile-looking black-and-white photographs he handed them to the older man who placed them in the waterproof pouch.

'Close the safe. Put the picture back.'

He did as he was bid.

'Thank you, Mr Maxwell. Now I'm going to ask you to take off your robe.'

Slowly, Maxwell obeyed. He touched the appliquéd blue 'Lady Ghislaine' on the breast pocket of the dressing gown, gave the ghost of a wink to the photograph of the two boys.

'Are you ready?'

Maxwell looked around him, at the walnut panelling, the Louis Quinze escritoire, the luxurious fixtures and fittings. He'd survived the war, he'd survived the Nazis, he'd built and lost an empire. Now, naked, he stood before his killers.

What a story, he thought. What a front page!

He dictated his last headline.

'I'm ready,' he said.

ONE

The wind, a hard north-easterly from the Chilterns, picked up once again. It scoured the valley and whipped through the pines which stood guard over the 1st XV rugby pitch, flattening the players' shirts to their bodies. The light was fading; the towers and parapets of Bolingbroke's School were an indistinct grey on the skyline.

Neil Slater glanced at his watch. Another ten minutes, then he'd send the boys in for showers and high tea. They'd done well, and he had a fair idea of whom he was going to choose for Saturday's match against Wellington.

Bracing himself against the wind, Slater watched as a slight sixteen-year-old American named Reinhardt intercepted an opponent's pass, made as if to pass in his turn, dummied, wrong-footed his opposite number, and raced for the try-line. A metre or two behind Reinhardt, a Saudi boy named al-Jubrin kept effortless pace.

The opposing full-back moved to block Reinhardt. His pile-driving tackle drove the breath from the American's body, but by then the ball was sailing

towards al-Jubrin. That the athletic young Saudi
would pluck the ball from the air without breaking
step was a foregone conclusion, as was the subsequent
try. Masoud al-Jubrin was born to play rugby.

al-Jubrin dropped the pass. There was no try –
instead the ball spun away into touch.

'Good, Paul!' Slater called out to Reinhardt as the
boy picked himself up. 'Masoud, what happened? You
don't usually drop those – you'll have to do a sight
better than that if we're going to beat Wellington on
Saturday.'

The Saudi pupil was silent. The wind plucked at his
neatly cut hair and snatched away the pale vapour of
his breath.

'What's wrong, Masoud?' asked Slater.

al-Jubrin shrugged. 'Nothing, sir.'

Slater put his hand to the boy's forehead, noted the
feverish brightness of his eyes. 'You're burning up.
How long have you been feeling like this?'

'Sorry, sir. Since this morning, sir.'

'Why the hell didn't you tell me?'

'Sorry, sir. Thought it would . . . go.'

And worried you'd be dropped from the team if you
mentioned it, thought Slater.

'I want you in that three-quarter line on Saturday,'
he told the boy. 'Now cut along and see Matron – my
guess is she'll put you in sick bay for the night. I'll look
in during the evening, make sure you're OK.'

al-Jubrin looked at Slater, opened his mouth to
protest, then thought better of it. Nodding, he headed

off towards the track suits piled on the touchline.

'And while we're at it, I'd like you to report to Matron too, Ripley. Have her take your temperature.'

Ripley, the son of a Midlands property developer, stared angrily at Slater. At six foot one, he was already two inches taller than the games master.

'I'm fine, sir. Honestly.'

'To Matron, Ripley. I'll be checking with her.'

'Sir, I can't miss this evening's prep. I've got a history project I've got to—'

'You heard me, Ripley. I want you lean and mean for Saturday.'

The boy bit his lip, nodded, and loped off. Sometimes, thought Slater, these rich kids had it hardest. Would Ripley — basically a decent lad — be ruined by the privileges that he would undoubtedly inherit? And Reinhardt, he wondered, seeing the American limping towards him. How would he be ten years from now? Would that cheerful sportsmanship survive whatever corporate hell was waiting for him?

'All right Paul?'

'Cream-crackered, sir.'

Slater smiled. If nothing else, an English education had broadened the boy's vocabulary. 'Train hard, fight easy, Paul — who said that?'

Reinhardt frowned. 'You've got me there, sir.'

'General Suvorov,' said Slater, and for a moment he saw the words painted on the adjutant's door at the old regimental HQ, smelt the gun-oil in the armoury.

'Who was General Suvorov, sir? I'm afraid my modern history's a bit shaky.'

Slater looked at the boy, at his narrow shoulders and mud-caked knees. God, he thought, they were so young. 'Look him up, Paul,' he said gently.

Watching the rugby squad trudge back to the school, Slater wondered if he was ever going to find life at Bolingbroke's School normal rather than freakish. On paper his was a good job. Games master to a school like Bolingbroke's was not a position to be sneezed at – on a good day the 1st XV could give Sedburgh or Ampleforth a run for their money. And the boys were good kids, for the most part. Too bloody rich and too bloody foreign, one of his colleagues had confided to Slater during his first staff tea, but Slater liked them. In many ways, he found the foreign kids – the Saudis, the Kuwaitis, the Indians – easiest to get along with. Away from their over-indulgent parents they had a hunger to prove themselves as individuals. They had no real understanding of the British class system, and they treated Slater exactly as they treated the other teachers: with an earnest, if at times joshing, respect.

Like Slater, the foreigners had started out as outsiders. Unlike Slater, however, they soon discovered that wealth and privilege confers its own insidership. For all the importance attached to rugby and cricket, games masters did not rank highly in Bolingbroke's pecking order. Slater was considered a cut above Jimmy McCracken – the semi-alcoholic groundsman who tended the pitches and was known to staff and pupils alike as 'Windy' on account of his dodgy colon – but well below any of the other teachers, most of whom were Oxbridge graduates and former public schoolboys. When he had first arrived at the school Slater had wondered whether he should imitate them, with their leather-patched sports jackets, their polished brogues and their baggy corduroys. He'd dismissed the idea immediately – he'd never get it quite right. To carry off that that kind of upper-class shabbiness you had to be born to it.

And Slater, as was regularly made clear to him, hadn't been born to it. He wore civilian clothes – as one of the warrant-officers had memorably pointed out on the first day of his undercover course – like a squaddie on the piss. He'd never quite sorted out the whole clothes thing. Or, for that matter, the accent thing. Or the posh restaurant and vintage wine thing that was supposed to work so well with women. Or any of that host of other 'things' that made for an easy progress through life.

But he did, Slater mused ruefully as the cold dusk gathered around him, have certain skills. At this moment there was a hot shower waiting for him and with luck a pot of tea and a plate of Jammy Dodgers in the staff room. If he ended up drinking the tea alone, well, bollocks to the lot of them. It was a billet, and all things considered, a comfortable one.

He pulled on his sweatshirt. With a fair wind behind them Masoud and Paul and the rest of the lads should punch holes through the Wellington defence on Saturday. Train hard, fight easy.

As he made his way towards the school buildings, Slater's attention was caught by a vehicle on the public road beyond the boundary wall. It was a Cherokee four-wheel drive, proceeding at about twenty miles an hour. Even given the warning signs outside the school, this seemed unnaturally slow for the road, and Slater realised that he had noticed the vehicle driving in the same direction and at the same speed earlier in the day. The Cherokee was a maroon colour, he remembered, although now in the failing light it looked almost black.

For a moment he wondered if the driver was a parent. A lot of the parents had Cherokees – it was pretty much Bolingbroke's signature vehicle – but not many went for the tinted window option. What was the point of spending all that money, after all, if no one could see who you were? And none of the parents considered themselves bound by the local speed restrictions, as this driver clearly did. Slater watched as the four-wheel drive crested a rise and passed out of sight. He had memorised the number.

Anxious to unload his misgivings and forget the incident with a clear conscience, Slater walked over to the main gate, where a white Mondeo, bearing the mailed-fist logo of a private security company, idled at the verge. The car was more of a public relations stunt than anything else, in Slater's opinion. All it served to

16

do was to underline the fact that the children of some very rich people were in residence – a fact which the blue and gold school notice-board (motto: Fortitude, Truth, Valour) made clear at a glance.

It was Bolingbroke's proximity to Heathrow – less than fifty minutes in a chauffeur-driven Lexus – which attracted the overseas customers. Summer visits were especially popular. Parents could fly in in the morning, take in a lunchtime meeting and a dash down Bond Street, and then spend a lazy couple of hours in a deckchair pretending to understand the rules of cricket. Rather fewer of these parents, Slater had observed, volunteered for duty on the rugby touchline. In the winter months, he supposed, parents were happy for the formation of their sons' characters to proceed on trust.

But there were real security issues, as there were wherever the children of the super-rich gathered. And while the school did not wish to turn itself into a high-tech prison – much of its commercial appeal lay in its traditional appearence and atmosphere – it wished to make clear that it took these issues seriously. Hence the white Mondeo.

And hence, Slater assumed, the chugging exhaust. What made people leave their car-engines switched on for hours at a time? He knocked on the driver's side window, which was blurred with condensation.

The driver lowered the glass, releasing a warm odour of fart and processed food, and regarded him suspiciously. Beyond the driver a second man was leafing through a pornographic magazine.

'Hi! My name's Slater. I'm the games master.'

The driver, a heavy-set man in a Barbour jacket, said nothing. A half-eaten meat pie sat in its foil dish in his lap. Pastry crumbs speckled his thighs.

'Did either of you notice a maroon Cherokee passing here a minute ago?' Slater continued.

'Why would you be concerning yourself with a maroon Cherokee, sir?'

'It's been past at least a couple of times today. Going very slowly. Looked to me as if it was scoping the place out.'

The second man turned his magazine through ninety degrees. 'Fuck me!' he said, grimacing with disbelief. 'Look at the state of that!'

The driver glanced at the magazine and turned back to Slater. 'A slow-moving maroon Cherokee that you think you've seen before.'

'And these have got to be silicone,' murmured the second man. 'They're all over the fucking shop.'

'I took the number,' said Slater, ignoring him. 'You might want to get it checked out. Here, I'll put it on your pad.'

Smirking, the driver handed Slater his pad. It was blank. Slater wrote down the number.

'Don't worry, sir,' said the driver, returning the pad to his pocket without looking at it. 'We're professionals. But thanks for the tip.'

'As the actress said to the bishop,' added the second man.

As Slater made his way up the drive, he heard both men laugh.

The Cherokee was parked in a lay-by 500 yards down the road.

In the driver's seat, smoking nervously, was a twenty-year-old man of Pakistani descent in an Umbro tracksuit. He was good with cars, and over the painful course of his teenage years – five convictions for taking and driving away, thirty offences taken into consideration – had refined his skills to the point where he was now considered one of the top wheel-men in the Gateshead area.

In the back seat sat two slightly older men, both bearded, both dressed in black windcheaters, jeans and hiking boots. They were Shi'ite Muslims from al-Ahsa, in Saudi Arabia's eastern province. The men were cousins; their mutual grandfather had emigrated from the Iranian Gulf port of Basra in 1925 and, unlike their Saudi neighbours, the two had been brought up strictly in the tenets of their faith.

They were followers of a radical Shi'ite holy man named Shayk Nabil Rahmat. Rahmat was the founder of a revolutionary faction called al-Hizb al-Makhfi – the Hidden Party. Acting with the utmost secrecy, and guarding its identity closely, the Hidden Party had carried out bombings in Riyadh, Jeddah, and even the Prophet's own city of Medina.

The Hidden Party, however, had been dealt a severe blow. Seven of its members had been convicted of terrorism by a religious court in Ahsa province, and condemned to death by beheading. Only the decision of a senior judge sitting on the Court of Cassation, the final court of appeal, stood between the seven party members and the execution of sentence.

And unless extraordinary pressure was brought to bear, that decision was a foregone conclusion. The judge in question was known as one of the most conservative members of the Saudi judiciary, and vehemently opposed to everything that Rahmat and his followers stood for. His name was Shaykh Marwan al-Jubrin. He was Masoud al-Jubrin's father.

The two men in the Cherokee had come to England in order to set in motion the applying of extreme pressure on the old judge. They had secured false Turkish passports from the intelligence services of the Islamic Republic of Iran, flown from Tehran to Rome, and then travelled across Europe by train to Denmark. In Copenhagen they had embarked on an overnight ferry to Newcastle, where they had shown their Turkish passports and been met by a local sweet-manufacturer. This man, a devout Shi'ite who had once burnt an effigy of Salman Rushdie for the benefit of an ITV news crew, had placed his spare bedroom at their disposal. At dawn, having picked up the driver, the sweet-manufacturer had driven the cousins to a lock-up garage where the stolen and replated Cherokee was waiting. Concealed beneath the driver's seat were the two weapons they had requested: a loaded Smith and Wesson Model 25 revolver and a sheathed Gerber Patriot knife with a six-inch oxidised blade.

The trio had begun the drive south immediately and by 2pm, after an unpleasant meal consumed at a service station outside Henley-on-Thames, had begun to recce the roads around Bolingbroke's School.

The cousins waited in the car, smoking, until it was fully dark. Then they embraced, whispered a prayer, took a weapon each, and climbed out into the icy cold of the lay-by. Their point of entry to the school, selected two hours earlier, was close to the rugby pitch where the 1st XV practice game had taken place earlier.

Within minutes both men were crouched outside the seven-foot perimeter wall. A leg up, a grunt of effort, a helping hand and they were both over, falling with a soft crunch into the frosted bracken. Purposefully they made their way towards the school buildings, by now a blaze of light. Their afternoon's reconnaissance had told them they had little to fear from the security guards and they moved fluently from shadow to shadow, eventually vanishing from sight among the ground-scraping branches of an elderly yew tree. A gravelled path led past this tree – a path joining the main school building to the modern refectory block. The two men settled down to wait.

For twenty-five minutes the darkness reshaped itself round them. Boys passed by, but always in twos or threes. Finally a solitary figure appeared, a slender fair-haired youth of about fourteen carrying a Game Boy.

Apparently heedless of the cold, the teenager paused beneath one of the lighted refectory windows, his fingers stabbing at the little console. The two men's eyes met. Soundlessly they climbed to their feet.

It was skilfully accomplished. Within seconds the boy had been bundled into the blackness beneath the yew. One man held him, clamping a strong hand across his mouth, the other urgently motioned silence. Eyes wide with terror, the boy nodded. To reinforce the need for silence one of the bearded figures produced the Smith and Wesson. In response the boy wet himself and began to shake.

'Listen, my friend,' whispered the second man. 'We are not going to hurt you – we just wish to talk. Now, what is your name?'

'C-Christopher,' the boy managed.

'OK, Christopher, when I give the word we are going to walk down the hill towards the games fields. Like I said, we will not hurt you but you *must* keep silent. Do you understand?'

The boy nodded, still shaking.

'Good boy. Let's go.'

The two men led the boy back in the direction they had come. Soon they were below the perimeter fence again. Getting him over was not easy. An icy frost now coated the stone, and terror seemed to have robbed the boy of all co-ordination. Eventually, however, they managed to bundle him up and over.

'Are you hurt, Christopher?' hissed one of the men as they landed to either side of him.

The boy shook his head.

'Just walk then,' said the man. 'Like normal, OK?'

In the Cherokee they turned on the ignition and the heater. The man with the Smith and Wesson pocketed his weapon and took out a small mobile phone.

'OK, Christopher. I want you to ask to speak to Masoud al-Jubrin. I'm going to dial the number of his mobile, and I want you to arrange to meet him in the same place that we . . . that we met you.'

'But I don't know Masoud. At least, I know who he is but—'

'It doesn't matter. Just say you have something of great importance for him. Something you have to give him in person.'

'Are you going to hurt him?'

'No. We just have to speak to him. To give him a message. That is all.'

The boy frowned doubtfully at the windscreen. At his side, the black-clothed figure punched out a memorised number and handed him the little Motorola.

A murmured conversation ensued. A more confident tone was returning to the boy's voice, especially now that the revolver was out of sight.

'Masoud's in the sick bay,' he said eventually, lowering the phone. 'He's got a flu bug or something.'

The men looked at each other.

'I'd like you to take us there, Christopher,' said one.

The Delves house prefects were watching a

documentary about the artist Tracey Emin in their common room. In theory they were supposed to be in their dormitories by ten; their minds and bodies, the headmaster insisted, needed proper recovery time if they were to handle the combined demands of competitive sport and the A-level syllabus. In practice, however, they could request late TV time if the programme in question was deemed to be of sufficient cultural value. As deputy housemaster of Delves, it was Slater's duty to police this system. He had never heard of Tracey Emin but had given the programme the nod anyway.

When he stuck his head into the common room there was a pair of soiled knickers on the TV screen.

'What's this?' he asked one of the boys, a rangy computer-fanatic named Tyrell.

'It's the documentary I asked you about, sir,' said Tyrell.

The camera panned across a wrecked bed, paused to examine a discarded condom.

'How much longer has it got to go?' If Latimer, the Delves housemaster, came in now there would be questions asked.

'About fifteen minutes. Do you agree that this is art, sir?'

An unshaven man in square-framed glasses was now standing in front of Tracey Emin's bed. 'Bad sex, skid-marked sheets – today it's all up for grabs,' he was saying.

'I'm afraid it's not my special subject, Tristram,'

Slater replied. It was a weak answer and he knew it. He should watch this business of Christian-naming the boys, too. The other staff-members didn't like it, and he'd been warned about it more than once. Undercutting discipline, he'd been told.

Tracey Emin was now on screen, topless.

'What do you think of that, sir? She's quite fit, isn't she?'

'I'm sure she'd value your approval,' said Slater drily. He glanced round the room. All eyes were on Tracey. 'How did you goons get to be made prefects, anyway?'

'Born to it, sir,' drawled a general's son named Springell, looking pointedly at Slater. 'Natural selection.' Running his fingers through expensively barbered hair, he turned back to the screen. 'Oh, you dirty, dirty girl . . . Bloody hell, that's a used Tampax, isn't it?'

'I think you should discuss it with Mr Parry in the art room, Springell. And less of the bloodies, please.'

'It's not my Tampax.'

'Don't wind me up Springell, OK?' Suddenly Slater's voice was raw steel. The temperature in the room seemed to drop several degrees. The boys stared at the TV screen, where Tracey Emin was dancing and laughing.

'How're al-Jubrin and Ripley, sir?' Paul Reinhardt said eventually.

'I don't think Masoud's going to be in that three-quarter line on Saturday, if that's what you mean. Gary Ripley should be OK.'

Slater was grateful for the change of subject. Even after fifteen years hard soldiering he was still vulnerable to the suggestion that he had been put on Earth for the casual amusement of the likes of Springell. I'll give him natural fucking selection, he thought.

Reinhardt's question also reminded him that he had promised to look in on the flu-stricken team-members. It shouldn't be too late.

'How much longer does this go on?' he asked for the second time.

'Fourteen minutes now, sir,' said Tyrell.

'Right. I'm just going over to the sick bay and when I come back I want you all upstairs in your rooms. Springell, you're responsible for making sure everything's turned off. TV plug out of the wall, please.'

'Sir,' said Springell, injecting the single syllable with all the irony he could muster.

The sick bay was at the back of the main building on the top floor, well away from the classrooms, kitchens and other centres of activity. Pupils were only ever detained there with minor conditions. Anything that exceeded the expertise of Matron – a corpulent body who regularly contacted her late husband by means of a spiritualist – demanded a visit from the Henley GP or transfer to a hospital in Reading. That, in turn, often meant a second transfer to a private clinic in London; the school had given up trying to explain to foreign parents that for most conditions the local NHS hospital was a better and safer bet than even the most expensive clinic.

The lift was waiting on the ground floor. Slater thought this strange: it usually remained on the top floor once Matron had retired to her quarters for the night. She slept next to the sick bay. There was also a night nurse, a willowy redhead named Jean Burney. Slater had caught Jean's eye once or twice and detected a definite twinkle. Since she was always on duty in the evenings, however, he had not had the chance to follow it up.

He stepped out of the lift, heard the doors slide shut behind him. The sick bay was arranged around a square lobby containing a pair of sofas, a low table and the night nurse's desk. On two sides of the square were curtained-off enclosures; these were for junior boys, and none appeared to be occupied.

Nor was the night nurse's desk. Perhaps Jean Burney had gone to the toilet. Slater decided to go straight through to the sixth form bay. Passing the desk, however, he saw that a table lamp had fallen and smashed, leaving curling fragments of glass on the white linoleum floor. Among the glass were smears of recently shed blood. More splashes led towards the door to Matron's quarters and the sixth form bay. Had Jean accidentally knocked the lamp to the floor and then cut her hand on the broken glass? She didn't look the clumsy type.

And then, at the edge of a smear of blood by the door, Slater saw a faint chevron-shaped imprint. It was no more than an inch long, but he recognised it instantly. No member of the teaching or medical staff wore commando-soled boots, and the boys all wore regulation lace-ups.

He froze, instantly alert, felt the familiar thud of his heartbeat as the adrenaline kicked in. For a moment he paused, ears straining for the slightest sound, and then moved at a crouch to the passage door. It opened, but not easily. Something heavy had been laid against it. Silently he raised himself to the level of the glass panes in the upper half of the door. The lights were off in the corridor but he made out a human shape – two bare legs, the faint scrabbling of fingers. Gently, Slater forced the door open, pushing the figure away from him until there was room to squeeze through.

It was Jean Burney. Slater recognised her by her hair. She had been blindfolded and gagged and her wrists were taped behind her back. Drying blood ran from both nostrils, her lower lip was split, and her nose looked broken. She was unconscious.

She was breathing, though, and Slater quickly ripped off the gag and the blindfold and cut the tape from her wrists with the Mauser penknife he carried on a lanyard in his trouser pocket. For the moment this was all he dared attempt. The intruder, or intruders, could still be in the building.

There was sufficient light for Slater to see that all three sick bay doors were closed. An attempt to enter any of them could invite a bullet. The fourth door bore a nameplate marked MATRON – Mrs T Mackay.

Silently, he turned the handle and slipped inside. He had barely closed the door behind him when a bedside light snapped on and a nightie-clad figure struggled to an upright position.

'Yes?' she began sleepily, assuming Slater to be Jean. Seeing that he wasn't her tone changed to alarm. 'Mr Slater, may I ask what on Earth—'

'Keep quiet!' he hissed. 'There are—'

'Come any closer and I'll scream,' hissed Mrs Mackay. 'What the hell's going on? What are you—'

'Intruders. They've knocked Jean out. I think they're after one of the boys – probably already taken him. I want you to ring security, the police and the headmaster in that order. And I need a weapon.'

'You *what*? Mr Slater, they might be—'

'Armed? I know. They could also be getting away with one of the boys.' His eyes searched the room, alighted on the reproduction Hepplewhite chair in which Mrs Mackay liked to watch *Emmerdale* and *EastEnders*.

A hard, downward stamp and a violent wrench before the Matron's horrified eyes, and Slater was hefting one of the chair's curved mahogany legs. Shreds of yellow damask trailed from the heavy business end.

'Phone,' he whispered, and slipped from the room.

In the corridor he stopped and listened again, all his senses racing. Jean Burney still lay unconscious by the doors. From the furthest sick room came a broken, murmuring sound.

Slater kicked open the three doors, the chair-leg raised to fend off any attacker. In the first, he found only darkness and silence. In the second, gagged as Jean Burney had been but half-conscious, he discovered a boy he recognised as Christopher Boyd-Farquharson – a dreamy fourteen-year-old excused from games on account of his asthma. The boy had received a nasty bang on the head, and judging from the confusion in his eyes was badly concussed, but – thank God – appeared to be breathing more or less regularly. Cutting him free, whispering to him that on no account was he to leave the room, Slater hurried on.

Behind the third door he found Gary Ripley and an empty bed. Ripley, twisted beneath a grey school blanket, had been beaten badly; his face was bruised and lacerated and he was bleeding from one ear. His knuckles, Slater noticed, were also bleeding and there was blood beneath his fingernails. He had not gone down without a struggle.

'How many men?' Slater asked gently.

'Two.'

'They took Masoud?'

Ripley nodded, a movement that was clearly agonising. 'I did my best, sir,' he whispered. 'One had a gun.'

'Describe the gun, Gary.'

'Revolver . . . heavy revolver. Other had a knife.'

'And the men?'

'Two Arabs. In black. Beards . . .' Tears of pain and helplessness began to run down the boy's cheeks. 'My stomach, sir. Could you . . .'

Slater pulled back the blanket. A black, inch-long slit gaped just below the boy's navel. Blood pulsed from the wound. The sheets and the boy's cotton pyjamas were dark with it. Grabbing a towel from the handrail, Slater pressed it to the stab-wound. Ripley gasped and his eyes rolled backwards.

'Gary, you've done well. You've done fucking well. Now you've got to hang in there, understand?'

'I'll be OK, sir. You go on.'

But the voice was barely audible, and as Slater raised himself from the bed the boy began to shake. Slater knew what was coming. He'd held men on the edge of death before, seen them move from this world into the waiting room of the next. Convulsing, Ripley lost consciousness.

Mrs Mackay, her nightdress smeared with Jean Burney's blood, stood in the doorway. Taking in the scene at a glance she moved swiftly to the bed and held a finger to Ripley's neck.

'I've rung an ambulance for Jean, but it's got to come from Reading. This boy's not going to last that long.'

Slater pulled a pen from his pocket and scribbled a number on the pillow-case. 'Get back on the phone. Tell whoever answers there's been a kidnapping and stabbing, that there are firearms involved, and that we need an emergency services helicopter immediately. Say you're calling on behalf of Neil Slater from B Squadron.'

Mrs Mackay looked at him uncertainly. 'What is this number?'

Slater picked up the chair-leg. 'It's the headquarters of the Special Air Service.'

'And you're . . .'

But Slater had already vanished.

Ignoring the lift, he ran headlong down the stairs to the bottom of the tower, then at full speed along the road fronting the main school buildings. The security team was based in a small ornamental lodge half-way up the drive – previously the domain of the estate's head gardener. During the day two men manned the main gates in a car, and at 7pm, when the main gates closed, the night team took over in the lodge, keeping watch over a bank of monitors.

To Slater's eye the system was all but useless, and he had told the headmaster as much within days of his arrival. Apart from loudly advertising its function, Slater had pointed out, the lodge was at least 200 yards from the main school buildings and highly vulnerable to assault. At the very least the operations centre should be moved indoors. The head had heard him out and then informed him that the system had been set up by a company owned by a school old boy. The old boy in question – and here the head had tapped the side of his nose meaningfully – had spent some time in one of the hush-hush departments, and jolly well knew what was what.

Slater had shut up. The lodge, with its imposing

bank of screens, was clearly a selling-point for nervous parents, and – equally important to the management – meant that the security teams could be kept at a distance; the staff and pupils didn't have to suffer their chain-smoking and filthy jokes.

Pushing the lodge door open with the chair-leg, he peered quickly inside. The monitors were blank, and both men were slumped forward against the control system console, which was running with spilt tea and blood. A holed and crumpled parka jacket lay on the floor. One of the men had crapped himself before he died – probably when witnessing his companion's fate – and the stench in the small overheated room was overwhelming.

Slater visualised the scene. The terrorists would have burst in. The man with the knife would have held Masoud while the gunman – his weapon muffled in the parka – would have immediately shot one of the security men. The second man, all but paralysed with fear, would then have been ordered to open the electronic gates before suffering the same fate as his partner – a single shot below the ear. With Masoud in tow there wouldn't have been any question of disabling or gagging; the security men had had to die. This far from the main building, no one would have heard anything.

Slater leant over the dead men and flicked the monitors back on. Nothing, just the darkness and trees twisting in the wind. The main gate, as he had suspected, had been opened. But Slater knew he wasn't far behind the kidnappers, and with luck, assuming their vehicle was laid up away from the gate, they hadn't got Masoud into the vehicle yet. Would a driver be waiting there?

Still carrying the heavy chair-leg – the security men were not permitted to carry firearms or any other salvageable form of weapon – Slater sprinted down the grass verge at the side of the drive. The frost was hard now, and he was grateful for the treads on his Timberland boots. The high winds had dispersed the cloud cover, and the moonlight glimmered on the hard-frosted landscape. He could see tracks on the drive now – two pairs of cleated soles and one much smaller pair of bare feet – and it was clear from the erratic pattern that Masoud was resisting hard. Good lad, thought Slater. Slow them down. Make it hard for them.

As he ran, Slater cursed himself for not having followed through on his suspicions about the Cherokee. How could he have been so stupid as to think those security guards would take the threat seriously? He'd known so-called hard men like them all his life – over-the-hill ex-regulars who pitched up with their thickening bodies and their Aldershot tattoos, sitting around on their arses, telling war-stories and hoping that nothing would happen.

At the open gates the tracks swerved to the left. The lay-by, thought Slater, his mind racing – that's where they've got the vehicle. If I follow them down the quarter-mile along the road they're going to see me –

they could easily risk firing at me, and there's no bloody cover of any kind. If I go through the school grounds, on the other hand, I'll be covered by the wall.

He broke back into a fast run, jumping brambles, hedgerows, dead bracken and frozen ditches. Four hundred yards to go. Despite the extreme cold, he could feel the sweat coursing down his back. At one moment he stepped calf-deep into an ice-crusted stream – but barely registered it. The pounding of his feet echoed that of his heart. His breath sawed in his chest. His hands and face burnt with the cold. Two hundred yards to go. So fucking *go*, he told himself. Push it harder. Lengthen your stride. Forget the pot-holes and the rabbit-holes and the broken ankles. Push it. *Push it!*

And then a faint cry reached him on the wind.

He froze, and heard it again.

'Itrukni li-hali! Itrukni li-hali!'

Slater was no linguist but he had picked up enough on missions in Saudi Arabia and Oman to understand Masoud's words. 'Leave me alone!' he was shouting. 'Let me go!'

Masoud was behind Slater. He'd overtaken them.

Fight, he willed Masoud. Slow them down.

He pounded through the darkness, brambles flailing at his hands and ankles. The voices on the other side of the wall were still a hundred metres away or more. If he crossed the wall now, fifty yards or so beyond the Cherokee he reckoned, they might not see him.

Over we go. Lobbing the chair-leg over the seven-foot wall, he ran at it – gave it his best shot. His hands found slick ice. His fingers scrabbled desperately, found no purchase, and he fell back to the bracken.

Squinting, he searched the darkness for an alternative run-up. Was there a bush or something against the wall – something he could climb?

Nothing.

The cries again. Nearer now.

Desperately he repeated his first attempt. Again the frosted bricks resisted his hands and again he fell defeated to the brambles. It was just too high.

Breathe. Use the desperation.

Focus.

Do it.

In his mind's eye he was back on selection at Hereford. His twelve-strong cadre had been beasted senseless for forty-eight hours – the previous night's exercise had included a frozen river-crossing in full kit – and they were almost hallucinating with fatigue. Promised a brew and a ration-break, they'd suddenly been ordered off on another thirty-click tab over the hills – any waverers to be immediately RTUed.

'You'll do it,' came the staff sergeant's voice, 'or ye'll fuck off back to whatever crap-hat outfit was misguided enough to waste this regiment's time with ye!'

And Slater had done it. He'd got round. Somewhere, he'd found the reserve.

Ah, came a tiny voice, but you were twenty-three then. You're thirty-six now, and . . .

Banishing the voice, Slater emptied his mind.

There was only the wall.

The wind roared at his ears as he ran, felt the brickwork kick at his chest, the icy flailing of his hands, the desperate swing of his legs.

And was over.

He'd judged it spot-on. The Cherokee was immediately in front of him. Picking up the chair-leg from the grass verge, he ducked behind the vehicle's radiator.

He could see as well as hear the kidnappers now: they were fifty yards up the road towards the school, thirty yards short of the Cherokee, and Masoud was kicking and struggling violently. '*Ib'id yadak!*' he screamed to the night air. '*Let me go!*'

Pulling the Mauser knife from his pocket, Slater stabbed the inside wall of each front tyre. Gently, the four-wheel drive sank forwards. Could he get to the back tyres?

Without warning, a car came hurtling from behind him, lights at full beam. The driver must have thought Masoud was a drunk being assisted by friends; the horn wailed conspiratorially and the darkness returned.

Clearly alarmed by the closeness of the encounter – a police car would certainly have stopped – the man with the Smith and Wesson hit Masoud hard on the head with the heavy butt. The boy's knees gave way, he was silent, and the black-clad kidnappers ran him to the rear of the vehicle.

From his position by the radiator, Slater watched

their legs moving between the back wheels as they got the rear doors open. His breathing was even, now, and his hands steady – fatigue had been replaced by a terrible clarity. Releasing the Mauser knife from its lanyard, he transfered it to his left hand. The blade was short, but it should serve its purpose.

Quietly, he crept along the verge by the vehicle. Having achieved their objective, the terrorists were making no attempt at silence, and were conversing in breathless Arabic as they bundled Masoud into the luggage area. Slater guessed that they were arguing as to whether they should gag the boy, hit him again, tie him up, or all three. He had no idea which man had the gun and which man the knife. The basic rule was to assume that both men had firearms. He was two yards from the nearest man now.

One yard.

With the rear doors open all that Slater could see was a waist and a pair of legs. The black windcheater had ridden up, showing two inches of T-shirt above the unbelted jeans. Light flooded from the interior of the vehicle.

With precision, Slater planted the four-inch Mauser blade to its hilt in the nearer man's spleen. In the same movement, letting go the knife, he brought down the carved prow of the chair-leg on the sacro-iliac joint at the base of the second man's spine.

The nearer man froze, almost senseless with pain, and Slater jammed the half-door of the Cherokee against his back. Bellowing, the second man reared towards Slater, feinting with the knife. But his pelvis and sacrum had been smashed by that first, terrible blow. Will power propelled him a further step and then, twisting in agony, he fell to one knee.

The first man, eyes dulled with shock, was straightening up in light from the back of the Cherokee now, and this time Slater saw the dull glint of gun-metal. Half-turning, he swung his improvised club in a scything back-hander, felt the splintering crunch as it connected with the side of his attacker's skull. The firearm clattered to the road.

Both men were down. The knifeman appeared to be praying, the gunman's prostrate body was shaking as if in the throes of some desperate rape.

Who hesitates, dies. Think detonator. Think grenade.

Slater, his system screaming with adrenaline, didn't hesitate. Snatching up the Smith and Wesson from the gutter, he put two .45 rounds into the base of each man's skull.

For thirty seconds, heart pounding, he stood there with the dead men at his feet. The police would be along soon, he was sure – assuming, that was, that Mrs Mackay had done her stuff. If necessary he could flag down a car, although not that many cars used this road at night. Apart from the school and a few farms, it didn't really go anywhere.

Masoud, he thought. I must see what those bastards have done to Masoud. He took a step towards the Cherokee – and to his horror saw it begin to move away in a cloud of exhaust, rear doors flapping.

Sweet Jesus, thought Slater. There was a driver. But where . . . ?

He must have seen him come over the wall, he realised. Flattened himself in the front of the car. And hearing the shots had decided – entirely sensibly – to get the hell out.

With two flat tyres, however, the Cherokee wasn't going anywhere. It managed twenty yards and then came to a halt.

Running, Slater caught up with the vehicle. He waited a half-dozen yards behind it, the revolver pointing at the doors, which had swung shut on the recumbent form of Masoud.

A half-minute passed, and then a male voice, Geordie-accented, came from the rear compartment.

'I'm coming out.'

The rear doors opened once more. Against the light Slater could not see the man's features – only that he was wearing a fur cap with ear-flaps and holding a barely conscious Masoud by the collar. Condensing breath rose smokily from both figures. Was the driver armed? Slater had to assume he was, that a weapon was pressed to the small of Masoud's back.

Arms outstretched, he thumbed back the revolver's hammer and trained the inch-long barrel on the driver's head. He'd made this shot many times in training – the shot through the chin that passed through the hostage-taker's lower skull and obliterated the cerebellum, ensuring that not even the slightest reflex movement threatened the hostage's life. Out here in the dark, however, it was a desperately risky play: the heavy Smith and Wesson was the last weapon he would have chosen for precision shooting in low light conditions. An inch off target and he'd blow Masoud's head apart.

And then a faint, rhythmic pulsing at the horizon was suddenly everywhere around them and the scene was flooded with light.

'Drop your weapons,' came a disembodied voice. 'I repeat: drop your weapons.'

Dead leaves and frost particles whirled in the police helicopter's rotor-wash. Opposite Slater, Masoud slid to the ground and the Cherokee's driver, a young Asian in a track suit who couldn't have been more than eighteen, slowly raised his hands. There had been no gun.

Releasing the hammer with his thumb, Slater flipped the Smith and Wesson to the frozen verge. Placed his hands on his head.

Waited.

TWO

The custody suite at Henley-on-Thames police station, Neil Slater mused, was not designed with comfort in mind. The bedding was thin, a drunk in the next cell had alternately howled and sobbed all night, and there was an all-pervasive smell of vomit overlaid with disinfectant. Slater had been tempted to sit up replaying the events of the evening in his mind, but had opted instead to try to sleep and clear his head.

The shakes had come soon after midnight, as Slater had known that they would, along with the fatigue and depression that invariably follows the adrenaline rush of violent action. He'd ridden them out as best he was able and had finally nodded off at about 2.30. His drift into unconsciousness had been eased by the certainty that his actions, given the circumstances, had been the correct ones.

In a counter-terrorist engagement, it had been drummed into him, you didn't leave wounded members of the opposition lying around where they could reach for a concealed grenade or detonator. If he'd had some armed assistance, perhaps the men's lives might have been spared. As it was, he'd had no choice.

For the terrorists themselves he felt not a gram of sympathy. They'd knifed Gary Ripley in the guts when he threatened to hold them up and they'd shot the unarmed security guards without a thought. Had they encountered Jean Burney and Christopher Boyd-Farquharson after kidnapping Masoud rather than before, the nurse and the boy would probably be dead too. No, by the time Slater had reached them, the two men had sacrificed any right to mercy or to any benefit of the doubt, and they'd known it.

But there was still, Slater was well aware, a price to be paid. A couple of hours' lost sleep was not going to be the end of it. There would be the flashbacks and the mood-swings that invariably follow a face-to-face killing. Alcohol took the edge off the process, but fucked you up in other ways. And there was no one, ever, that you could talk to about any of it.

Once, as a newly badged trooper, he'd gone into a wine bar in Hereford in search of others from his intake. There had been a tight knot of NCOs standing around the bar, and a staff sergeant had called him over, stood him a bottle of Michelob, and introduced him to the others. Among them was a corporal with conspicuously long hair who had just returned from a tour of duty in Belfast. The group had been welcoming, asking how he was settling in, but then an inoffensive-looking civilian in a windcheater had brushed past the long-haired corporal, nudging the arm that held his bottled beer.

The reaction was instantaneous. Grabbing the man by the lapels, the corporal had slammed him against the bar. 'Who the fuck do you think you're pushing around?' he'd whispered, his face an inch from the terrified civilian's. The others had pulled the corporal back, pinioning his arms, and Slater had seen that he was quivering with rage, his eyes narrowed and his teeth bared like a dog's.

The incident was swiftly over. While the senior NCO apologised profusely to the shaken civilian, the others calmed down the corporal. Two men were deputed to walk him back to Sterling Lines but the corporal shook them off, insisting that he was fine, that it had been a mistake, that there would be no more trouble.

He carried on drinking – they all did – and the NCOs talked Slater through life in the Regiment – where to find the best bars, the cheapest cars, the prettiest girls. And then the corporal, who had been standing in silence, drinking bottle after bottle of Beck's, looked Slater in the eye. 'It's shite,' he said quietly. 'The whole thing's fucking shite. The Regiment's shite, the job's shite . . .'

For a moment, the others fell silent.

'You want to know a secret?' the corporal continued in the same flat, undemonstrative tone. 'They don't die. You shoot them, you stab them, you do what you like, but they don't fucking die.'

'All right, that's it!' snapped the staff sergeant. 'Tony, Stevo, get him back to the Lines.'

The trio swiftly disappeared and the staff sergeant shook his head. 'He's had a bit of a rough tour. He's still in the old Darkland.'

'Darkland?' Slater enquired.

The sergeant glanced at him for a long moment, expressionless, and then returned to the inspection of his drink. It became clear that no answer was forthcoming.

But Slater had remembered the expression.

Darkland.

He'd never seen the corporal again.

Breakfast was an Egg McMuffin from the high street and a mug of the desk sergeant's tea.

'Just had that headmaster of yours on the phone,' he told Slater with cheerful satisfaction.

'Pembridge,' said Slater.

'That's the one. Sounded like a *very* unhappy man!'

'Have you met him?'

'Once or twice, yes. A couple of years ago he tried to make the case that we should have a permanent detachment guarding the school. When the super suggested to him that he put his hand in his pocket for the privilege he . . . got rather irate. Started spouting on about foreign policy by other means, invisible exports, defence sales to the Middle East – all bloody sorts.'

'And ended up going private,' said Slater.

The sergeant rolled his eyes but kept his opinion of the security arrangements to himself. At the desk the phone started ringing. 'No rest for the wicked,' he grumbled, retrieving Slater's empty mug.

'Oh, I don't know about that!' murmured Slater, stretching out on his mattress.

He was not feeling as bullish as he sounded. Two dead men, considered in the cold light of day, meant some very serious aggravation. No one would have blamed him if he had merely dialled 999 from the Matron's phone and left it at that – technically speaking, in fact, that was precisely what he should have done. But whether Masoud would have survived if he'd done so was another matter. By the time marksmen and a hostage rescue unit had been activated, the snatch team would have been long gone. And even if they'd located them, the Arabs hadn't looked like men who'd come out with their hands up – no matter how politely they'd been asked.

How would the school view the incident? Badly, that was for sure. When Slater had joined Bolingbroke's staff six months earlier he'd told Pembridge that he'd spent the majority of his service career with the SAS, and indeed had played rugby for the Regiment, but had requested that these details were kept quiet. Pembridge had agreed, and the story was put about that Slater had been a physical training instructor with the Royal Engineers – his parent regiment.

If an inquest on the dead men revealed Slater's true identity to the press, there were going to be some very angry faces on Bolingbroke's Board of Governors. Any coverage would be damaging enough; an SAS connection would punt the story straight to the front page and keep it there.

The Regiment themselves, he guessed, would probably be understanding. Not happy – the SAS hated seeing their name in print in any connection – but understanding. They would know that whatever Slater was, they had made him.

It was for this reason that he had rung Lark as soon as he'd arrived at the station in the early hours of the morning.

Lark was a clean-up man, a conjuror in pinstripes who made things disappear. If some chopping had to be done – as it had had to be done in Gibraltar and on several less-publicised occasions – then Lark was the man who smoothed out the rough edges afterwards. He was a Treasury Solicitor, one of a highly secretive elite working out of the Metropole building on Northumberland Avenue, where a small band of high-flyers concerned themselves with the legal interests of the Ministry of Defence. In the last two decades he had represented the difference between jail and freedom to at least a dozen SAS soldiers and other security services operatives. If Lee Clegg and his mates from 3 Para had had access to Lark after gunning down a joyrider at a Belfast check-point, Slater mused, they wouldn't have ended up being banged up.

Lark presented himself in the Henley-on-Thames custody suite at precisely 9am, carrying a Thermos of fresh coffee and a folded copy of the *Daily Telegraph* –

details which Slater appreciated. As usual Lark was impeccably dressed. His tie was that of one of the older civil service rowing clubs.

'Mr Slater,' he began, extended a well-manicured hand, 'I hadn't expected to see you again . . . quite so soon.'

'We do have to stop meeting like this,' Slater agreed wryly, running his hand over his chin. The lawyer's immaculate grooming made him feel like a rough-neck. His mouth tasted sour and he needed a shave.

Lark smiled – or at least the corner of his mouth momentarily flickered – as he loosened the lid of the flask. 'Usual drill, Mr Slater,' he said. 'Tell me everything. And I mean everything.'

Savouring the coffee, Slater started at the beginning; Lark made notes.

When Slater had finished, the Treasury Solicitor steepled his fingers. 'I'll tell you the bits I don't like,' he said thoughtfully, wrinkling his nose as if tasting a mediocre sherry. 'For a start I don't like the chair-leg – it argues premeditation of assault, I think . . . I think that what you actually took from that room was a torch – a big fifteen-inch Maglite, perhaps. A torch would have been an entirely prudent thing to take outside with you. If you were later taken by surprise and forced to defend yourself with it, well, that's something else – do you take my point?'

Slater indicated that he did.

'I think it's possible that a friend might drop in with just such a torch later today and that you might have a look at it — handling and fingerprinting it fairly extensively in the process.'

Slater nodded. Relief flooded through him. They were going to give him the full five-star service — exactly as if he'd still been 'in'.

'It won't be found at first, of course. We'll give it a night or two. And I rather think that someone's going to have to have a quiet word with Matron about that chair. Any feelings about what line we should take with her?'

'The truth?' hazarded Slater.

Lark looked appalled. 'I'm not sure that we—'

'Listen, she's seen one of her patients abducted and one of them stabbed, she's had a fourteen-year-old boy and a nurse beaten senseless just because they happened to be on her wing. She doesn't need to be threatened or bribed, she just needs to be put in the picture. She'll say what needs to be said.'

Lark pursed his lips doubtfully and then nodded. 'The second thing I'm not very keen on,' he continued, 'is the impression — a false impression, I'm sure — that your reason for pursuing these men down the school drive was to provoke a confrontation. I put it to you that your original intention in leaving the school grounds was to ascertain the registration number of the kidnappers' vehicle from a distance in order to convey this information to the police. Would this interpretation of your actions be an accurate one?'

Slater assured him that it would.

'And that having come upon their vehicle

49

apparently untended, you attempted to disable it by slashing the front tyres. Unfortunately, while doing so, you were discovered – knife in hand – by the kidnappers . . . '

Slater nodded.

'A fight ensued . . .'

Slater nodded.

'You see, the impression I really want most strongly to dispel is that you effectively mounted an ambush on these men.'

'Absolutely,' said Slater.

For two unbroken hours they went through every move, every gesture, trimming the action so that no legal blame could adhere to Slater. A phone call by Lark from the front desk established that Ripley was in intensive care in Reading, but expected to make a full recovery.

Lark excused himself at 11.30, leaving Slater with the *Daily Telegraph*. Slater read the newspaper from cover to cover, unsuccessfully attempted the crossword, and eventually tried to sleep. And then, at 2.00, the door of the cell was unlocked, and his effects were handed back to him. 'Whole thing's been taken out of our hands,' the desk-sergeant told him resignedly. 'Security implications, apparently, whatever that means. I'm to tell you' – he glanced at a Post-It note attached to the counter – 'that you'll be contacted in due course by Mr Lark, vis-à-vis a witness statement and possible Court of Inquiry.'

Slater nodded gratefully. This was exactly what had happened on previous occasions. Lark had spent a few days hammering out a suitable statement, he'd been called in to sign it, given a copy to memorise – to 'internalise' as Lark put it – and the whole dossier had then been consigned to some dusty drawer at the MOD. Classified for reasons of national security. As a system it wasn't watertight – there were increasing demands in the left-wing press for the 'accountability' of the security services – but it had seen Slater right so far.

A police driver returned him to the school in an unmarked car. The system, it seemed, had once again come to Neil Slater's rescue.

At Bolingbroke's, far from the confusion that Slater had expected, all was ordered. A tape barrier had been erected around the security lodge and there was a black Range Rover parked on the drive beneath the sick bay, but that was all.

As Slater approached the main entrance the 1st XV rugby squad clattered down the steps past him – minus Ripley and al-Jubrin.

'Thought I'd take them for some circuit training,' one of the assistant games masters called out. 'Hope that's OK.'

'Fine!' Slater managed. 'Great!'

'No problem. Hope you feel better soon.'

Slater watched the squad jog down towards the athletics track. What the hell have they been told? he wondered.

Before he had time to surmise further, the

headmaster, Pembridge, materialised in the entrance. His gesture indicated welcome, but there was considerable strain apparent.

'Mr Slater. Good. My study, if you would be so kind.'

They proceeded up the wide stone passage in silence. Pausing in the anteroom to his study, Pembridge informed his secretary that he did not wish to be disturbed.

'Mr Slater,' he began when the doors had closed behind them. 'I – we, Bolingbroke's – owe you a debt of thanks. Your very resourceful actions last night quite possibly saved the life of one of our boys. Thank you.'

He extended his hand, which Slater shook.

'I also understand that you made a report concerning your suspicions of a certain vehicle to the afternoon detail of MailedFist Security, and that no action was taken in this regard.'

'Yes, sir.'

Pembridge walked to the study window. 'Mr Slater, I will speak frankly. Had MailedFist acted on your report and telephoned the police as you suggested, we would not be having this conversation. I recall very well your reservations concerning the company, and I recall my . . . possibly rather high-handed reaction to these reservations. In apology, and in thanks for your bravery, I would like to make you a small presentation.'

He returned to his desk and handed Slater a small box. Inside was a pair of gold cufflinks, engraved with the crest of Bolingbroke's School.

Apart from formal mess–dress, Slater had never owned a shirt requiring cuff–links, but he smiled appreciatively. 'Thank you. They're beautiful.'

And now for the bad news, he thought, pocketing the box. It was never going to be this easy.

'Unfortunately, Mr Slater, there are more people involved than just you and me . . .'

Here we go, thought Slater.

'And Bolingbroke's – although at times we may wish that it did – does not exist in a constitutional vacuum. There is a board of governors to be considered, and there are the laws of the land . . .'

Get on with it. If you want to bin me, then say so.

'. . . and admirable as your behaviour might seem from a certain point of view, the fact remains that you have caused the violent deaths of two men while serving on the staff of this school. Caused their deaths, moreover, in circumstances which do not appear to permit an argument of self–defence.'

'Mr Pembridge—'

'In the final analysis, Mr Slater, the fact that you are a former SAS soldier gives you no special rights. Upon discovering the state of affairs in the sick bay, you should have rung the police, who are not quite the plodding incompetents that you seem to assume. For your information – and I have been given dispensation to tell you this – the two young men that you killed were under surveillance by Special Branch. By all accounts a major operation has been compromised.'

Slater stared at him, disbelievingly. 'Compromised!

Two members of your security staff are shot dead. A boy is kidnapped at gunpoint. Another boy who tries to defend him is stabbed in the guts—'

'Mr Slater, there is no need to raise your voice.'

'And you talk about an operation being *compromised*?'

'Mr Slater, you will kindly keep your voice down. The school is aware that some sort of incident occurred last night, and that it related to a break-in at the sick bay, but that is all. The story doing the rounds at the moment – a story I have not discouraged – is that a member of the security staff intercepted a burglar.

'Now, as you know, there are only two and a half weeks of this term left to run. Miss Burney and two of the boys involved in last night's débâcle – Ripley and Boyd-Farquharson – are in hospital in Reading, and upon their release they will go straight home. Masoud al-Jubrin is being flown to Saudi Arabia as we speak, and Mrs Mackay will be taking extended leave. None of those involved will be returning to Bolingbroke's until the beginning of the January term.'

'And me?' asked Slater sourly. 'How extended is my leave to be?'

'Mr Slater, a cheque is waiting for you in the bursar's office. To your back pay, the school has added the sum of £20,000. Before you take possession of this cheque, however, we would ask you to sign a prepared form stating that your contract with Bolingbroke's School has been terminated by mutual consent. You will also – although this has not been put in writing – agree never to mention the events of last night outside of such inquests and courts of inquiry as may demand your co-operation. This school has many friends, Mr Slater, and those friends would be very unhappy if adverse publicity concerning Bolingbroke's were to be broadcast. So unhappy, in fact, that not even your Mr Lark would be able to help you. Do we understand each other?'

'I think so,' Slater said coldly.

'I'm sorry it has come to this. You have done good things for the rugger team. I fully expect us to beat Wellington.'

Twenty-four hours later, Slater was coaxing his ten-year-old Saab down the drive for the last time. The barriers around the lodge, he noticed, had been removed. On impulse he stopped the car and peered in through one of the windows. The interior was deserted and the monitor screens were blank. There was no sign that two men had died violently here, or indeed that the place had ever been occupied.

'Took 'em away in a van,' came a quiet voice from behind him. 'Big fellers, the both of them.'

It was the groundsman, Jimmy McCracken. He was holding a quarter bottle of Teacher's whisky, and it was almost empty.

'What did you see, Jimmy?' asked Slater.

'There's a lot of blood in a man,' McCracken said obliquely.

'That there is,' said Slater. Five hundred yards away

a crowd of warmly wrapped spectators was assembling on the touchline of the 1st XV rugby pitch. 'How long have you worked here at Bolingbroke's?' he asked.

The groundsman slipped the bottle thoughtfully into his pocket. 'Twenty-eight years now, it'd be.'

Slater reached into his own pocket. 'Well, I have something for you.'

'You'll not be staying, then?'

Slater shook his head.

McCracken opened the box with unsteady fingers and peered at the chain-linked gold cufflinks. 'You know, I've been meaning to get some of these,' he said.

THREE

Neil Slater looked round the studio flat that, for the time being at least, was his home. It was small, and at some point he really had to give it a lick of emulsion, but at least he now had somewhere to unpack his things. It was a top-floor walk-up in a Victorian terrace to the east of Highbury Park, and Slater had chosen it for its proximity to Arsenal tube station. He wasn't a football fan particularly, but he had heard that the fortnightly rampage of fans through the area kept rental prices down.

He'd arrived in London a week earlier after spending Christmas with an ex-Regiment friend and his wife. Dave and Linda Constantine owned a farmhouse outside Hereford, and had recently converted it to provide bed and breakfast. Slater had had visions of long walks on the hills and companionable mealtimes at the scrubbed-pine kitchen table, but in the event things hadn't worked out like that. The Constantines' marriage had been under strain – money problems, mostly, but Dave's drinking came into it – and Slater found himself on the receiving end of two well-rehearsed sets of grievances.

Dave's was a very familiar problem, and afflicted most long-serving SAS soldiers. The time came when you had to move on, when you just couldn't carry the weight of regimental life any more. You looked around and you saw normal people living normal lives and it just looked like the best thing in the world. And so you handed in your warrant card and you walked out of the gates and you tried it, and you discovered that normal life – or what you'd taken to be normal life – was actually a very difficult, very elusive thing. None of your military experience was any help, you couldn't capture happiness and financial security by lying in wait for it on an icy hillside, and the attributes of toughness and self-reliance that had served you so well now started to seem like crippling deficiencies. You needed a new set of skills; you needed all that touchy-feely interpersonal stuff that you'd spent so many years sniggering about with your mates.

Slater himself had attempted to address these issues by applying for the post at Bolingbroke's. He'd come with a glowing letter of recommendation from his former CO (a Bolingbroke's old boy, usefully) and a determination to make a success of his new life. If this involved a few humiliations along the way, then so be it. If some of the parents and teaching staff chose to see him as their social inferior, then let them – it would be their problem, not his. He'd make a new life for himself on the rugby touchline, have his own chair in the staff room, fix himself up with a local girlfriend, become part of the establishment. And if he'd had his doubts – if, at times, it had occurred to him that he was merely exchanging one barracks for another – well, there were worse things than institutionalisation.

Dave Constantine had laid claim to less modest ambitions. He had invested his entire twenty-two-year service gratuity of £37,000 in a private security company named Radfan that another former Regiment member was setting up. Things had looked good for a while, but then the microchip fabrication plant which was Radfan's biggest corporate client went bankrupt and defaulted on a large sum owing. Radfan's financing had been shaky from the start – they had badly overextended themselves buying hi-tech surveillance equipment – and the bad debt finished them off. Of his £37,000 Dave Constantine recovered just £1200. Severely depressed, he spent the money on reslating the farmhouse roof and upgrading the plumbing. You could charge more for bed and breakfast if you had power showers, Linda had heard.

And so Dave had found himself turning back the bed-sheets and plying the Toilet Duck. The guests had come in twos and threes in the summer months, but the venture had never really taken off. The fact that the proprietor smelt of whisky at breakfast-time probably didn't help. Nor did Linda's tense and sometimes bruised countenance.

To escape the recriminations and the silences Slater went running, pounding the icy country roads for hours at a time, often returning well after dark. His stay at Wormbridge had come to an end after a joyless New

Year's Eve party at the farmhouse. After announcing that he had decided to accept an offer of work as a mercenary in Sierra Leone, Dave had passed out cold. A tearful Linda had then invited Slater into her bed. He had turned her down as tactfully as he was able, but hadn't been able to face the couple the next day. Leaving a note and a generous contribution towards the household budget, he had slipped away at first light.

He'd driven straight to London, and used the remainder of the day scouting the Highbury area. At nine o'clock the next morning, after a night at a cheap hotel, he'd visited the first estate agent. By midday he was pocketing the keys to 28 Mafeking Terrace, and forty-eight hours later, after hiring a van and scouring the Holloway Road's second-hand furniture and kitchen shops, he had the place in working order. The fridge had a weird shuddering hum that no amount of tinkering seemed to fix, and he preferred not to think too closely about the provenance of the cooker – but it was a base.

The other reason – apart from affordability – that he'd chosen the area was that it was on the Piccadilly underground line. Although he'd been unwilling to involve himself with bodyguard and private security work when he'd first left the Regiment – the work hadn't promised the clean break he'd been looking for – Slater had reviewed his options over the course of those long runs through the Herefordshire hill-country. The pay-off from Bolingbroke's wouldn't last long and his choices were few. Working as a bodyguard had its down-sides – you had to wear a suit, for a start – but by all accounts the money was good. The Piccadilly Line ran through Mayfair, Knightsbridge and Belgravia, which is where most of the work was. Bodyguarding hours were long, and Slater didn't want to spend a second more than necessary getting to and from work.

His time at Bolingbroke's was now a distant memory. Ever-present, however – despite Lark's involvement – was the nagging worry that the affair at the school would have serious consequences for him.

The Saudis, he was certain, would not wish news to get out about the attempt on Masoud al-Jubrin, and it was probably to accommodate the Saudis that the police had been stood down and the terrorists' and the dead security men's bodies had been spirited away by an MI6 cleaning team. No sense jeopardising an entire arms-sales programme because of a local unpleasantness – especially one that that would reflect so poorly on all parties.

Pembridge, in his turn, would do all that he could to hush up the affair for the sake of the school. But that still left a lot of mouths to be stopped: Mrs Mackay, Jean Burney, the Ripleys, the Boyd-Farquharsons, the families of the security men . . . If any one of them went to the press then there would be some very hefty deals to be brokered. And the security services, as Lark had impressed on Slater on more than one occasion, really hated to do deals of that sort.

No, Slater would be made to take the drop if there was a court of inquiry. There would be a lot of talk about post-traumatic stress and the difficult circumstances of his departure from the Regiment, but in the end they'd leave him swinging in the wind. He just had to hope that it never came to that. It was a worry, though, and a serious one.

How should I dress for the interview? he wondered.

Minerva Close Protection was a small but very successful company set up by a former Guards officer. Based in Knightsbridge, the company employed a number of ex-SAS soldiers, among others, to guard and otherwise minister to its stable of super-wealthy clients. The work often involved counter-surveillance and evasive driving in addition to straight body-guarding – if Minerva clients appeared in the newspapers, they prefered it to be at a time and in a context of their own choosing.

Slater had been recommended to Minerva by Tommo Goss, an ex-Coldstream Guardsman who had spent two years with G Squadron. There was a large number of private security companies based in the West End, Goss had explained to Slater over a pint, but there was a limited amount of really top-drawer work. And a lot of companies ripped you off, charging up to a thousand pounds a day for your services and only passing on a quarter of that figure to you. Minerva played fair, Goss said, and if you played fair in return you could expect to make a lot of money.

'What do you mean, "play fair in return"?' Slater had asked.

'Don't cut out the agency by offering to deal direct,' Goss answered, 'and don't dip the quill in company ink.'

'Dip the—'

'Don't bang the female clients. Those are the two basic rules. And the boss, Duckworth, is a canny bugger – he'll find out if you're playing around. He won't say anything, but you won't hear from him again either.'

Slater decided to attend the interview in the clothes he stood up in. No point in trying to go smart – he'd only get it wrong.

Within thirty minutes of leaving Mafeking Terrace he was entering an anonymous block overlooking Hyde Park. The offices, which were on the eighth floor, were quietly expensive. A receptionist showed Slater to a waiting area containing a large abstract painting and current editions of *Vogue* and the *New Yorker*. Nothing suggested that this was a company staffed principally by ex-special forces soldiers and secret service personnel.

Five minutes later the receptionist was back. She was very pretty – the almond-shaped eyes and wide smile giving the lie to the severely tailored grey suit. She also, Slater guessed, represented a test for potential employees like himself. If you couldn't resist trying it on with her, you were probably not suitable bodyguard material. Tearing his eyes from her trim figure, he tried to give an impression of watchfulness as he followed her across the silent carpet past a series of closed doors.

Peter Duckworth was a tall, languid figure in – Slater guessed – his early fifties. His hair was silver and his suit of exquisite cut. His eyes twinkled.

'Mr Slater – Neil – come in. Coffee?'

Slater was not deceived by the affable manner. There was something lethal about Duckworth.

For ten minutes the former Guards officer quizzed Slater about his SAS activities. Slater's responses were neutral and in several instances he felt it prudent not to answer – the man was a civilian, after all.

'And I understand that you're a close friend of Tom Goss, is that right?'

'We were in Belize together, instructing on the jungle warfare course,' said Slater.

Duckworth nodded and helped himself to a biscuit from the tray at his side. 'Good. Lovely. Well, let me tell you a bit about what we do here . . .'

Duckworth spoke for twenty minutes. Slater guessed he had given the same talk, word for word, many times before. The company's clients, he explained, were people of wealth – he used the phrase as if it were a form of victimhood. Their lifestyles were not ordinary lifestyles, their needs were not ordinary needs, their behaviour was not ordinary behaviour. 'Nevertheless,' said Duckworth, 'you will behave at all times as if it was. You will not be petulant, and you will not stand upon your dignity. You will refuse a client's request only if, in your judgement, to accept it would compromise that client's security. Do you understand?'

'Yes,' said Slater, deliberately withholding the 'sir' that years of non-commissioned service otherwise brought automatically to his lips.

'Good,' said Duckworth with a quick smile. 'Very good. I'm sure you'll . . . fit in.'

'I'm sure I will,' Slater said.

Duckworth nodded. 'Just before I ask Josephine to run through the paperwork with you, Neil, I'd like to read you a few lines of poetry. You may make of them what you will.'

Slater, who was studying a framed painting of an Arab boy with a snake draped around his neck, tried to look intelligent.

Duckworth removed a book from a drawer in his desk.

'*When the Himalayan peasant meets the he-bear in his pride,*

He shouts to scare the monster, who will often turn aside,

But the she-bear thus accosted rends the peasant tooth and nail . . .'

Hesitating, Duckworth glanced at Slater.

'*For the female of the species*', Slater obliged him, '*is more deadly than the male.*'

'You know it!' said Duckworth.

'My father used to read me Kipling when I was a child,' said Slater. 'He was a Royal Engineers RSM. *Mandalay* and *Gunga Din* were the nearest I ever got to nursery rhymes.'

'And your mother?' Duckworth asked delicately.

'She was knocked down and killed by a police car in Hong Kong when I was six.'

'Brought up by the army, then.'

'Pretty much.'

'There are worse parents, as any bodyguard will tell you.'

Abandoning any pretence of interest in Slater's beginnings, Duckworth shifted his attention to the screen of his computer. 'Are you free to work on Wednesday? I've got a rather interesting one for you.'

As he stepped out of the marble atrium into the street, Slater heard his name called. A smiling dark-haired figure, tough-looking beneath the fashionably cut suit, was waving and hurrying towards him.

'Andreas!'

'Neil! How are you, man?'

'I'm OK. Wow! It's good to see you. Are you here to . . .' he nodded up at the building he had just left.

'That's right. I've just been on a job in Europe for them. You?'

Slater nodded, and looked the other man up and down. Andreas van Rijn was recognisably the same person that he had served with in the SAS. The same square features and amused brown eyes, the same swagger, the same air of being up for anything. But something had changed. Some subtle smoothing-out process had taken place.

66

Until his departure five years earlier, Andreas van Rijn had been one of the Regiment's more colourful characters. Good-humoured in the vilest of conditions and a supremely efficient soldier, he had always seemed to Slater to represent the best that the SAS stood for. The two men had been good friends, serving together in Northern Ireland, the Gulf, Libya and Sri Lanka. They had shared more hangovers than either of them cared to remember and probably, it occurred to Slater, the odd girlfriend too.

Andreas had left the Regiment after an Overthrust exercise.

Overthrust was an inter-service co-operation programme between the special forces and MI5. Slater, Andreas van Rijn, Dave Constantine and a handful of other NCOs had been sent to London, dressed in plain clothes, and placed alongside the Box agents (in military circles MI5 was known as 'Box' after their old PO Box 500 address, just as MI6 were invariably 'the Firm'). On balance, Slater reckoned, the soldiers had shown up the spooks. Northern Ireland had sharpened them, and they were more aware of the consequences of not doing the job properly. Dave Constantine always claimed that he'd been on a surveillance detail in North London with a Box agent when his companion had glanced at his watch, said, 'Right, five-thirty, that's me off home,' climbed out of the car, and disappeared. While Slater only half-believed the story, he had not particularly enjoyed the Millbank atmosphere. For his money there were too many smart-arsed, number-crunching twenty-three-year-olds about the place.

Andreas, on the other hand, had appeared impressed by the set-up, and the general assumption in Hereford had been that he had been cross-recruited.

'Listen,' he told Slater now, still smiling, 'are you free for lunch? Because if so give me half an hour . . .'

They arranged to meet in Harvey Nichols, at the fifth-floor restaurant. En route, Slater visited a shoe shop. He had a good suit, bought at Austin Reed out of his SAS clothing allowance, but if he was going to be pounding pavements he needed new shoes. He settled for Church's black Oxfords. The price made him wince but if there was one thing that Slater had learnt in his years of soldiering, it was that you had to look after your feet. In Harvey Nichols he added a couple of plain white shirts and a black, knitted silk tie to his shopping basket. You couldn't go wrong with black and white, he reasoned. It was discreet, as bodyguarding demanded, but it also had that sixties retro look he'd seen advertised in the magazines in the Minerva offices. Next time he came face to face with the delectable receptionist, he decided, he'd look the part.

At the table, Andreas immediately ordered them a glass of Champagne each. Slater eyed his narrow-stemmed tulip-glass dubiously. The swanky restaurant and the Champagne obviously represented some sort of attempt to impress: in the old days they'd have made straight for a pub.

'So Neil!' Andreas began. 'How have you been?'

'Well, I'm out of the Regiment,' Slater began. 'I left just before Kosovo. Since then I've been working at a school, coaching the rugby team.'

'And how was that?' asked Andreas. 'A bit low-gear for a man of your talents, I'd have said.'

'Well, it didn't really work out in the end,' said Slater. How much did Andreas know? he wondered. If he was working for Minerva, presumably he wasn't still working for Box. If, indeed, he ever had worked for Box.

For a time they talked of mutual friends and old times. Slater reminded Andreas of an incident that had nearly seen them both RTUed, when an intelligence team known as the Forces Research Unit had discovered that a Provo sniper unit was assembling at a location near the border and had tried to scramble the SAS. To their fury and frustration the FRU were told that the Lisburn duty officer could get no response from the unit. Little wonder – the entire team, including Slater and Andreas, had been at a Def Leppard concert in the Belfast city centre. If any of them had heard their pagers over the ear-numbing wall of sound it would have been little short of a miracle.

'This is good,' said Slater, indicating the shining tranche of swordfish on his plate.

'It's metropolitan food,' smiled Andreas. 'You've been on ration-packs and school cabbage for too long. How did you find Minerva?'

'The money seems pretty good. And the work sounds pretty painless. How do you find it?'

'Well the fact is, Neil, I don't actually work for Minerva. I was looking for you.'

'Me? How did you know I was going to be there?' The moment he had spoken Slater realised how naive his words sounded.

'Everything connects, Neil. You know that. How about another glass of Champagne?'

'I'd have preferred a beer, but yeah, OK.'

Andreas smiled, beckoned him closer and brought him up to date. After the Overthrust exercise he had – as Slater had guessed – crossed over. He'd been ready for a change of scene. Had had enough, frankly, of freezing his bollocks off in all weathers.

And he'd enjoyed what he'd found, he told Slater. Plenty of brain-work, plenty of weirdness, and a lot of autonomy. 'I plan my own operations,' he explained. 'Get the word from upstairs and set things up in my own way.'

To Slater the whole set-up sounded unappealingly corporate. 'I'm glad it suits you,' he said. 'Personally, I'm looking forward to the freelance life.'

'You've never done BGing, before, have you?' asked Andreas, indicating Slater's empty glass to the waiter.

'Not outside of the Regiment,' admitted Slater.

'It sounds good,' said Andreas. 'You turn up at some fabulous apartment, pick up the lady of the house, have lunch, perhaps do a little shopping . . . But the truth is,

Neil, that a switched-on guy like you will go nuts in five minutes. You realise that you're a nanny, that you're an arse-wiper, that you're a trolley-pusher — basically that you're a servant. And a servant for the kind of people you wouldn't give the time of day to. Corrupt businessmen. Spoilt rich kids. Vulgar, uneducated women who haven't done a day's honest work in their lives.'

'All the more reason to take their money,' said Slater reasonably. 'At least I know that at the end of the day I'm my own man. I can say no to anything I don't fancy.'

'You won't last long if you do say no,' Andreas retorted. 'Close protection's a service industry. It's all about saying yes. Did Duckworth read you the poem?'

Slater admitted that he had.

'He does that with all the guys. Then when they complain that some arms-dealer's wife has given them a bad time he can quote it back at them. In fact, like a lot of queers, Duckworth adores rich women. He genuinely thinks that—'

'Did you say queers?' asked Slater.

'Yes. Didn't you figure that out? Your antennae are going to have to sharpen up, my friend.'

'I guess they are.'

Andreas, his eyes shining, leaned forward conspiratorially. 'Neil, junk Minerva and come and work with us. It'd be like old times, but without the beasting and the bollockings and the trenchfoot. We were a great team then, we can be a great team again.'

'Doing what, exactly?' asked Slater. Faced with Andreas's enthusiasm, he could feel his resolve wavering. And the other man was right – they *had* been a great team.

'Doing what we both do best,' said Andreas, gesturing to the waiter to take their plates away. 'Look, I'll put my cards on the table. You remember the stuff the special projects teams used to do?'

As if he could forget.

'That's what I do. I'm part of a sort of inter-service special projects team. There are only a handful of us – half a dozen all told – but what we do is important. It saves lives. I can't give you details at this stage, but I have been authorised to make an approach to you.'

'Why me?'

'Because you're very good. Because you're . . . experienced. Because although you probably don't want to go back to the Regiment you're missing something. Something you can't quite put your finger on. Something to do with the excitement of planning an operation and seeing it through, of living a certain sort of life, of *being* somebody again.'

'Look, Andreas, I arrived in London a week ago. All I want is enough work and enough money in the bank to keep me going. I'd like to hang out with normal people and do normal things like shopping and playing sport and going to the cinema. I'm thinking of doing an Open University degree. I don't need all this covert operations stuff.'

'But Neil, you don't know any "normal" people, as

you call them, to go shopping with. You don't know anyone to go to the rugby with, or to take to the cinema. Look what happened last time you tried living in the normal world – there were corpses strewn over three counties. The covert world *is* the normal world for you.'

So, he knew about the school.

'We need you, Neil, and right now I think that you need us.'

Join us, in other words, if you want Lark to get you out of the shit.

Looking back, Slater remembered that there had always been this manipulative side to Andreas van Rijn. He had always enjoyed power games – always liked trying to freak people out, to control them.

The trouble was, although Slater was loth to admit it, much of what Andreas said was true. He didn't really know anyone outside the covert world. And there was a side to it all – a sharp needle of excitement – that he missed . . .

'I need to get on with my life, Andreas. That's all. I wish you well, but I'm not going anywhere near your department. I'm out of the system now.'

Andreas smiled. 'And you think the system's out of you?'

He left the question hanging.

Two days later Slater was standing on the steps of the Hyde Park Hotel, waiting for the man he was to be guarding for the day. In the morning, he had been told, the principal would be shopping for clothes in the SW1 area, and in the afternoon he would be watching a home game at Spurs' White Hart Lane football ground. At 7pm the principal would be attending a drinks party followed by dinner at a private house from where a car would be collecting him and driving him home.

At 10am precisely a dark green Rover swept to the kerbside and the principal climbed out. Slater recognised Salman Rushdie immediately from the many newspaper portraits that had been published over the years. Today, the novelist was swathed in a long belted overcoat and wearing a Parisian beret.

'Mr Rushdie, I'm Neil Slater.'

Was it Lord Rushdie? Had he read somewhere that the writer had been made a life peer? Had he made a fool of himself with his first word?

But Rushdie still seemed to be smiling his oblique smile. 'I think we might start with some coffee,' he said. 'Just to fortify ourselves.'

Slater looked around. No obvious assassin had presented himself. There were no cloaked anarchists carrying bombs, no wild-eyed sword-wielding dervishes. He led Rushdie up the hotel steps, into the large, ornate foyer, and thence to the dining room. Again, the place looked safe enough.

'Why don't you sit here?' said Rushdie, pointing Slater to a window seat facing the door.

Slater sat down. From the security viewpoint the position was a sensible one.

'It occurred to me recently,' the novelist continued, 'that if people were to stop reading my books, I could go into the bodyguarding business myself. I've probably as much experience as anyone.'

'I'm sorry it's been necessary,' said Slater.

Rushdie nodded. 'Me too. Me too. Now, how do you take your coffee?'

Slater had never guarded a celebrity before. With the Regiment he'd been assigned occasional protection duties, but never of a recognisable figure. As he and Rushdie made their way through Harrods ten minutes later he realised just how complex his task was to be. A lot of people recognised the novelist, and many of them stared. Some manoeuvred themselves into positions from where they could take a second look. Whether any of this attention was hostile was almost impossible to determine. Rushdie had insisted on proceeding on foot – he liked window-shopping, he told Slater, and he liked to see the faces of strangers close up – and the best that Slater could do was to interpose himself between Rushdie and anyone who might conceivably be an Islamic militant.

For more than a decade the novelist had been the object of a *fatwa* issued by Iran's supreme leader, the Ayatollah Khomeini. This edict urged that Rushdie be killed because of supposed blasphemy in one of his novels. A year ago, however, a less puritan Iranian government had announced it intended no harm to Rushdie, and for a time it had seemed as if he might resume normal life. And then a report had appeared in the Iranian newspaper *Kayhan* that over 500 Iranians had pledged to sell their kidneys to raise money for the writer's murder. According to intelligence sources the plan was devised by Islamic militia members in the Iranian holy city of Mashad.

Slater, for whom anonymity was the very breath of life, sympathised with Rushdie. He had seen photographs smuggled out of Iran of mass public hangings from the arms of cranes, and from Algeria of the mobile guillotines driven from village to village by Islamic fundamentalist death-squads. And in Iraq, of course . . .

'Do you mind', said Rushdie, 'if we just look in here?'

It was the book department. Shoppers were browsing among the shelves and standing in line at the till, but no one made any sign of having registered Rushdie's entrance. In fact, Slater was certain, they had all noticed him. They just weren't so uncool as to stare.

On a small, circular table close to the aisle was a display of a new John le Carré novel. On the far side of the table, facing the interior of the room rather than the aisle, was a similar display of Rushdie's new book. A visitor passing through the department would certainly see the Le Carré display, but probably not the Rushdie. Deftly, the author revolved the table through 180 degrees.

'What's the book about?' asked Slater, amused.

'Rock 'n' roll,' Rushdie answered. 'Would you like a copy?'

'Very much,' said Slater.

'Help yourself, then. Steal one.'

'You're kidding!'

'I dare you,' said Rushdie, with the ghost of a smile.

'I'm not in the daring business any more,' said Slater. 'Let alone the getting-arrested business. Apart from anything else we're on closed circuit TV. And that guy over there in the blazer is a store detective.'

'How can you tell?'

Slater shrugged. 'The way he stands. The way he isn't actually looking at the books.'

'I see what you mean. Do you think he knows what you're doing here?'

'Yeah, definitely he does.'

An assistant approached them.

'Have you got Geri Halliwell's autobiography?' Rushdie asked.

Ten minutes later they were in the Armani shop on the Brompton Road.

'What do you think?' asked Rushdie, holding up a shirt in heavy olive-green wool.

'I'm not a good person to ask about clothes,' replied Slater, his eyes scanning the store. 'But it looks OK to me.'

Rushdie held up the same shirt in grey. 'And this one?'

'That looks OK too.'

'Which would you buy for yourself?'

'The grey. I've spent half my life in dark green.'

As Rushdie signed the credit-card slip, Slater held out a copy of his novel. 'While you've got your pen out,' he said, 'would you mind signing this?'

Rushdie stared at him in amazement. 'Now how the hell . . .'

'I never could resist a good book.'

With the clothes-shopping completed they had lunch in a pub in Beauchamp Place, where Rushdie questioned Slater about the Gulf War. 'What was your worst moment?' he asked.

Slater considered. 'Well, the most frightening moment was probably during an anti-Scud mission.'

'Go on,' said the novelist, forking Branston pickle on to his cheese roll.

Slater sipped at his Coke. 'Well, we'd got satellite pictures in, showing activity near a place called al-Anbar, west of Baghdad. The theory from the intelligence people was that a number of missiles were being grouped there before moving them on to their mobile launchers. They didn't know how long they'd all be in one place, so the word was we had to check them out fast and if possible help knock them out.

'Four of us went in. They dropped us off by helicopter at night and got out as quickly as possible. Al-Anbar was surrounded by anti-aircraft batteries, there were tanks in the area, and there were rumours of a concealed airbase. It was also fantastically cold. We'd been expecting the Costa del Sol, but we found the coldest January for thirty years. Snow was expected and the wind-chill was murderous.

'We moved up on the target. Air-reconnaissance pictures had shown there was a small berm – a kind of banked-up dugout – a couple of hundred yards from where we thought the Scuds were, and the theory was that this was for the ground-crew to shelter behind when the missiles were fired. It was a risk, but we decided to make the berm our observation post.

'It took a lot longer than we thought. We knew from prisoners we'd interrogated that all the sentries would have night sights, so we couldn't take any chances. The trouble was there was no cover, just bare rock, and we were like flies on a table-top. In the end we made it to the berm about an hour before dawn, and at that point it began to pour with rain. By then, though, we'd been able to confirm via our own night sights that there were definitely Scuds on the base. They were well concealed, but they were there.

'I radioed through the confirmation to the base in Saudi and we were ordered to sit tight. The air attack would come after dark that night. Between now and then we were to dig in and observe any movement.

'It got light. The Scuds and the trucks had been netted up for the day and were pretty much invisible. The only sign of life was two low, camouflaged tents which we guessed housed the missile and anti-aircraft crews. So we just hunkered down in the berm with one man on stag and the rest trying to sleep. There was nothing else to do. If any sentries had come along we'd have been dead, but none did, and gradually we got a bit of warmth back in our bones. By eleven o'clock we were beginning to think we might even make it through to nightfall. And then everything changed.

'I was on stag. There had been no movement for an hour. And then, on the horizon, I saw a dust-trail. It was moving towards us, and soon I could make out a pair of Panhard landcruisers. Landcruisers usually meant someone important, and twenty-four hours earlier the intelligence people in Saudi had intercepted a message announcing that the al-Anbar base was due to be visited by some high-up code-named Marwan. No one was quite sure of Marwan's identity, but the popular theory was that he was an Iranian scientist who had defected during the Iran-Iraq war and was now running the missile research plant at Sa'd 16, up in the north. If this theory was right then he was a real prize: it was the Sa'd 16 team who had designed the al-Husayn – the long-range version of the Soviet Scud that you could fit with chemical and biological weapons.

'And then I saw that the dust-trail was more than a couple of visiting high-ups in landcruisers. Behind them, over the horizon came this vast convoy of T-55 tanks. They were heading straight for us, and there wasn't a thing we could do about it except cover ourselves with stones and dirt and camouflage netting and hope they didn't notice us. I was the last to get under cover and I've never seen anything more terrifying than those T-55s. They looked like monsters

– old and black and pitted with shell-scars. The whole desert was roaring and grinding, and all that we could do was lie there – I had my head jammed up against one of the other guys' arses – and hope that they kept moving. But they didn't. They clanked to a halt, in formation, all around us. We could hear them opening their turrets and we could hear their radios, and eventually we could hear their voices. And then a couple of them came over and I thought well, that's it. We're dead. And then they pissed on us. I felt it running down my neck. They must have thought the berm was some kind of rubbish tip where they threw the old cam-netting. We were there, not moving a hair, for four hours, and I can't even begin to describe to you what that was like, or what that kind of fear does to you.'

Slater returned to the present to find Rushdie watching him.

'You see, you're looking at me right now – you know how the story ends. In that berm we didn't know how the story was going to end. There had been stories about spies being stoned to death, castrated, hung from wire nooses . . . you name it.'

'So what happened?'

'They went away. They started up their engines, locked down their hatches and went away. I radioed in a report about the tanks on my handset and we stayed there, not moving, for another three hours. The air-strike came in just before midnight, and boy, was it good to see that Scud jet-propellant blow!'

'And Marwan?' asked Rushdie. 'Did you ever identify him?'

'No one survived the attack,' said Slater. 'That was one of the things my team had been tasked to ensure.'

There was a long silence.

'How is it to know that you've killed someone?' asked the novelist. 'If you don't mind my asking.'

'How's that ploughman's lunch?' asked Slater.

The football went well. The stands tickets gave a good view of Tottenham beating West Ham two-nil, and Rushdie took notes assiduously throughout in a small, leather-covered book.

After the game, rather than look for a taxi, Rushdie suggested they might walk down the High Road to Seven Sisters tube station, as most of the fans did whenever Spurs played at home. To begin with they were swept along by a crowd of cheering, chanting Spurs fans. The air was heavy with fried food and beery good humour. The grey skies promised snow.

At intervals Rushdie stopped to note his impressions, glancing around him as he did so. This began to worry Slater: the writer was less likely to be recognised in Haringey than in Knightsbridge but his actions closely resembled those of a policeman and might easily be construed as hostile. He seemed impervious, however, to the stares he prompted.

'I think it might be an idea to keep going,' Slater said, when Rushdie indicated that, yet again, they should stop for a moment. The faces around them were those of West Ham supporters now, and their mood was visibly less benevolent than that of the victorious Spurs crowd.

'I'm a writer,' said Rushdie simply. 'And right now I have to write.'

'Can you wait until we get to that bus stop?' Slater asked.

But as they sat down, they found themselves surrounded.

'Know me again, would you?' asked an acned fatboy in a Hammers shirt.

Rushdie said nothing, but watched with detached interest as the group solidified around him. Slater, hoping that the situation would defuse of its own accord, remained silent.

'You deaf or sump'ink?' asked the fatboy.

Slater flickered a glance at the group. There were three talkers, he reckoned, and three fighters. The one to watch was the heavy guy at the back, who was even now flexing and curling his fingers.

'An' what's your fuckin' problem, wanker?' demanded the fatboy, sniffing.

Here we go, thought Slater. On the seat beside him Rushdie patiently studied his hands.

'I'm talking to you, cunt!'

'Are you going to let us carry on our way?' asked Slater mildly.

'You don't get it, do you pal?' It was the heavy guy at the back. His naturally ugly appearance had not been improved by the spider's-web tattoo across his neck.

Like the fatboy, his eyes were puffy and his nose ran.

They were all, Slater guessed, completely hot-wired on coke. They weren't about to walk away – they wanted a positive result to counterbalance the defeat at White Hart Lane.

'Is this a money thing?' asked Rushdie, speaking for the first time. 'Or just a football thing?'

His voice was steady. Slater was amazed at his composure.

'It's basically a stupidity thing,' answered Slater evenly. 'What we have here is a bunch of not-very-clever boys who've taken too many drugs.'

The taunt had the desired effect. Spider's-web, his eyes narrowing, took an angry step forward and drew back his fist.

But Slater was already rising to his feet. His first punch hammered into his attacker's lower ribcage, his second – as the thug doubled up – flattened his nose. Each blow was accompanied by the crack of fracturing bone.

Bloody drool running down his chin, Spider's-web sank to his knees.

'How about you?' Slater addressed the fatboy reasonably. 'Ready to put your money where your mouth is?'

The fatboy stared open-mouthed at the twitching figure at his feet. The other four took a step backwards.

'There's a hospital back there,' Slater continued. 'You'll probably want to get this ape to the casualty entrance. He'll have a broken nose and two fractured ribs. We'll be on our way.'

'Was there any other possible conclusion to that sequence?' Rushdie asked five minutes later as they descended the steps of Seven Sisters tube station.

'Not really,' said Slater. 'There comes a point from which, for certain people like that guy with the tattooed neck, retreat becomes physically impossible. You can see them flooding with adrenaline before your eyes. And at that point you have to fight or flee. Personally I'd rather flee, given the choice, but I suspect on that occasion we wouldn't have made it.'

'My four-minute mile days are behind me,' admitted Rushdie. 'Are you all right?'

'I could use a cup of tea,' admitted Slater. 'And I expect you'd like to write the whole thing up.'

FOUR

'Neil, be a darling and carry the bags, would you?'

'Certainly,' said Neil Slater. So far there were nine of them: two from Versace, three from Donna Karan, and four from Miu-Miu. Grace Litvinoff – and she was the first to admit it – liked to shop.

'Chanel, Neil!'

'Certainly, Mrs Litvinoff.'

'I don't need to tell you the way there do I?'

'Not any more, Mrs Litvinoff.'

And she didn't. He knew all her favourite places. And what was more, they all knew him. Grace Litvinoff had been in London for ten days now, and for most of those he had trailed her up and down Bond Street, Sloane Street, Mount Street, Brook Street, and all the other Streets where it was possible to spend a thousand pounds on a hallmarked scrap of silken or cashmere nothingness.

Now, when he followed her into one of those cool, perfumed establishments the impeccably groomed male and female staff nodded to him, smiled hello to him, and in a couple of cases stared with open and amused longing at his groin.

For Slater was not the raw provincial he had been two months earlier. He now looked as if he belonged in Prada or Fendi or Gucci or wherever whimsy and greed led his mostly female clients. His haircut had cost twice the price of a tank of petrol, the labels on his clothes were Italian, and he knew the menus at the Met Bar and Le Caprice off by heart.

On the down-side was the question of his own status. They knew him at all the metropolitan watering-holes, but they knew what he did too. They knew that he was being paid to fetch and carry and look out for trouble. And while it was one thing squiring a beautiful and glamorous woman like Grace Litvinoff round the West End, it was quite another running errands for some loudmouthed gangster's wife – or worse, some loudmouthed gangster's children, as he'd been called on to do once or twice. Andreas had been right – bodyguarding was a service industry.

But having said that, he was good at it. Since the incident with Salman Rushdie there had not been a hint of trouble. He had learnt an operating style which combined social deference with professional authority and had managed to retain most – if not quite all – of his self-respect in the process. Duckworth was pleased with him, and had said so.

It was a clear spring day, and the starlings were singing in the plane trees as Slater followed Grace Litvinoff into Chanel. According to her passport, which he had seen in the Litvinoffs' Mayfair apartment, Grace was thirty-four and had been born in

Singapore. Her husband, whom Duckworth approvingly described as 'stupendously rich', bought and sold communications companies.

David Litvinoff was some fifteen years his wife's senior, and the story went that he had been making a business stopover in Singapore in the mid-eighties when a colleague had persuaded him to visit one of the island's shirtmakers. The fitting had taken place in the morning in one of the myriad 'shop-houses' behind Raffles Hotel, and the half-dozen completed garments were delivered to Litvinoff's room at the end of the afternoon.

They were delivered by the shirtmaker's eighteen-year-old daughter, a girl fashioned by chance and genetic accident into a creature of extraordinary beauty. Like many Singaporeans she was slender and ivory-skinned, but unlike any Singaporean that David Litvinoff had ever seen her eyes were a dazzling tropical green. As soon as she walked into his hotel room the young New Yorker – already many times a millionaire – felt himself drowning in her gaze. They were married three months later.

Marrying Grace, it was said, was the first and last impulsive thing David Litvinoff had ever done. At his preliminary interview for the position of bodyguard, Slater had been struck by the man's remoteness. Litvinoff had barely spoken, raising his eyes from his paperwork for no more than a few seconds at a time and indicating his final approval of Slater with a nod. What he and his wife had ever had in common was hard to imagine.

For the Singapore shirtmaker's daughter had become one of the international set's most dazzling and extrovert stars. As a child she had seen glamour at a distance – now she wanted it for herself. And she got it. She spent her husband's money with reckless panache – buying art in Manhattan, enlightenment in Tibet, *haute couture* in Paris, and holiday homes in St Kitts and Aspen. She was a particular darling of the fashion houses, for unlike ninety-nine per cent of the face-lifted harpies who occupied front-row seats at the shows, Grace Litvinoff was beautiful. The waist-length curtain of raven-black hair had been replaced by a chic little bob and the long green eyes were perhaps a little more knowing than they had been when her husband had first encountered them sixteen years ago, but otherwise time had stood still. Her skin was still as delicate as the petal of an orchid, while her body – toned and streamlined by hundreds if not thousands of hours of gym workouts, yoga, tai-chi, hydrotherapy and deep-tissue massage, was as lithe as a panther's.

For twenty minutes, as she tried on outfit after outfit, Slater watched the shop's Bond Street entrance from a well-stuffed chair. Where, he wondered vaguely, would they be lunching today? Earlier in the week they'd visited the Mirabelle, and Marco Pierre White had joined them at their table.

From the far end of the shop, by the changing rooms, came the sound of female giggles.

'Neil, darling,' came Grace Litvinoff's mid-Atlantic drawl. 'We need you!'

Leaving the nine shopping bags by the counter he hurried over. His employer's sleek, elegantly-coiffed head protruded from one of the changing-rooms. Two assistants in gilt-buttoned suits stood on either side of the door. There was an air of stifled hysteria.

'We need a decision, Neil. For the reception tonight do I go *with* . . .'

She stepped out wearing a sheer, barely existent silk top over an embroidered lace brassiere.

'Or do I go *without*?'

She reappeared without the bra.

For a long moment he gaped at her, stared at the small, dark-pointed breasts trembling beneath the silk.

'Well, Neil? What do you think?'

The two assistants were smiling at him, enjoying his discomfort.

'I'm . . . I'm not sure,' he managed, looking away.

'I think Neil disapproves of me,' Grace Litvinoff cooed. 'I guess the decision will have to wait. Perhaps I'll wait and see how I feel.'

There had always been an edge of flirtatiousness in her dealings with Slater, but she had never, he thought, quite crossed the line like this before. God, but she was sexy though, with those lazy green eyes and that sly, spoilt mouth. And, of course, those edible little breasts. Wondering about the rest of her, imagining her nude – imagining her arching beneath him and murmuring his name – he felt himself harden.

And turned to the door of the shop. Get a grip, he told himself angrily. Get a fucking grip. He'd lost it then – dropped his guard and his concentration one hundred per cent.

'Am I *very* naughty?' she asked him, passing him the bag containing the silk top – so light it felt empty. 'Are you *very* cross with me?'

'I'm here to guard you, Mrs Litvinoff,' he replied carefully.

'Someone to watch over me . . . Do you know that song, Neil?'

'I'm afraid not, Mrs Litvinoff. Would you like me to take the bags to the car, or would you like to go on somewhere else?'

'I thought Valentino, perhaps. And then lunch.'

What was it, wondered Neil Slater, looking around the minimalist white-on-white dining room, that linked all these people? Why did they all look as if they knew each other – as if they belonged here by right? And why – Italian loafers or no Italian loafers – didn't he feel that way? Why did he always feel the outsider?

Perhaps it was that sense of outsidership – that sense that life's rules don't quite apply – that had linked them all in the Regiment. That was what had been missing from his life since leaving the army, he thought – the sheer satisfaction of bending the rules. As a Bolingbroke's employee, and now as Duckworth's man, there was no such satisfaction to be had, no such privilege to be enjoyed.

Thoughtfully, his eyes scanning the room for any

jarring note – for anything or anyone that shouldn't be there – he raised a glass of mineral water to his lips.

And held it there.

Something out of the ordinary was happening. Grace Litvinoff's hand was delicately – but very definitely – exploring his thigh. They were sitting in a corner beneath a tall, white-curtained window and she was leaning forward and confiding to him that what she really wanted – what she really *badly* wanted and wasn't prepared to wait any longer for – was for him to take her back to the flat and undress her and fuck her hard for the whole of the afternoon.

'Can we go now, Neil?' she whispered, her long fingers closing over him. 'Can we just pay the bill and get the car and go? I just can't wait any longer.'

Slater felt himself stiffening. His professional resolve evaporated before the need in her long green eyes. You can't blame a compass for pointing north, he told himself.

Her husband, he knew, was in Milan until Wednesday.

'Excuse me!' Grace Litvinoff waved breezily to one of the waitresses. 'We have to go.'

The waitress looked at the table, at Grace's fully charged glass of Krug Champagne, at their barely touched Lobster Newburg. 'Is everything all right, Mrs Litvinoff?'

'Everything's perfect,' she smiled, giving Slater an encouraging squeeze. 'We just have to go. It's kind of urgent.'

She dropped her napkin and stood up. Slater wondered if he dared do the same.

In the silver Lexus, as usual, she sat in the back while Slater sat in front with the driver. No word passed between the three of them. Grace Litvinoff, as she liked to do, chatted to friends on her Nokia, while Slater attempted to squash down the bulge in his trousers and went through the motions of monitoring the surrounding traffic.

The entrance to the Litvinoffs' building was in Mayfair Place, behind Piccadilly. Dismissing the chauffeur, Grace Litvinoff waited as Slater carried the dozen or so shopping bags into the hallway. In the lift, which was operated by a uniformed porter, she appeared to ignore him, but as soon as the gates closed behind them on the eighth floor she turned her face to his.

'Wait,' he told her, and unlocking the door to the penthouse apartment quickly disarmed the intruder alarm. Behind him she slipped the chain over the latch.

'I didn't get a chance to finish my Champagne,' she whispered. 'Would you be an angel?'

In the kitchen, Slater found a bottle of cold Dom Pérignon and a single crystal glass. She was waiting for him in the terrace room – a cool, light-filled space dominated by the view over Green Park. She took the glass, drank from it, and placed it on the mantelpiece. Then, wrapping her arms delicately around Slater's neck, she kissed him. The kiss took a long time.

Closing his eyes, Slater surrendered to the soft urgency of her mouth and the pliancy of her slender body beneath his hands. He had never in his life held a woman as impossibly exotic as this, never tasted a scent quite like her scent, never felt skin quite like her skin.

'You're so quiet, Neil,' she said, slipping her long fingers beneath his shirt. 'You hardly say anything.'

'I'm not so much of a talker,' he murmured into her hair. 'I'm more of a doer.'

'And are you going to . . . *do* me?' she asked.

'I think I am, yes.'

'Call me by my name,' she said, drawing her nails softly down his back. 'Look into my eyes and say, "Grace, I'm going to fuck you."'

'Is that what you want?' he asked, undoing the silk loops of her mandarin-collared shirt.

'That's what I want,' she breathed.

'In that case,' said Slater, moving his mouth to her breasts, feeling the dark nipples harden beneath his lips and against his tongue, 'you should wait and see what happens.'

'No words of love?' Her mouth was against his hair.

'No words.'

They undressed each other and he carried her through to one of the bedrooms. 'Wait!' she said, snatching up her handbag.

In the mirror he watched her rise and fall over him. The whole scene – the tall, white room, the sunlight at the windows, the slight, gasping figure straddling him – had an air of impossibility, of unreality.

'Grace,' he said.

'Tell me, darling,' she said quietly. 'Talk to me. Tell me how much you want me.' Her eyes were closed now.

'You know how much,' he said, moving his hips in time with hers. 'You know how much I want you. How much I've wanted you since the first second I saw you.'

'When did you want me most?'

'This morning, in the shop. That was . . .'

'Would you have liked those girls to watch us?'

'I wouldn't have cared.'

She leant over him, let her hair fall in his face. 'Do you love me, Neil?'

His hesitated for less than a moment, felt the slick, hard insistence between her legs. At that moment he would have told her anything. 'Yes. I love you.'

'Tell me that you do. Use my name.'

He reached for her hips, pressed them against him. 'I love you, Grace. You're the most . . .'

Her nails dug into his shoulders. 'Go on!'

'You're the most beautiful . . .'

'Go on, Neil!' she gasped, biting her lower lip. 'Tell me how . . .'

But Slater was beyond words. Flipping her on to her back, taking her rhythm for his own, he drove into her with a lost, desperate abandon. Beneath him he felt her tauten, cry like an animal, tear at his shoulders with her nails until at last they were riding the wave together.

Mouthing each other's names, laughing with

disbelief at the unexpectedness of it all, he fell exhausted to her side, watched the white room reform around them. She lay like a cat, eyes closed, and tentatively he drew his tongue across her breasts. What the hell am I doing here? he asked himself. What the hell have I done?

Smiling, she drew him to her.

'Do you really love me, like you said? If I was to get a divorce from David, would you . . . still want me? Would you still look after me?'

He looked at her, kissed the soft hollow beneath her ear, felt the coolness of her blue-white diamond stud earring against his mouth. 'Yes,' he said. His brain felt totally disconnected from his body. 'Yes to everything.'

That evening he accompanied her to a reception at the Tate Gallery. As he patrolled the crowd, mineral water in hand, he wondered if he was completely insane. If Duckworth got to hear that he'd spent the afternoon in bed with one of his best clients – or to be precise with the wife of one of his best clients – then his bodyguarding career was over. He'd committed the cardinal sin.

But it would have been worth it. God, but she was beautiful. Never in his wildest dreams had he thought he would ever see such an exquisite creature curled beside him, hear her whisper his name, beg him to make love to her again. And again. She was a tiger, green-eyed and insatiable.

Drained, drowsy with sex, they'd showered and dressed at six o'clock. He'd discovered he was ravenous, and raiding the fridge had discovered a pot of Astrakhan caviar, a mango, and a bottle of Japanese beer. Grace Litvinoff had recharged her batteries with a tiny cube of sushi, which to Slater's eyes looked as if it would barely sustain a weasel. 'You should eat more!' he told her, patting her flat little stomach.

'Then I'd look like everybody else,' she answered. 'And my clothes wouldn't fit. And you wouldn't want me.'

She looked at him, watched him wash up the plates and cutlery that they'd used. 'Neil, when did you last . . . sleep with anyone?'

'It's been quite a long time,' he admitted. 'I was a bit . . . out of things for a while. And that side of my life pretty much closed down.'

'Were you ill?'

'Something like that. I had a bad tour of duty across the water.'

'In the USA?'

'In Northern Ireland. And by the end of it things had come on top.'

'I came on top a couple of times this afternoon,' she said. 'It's not such a bad place to come!'

'Funny girl.'

They'd agreed on the ground rules. In public − anywhere except in the flat − they would behave as client and bodyguard. Not so much as an intimate look would pass between them. Slater would do his job exactly as before – given her husband's vast wealth the possibility of a kidnap attempt remained a real one. Meanwhile they would communicate using text messages on their mobile phones.

The paintings at the reception were very large, and showed hugely enlarged parts of the human body. There was a vast and filthy fingernail, an arsehole the size of a dustbin-lid, a weeping appendectomy scar, and several square metres of acned buttock. For the most part the 200 or so guests were standing with their backs to these paintings, although each new arrival gave the exhibition a cursory glance. To Slater's eye they were a creepy, vampiric bunch – especially the men, with their too-short hair and their tight-lipped, puritanical expressions. Grace, as he watched, was greeted by two of them – zombies in their mid-forties with plucked eyebrows and the over-pink faces of habitual amyl nitrate users. Having discussed her outfit in detail – an outfit Slater had helped choose – they took an arm each and steered her from exhibit to exhibit.

'Are you having a good time?'

At first Slater was unaware that the voice was addressed to him.

'Lost for words, are we?'

Slater nodded, and turned away. The speaker was a carefully groomed man in his fifties with a goatee beard.

'Do you like the paintings, then?'

'Not a lot. At least I wouldn't hang them on my

walls, if that's what you mean. Not that they'd fit on my walls.'

'I'm sorry to hear that.'

'Well, it's a small place. Not bad though, for the money.'

'No, I'm sorry to hear you don't like the paintings. What *do* you put on your walls?'

Slater frowned and pretended to consider. 'Well, you know that poster of the tennis girl scratching her arse?'

The other man raised an eyebrow. 'Yes, indeed I do.' He nodded vigorously. 'Well, I must be circulating.'

'Good luck,' Slater called after him. Wanker, he added mentally.

A soft, familiar voice behind him. 'Neil, I'll be another half hour or so, OK?'

It was Grace, with her two hangers-on.

Slater nodded. 'Sure. No problem.'

'Did I just see you talking to Daniel Sweeting?' she asked, indicating the departing man.

'He asked me if I liked the paintings.'

'And you told him?'

'I said I didn't.'

The hangers-on looked at each other, their eyes widening in horror.

Grace smiled. 'He's the artist. He's also a friend of mine, so try not to give him too hard a time if you run into him again.'

'I'm sorry,' said Slater levelly.

'Neil looks after me,' Grace told her two companions. 'He keeps me safe. He's my desert island luxury.'

They looked him up and down. Particularly down.

'I suppose this must all seem very strange to you,' said one.

'I've seen stranger,' said Slater, his eyes moving around the room.

'So where did you train?' said the other. 'Is it like a social work thing?'

'Sort of,' said Slater. On the other side of the room Salman Rushdie and Geri Halliwell were walking arm-in-arm. Seeing Slater, the novelist raised a hand in greeting.

'Neil knows everyone,' said Grace.

She left him alone after that, and Slater tried not to stare too intently after her. Already he wanted her again, and more badly than he could begin to put into words. He was grateful to his job for having enabled them to meet, but Andreas's crack about bodyguarding being a service industry still reverberated in his mind. These people regarded him as being of lower status than themselves, he mused, and even though they met as equals in bed, Grace surely felt the same. Her husband paid for him to be delivered to her door every morning, after all.

Was this really how a former SAS soldier should be occupying himself? As a glorified male escort? He thought of Dave Constantine cleaning lavatories and unblocking plug-holes in Wormbridge. Dave was probably in Africa by now, sweating out the last two years' alcohol and cursing himself for having walked out on Linda. But he was also doing the thing that he'd been born to do – the thing that they'd all been born to do.

'You're a Minerva BG, aren't you?'

Slater snapped out of his reverie. The questioner was of about the same age as himself – a tough-looking man with a crewcut and a closely controlled moustache.

'Yes,' said Slater. 'You too?'

'Yeah. I'm looking after Mr Rushdie. How long have you been working for Duckworth?'

The two men compared notes. Tab Holland was a former Military Policeman, and like Slater was not greatly impressed by the antics of some of the moneyed classes. He'd spent the last week looking after a pop group, and described how he'd had to carry tampons with him at all times – the lead singer's cocaine habit had caused her to haemorrhage from the nose on a daily basis.

Holland was interested to hear that Slater had been in the SAS. 'Did you see the *Evening Standard*?' he asked, and Slater shook his head.

'A bunch of your guys lifted Radovan Karadjic. They'd been watching his place in Bosnia – some farm, I think – and followed him when he and some of his guys were driving towards the border into Montenegro. Bloody great firefight, apparently –

thousands of rounds expended – and at the end of it, after losing six guys, the Serbs came out with their hands in the air. Next stop the War Crimes Tribunal in the Hague. Fucking brilliant result!'

'I'll drink to that,' said Slater, raising his mineral water. Shit, he thought, that would have been a good one to be on. The lads'll be pissing it up tonight, that's for sure. He felt a hot stab of jealousy and regret.

'Who dares wins, eh!' said Tab Holland.

'Yeah,' said Slater. 'I guess that's about the long and the short of it.'

He looked around him. Precious little daring here. Precious little winning. And then he saw Grace Litvinoff, caught her eye for a second as she air-kissed Geri Halliwell, and his heart went into free-fall.

Four hours later, after a seemingly endless dinner for twelve at the River Café – he and Tab Holland had been consigned to a table of their own by the door, where they picked at spaghetti carbonara and swapped war stories – Slater was walking her to the car.

'Were you *very* bored?' she asked him, her voice slurring slightly.

'I was fine,' said Slater. He dropped his voice. 'Shall I stay tonight?'

'I haven't got you tomorrow, have I?'

'No. I've got some Indian family to take to the zoo.'

'Stay, then. I can't wait till Friday.'

When they reached the Lexus, Slater climbed in front with the driver.

'Drop you home, mate?' the driver asked when they reached Mayfair Place. The pattern on other nights had been that Slater accompanied Grace Litvinoff up to the flat and then the driver, who lived in Walthamstow, gave him a lift up to Highbury.

'Not tonight, thanks,' answered Slater. 'I've got to go on somewhere.'

'Right, mate. Sure,' the driver replied. 'See you Friday, then.'

From the man's faint smile, Slater could see that he had guessed the score.

'See you Friday.'

Expressionless, Slater walked round the silver bonnet of the Lexus and opened the door for his principal.

In the flat they started undressing each other the moment the heavy Banham latch clicked shut behind them. A trail of clothes described their erratic progress to the bedroom.

By 1pm the next day, Slater's mood was beginning to fray. He had arrived at the Chabbrias' Bayswater Road apartment at nine, after an early morning dash home from Mayfair for a change of clothes. The idea was that he should accompany the three Chabbria children to the zoo, but by 11am there was no sign that this was going to happen. One of the children, a pale, overweight twelve-year-old named Sweetie, had refused to get out of her nightie until her *Xena, Warrior Princess* video was finished, eight-year-old

Lallu had installed himself in front of his Playstation and announced his intention to play Mortal Kombat all day, and the youngest – Chunky – was still throwing his breakfast at the Norland nanny. None of them paid Slater the slightest attention except the nanny, a West Country girl named Alison, who managed to break away from feeding Chunky for long enough to make him a cup of tea.

'Nice, unspoilt children,' murmured Slater.

'Couldn't you just eat them up?' agreed Alison with a wan smile.

Brief excitement was caused by the arrival of the post, and with it several mail-order catalogues. Sweetie put *Xena* on pause and Lallu halted his game and both children then placed several orders for CDs and computer games on their mobile phones. 'Are you sure you've got Mummy's Visa number right this time?' asked Alison. 'We don't want any more lost tempers, do we?'

Mummy, bleary with sleep, made an appearance shortly after midday. Like Sweetie, she was dressed in a nightie and a quilted nylon dressing gown. Her make-up had not weathered the night well.

'Where's the cook?' she demanded abruptly of Alison.

'It's her day off, Mrs Chabbria. Can I get you anything?'

'No,' she yawned. 'God, so lazy these people – they just come and go without a care. *Nightmare*, this servant thing. Who's this fellow?'

'I'm . . . I've come to take the children to the zoo,' said Slater. 'Or wherever they want to go.'

'Oh, I see. Bodyguard, *yaar*?'

'That's right.'

'OK, make yourself useful. Go out and get me a Slush Puppie and a Family Bucket of KFC. Any of you kids want anything?'

None answered.

'Edgware Road,' mouthed Alison. 'Just up from the cinema.'

Slater nodded. It was clearly going to be a long day. Passing a newsagent's he picked up a paper for details of the Karadjic snatch. Soldiers from 22 SAS, he read, had followed the indicted war criminal from Belgrade to a farm near Foca in Eastern Bosnia. There they had kept watch from the minefields on the outskirts of the property until their target, accompanied by twelve associates, had ventured out under cover of darkness, heading for Montenegro. Less than two miles from the open border, the Serbian cars had found their passage blocked by an articulated lorry, which had apparently slewed in the road. Behind them, a truck had raced down a farm-track to block their exit. Karadjic's guards had immediately opened fire and a fierce gun-battle had ensued in which six Serbians had been killed and two seriously wounded. The remainder had surrendered along with Karadjic, who according to the paper had sustained a flesh-wound 'in the upper thigh'.

This news reflected well on the Regiment – none of the other peacekeeping nations had got close to this most elusive of targets. All that was needed now was to nail General Ratko Mladic. What a left and right that would be!

Ten minutes later he presented himself back at the flat with the fried chicken bucket and the Slush Puppie. He presented these to Mrs Chabbria, who by then had joined Sweetie on the sofa. After the cold air outside the flat seemed stiflingly hot. Electronic bleeps and Chunky's howls filled the air.

'You know,' said Sweetie, fast-forwarding through the trailers on a new video. 'I quite fancy a Slush Puppie too. But the mint one, *yaar*? The green one?'

'Sure,' said Slater, injecting as much good humour into his voice as he could muster. 'Anyone else want anything while I'm out? Last orders ladies and gents . . .'

When he returned, there were two new arrivals – a boy and girl of around seventeen and sixteen respectively, both dressed in matt black couture-line Versace.

'Watch out,' whispered Alison, as Slater passed her at the ironing-board.

'Hey, Sweetie!' said the teenage boy, grabbing at the twelve-year-old's Slush Puppie. 'Give it up, *yaar*.'

'Bugger off, Vinny!' Sweetie protested. 'Send the man.'

'You!' mouthed the boy in Slater's direction. 'Get the same again. And pick up some fries, too. Bimla, you want something?'

Bimla, the teenage girl, shook her head.

'Got that?' asked Vinny.

'I've got it,' said Slater evenly.

'OK, *chalo*. Move!'

In a way, thought Slater, as the lift whirred downwards yet again, the last couple of months had served as quite an education. He'd met some arrogant types in the army – Ruperts, they were universally known as, with their braying voices and their shrieking, Sloaney girlfriends – and he'd met some appalling snobs among Bolingbroke's parents, but they'd been rank beginners compared to the people he'd met while working for Minerva. People like these Chabbrias, for example, for whom manners and courtesy appeared to count for nothing at all. People who considered that money gave them a licence to behave exactly as they pleased.

But perhaps it did, Slater mused. Perhaps the fact that people like him and Alison took their employers' arrogance on the chin sent the message that it was just fine to order people around like that. Perhaps the fact that he didn't slam that overdressed turd Vinny up against the wall and teach him a lesson in manners meant that the next employee would be treated even worse.

Tough. He needed the money, so he would put up with it. Sticks and stones, he told himself. Sticks and stones.

'Didn't you listen?' said Vinny angrily when Slater returned to the flat carrying the Slush Puppie and the french fries. 'Bimla, what did you ask for?'

'A smoothie,' said Bimla, yawning. 'A strawberry smoothie.'

'I'm sorry, Vinny,' said Slater. 'I didn't hear her.'

The boy stared at Slater. 'What did you call me?'

'Vinny,' said Slater. 'Why, isn't that your name?'

The boy clicked his fingers. 'Come out here.'

Slater followed him into the hallway, giving Alison the ghost of a wink *en route*, and waited while Vinny lit a cigarette with a gold Dunhill lighter.

'How much does your agency pay you?' the boy began, turning the lighter between his fingers.

Cool it, Slater told himself. Don't let this little tosser wind you up.

'Mr Chabbria pays the agency six hundred pounds a day. I get three hundred of that.'

'Three hundred pounds a day. Right. Well my father earns that sum in two minutes. And that's without getting out of his fucking chair. So you'll understand, butthead, that you don't call me by my family name – or even Vinod – until I invite you to, OK?'

Slater took a deep breath. 'Fine,' he said. 'What do I call you?'

'Mr Chabbria will do.'

'Mr Chabbria it is, then. Shall I go and buy Miss Chabbria her smoothie now, Mr Chabbria?'

In the end, no one went to the zoo or even left the flat. Slater went backwards and forwards collecting snacks and DVDs, and the Chabbrias lounged about, eating and watching the flickering screens. Slater's elaborate courtesy seemed to infuriate Vinod Chabbria even more than his easygoing approach had, and the boy had had to smoke several joints to calm himself down. Meanwhile Bimla, altogether a nicer piece of work than her brother although no less spoilt, had been darting thoughtful glances in Slater's direction.

Don't even think about it, he told himself. Don't even fucking think about it. He was in deep enough already. Why on earth had he told Grace Litvinoff that he loved her – a statement that he'd never made to any other woman? Grace was amazingly stylish, certainly, and by far the most beautiful woman he'd ever slept with, but how could he say that he loved her? He and she occupied different worlds. They could spend a lifetime together and not begin to understand each other.

On one of his sorties to the Edgware Road he checked his text messages: 'D KARAN THUR 11AM'.

She knew that he was free but had told him that she was spending the day with a friend. The arrangement had been that they would see each other on Friday, when he was officially booked to look after her. Still, he would meet her in Donna Karan tomorrow if that's what she wanted. His heart quickened at the thought of her, was wrenched at the frustration of not being able to see her tonight. She was going to an opera gala at Covent Garden with her husband, and one of the other Minerva bodyguards had been booked to accompany them.

In the end, before returning to the Chabbrias' flat for the last time, he rang Tab Holland and arranged to meet him for a drink. The ex-RMP was working in South Kensington and they agreed to meet in a pub near the tube station.

Holland had spent the day at the French Lycée, guarding the daughter of a French publisher who had received death threats from Algerian terrorists.

'At least you were doing something valuable,' said Slater, downing the best part of a pint of Guinness in a single, desperate swallow. 'I tell you, another hour and I would have ended up chinning that fucking Vinod. And the worst of it is, I reckon, that by taking his shit rather than sorting him out I've made him worse. I've made myself at least partly responsible for the bad time he gives the next guy.'

'You can't think like that,' said Holland. 'You've just got to walk away from arseholes like that and forget them. Life's too short.'

'How long have you been in the bodyguarding game, Tab?' Slater asked, beckoning to the barmaid to refill their glasses.

'Too bloody long,' said Holland. 'Eight years odd.'

'And in all that time, have you ever broken the rules? I mean have you ever . . .'

'Hit a client? No.'

'No, I didn't mean that as much as . . .'

'Get involved with a client's wife?'

'Yeah. Have you ever done that?'

Holland paused. He was older, Slater saw, than he

had originally seemed.

'Let's just say that it happens, OK? But let me give you a word of advice. If it ever happens to you . . .' He regarded Slater meaningfully. 'Don't tell your colleagues. You're not in a regiment now, and there's no mates' code of honour to protect you. One of the other BGs'll grass you up to Duckworth and that'll be the end of it. No work, no mortgage payments, no *Star Wars* stickers for the kids.'

'Should such a situation ever arise,' Slater said wryly, 'I'll remember what you said.'

'Do that,' said Holland.

'What would you do if you weren't BGing?' Slater asked him.

'The dream's to start a little gardening consultancy in the Chichester area,' said Tab. 'Installing fountains and water-features and that. Statuary.'

'So when's that going to happen?'

'I told the wife it'd be this year. Trouble is, the money for BGing is just too good. There's always just one more job you can't turn down. And then one of your kids asks for the new Man U strip and you have a conversation with the bank manager and that job turns into one more season you can't turn down . . .'

He drained his glass and pushed it towards the Guinness tap. 'What I'd really like, to be honest, is a good war. Nine months or so of total fucking mayhem. If I could just have that, and survive, I'd cheerfully install precast concrete sundials for the rest of my life.'

Slater laughed. '*Vive la mort, vive la guerre . . .*'

'*Vive le sacré mercenaire!*' they roared in unison.

By the time the pint glasses had each been refilled four times over, Slater was feeling a bit more like a warrior and a bit less like a domestic servant. He and Tab Holland had worked out how, for an investment of less than £100,000, they could kidnap the radical Islamic leader Osama bin Laden from Kabul in Afghanistan and claim the $5 million reward supposedly on offer.

After a couple of large drams each of Jameson's Irish whiskey, the barman had somehow been recruited into the scheme. When trying to remember the details later − details which had appeared watertight at the time − Slater would be able to remember only that a scuba kit and a plastic dustbin were involved.

'You're not driving are you, gents?' the barman had asked them at the point at which they'd switched to brandy.

'No mate, public transport!' Slater had replied. For some reason it had seemed the saddest, funniest answer in the world.

FIVE

Slater woke to a bad hangover – the worst since New Year's Day – and the insistent ringing of the Motorola.

'I'm sorry if I woke you, Mr Slater. It's Lark here, from the Treasury Solicitors' office.'

The hangover was immediately overlaid by dread. 'You didn't wake me,' Slater lied. 'What's up?'

'Well I won't beat around the bush. There have been a number of developments in the Bolingbroke's School case and I'm afraid it looks as if there's going to be an inquiry, at the very least.'

Slater's stomach churned. 'What exactly does that mean?' he asked.

'In the first instance it means that you and I should meet. How are you fixed for, say, tomorrow?'

Tomorrow was Friday. He was booked to look after Grace. 'Would Monday be too late?'

'No, Monday would be . . . fine. Shall we say ten o'clock here at Northumberland Avenue?'

Slater pressed the off button and flipped the little mobile on to the bed. This was seriously bad news.

For ten minutes, mind and body screaming, he stood under a cold shower. Trust in Lark, he told himself. Lark had always come good in the past. But he wasn't inside the system any more, and something distant in Lark's tone told Slater that this made a difference.

Pulling on a track suit and trainers, pocketing his keys, he went out for a run. He felt terrible, but experience told him that exercise and fresh air were the only effective counter to a hangover. Soon he was sweating, lengthening his stride as he pushed himself round the cheerless perimeter of Finsbury Park. His head pounded, but he ignored it.

A second shower – hot this time – and he was beginning to feel human again. The worry about the inquiry had receded to the point where he could think about it clearly, rather than in a state of sick panic. They *had* to bale him out, he told himself. They bloody well *had* to.

But of course he was being childish. They didn't have to do anything. If it suited them, and if more serious considerations than his own well-being were at stake, they'd bang him up without hesitation. He made a decision. If he went down for murder, or even for a long manslaughter stretch, he'd top himself. Open a fucking vein. He wasn't rotting away in a cell for anyone.

After arriving at this decision, and imagining for a morbid minute or two his blood flowing darkly and secretly into a prison mattress, Slater felt better. Dressing himself in off-duty clothing – jeans, a sweatshirt and his old leather jacket – he left the flat in search of a full English breakfast.

At eleven o'clock, as requested, he presented himself at Donna Karan in Bond Street. A glance inside the shop showed no sign of Grace Litvinoff, nor was the silver Lexus anywhere in sight.

'Can I help you?'

'Has Mrs Litvinoff been in today?'

The male assistant consulted a pad. 'Are you Mr Neil Slater?'

He nodded.

'Mrs Litvinoff isn't coming in today, but she's left us certain instructions. We're to provide you with some clothes.'

Slater gaped. 'Provide *me*?'

The assistant smiled. 'Let me get Alexia, who spoke to Mrs Litvinoff.'

Slater waited, and a minute later a svelte figure in form-fitting grey was shaking his hand.

'You're Neil, right? Grace gave me a list of what you needed. And she asked me to tell you that there are some other bits and pieces to be collected from . . .' she consulted her list – 'Prada. OK?'

Dazzled by her smile, Slater could only nod his assent.

'Do you have the prices on that list?' he asked her uncertainly.

Alexia laughed. 'Grace said you weren't to be given any prices. She said you'd only make a fuss.'

Slater stared about him in disbelief, digesting the airy grandeur of the place. Not long ago he'd have felt acutely uncomfortable even standing somewhere like this, and while he'd begun to learn the laws of the Mayfair jungle, he was still capable of finding himself at a disadvantage.

'Shall we do it?' asked Alexia, still smiling.

For ninety minutes, without daring to consider the cost, he tried on a dark and gorgeous array of suits, jackets, shirts, ties, trousers and shoes. Sometimes Alexia nodded her approval, sometimes she stood birdlike and thoughtful, sometimes she made a note or added a pin to a trouser-leg, sometimes she shook her head dismissively.

For Slater, the hour and a half was an education. His own clothes seemed cheap, shapeless and dowdy in comparison to this finery. Luxury was a ratchet. It only turned one way.

'So what do you think?' Alexia asked him when the session was finally completed and he stood there surrounded by crisp, neatly aligned bags. His own, for once.

'I'm lost for words,' he told her. 'What do *you* think?'

She folded her arms. Gave him the full-beam smile. 'I think Mrs Litvinoff has . . . great taste. I'm glad we've been able to help.'

Half an hour later, with several Prada bags added to his haul, he was sitting on a bench reading a newspaper and wondering about lunch. His hangover was no more than a memory now, and he had decided to put the whole business of the inquiry out of his mind. There was nothing he could do to change anything – it was all up to Lark. On Monday he would start worrying. For now he would think about Grace.

He checked his text messages.

'LOOKING GOOD? LOVE U.'

He shook his head admiringly. She was just too much.

'They're very cute those things, aren't they? Especially for love affairs.'

Slater turned his head. Behind the bench, vaguely piratical in an old grey leather Luftwaffe flying-jacket, stood a grinning Andreas. At his side was a woman of about thirty in a long black coat. Where Andreas looked somehow actorish, like a terrorist glamorised for TV, the woman looked entirely businesslike. Her eyes were a pale sea-grey, her strong, neatly made features were devoid of any obvious make-up, and the dark blonde hair that fell to her collar was quietly but expensively styled.

She watched Slater in polite silence. There was no way that they were a couple, you could sense that at a glance. They had to be colleagues. If he had to bet he would have said that she was the senior one of the two, but he couldn't be sure of it. She radiated the cool assurance that came with a privileged Home Counties upbringing and expensive schooling, but then so did some of the most stupid people Slater had ever met.

Turning off his phone, he pocketed it. 'Andreas,' he

said resignedly. 'Now just what is it that tells me this meeting isn't completely accidental?'

Andreas van Rijn turned to the woman in the coat. 'This guy,' he told her apologetically, 'is just the most cynical . . .' He dropped his voice. 'Let me present Neil Slater, lately of Her Majesty's Special Air Service, more recently poodle-walker to ladies of a certain age.'

'Hi,' she said, turning an amused smile on him. 'I'm Eve.'

The accent – suggesting first-floor flats in Kensington and weekends in the country – went with the coat. And the haircut.

'Neil Slater. And you mustn't believe Andreas. I've yet to walk my first poodle.'

'But obviously not doing too badly,' said Andreas, bending over the Prada bag. 'What's this? A wallet? And three belts? And . . .' he peered into some of the other bags, 'shoes, and a suit, and a . . . Bloody hell, Neil, there must be thousands of pounds' worth of stuff here.'

Slater shrugged. 'I have to look good. The clients expect it.'

'You don't have to look this good. At least . . . you fox, Neil, you've been snaking one of Duckworth's clients!'

Slater was a little embarrassed by Andreas's crudeness.

'That's a rather unlovely metaphor, Andreas.' Eve turned her level, grey gaze on Slater. 'We were just thinking of getting a bite to eat. Will you join us?'

'Why not?' said Slater, amused at the directness of her approach and impressed by the way she took Andreas's laddish remarks in her stride.

He followed them up Bond Street to Stratford Place. 'We're going to the Oriental Club,' explained Andreas. 'I seem to remember you being a bit of a curry addict.'

The club was old and quiet and smelt of furniture polish. Paintings of colonial administrators and engravings of battle scenes hung from the walls.

'Are you a member here?' Slater asked Andreas, as the hall porter removed his bags. It seemed unlikely.

'I am,' Eve answered. Beneath the coat she was wearing a darkly anonymous business suit. Neither she nor Andreas handed their briefcases to the porter.

In the dining room, when they had placed their orders, the three of them sat for a moment in silence.

'So, tell me, Neil, how's it going?' Andreas asked eventually. 'Do you think bodyguarding's going to be your future?'

'Not necessarily,' said Slater. 'But it'll do for now. It's got its down-sides, but the up-side is that I'm in charge of my own life. If I don't want to do a job I can just walk away from it.'

'Did you read about the Karadjic snatch?'

'I did. Do you know who did it?'

'Some of the guys from A Squadron. Ray Mortimer led the team, apparently. The boss is over the moon – it was a real result. And I'll tell you this for nothing.' He levelled his gaze at Slater. 'There certainly aren't going to be any prosecutions on behalf of those Serbs they wasted. Cheers!'

Thoughtfully, Slater raised the glass of Kingfisher lager the waiter had placed in front of him. Eve, he saw, was drinking mineral water.

'So how do you know Andreas?' he asked her, although by now he was certain what the answer would be.

'We work together,' she answered, her expression neutral.

'I see.' She was the watcher, Slater realised, and Andreas was the talker. What would the deal be this time? he wondered. What were they offering?

They waited in slightly awkward silence as their curries were laid out on the hot-plate at the table's centre. When the waiter had finally withdrawn Andreas lifted his fork and examined the insignia stamped into the heavy silver.

'Neil, vis-à-vis that school stuff, you're in trouble,' he said quietly. 'I spoke to Lark last night and his words were that there was only so far his department could stick its neck out for a civilian. Now this doesn't mean that everyone doesn't want the whole thing to go away – everyone does, and the Saudis in particular. They're supposed to be the Islamic state we can do business with, not some bunch of whacko trigger-happy fundamentalists. So they'll be throwing plenty of time and money at the thing. But the bottom line is that the Firm protects its own. Without some commitment on your part, they can't promise to go the distance for you. Given the way the press works these days, it's just too risky.'

'I see,' said Slater. He was quietly furious. Who the fuck did these people think they were – following him about and, for all he knew, intercepting his phone calls too? Did they know about Grace? They could hardly fail to.

Expressionless, he turned to Eve. 'So which is the chicken jalfrezi?'

For five minutes they busied themselves with their food. The other club-members and their visitors tended to be male, blazer-wearing and of a certain age. A couple of Gurkha Rifles ties were in evidence. A journalist of either sex would have been very visible indeed.

'Is this one of your department's places?' Slater asked Andreas.

'No, it's more one of Eve's places.'

'Not a very feminine establishment,' Slater ventured.

She turned amused grey eyes on him. 'I'm not your stereotypical girly girl, Mr Slater. More pilau rice?'

When they had finished their meal Eve asked for coffee to be brought to them in the reading room. There, she selected a table some distance from the fireplace and from the other club members. Andreas ordered a glass of Cognac.

'So tell me,' Slater asked her warily as he stirred his coffee, 'what exactly do you and your department mean by commitment?'

'Basically that we'd like you to join the department.'

'Why? There must be scores of ex-Regiment blokes like me doing the rounds. And who are you people, anyway?'

'In answer to your first question let's just say for the moment that you come highly recommended. As to who we are, well . . .' She thought for a moment. 'How's your modern history?'

'Uneven,' admitted Slater.

She smiled. 'OK. Basically we're a department of MI6, based at Vauxhall Cross. Our official title is the Operational Research Cadre, but we're usually just known as the Cadre. Like all such departments we've had several identity crises over the years. We started life during the Second World War as a subsection of the escape and evasion unit known as MI9, whose role was to set up ratlines for agents and POWs in occupied Europe.'

Slater nodded. He'd been introduced to a couple of wartime agents at the Special Forces Club behind Harrods. They'd been watchful, belligerent men, he remembered, unsoftened by the passing of the years.

'When the war ended,' Eve continued, 'the unit's infrastructure remained in place but its role changed. Until the early fifties its principal activity was the tracing and processing of former Nazis. And then, at the time of the Korean War, with the Cadre reduced to a single office at SIS headquarters, a decision was taken to run a major network of covert operatives in South East Asia. So new faces, new money, and a new role.'

122

'Working alongside the CIA and the US Special Forces?' Slater hazarded. 'The Vientiane connection?'

'That sort of thing. Those were the Cadre's Dark Ages, I guess. You hardly ever meet anyone from that time; most of them just kind of, I don't know, *vanished*. Into the jungle, I suppose.'

'Strange days!' said Andreas, swirling his Cognac in its balloon glass.

'And now?' asked Slater.

'Now the Cadre is an autonomous, fully-funded research unit within Six.'

'Research?'

Eve shrugged. 'It's as good a name for what we do as anything. Basically we're problem-solvers. People – other departments, other services – come to us with . . . very intractable problems. And we solve them.'

'I'm not sure that I like the kind of problem-solving you're talking about,' said Slater. 'I'm sure we wouldn't be having this conversation if you hadn't done your homework, so I assume you've seen my service record.'

Eve nodded.

'Then you know about the circumstances surrounding my leaving the army?'

She nodded again.

'Then you'll know that I don't do that sort of work any more. I don't like it. And I don't need the nightmares.'

Andreas leant forward. 'Neil, like you said – and like we both know – there are scores of ex-Regiment guys like us doing the rounds. But most of them left the Army for a damn good reason – they were burnt out, they'd screwed up, they'd lost their nerve. That or they were so overwound that they wanted to put a bullet through everyone who so much as looked at them. But you're not in that boat. You had a bad time, you got lost in the old Darklands for a while, but you pulled through. You must have pulled through to have done that stuff at the school. And for all that line you fed me in the New Year about getting shot of the system, I could tell straight away that you hadn't really changed. Not deep down. Deep down you were the same old green-eyed boy I used to know in B Squadron.'

'I'm not sure that I am that person any more, Andreas.' Slater drained his coffee. 'I'm really not.'

Eve leaned forward. 'Look,' she said. 'Can I make a suggestion? Why doesn't Andreas drive all your shopping home for you? And why don't you come back to Vauxhall Cross with me? Just for an hour. There's something I want to show you.'

If Andreas was irritated at being relegated to the role of bag-man he didn't show it, merely leant back in his armchair with the remains of his Cognac.

For several moments Slater avoided Eve's gaze. The fact that he was very obviously being flattered didn't detract from the fact that the department's offer had real temptations – the most immediate of which was the chance to stop agonising about the outcome of the Bolingbroke's inquiry. And he'd never been inside the

MI6 headquarters. He felt a crawl of curiosity.

'No strings?'

She shook her head. 'No strings whatsoever.'

Slater felt in his pocket for his keys. There was nothing revealing or incriminating at the flat.

'I doubt I need to give you the address,' he said drily.

Eve and Andreas smiled.

The MI6 building towered over Albert Embankment and the Thames with a kind of colossal arrogance. Here we are, it said, in plain sight. Make of us what you will.

For all its visibility, and for all the supposed new openness and accountability demanded of the security services, Slater knew that the building housed one of the least transparent organisations in the world. The public were given the impression of inside knowledge in the same way that audiences were let into a magician's act – for no other purpose than to distract them from the main order of business. Even the windows were opaque.

'Welcome to Ceausescu Towers!' Eve said drily, and Slater followed her through the tall glass doors into the atrium, where he filled in a security form and was handed a visitor's pass to clip to the lapel of his jacket.

The lift door opened with a sigh on to a bare air-conditioned corridor with small, high-set, triple-glazed windows. At the far end was a door marked ORC (9). Swiping a card and punching a code into the keypad, Eve gestured that Slater precede her into a small, open-plan office containing several computer terminals. At one of these a man in heavy black spectacles was listening to a head-set and making notes. At another a woman with a spiky punk hairdo was scrolling through aerial photographs. Each raised a hand in silent greeting as the pair entered.

'Has anything come in for me?' Eve asked, hanging her coat on a stand by the door.

The spike-haired woman nodded. 'Couple of things. Nothing urgent. And I've got those pictures you asked for.' She handed Eve a black envelope.

'Thanks.' Eve turned to Slater. 'Let's go into the briefing room.'

The room was windowless and spotlit. Half a dozen chairs stood at a rectangular mahogany table.

'Have a look at these.'

She took two colour photographs from the black packet. One showed a clean-shaven young man in a sheepskin jerkin and military fatigues, the other was a blurred portrait of a lightly bearded figure in a Mujahidin cap.

'You may or may not recognise these men – they're the ones who tried to kidnap Masoud al-Jubrin. The one on the left is Ali Akbar Dilshah, and this one is Riza Talibi. They were council members of the Hizb al-Makhfi, a Saudi-based terror group which has carried out actions in several countries; most recently, of course, in the UK. Six has been watching these men for some time now. They were both trained at camps in the Dasht-i Lut desert in Iran, and both spent several years fighting alongside the Taliban in Afghanistan. There's also an Algerian connection. These were not amateurs.'

'I was pretty sure they weren't,' said Slater.

'I'm sure. But just in case you've got the slightest regret about what you did to them, I'd like you to look at the other pictures. They show the specific acts of violence for which these men and their group were responsible.'

Slater went through the pile. It was as bad as anything he'd ever seen. The first picture showed a shopping arcade in which a bomb had exploded. There were several corpses, some of them barely recognisable as having ever been human. Other victims, maimed but not yet dead, scrabbled in agony amongst the blood and the glass. The second photograph showed a line of blank-eyed teenage girls propped up against the dusty mud wall of a building. Their throats had been cut from ear to ear and their chests were sheeted with blood.

'The girls went outside the house without a veil,' said Eve.

Slater nodded and continued through the pile. An elderly couple lay face down and naked at a roadside; it was clear they had been whipped to death. There was another bomb-scene: a screaming woman clutching a dead child, a young man staring incredulously at the mess of flesh, bone and denim that had once been his legs. The final photograph was of a young woman lying on a table, her head severed from her body.

'That was Riza's sister,' said Eve, her grey eyes expressionless. 'He killed her when a rumour started that she'd been seeing a Christian male nurse attached to one of the hospitals.'

Wearily, Slater replaced the photographs in the packet. He said nothing.

'Sometimes people just have to be stopped,' said Eve. 'Their actions amount to a declaration of war, and the only rules you can apply to them are the rules of war. But I hardly need to tell you that, do I?'

'No,' said Slater. 'You don't need to tell me that.'

She got to her feet. 'Come with me.'

He followed her from the room and into a side office whose floor-to-ceiling windows afforded a dizzying view towards the north-west. Like those outside in the corridor, the windows were triple-glazed and treated against laser penetration and radio frequency flooding. Far below them, its steely surface galvanised by an erratic spring wind, was the Thames. Beyond the river, their grey mass softened and illuminated in the sunshine, were the towers of Westminster, Belgravia and Whitehall. Beyond these, fainter, St James's Park, Constitution Hill and Buckingham Palace.

'There's a place for you here if you want it, Neil,' Eve said quietly. 'What more can I say? The work's hard, the company's good, the money's crap to middling and there's a not bad canteen.'

He felt his phone vibrate against his hip. 'Excuse me,' he said apologetically, and glanced downwards.

'FREE TONIGHT? RING ASAP.' He smiled to himself, and flicked off the display.

'Good news?'

'I think so.'

Eve ran her fingers through her blunt-cut fair hair. 'I'm going to give you a number,' she said. 'Ring it if you want to get hold of me. Any time, day or night, OK? Any time.'

He took the card.

From Vauxhall to Green Park took five minutes on the Victoria Line.

'Neil,' Grace said when she saw him. 'You're not wearing a single—'

'I came straight here,' he told her, looking down at his jeans and desert boots. 'I haven't had a chance to change. And by the way, I'll be paying you back for all that gear.'

She slipped her arms around his neck. 'Darling, don't even think about it. You are free tonight, aren't you?'

'Yes. But what happened? Where's your husband? I thought he was supposed to be in London tonight.'

'He rang half an hour ago,' she said, flipping open the waist-stud of Slater's Levis. 'From Frankfurt.'

When they finally lay still the light had gone from the sky. As Slater lay half asleep on the ruined bed Grace gently raked her nails up and down his back.

'So, do you fuck any of your other ladies?' she whispered, nipping his ear between her teeth.

'Uh–uh.' He shook his head.

'I bet you do,' she said. 'I bet you make them scream.'

He opened his eyes a fraction. 'Are you being serious?'

'Tell me about all those fat Middle-Easterners,' she breathed. 'What do you do to them? And all those Manhattan social-register types, how do they like it best?'

'Do you seriously think that's how I spend my time?' Slater murmured.

'I wouldn't mind, necessarily. As long as you were here whenever I wanted you. And you told me about all the others. In detail.'

He raised himself on one elbow. 'Grace, there aren't any others to tell you about. There's just you. I'm . . . I'm amazed you could think I wanted to see anyone else.'

'So, what do you do all day with them?'

'I follow them about. Like I did you.'

'But they must want more, some of them.'

He let his head fall back to the pillow. 'I've got no idea.'

She climbed across him. Straddled his drowsy form. 'Neil, darling, don't be cross with me.' Slowly she began to rock her pelvis back and forth. He made a point of not responding.

'You're cross with me, aren't you?' She closed her eyes and continued the movement. 'Mmm . . . but maybe not *that* cross!'

Furious, he felt his body betray him.

'Go on, Neil,' she gasped. 'Turn me over. Fuck me like I was a prostitute . . . Tell me I'm a whore. Tell me I'm a filthy backstreet whore.'

He could do the actions, but he couldn't make himself say the words. For the first time, he found her unreachable. After a few minutes she gave up the ghost. Subsided next to him. Said nothing.

'What would you like to do this evening?' he asked her eventually.

She looked at him quizzically, and he gently touched her cheek. For a moment she seemed to flinch at his tenderness, and then she gave a small laugh.

'Well . . .' she began brightly. 'Madonna's giving a party at Chinawhite. We could go to that. There might be some amusing people there.'

He hesitated. 'With me going as what?' he asked her. 'Your bodyguard? Your lover?'

'What would you like to go as?' she asked him, raising an exquisitely shaped eyebrow.

'Well, I'd like to go as your boyfriend, but I'm risking my job if I'm seen. And I don't expect your husband will be too happy if he hears we've been out on the town together, either.'

'Don't worry about David. David just wants me to be happy. He expects me to go out and have a good time.'

More fool him, thought Slater.

'But of course we shouldn't endanger your career, should we?'

'We'll go,' said Slater. 'We'll go to the party. With you as my lover. How's that?'

'That's nice,' she said, touching his cheek. 'As my lover, then, rather than as my bodyguard, would you go and find me something from the fridge? Fucking always makes me so hungry.'

He took the tube home to change. The flat was as he had left it: neat and Spartan. The bed was made with the blankets stretched drum-tight across the mattress, as he had learnt as a seventeen-year-old squaddie.

Andreas, he discovered, had taken his designer clothes out of their bags and squared them up on the bed in their tissue paper as if for a kit inspection. The silver and crocodile belt lay where his webbing belt had once lain; the Prada shoes stood where his Northern Ireland boots had once stood. The ex-NCO's message was brutally clear: you're still following the orders of your betters – the only difference is in the design of the uniform.

'Well, bollocks to you, Andreas van Rijn,' Slater said aloud, kicking off his desert boots. 'I'm going to Madonna Ciccone's party and you're not.'

He dressed carefully, combining the clothes precisely as Alexia had suggested.

On the tube he stood. The seats were filthy.

Grace seemed pleased with Slater's new look. 'That's so much better,' she told him. 'You look like you belong.'

The driver dropped them off in Glasshouse Street.

Outside the club the police had erected a barrier to keep the paparazzi and inquisitive members of the public at bay; behind this at least a hundred bodies pressed and struggled. As Slater and Grace Litvinoff entered the club a ragged storm of flashbulbs burst about them.

'They take pictures of everyone,' shouted Grace, amused, as they hurried into the club's foyer. 'Don't worry, you're not going to make the front cover.' She stood back from him. 'Although, who knows? You look good enough!'

Slater caught sight of himself in a mirror. Dressed as he was in the best part of two thousand pounds' worth of clothes and accessories – slate greys, anthracite, midnight blue – he had to admit that he damn well did look good enough.

Inside, the club was packed. 'Madonna must have a lot of friends,' he told Grace, steering her towards the bar, and she laughed. On the way they passed the actress Jennifer Ehle, who was deep in conversation with Tara Palmer-Tomkinson. Both seemed to recognise Slater. It must be the clothes, he realised, when at least the tenth person had nodded or waved to him. They must assume that if I'm dressed like this I'm one of them. Either that or I have a double.

At the bar they were swooped on by one of the zombies from the Tate.

'It's Grace and her carer!' he crooned, running a finger down Slater's lapel. 'I must say, dear, you've done him out very nicely!'

Grace laughed. 'Zoltan, darling! How are you?'

'What would you like to drink, Grace?' Slater asked her pointedly, ignoring the zombie.

'Oh . . . surprise me!' she said absently, staring over his shoulder.

Pushing irritably through the crowd, he encountered another familiar face. 'Nice threads!' said Salman Rushdie.

'Thanks. How's the football?'

'I went to Brentford on Wednesday. They've just signed a new striker from Grasshopper Zurich.'

'Any good?'

'No, rubbish. You know Geri, don't you? And this is Martine McCutcheon.'

'Hey!' said the former soap star. 'Didn't I see you in something last night?'

'I was in the Roebuck last night.'

'That must have been it. You were really good.'

'I'm just going to the bar,' said Slater. 'Can I get anyone anything?'

'Surprise me,' said Martine McCutcheon.

In the end he got four dry Martinis – two for himself – and a tray. When he eventually got back to where Grace had been, she had disappeared. He eventually spotted her at the centre of a group of men – he assumed they were men – in pinstriped suits and rubber bondage masks. She already seemed to have a drink. The conversation looked both hilarious and impenetrable. Taking a seat at a nearby table, he placed the three remaining Martinis in front of him.

Thoughtfully, as the party swirled around him, he lifted the first. The music rose and fell. Flash-bulbs bloomed.

At the far end of the room, he discovered some time later, was an inner sanctum. A VIP area. He'd been roaming the floor for a while now, having overlaid the Martinis with a pint of something gassy and Japanese at the bar, and although he hadn't smoked for several years a Cohiba cigar seemed to have found its way between his teeth.

The object of his quest was Grace and, if possible, Madonna – in some curious way the two women seemed to have become one in his mind. The VIP area was guarded by a tall, suave-looking black man in a dinner jacket, and some distance beyond the velvet rope Slater thought that he saw Grace. Was that Madonna she was talking to? It could have been.

'I'm sorry, sir. Special invitations only.'

'That's my girlfriend in there,' said Slater. 'I have a special invitation.'

'What name was that, sir?'

'Um . . . Litvinoff.'

The man consulted a clipboard.

'I only have a Mrs Litvinoff down here.'

'I'm with Mrs Litvinoff.'

'I'm sorry, sir. If I don't have your individual name down here I can't let you in. I'm sorry, sir.'

Slater shook his head. 'Give us a fucking break, man. Go and ask her.'

At that moment a wild-eyed girl of about sixteen in a see-through top pressed past him. Tears and mascara streaked her face. 'I have to speak to Madonna!' she moaned. 'Please! I have to.'

'Sorry, ma'am,' said the bouncer firmly, intercepting her dash for the inner sanctum with a broad forearm. 'Special invitations only.'

Beyond the weeping girl and the velvet rope, Grace suddenly seemed to be swallowed up in a melee of shining hair and glittering clothes. At Slater's side the girl, sobbing now – was attempting to claw the bouncer's eyes out. Catching her wrists, the guard attempted to subdue her, and seeing his chance Slater barged past him into the tented enclosure.

This area – much darker than the rest of the club – was done up like a scene from the Arabian Nights. Mirrored and tasselled cushions lined the carpeted floor on which guests lounged like pashas – talking, flirting and smoking. Pale shafts of coloured light pierced the air from Algerian lamps. Accepting a glass of green absinthe from a passing waiter, Slater toured the cushions, peering at faces as he passed.

No Grace.

And for that matter, no Madonna. He exchanged his empty absinthe glass for a full one.

And then he understood. He wasn't there yet. At the end of the tent, a series of overlapping hangings concealed a further entrance. Within this inner sanctum was an inner inner sanctum. A VVIP lounge.

Glass in hand, Slater moved towards it.

A second security guard – possibly the older, larger brother of the first – seemed to materialise before him. 'Hi there!' he said, as if genuinely pleased to see Slater. 'How's it going?'

'Can I go in?'

The guard smiled. 'I know your face, man,' he said. 'I know your face *of old!*'

From beyond the wall of drapery came the sound of female laughter.

'You like that crazy ol' green witch?' asked the guard, indicating Slater's absinthe.

Slater shrugged. The ground lurched beneath his feet. 'Can I go in?' he repeated.

The guard narrowed his eyes. 'You wanna go in there?'

'Yeah . . . no.' He shook his head. Another mistake. 'I just want to know if Grace is in there.'

'Grace is a universal attribute, man, but I can check for you if you want. Wait here.'

Behind the hangings, Slater heard the conversation trail to silence. A moment later Grace appeared.

'Neil,' she said vaguely. 'What is it? What do you want?'

'I lost you,' said Slater, and then couldn't think of anything further to say. Her face seemed to swim before his eyes.

'Take the key,' she said. 'Wait for me at the flat, OK?'

He walked back.

In the flat he put on some music and took a bath. Re-dressed himself.

Grace Litvinoff pressed the doorbell at about one o'clock. In her voice, as she identified herself, Slater sensed an excitement, an anticipation. His negative feelings about the evening began to fall away. He thought of her body, felt himself hardening.

She was standing at the door with two men. One was a very tall, very fair young man in a transparent T-shirt, who Slater thought was probably a model, and the second was the larger of the two black security guards. Both regarded him with amused anticipation.

He raised an interrogative eyebrow at Grace, who smiled. 'This is Simon,' she said, indicating the blond man, 'and this is Oke. I thought the four of us might . . . have some rather naughty fun.' She narrowed her eyes at him kittenishly 'Why don't you start by fixing us all a drink?'

Slater stared at her. The alcohol roared at his ears. 'Are you serious?' he demanded.

'No, darling!' she said woozily. 'That's just the point. Unlike you I'm never serious.' She ran the heel of one hand slowly over the security guard's tightly-bound crotch and with the other squeezed Simon the male model's buttock. 'Haven't you heard the song: "Girls just wanna have fun . . ."'

'Chill out, man,' Simon grinned at Slater, rippling his gym-toned pectorals as he felt in the pockets of his impossibly tight trousers. 'I've got some fantastic coke somewhere.'

Slater ignored him. 'You get rid of this pair of clowns right now or I'm walking, OK?'

'Fine!' she said, folding her arms. 'Walk. Who the fuck do you think you are, anyway? You're just the hired help. How dare you criticise my friends?'

'Fuck your friends!' shouted Slater.

'That's exactly what I intend to do. So why don't you run off home and leave the grown-ups in peace? And send the driver home while you're at it. Simon and Oke will be staying the night.'

Slater considered beating both men up, dropping the stone Buddha from the mantelpiece through the glass table-top and then pissing on the carpet, but in the end he simply walked out.

The driver was waiting in the Lexus, listening to the radio and smoking. From the expression on his face, Slater could tell that he had guessed what had happened up in the flat.

'Highbury, is it mate?' he asked sympathetically.

'Thanks.'

The motion of the car made Slater feel nauseous. The journey seemed to go on for ever. When he finally climbed out in Mafeking Terrace, the driver wound down the electric window.

'If it's any consolation, mate, you're not the first – nor likely to be the last. She's a bit of a greedy girl is our Gracie.'

Slater, swaying, stared at him in silence.

'You're not going to tell me you thought it was the real thing, are you?'

139

'No,' said Slater, looking down at his Prada shoes. 'I'm not going to tell you that.'

As the car vanished into the night he spread his legs, the better to avoid splashing himself, and threw up into the gutter.

SIX

The next morning Josephine rang Slater from the Minerva office. Grace Litvinoff, she told him, had decided to leave town for a few days and would not be requiring his services after all. He would be paid a cancellation fee for the lost day's work.

Slater had been expecting the call. Bagging and wrapping his unworn designer clothes, he returned them to the bemused sales assistants who had supplied them. There had been a mistake, he explained to them, and Mrs Litvinoff should be recredited for the goods. The clothes that he had worn the night before he took to the local Oxfam shop, who were delighted to accept them.

On the Monday he kept the appointment with Lark. For two hours, once again, he went over every detail of the events at Bolingbroke's School with the Treasury Solicitor. A smooth-jowled, pinstriped figure whom Slater estimated to be in his late forties sat in on the interview. He remained silent throughout.

This time, although the same ground was covered, Lark seemed a little more concerned by Slater's account than he has been in the police cell. As Slater

141

described breaking off the chair-leg and setting off down the school drive in pursuit of the kidnappers, he frowned, touched his gold propelling pencil to his lips, and shook his head. As Slater recounted how he drew his knife and stabbed the first Arab, Lark steepled his fingers and rocked back and forth in his chair, expressionless, before leaning forward and making copious notes.

Finally Lark indicated that he had all the answers he required, and the man in the pin striped suit left the room. At no point in the interview had he acknowledged Slater.

'You were informed of the possibility of a court of inquiry?' Lark asked Slater when the other man had gone.

'Of the possibility, yeah,' answered Slater. 'Why, has it become a probability?'

'Not as yet,' Lark replied levelly. 'So far we've kept the lid on. I'd encourage you, though, to do everything that you can to prevent things going any further.'

'And how can I do that?' Slater asked frustratedly.

'I'm sure ways will suggest themselves in due course, Mr Slater,' said Lark quietly. He rose to his feet. The interview was over.

They were playing with him, thought Slater bitterly. They were pissing him around, winding him up, rattling his cage. Well, they could fuck themselves. If he was prosecuted he'd bring down the whole house of cards, tell the court that the Regiment had taught him to shoot to kill and that he could no longer control his reactions. He'd play the post-traumatic stress card, force them to question him about Operation Greenfly. That'd set set the cat among the pigeons and no mistake.

Basically, he told himself now, he wanted to steer well clear of any involvement with the security services. They could bring him nothing but grief. He had to prove to himself that he could live a self-sufficient life.

For all his anger, however, and for all his determination not to bow to the system, at heart Slater was afraid. He was no David Shayler: he wasn't good with words and he didn't have the whistleblower mentality – at heart the habit of loyalty was just too deeply ingrained. If push came to shove and there was a court of inquiry, he was pretty sure he'd end up being the fall-guy. They'd plead national security and bang him up somewhere he couldn't be seen or heard, and that would be it. He just had to try and put the whole business from his mind and hope against hope that push never did come to shove.

That afternoon he visited a DIY warehouse in Walthamstow. He bought paint, decorating materials, cleaning equipment and kitchen goods. That afternoon he started work on the flat. By the end of the weekend he had the place how he wanted it – comfortable but anonymous.

Over the two months that followed Slater accepted every bodyguarding job that he was offered. He was polite, he was biddable, and he was obedient. He kept his distance from his clients emotionally, but provided a discreet and professional service. He was involved in only two confrontations – both with paparazzo photographers. In each case the photographer handed over the film and backed off.

He started a desultory affair with a woman who lived on the floor beneath him. He met her when he knocked on her door one Saturday morning to apologise for the noise he was about to make with an electric floor-sander that he had hired. That evening they went out for a meal at a Turkish restaurant in Highbury Grove. Her name, she told him, was Lauren Vail, and she was a nurse attached to the Royal Free Hospital in Hampstead. She loved the work but the money was terrible, and she'd been considering going private – maybe in one of the Gulf States.

He told her in his turn that he worked in the security industry, that the work was dull but regular, and that he was saving up to buy a small business. What sort of small business this would be, he hadn't yet decided.

After the meal, in the course of which she drank two glasses of white wine and he drank a bottle and a half, they returned to Mafeking Terrace. She showed him round her flat – a tour lasting less than a minute – and left him asleep in her bed the next morning.

He took to staying with her two or three times a week. They got on well, but it soon became clear to Slater that she wanted more than a drinking companion and occasional sex-partner.

One evening she came back from work to tell him that she had signed on with an agency providing nursing personnel to hospitals in Oman and Abu Dhabi. As she spoke to him she scanned his face for any sign that this news saddened him, waited hopefully for him to ask her to stay.

He said nothing. Remained expressionless.

'It's not going to happen between us, is it Neil?' she said regretfully.

'We have more than a lot of people have,' he told her, turning to the window. 'We've never treated each other badly.'

'That's not enough, though, is it? I can't get anywhere near you, really. Not the real you. I probably won't ever know what . . .'

'What?'

She took a deep breath. There was nothing to lose now. 'What's "Greenfly", Neil?'

His face blanked, turned to stone. 'Where did you hear that word?'

'You talk in your sleep, Neil. Especially . . .'

'Especially?'

'Especially on the bad nights. Neil, you sit up in bed and *shout*. I had to tell Ray and Dave next door it was the TV – some late-night cop show.' She hesitated. 'I'm not trying to force my way into your life, I promise you, I'm just trying to help. Can't you . . . can't you let me do that?'

He smiled at her. Placed his arm round her shoulder.

'Forget it, Lauren. It's nothing. Nothing I can talk about, anyway.'

She shook off his arm. 'I'm not a child, Neil. I know you're . . .'

'You know I'm what?'

She stared wretchedly at him. 'I know you move in a pretty weird world.'

'None of it means anything, Lauren. Forget about it. Live your life. Move on.'

'You're a real one-man no-go area, aren't you?' she said angrily. 'No wonder you're stuck up there by yourself in that sad little flat.'

'I was going to suggest we went out for a bite to eat.'

'I'm not hungry,' she told him curtly, and closed the door.

For the most part, Slater was indifferent to the clients that he guarded. He performed his job efficiently and asked no questions about the source of their wealth. Wealth, in fact, was the only thing that Minerva's clients had in common, and Slater was aware that for much of the time his presence was purely cosmetic. In the world of fifteen-minute junk celebrity there was considerable cachet in the suggestion that you were under physical threat.

Howard Berendt was different. Howard Berendt employed Minerva bodyguards because he genuinely believed his life to be under threat, and because he could no longer trust the slags – the underworld gorillas – that he would normally have relied on.

Berendt was an Essex property dealer who had diversified into lap-dancing clubs. His ambition was carrying him westward, and the leery sweep of his empire now extended almost to the Tottenham Court Road. Berendt's rise, however, had irritated a lot of people. He had trodden on corns. He had angered people whose anger had been known to manifest itself in acts of extreme violence.

Duckworth was well aware of Berendt's low popularity quotient in the criminal underworld, and charged for his bodyguards accordingly. For a week on the job with Berendt an operative could hope to take home the best part of £2000.

To Slater, this sounded like excellent money. His landlord had decided to sell the property in Mafeking Terrace, and had offered Slater first refusal on the top-floor flat. It galled Slater to know that he himself was responsible for the flat's 'pristine condition', as it was described in the agent's details – but he had decided nevertheless to try and raise the deposit. He accepted a week's work guarding Howard Berendt without hesitation.

The first few days were intense. Berendt, a squat, powerful-looking figure with the boiled skin and discoloured eyes of the heavy spirits-drinker, travelled from business location to business location in a mid-seventies Rolls-Royce Silver Cloud – a vehicle he described as a 'classic fuck-off motor' – distributed tips with vulgar lavishness wherever he went, and generally and forcefully announced his presence. Anyone wanting to whack him, thought Slater, just had to follow the cigar wrappers.

In fact, to his surprise, and for all the man's loudness, Slater found that he did not dislike the Essex entrepreneur. There was a red-blooded vigour about him that had long departed most of the clients of Minerva Close Protection. He told a good joke too.

In the days before running to fat and falling prey to habitual sweating, Berendt had been a paratrooper. He was impressed by Slater – he'd once thought of trying Regimental selection himself – and although he did not know quite as much about the subject as he thought he did, he lost no opportunity to discuss esoteric weaponry with the ex-SAS soldier. The day's work often ended in a pub with Berendt and his cronies, and on these occasions Slater took care never to drink anything stronger than bitter lemon. Berendt's girlfriend Kat, formerly a dancer with the Royal Ballet and now a star performer at one of his lap-dancing clubs, often turned up to join them before taking a cab on to work.

On the final evening of the contract, Slater detected a strange atmosphere among the group gathered in the Porcupine, one of Berendt's haunts in Old Street. It was eight thirty, Kat had departed half an hour earlier, and there was an air of anticipation, of nervousness, and of stifled amusement.

Slater felt the uncomfortable sensation of being the only person present not in on the joke. He would have liked to be able to leave, to get back home and go out for a drink or three, but his contract stipulated that he remain until eleven o'clock every evening. There were two and a half hours to go.

'Why don't we drive back to the flat and get some take-away?' Berendt suggested, and there was more back-slapping, more sniggers. 'Got a treat for you, mate,' he said to Slater. 'Oh yes indeed!'

Berendt lived in a large, well-fortified flat off the Edgware Road. Half of the group drove there in Berendt's Rolls-Royce, the others followed in the cherry-red Jaguar owned by Berendt's accountant, Ossie Oswald. In the flat, whose heavy modern furniture and bar was covered in more beige calf-skin than can ever have been assembled outside an abattoir, the group made itself at home. They were an unattractive-looking bunch with the same drinkers' faces and run-to-seed bodies as Berendt himself. Between the six of them, Slater calculated, they were probably wearing the best part of a pound of gold jewellery.

Declining all offers of drinks, Slater positioned himself by the front door. Judging by the increasingly hysterical mood in Berendt's lounge he was in for a bumpy ride. He suddenly felt very hungry; he hoped all the talk of a take-away meant that a decent curry was on its way.

'Ossie, take a couple of the boys and sort us out,' announced Berendt cheerfully. 'Don, give us a fucking bevvy, mate. Some of that single malt. And give one to Neil, too. Can't ignore the poor bloody infantry.'

To buy himself fifteen minutes of peace, Slater accepted the drink. Borrowing an entrance key, he made a quick tour of the approaches to the flat, made himself think like a possible assassin. If he was going to whack someone like Berendt, he thought, this wouldn't be a bad time to do it. Lots of noise, lots of laughs, people coming and going. He'd just rock up to the front door – maybe get a woman to press the bell and wave at the security camera – burst in with a silenced weapon, find Berendt, waste him, and get back on his bike and vanish into the traffic. Well, maybe it wouldn't be precisely the way he'd do it but it was a possible scenario.

Re-entering the flat, he eyed the Islay malt in its crystal tumbler. He hadn't meant to touch it – had meant to pour it down the crapper, in fact – but he couldn't resist a quick slug. For a moment he stood there, tasting the smoky complexity of the malt, feeling the strong clean alcohol course through his veins.

'Liquid fucking gold, isn't it?' smiled Berendt. 'I got a half-dozen cases in before Christmas.'

'It's very good,' agreed Slater. He frowned. 'Mr Berendt, you'll remember what I told you about not opening the door to anyone you don't know. Well, that includes women who claim they have messages for you. It's just a thought, but there have been a couple of cases this year of entry to premises being gained by women who then let heavies in after them.'

'A sort of "Trojan whores" scenario,' said Berendt, and laughed uproariously. 'That's not bad, is it? Trojan whores? I must tell the lads.' He swung heavily away. From the lounge came laughter, then an amplified grunting and the wet slap of flesh. Someone had found the porn collection.

Ossie Oswald's face swum into view on the entry-phone monitor. Although he had departed with one man, a casino manager named Ray Gedge, there now appeared to be five of them.

'Mr Berendt, I think you've got visitors,' said Slater, sticking his head into the lounge where, on the TV screen, a tattooed woman was being vigorously penetrated by several men in Wolverhampton Wanderers football shirts. 'Would you just OK them before we let them up?'

'Relax, Neil,' said Berendt, glancing at the entryphone monitor. 'It's just Ossie with the take-aways. Including yours.'

He re-admitted Gedge and Oswald. Following them were three girls. Their clothes were threadbare, their faces and limbs were marbled with the cold – all three were wearing miniskirts – and they smelt of the streets.

Oh, bloody hell, thought Slater. No. Please, *no!*

They were children. Average age what? Fifteen?

The girls, visibly nervous, were led through into the lounge, where they looked furtively around them. A small cheer and a whistle went up as they entered. A large whisky and a fifty-pound note was handed to each of them. I can't be part of this, thought Slater. I just bloody well can't.

'So take your pick, Neil,' said Berendt. 'Go on, son. You can do anything you want. No one here's going to tell.'

There was laughter. The assembled faces looked up at him, flushed, wreathed in smiles, boozily conspiratorial. The three girls huddled in silence.

Ray Gedge stood up. 'Go on, mate. Which is it to be?' One by one he wrenched the girls' tops up. They shrank from him but remained there with their breasts exposed, not yet fully afraid. Smackheads, thought Slater.

'I don't want any part of this,' he told Berendt. 'These are kids.'

'Choose one,' said Berendt patiently. 'And take her to the first bedroom on the right.' He eyed the girls. 'You can do anything you want,' he whispered. 'And I mean *anything*. No one's going to come looking for this lot.'

Slater shook his head. 'I can't guard you from a locked bedroom.'

Berendt rolled his eyes. 'Neil, I want you to stand down, OK? Full pay, obviously, but you're relieved of all duties for half an hour. How's that?'

Slater decided to pretend to go along with the game. He'd lock himself in the room with one of the girls for half an hour and they'd sit the whole thing out together. To object to a client's behaviour, or even to imply disapproval of a client's behaviour, was to kiss goodbye to a career in bodyguarding. Berendt was a high-paying client, Slater told himself, and saving underage runaways from a life of prostitution was hardly part of his brief. Still, he could give one of the girls a break.

Taking the smallest and most pinched-looking by the hand, he led her to the bedroom Berendt had indicated. Ragged laughter followed him as he closed the door. 'Fill yer boots, son!' he heard Berendt shout after him.

'What d'yer want, mate, a gob or a fuck?' the girl asked, mechanically reaching for his belt-buckle. She had a Liverpool accent and a dark bruise on her left cheekbone.

'What's your name?' he asked her.

'Bethany.'

He didn't bother to ask her age. A quick scan of the room showed him what he'd half-guessed would be there: the framed mirror attached to the wall. If you knew what you were looking for – a particular kind of glassy opacity – one-way mirrors were easy to spot. Most customs halls used them, as did the police in custody suites adapted for identity parades.

Slater gave no sign of having recognised the one-way mirror but mentally he shook his head in disbelief. How stupid did Berendt think he was? The idea, obviously, was that they give him a couple of minutes with Bethany and then move into the next-door bedroom for the show. Maybe even video the whole performance.

Basically, he guessed, it was a machismo thing. A get-out-your-dick exercise. In terms of toughness and military expertise Berendt felt that Slater had the edge on him, and the fact that Slater was Berendt's employee didn't change that fact. To see Slater – or better, film him – having sex with an underage prostitute would go a long way in Berendt's mind to redressing that imbalance.

Slater felt a slow fuse of anger begin to burn.

'Pull your top down, Bethany,' he said quietly, moving the girl's hands away from his groin. 'I want you and your friends out of here.'

She stared at him. Suspicion clouded the thin features. 'Are you's going to fuck us or what?'

'Listen to me, Bethany—'

'Gi'us another twenty, you can go up me arse.'

There was a short but definite scream from the lounge. Bethany frowned, as if she dimly recognised the sound. Slowly she pulled her cheap spandex top down.

'Listen!' Slater told her, furious with himself for allowing the situation to develop this far. 'There's something I've got to look after. I want you to wait here, OK?'

There was another scream, followed by the sound of a hard slap.

Bethany nodded, but looked as if she was having trouble understanding his words. 'You'll say you fucked us, yeah? So they don't ask for the money back, like?'

'Don't worry about the money,' said Slater urgently. 'Just wait here, OK?'

She looked at him blankly and nodded.

There were six men in the lounge. One of the girls, naked, was bent over a heavy glass-topped table. From behind her Ray Gedge pounded into her, his trousers round his ankles. At intervals he wrenched her head up by the hair and slapped the side of her face. Her nose and her mouth were bleeding, and she was crying. Two other men, appreciative spectators of this scenario, stood at her side.

The other girl, also naked, was bent over Ossie Oswald's lap. Her hair was pulled taut between his fingers. As Slater walked into the room Berendt's partner Don Parry was unzipping his trousers behind her.

From the room's deepest armchair, a seven-inch Macanudo cigar clamped between his lips, Howard Berendt surveyed the revels.

Without saying a word Slater sauntered across the room, collected a heavy onyx table-lighter from a display-case, walked over to Ray Gedge, hefted the lighter briefly in his right hand, and swung it full force into the hinge of the casino-manager's jaw.

A look of stupefaction crossed Gedge's face as he sank to his knees. Amazed, he watched as several bloody teeth fell from his mouth to the white carpet. Attempting to articulate his broken jaw a moment later, he fainted.

Leaving Gedge where he was, Slater crossed the room to Berendt, took the smoking cigar from his unresisting fingers, and approached Ossie Oswald.

Eyes widening in terror, Oswald pulled his rapidly deflating penis from the teenager's mouth, disentangled his fat fingers from her hair, and made desperate moves to fasten his trousers. In no apparent hurry, Slater kicked Oswald's knees from under him, and as the grovelling accountant attempted to right himself, ground the glowing coal of the cigar into the hairy junction of his buttocks.

Scrabbling at his anus, Oswald screamed and writhed. Don Parry, mutely shaking his head, raised both hands above his head in terrified surrender. Howard Berendt sat frozen in his armchair.

'Get dressed!'

The girls both appeared to be in shock.

'Get dressed!' Slater repeated, and slowly they began to gather their clothes from the carpet.

'Does Kat stay here?' Slater asked Berendt.

Berendt nodded.

'Go and get some clothes,' Slater ordered. 'I want jackets, trousers and sweaters – the best she's got. As for the rest of you rapists and conspirators-to-rape, I want cash on the table. We're going to have a collection for these children. Anyone disagree?'

He looked around the room. Gedge was still unconscious on the carpet. Oswald, tears running down his cheeks, was agonisedly pulling on his underpants. Don Parry was undergoing an attack of the shakes. No one disagreed.

Slater took a wallet and a handful of cash from each of the six men. One – an enthusiastic spectator of

Gedge's sadism – hesitated for a moment before handing over his money.

'Give it to me,' said Slater quietly, weighing the heavy table lighter in his hand. 'Or I'll break your fucking jaw too.'

The man nodded.

In the end there was over £600 on the table. When the weeping, bloody-nosed girl had dressed herself, Slater dispatched Don Parry to clean her up in the bathroom and called Bethany to come out from the bedroom. The third girl, eyeing Oswald with loathing, took a swig of malt whisky, gargled, and spat the result on to the carpet.

When Berendt returned with an armful of Kat's clothing, Slater allotted each girl £200, a cashmere sweater, a pair of leather trousers, and a coat.

'Range Rover car keys, please,' he demanded. Terrified, Oswald produced them from a pocket.

'This isn't a good idea, Slater,' said Berendt levelly, the first vestiges of colour returning to his sallow cheeks. 'You'll never work in London again, I can promise you that. And what the fuck you hope to accomplish for these little scrubbers is totally beyond me. The clothes and the money will go straight back to some smack-dealing nigger and that'll be the end of it.'

'You know what I'd really like, Howard?'

'I expect you're going to tell me.'

'I'd really like to know what you're going to tell Kat.'

*

Easing the Range Rover into third gear, Slater turned into the Edgware Road. The girls – who must have seen a thing or two in their young lives, Slater reflected – were beginning to find their voices.

'This is class fuckin' gear,' said Maxine, the oldest of the three, running her hands down the front of her new thousand-pound shearling coat. Bethany, for her part, was counting and recounting her wad of cash. Chanelle was still dabbing at her bleeding cheek.

'You're sure?' said Bethany to Slater. 'You don't even want us to gob yer off?'

'The fuckin' mouth on her,' said Maxine.

They drove on. They had been picked up, Bethany had told Slater, at King's Cross station.

'I suppose you're gonna tell us the deal's off with the money and the clothes if we don't go back to our parents and that,' said Maxine.

'There's no deal,' said Slater. 'What do you want to do?'

The girls looked at each other.

'I've got a mobile,' said Slater. 'Anyone want to ring home?'

There was a long silence.

'Give us it,' said Bethany.

'Don't be so fuckin' simple!' shouted Maxine. 'You know who's going to be waiting for you, soon as we get to King's Cross? Lennie.'

'Lennie's your pimp?' asked Slater.

'He's my boyfriend,' said Maxine.

'Lennie needn't be a problem,' said Slater quietly. 'I could have a word with Lennie.'

'He'd fuckin' kill yer.'

'I don't think so.'

'This is bollocks,' Maxine muttered. 'Stop the car. *Stop the car!*'

Slater braked. They were outside Madame Tussaud's in the Marylebone Road. Maxine threw open the Range Rover door and grabbed Chanelle's coat. 'Come on, Sha, leave yer face alone and get the fuck out. He's a fuckin' nutcase, this one.'

Wordlessly, Chanelle stumbled out of the car.

'*You're a fuckin' nutcase!*' Maxine screamed, slamming the door. '*Wanker!*'

Bethany watched them go, and then climbed into the front seat next to Slater.

'Where to?' asked Slater.

'I'll have to stop at the station.'

'Why?'

'I have to give Lennie that money. Maxie'll tell him I've got it and if I don't hand it over he'll really hurt her.'

Slater pulled out from the kerb. 'Like I said, I could have a word with Lennie.'

'Please,' said Bethany, urgency contracting her narrow features. 'He's got what I need.'

'How long have you been using?'

'Please,' repeated Bethany.

The blur of the London night swung past the smoked-glass windows.

Slater parked the Range Rover on a double yellow line in front of the station. Almost immediately he saw a black man in a leather coat pushing his way towards them.

'Thank you,' whispered Bethany. Leaning towards the driver's seat she touched her thin, papery lips briefly to his, then climbed from the car.

Slater watched her go. He left the Range Rover standing there with its headlights on, and tossed the keys down the nearest storm-drain. In the distance he saw Maxine and Chanelle climb out of a black cab, laughing.

Despair, or something very like it, washed over him. This was the bottom of the fucking barrel, and no mistake. How much lower could he go than acting as minder to a criminal? It seemed that he was about to find out – Berendt would make sure that Duckworth felt the full force of his displeasure.

Even if Duckworth believed his side of the story rather than Berendt's, Slater knew that he was finished as a bodyguard. You couldn't physically attack your clients just because you disapproved of their behaviour. He'd be blacklisted – there wouldn't be a security agency in London that would take him on.

Fuck them all, thought Slater. Fuck every last fucking one of them.

Turning away from the lights of the station he stalked off in search of a pub.

SEVEN

Slater woke to dusty sunshine. Blinking, he looked around him. He was on a camp bed, in a sleeping bag. A steel desk and filing cabinet stood against the opposite wall. An electric clock gave the time as 10am.

It was the ringing of the telephone on the desk, Slater realised, that had woken him. Was it for him? Shrugging himself out of the sleeping bag he reached for it. It was Eve.

'Neil. Good morning. How's the head?'

'Not too bad,' Slater told her, 'all things considered.'

'Good. I'll call for you in an hour. We're going down to the country to meet the boss. If you're up to breakfast I recommend the Cabin Café in Neave Passage, fifty yards down the road to the left.'

'At the risk of sounding very stupid indeed,' said Slater, 'where the hell am I?'

'Nine Elms Lane, SW8. If you look out of the window you'll see the fruit and vegetable market. The front door key's on the desk in front of you, the letterpad code is BASRA. See you in an hour. If you go to the Cabin I recommend the bubble and squeak.'

The phone went dead.

It had been a long night. After dropping the girls at King's Cross station Slater had found himself in a pub in the Caledonian Road. The pub had filled up as the night wore on, and he had found himself drawn into the beery embrace of a local women's football team. By 11pm, sadly, the Barnsbury Bantams had left, and Slater's ear was being bent by a party of carp-fishermen from High Wycombe. At 11.30 the landlord had locked the doors, and it was at that point – Slater was drinking Red Stripe with whisky chasers – that time and events started to blur. What was certain was that shortly after midnight he had rung Eve's mobile and suggested that she might care to join the party.

She'd arrived forty minutes later, by which time the landlord had thrown everyone out. She found Slater sitting on the pavement, nursing a final can of Red Stripe.

'Is this how it's going to be?' she'd asked him drily. 'You only ring me at closing time on Friday nights?' She was wearing a midnight blue evening dress, and looked considerably more glamorous than he remembered her.

'I'm sorry,' he had said, struggling to his feet. 'I didn't mean to . . .'

She shook her head. 'It was an official thing. I was leaving anyway.' She beckoned him to her car, an anonymous-looking BMW. 'So, what did you have in mind?'

He looked down at his crumpled trousers and

scuffed Ferragamo loafers, realised just how dishevelled he looked. 'Can I, um, tempt you to a drink of something?'

'I could go for a coffee. I'm driving tomorrow morning.'

They ended up at the Bar Italia in Soho. A boxing match played on the TV screen. They ordered large espressos.

'So, is this just a social call, Neil?' Eve asked him, settling the folds of her skirt around her stool. 'Or . . .'

'You know why I'm calling you.'

She raised her eyebrows. 'Do I? Tell me.'

He told her. Told her that he couldn't kid himself any longer, and that bodyguarding was – not to put too fine a point on it – a total load of shite. Told her that civilian life was driving him out of his mind. Told her that he wanted to be operational again.

'Is this the Special Brew talking?' she asked him.

'No. And it was Red Stripe, anyway. And a couple of measures of Bell's. Let me tell you what happened this evening. Have you heard of a man named Howard Berendt?'

He told her the story. She enjoyed it, especially the idea of Berendt looting Kat's wardrobe to dress the trio of underage prostitutes.

'But that apart,' she said soberly, 'it's all pretty depressing. You didn't honestly think you could change anything for them, did you?'

'I suppose not,' said Slater.

'And there isn't going to be any come-back, is

there? You didn't damage any of the punters too seriously?'

'No. They'll have to wire Gedge's jaw and Oswald won't be sitting down for a couple of weeks but that's about the limit of it. Berendt might hire a couple of big lads to come looking for me, I suppose, but I can't say I'm exactly quaking.'

She nodded. 'And you're positive you want to join the department? You didn't seem very keen last time I met you.'

He shrugged. 'Andreas was right. I am what I am.'

She looked at him hard, and nodded. 'OK, here's what we do. You don't go home tonight; instead I take you to one of our safe houses. Tomorrow, if you're still interested, you meet Mr Ridley.'

'So where are we going, exactly, to meet this boss of yours?' he asked as they sailed down the M3 in Eve's BMW.

'Not too far,' she smiled. She was wearing jeans and a tweed jacket. A well-worn Barbour coat lay on the back seat. Slater lay back with his eyes closed and allowed the warm breeze to pour in through the sunroof.

'And Ridley isn't the boss, in fact, he's the ex-boss. He's retired from the service now. He practically invented the Cadre, though, and spent most of his career running it, so he . . . he takes a continuing interest. It's just a courtesy thing, really, but we always introduce potential new people to him. He likes to run an eye over them.'

'How did you come to join the Cadre?' Slater asked her.

'I joined Box when I left Cambridge. Started off in Derry – source-handling with North Det.'

'Did you get down to the hangar for any of the piss-ups with our lads?'

'No, I was warned off!'

Slater laughed and shook his head. It had been an insane time: for all the talk of peace the secret war had been waged right up to the wire, with killings and reprisals covered up by both sides. There had also been some serious mistakes made; a strong mutual distrust had prevailed between the various security services, and this had led to a lack of communication which on more than one occasion had proved lethal.

'Have you ever worked with a woman?' Eve asked him. It was clear to Slater that they had followed the same train of thought.

'No,' he said. 'Except on surveillance jobs. And I worked with a couple of female bodyguards last month. But never operationally.'

'Would it worry you?' she asked.

'I don't see why it should,' said Slater carefully. 'But if it gets rough, to be honest, I'd be more comfortable with a couple of experienced blokes.'

'Because the women would need "protecting"?' she asked with heavy sarcasm.

'No, just because I've got a theory that women tend to go for their firearms faster than men do. They know they're going to lose a fist-fight or a kicking contest, so they pull out a weapon instead. And the thing escalates.'

'Have you got any evidence whatsoever to back up this cute little theory?'

'None whatsoever,' admitted Slater cheerfully. 'Nor for my other theory.'

'Which is?'

'That a man will surrender to a man, when he wouldn't to a woman. A lot of guys will literally risk a bullet rather than put their hands on their heads for a woman. It's a face thing.'

'I see,' Eve said tersely.

'They're just theories,' said Slater, 'but they're very good for winding people up.'

'Oh, that's where we are, is it? The wind-up stage?'

'You drive beautifully,' said Slater. 'I always feel safer with a female spook at the wheel.'

'Was that a compliment? I can't believe it.'

'Seriously,' said Slater, 'the answer to your first question is no. I have no trouble whatsoever with the idea of working with women, any more than I have with the idea of being ordered around by someone younger than me. All I think is that people should do the things they do best. The managers should manage, the planners should plan, and the doers should do.'

'That's all very well in theory,' said Eve, reaching in her bag for her sunglasses. 'But in practice we don't always have the people for that. In this department we all do all of those things.'

Slater nodded. 'Point taken. So how did you move over the river from Five?'

'I was . . . sort of recruited. My cover had been blown in Ireland, I didn't want to spend the rest of my career doing watcher duties, so I let it be known I was ready for a change. As it happened, the Cadre had just lost someone and were looking for a replacement.'

'Lost someone?' queried Slater.

'A job went wrong. My predecessor was killed.'

Slater stared at her. 'Killed. How?'

'In a firefight in a Paris car-park. I shouldn't be telling you this.'

'And am I replacing someone?'

'Yes. There are always six of us on permanent attachment. Plus two support.'

Eve pulled the BMW off the M3. Soon they were travelling along a sun-splashed country road overhung by trees. Village succeeded village – Nutley, Preston Candover, Chilton Candover – and the landscape seemed to broaden, to expand around them. As they emerged from a long tunnel of beeches and oaks Eve turned off the road on to a narrow track marked Dunns Ford Only. To either side fields of young corn stretched to the horizon. Dunns Ford proved to be a village of no more than two or three dozen houses – all of them old, all of them graceful, several of them large. Alongside the road the river Itchen wound its way over shining gravel and emerald-green weed.

The BMW drew to a halt.

'What do you think?' Eve asked Slater.

Slater shook his head. 'It's like a private world. What would one of these houses cost?'

'Oh, a million or so at least. More with land. More still with a stretch of river. Many, many years bodyguarding, I'm afraid.'

Slater nodded and looked down at his shoes. He would very much have liked the chance to change. There had been a washing and shaving kit in the safe house, but he still felt stale. This Italian gear might have looked cutting-edge in the West End, but in rural Hampshire it just looked flashy and inappropriate.

'Thanks,' he smiled sourly. 'I needed reminding of my lowly status. So, your Mr Ridley is a multi-millionaire?'

'No, he's a former civil servant who lives on his pension. He's lived here for ages – long before prices went mad. Are you ready?'

'As I'll ever be,' said Slater.

River House was bounded by high stone walls and set back some distance from the road. Eve rounded a small circular lawn, brought the BMW to rest in front of a pillared entrance, and pressed the brass bell.

The door was answered by a smiling, pink-cheeked figure with a scrubby white moustache and a keen gaze. He was wearing shapeless corduroys and a frayed country shirt, and Slater guessed him to be in his sixties or seventies. The two men shook hands.

'Mr Slater – Neil – it's very good to see you. Come on in, hope you're hungry, bathroom on the right if you want a wash. Eve, my dear, what a pleasure.'

He beckoned Slater into a stone-flagged hall. The place was comfortable rather than grand, and not especially tidy. Bookcases lined the walls, and where there were not books there were photographs: children on horseback, pre-war school cricket teams, officers in uniform, African servants, Scottish rivers and long-demolished houses. There were also mounted antlers and fox-masks, and from its case above the fireplace a vast and snaggle-toothed pike cast a glassy eye on proceedings.

Slater gave himself the once-over in the bathroom mirror, rejoined Eve and Ridley, and accepted a beer. A woman – a housekeeper rather than a wife, Slater guessed – was bringing food to the table.

'Do you fish, Neil?' Ridley asked.

'I did as a boy,' Slater admitted. 'Not . . . not the sort of fishing you do down here, though.'

It had been poaching, mostly, and eventually he'd been caught by the gamekeeper, a man with a reputation for punching you in the face first and asking questions afterwards. Until he went to Iraq Slater had never been as scared as he'd been when he felt his collar grabbed that night. His heart still turned over when he thought about it.

'What I thought we might do', said Ridley, 'is have a bite of lunch, and then potter out and spend a couple of hours on the river. OK by everyone?'

It was. Lunch was steak and kidney pie and a bottle of claret, followed by summer pudding. Slater had been right, the woman was a housekeeper. Ridley lived alone.

Department business was not discussed or even mentioned during the meal. Instead the conversation embraced – among other topics – the English countryside, soldiering, books, marriage, whisky and Far Eastern travel. Slater was fully aware that he was being interrogated, and that his answers were revealing more and more about his private loyalties and his secret and inner self, but the whole thing was so skilfully and sympathetically done that he offered himself up without resistance. Aware that Eve was watching him – unlike Ridley, he noticed, she had not yet learnt how to observe people without their being aware of it – he made a point of limiting himself to a single glass of wine, and of not quite finishing it.

When coffee was finished, Ridley led them through to his rod room. This was a pleasantly chaotic area with nineteenth-century prints on the wall, elderly Barbour jackets hanging on pegs, and waders and gumboots on the floor. And fishing kit. Reels and flyboxes cluttered a Victorian chest of drawers, nets hung from hooks, and dissassembled and partially assembled rods stood in every corner.

'Now, Neil, how are we going to kit you out? British traditional or American high-tech?'

The question, Slater knew, was a loaded one. 'I'll go for the Brit option,' he said.

Ridley nodded approvingly. 'Eve, would you be so good as to fix Neil up with the eight-foot split-cane Hardy and the Princess reel?'

Five minutes later, in a pair of Ridley's wellingtons

and with a borrowed bag of tackle over his shoulder, he followed the others through the garden. Ridley owned 500 yards of the fishing in the river Itchen – a stretch reached by crossing the bridge in the village and walking through a couple of water-meadows. Ten minutes later they stood at the foot of an ancient willow, with the gin-clear water streaming slowly past them.

'First,' said Ridley, 'find your prey. Now how about him?'

Twenty yards away, hard under the far bank, a dark shape wavered in the current. As Slater watched, it drifted upwards, plucked a fly from the surface, and returned to its station. Assembling his rod, selecting a fly from a battered tobacco tin and deftly attaching it to the end of a line of hair-like fineness, Ridley began to cast. The line snaked easily out and the fly landed with thistledown lightness a yard above the fish. Slowly, as Slater held his breath, it drifted downstream, and equally slowly the trout began to tilt upwards. Almost lazily it engulfed the fly, and then as Ridley tightened the line, the split-cane rod hooped, the reel screamed and the fish raced up-river with electric fury. It fought hard, but Ridley remained in control, and a few minutes later he slid the net beneath its shining, exhausted form. It was a beautiful fish, several pounds in weight, and Slater gazed wonderingly as Ridley released it. The trout hung in the current for a moment like a shadow and then, its instincts returning, raced for deep water.

'The wild brown trout,' said Slater. 'The subtlest of the freshwater fishes. If you can deceive him you can deceive . . .'

'Anyone?' ventured Eve.

'Why don't you have a go, Neil?' Ridley suggested. 'If an old fool like me can manage it, I'm sure you can.'

'I'm not,' said Slater, 'but I'll give it a crack.'

'Let's go upstream,' said Ridley. 'This one will have been disturbed by that last fish.'

Another pool, smooth as glass. And another fish, lying between two waving banks of green weed. Assembling the tackle as he had seen Ridley do, and allowing Eve to select and tie on a suitable fly, Slater began to cast.

Ridley had made it look so easy, but in truth fly-fishing proved nightmarishly difficult. Far from snaking effortlessly out over the river the line seemed to be everywhere. Within sixty seconds the fly had caught in the grass behind him, in a bush opposite him, and finally in the seat of Slater's trousers from where Eve smirkingly extracted it. On his second attempt the line lashed the surface like a whip, and the trout vanished in a puff of gravel.

'Don't be discouraged,' said Ridley. 'They're very . . . *educated* fish.'

At the next pool, at Ridley's suggestion, Eve stood behind Slater and guided his casting arm. Eventually, after a number of mishaps and tangles, he got the feel of it. He also got the feel of Eve's breasts against his back, but decided to file the sensation away for later retrieval. He was determined to catch one of these bloody trout.

'Why don't we split up?' Ridley suggested. 'Neil, you go upriver a hundred yards, Eve can stay here, and I'll go down to the bottom field. Oh and Neil, anything over a couple of pounds, knock it on the head and we'll have it for supper.'

Keeping well back from the bank, Slater walked up through the buttercups with the split-cane rod at his side. It was a hot afternoon, bees hummed, and bullocks regarded him incuriously. Finding the pool he had been directed to, he knelt down beside an alder bush in order not to silhouette himself against the skyline, and started to cast. There were two fish in view, swimming side by side in the centre of the river. With no obstruction nearby Slater managed to float his fly past them a dozen times, but they ignored it. Painstakingly he knotted on another on another fly, but with the same result. For half an hour he tried to cast as Ridley had done, but it was no good. The fish seemed to be laughing at him, hovering in the current and then lazily scattering as soon as he made a move towards them. Sometimes they didn't even bother to swim away, but merely ignored him. Perhaps, Slater mused irritably, you had to have been an officer for them to take you seriously.

But there had to be a way. He was damned if he was going to return to the house empty-handed. Improvise, he told himself – as you have spent your life improvising. If fair means don't get you where you want, try foul. On hands and knees now, he rounded a bend in the river and peered over the side of the bank. Below him, finning placidly over the gravel, was the long, ghostly form of a trout. It was the best fish he'd seen all day.

Retreating from the bank, he looked round and made sure that he was out of sight. Then taking the flybox from the bag that Ridley had lent him, he selected the largest fly he could find. Hooking its barbed point into a stick he took his lighter from his pocket and burnt off the feather hackles of the fly until only the bare hook remained. This he attached to his line. Crossing to the bullocks' field he found a splatter of dried dung. Beneath it, as there had always been in his boyhood, he found a colony of lively red worms. Six of these went on to the hook.

Returning to the bank, which overhung the river by a couple of metres, he pulled two or three yards of line off the reel. If he stuck the end of the rod over the bank, he guessed, the fish would spook. So keeping well back, he took the writhing bundle of hooked worms in his hand, and lobbed it a few feet upstream of where he had seen the fish.

For a second nothing happened, then there was a loud *gloop*, and the fly-line started snaking through the grass. Seizing the rod, Slater held hard. The split-cane bent double, and then line started zipping through his fingers. The fish was thirty yards upstream before he managed to turn it, and this was only the first of half a dozen such runs.

Finally the trout lay beneath him, beaten, but here the bank was too high – five or six feet above the water – to reach it with the net.

Only one thing for it – and Slater slid feet-first into the river, feeling his Italian trousers rend as he went. He went in up to his waist, and finding his feet, quietly netted the fish. It was a beautiful thing, perhaps three and a half pounds in weight, and Slater watched it for a few moments. Then walking into shallower water he reached for a large stone and struck it sharply on the head. The trout shuddered briefly, and was dead.

Climbing from the river he laid the fish and his tackle among the buttercups. Water streamed from his trousers as one by one he emptied his wellingtons. He was wringing out his socks when a shadow fell across him. It was Eve.

'What a fantastic fish! I'm impressed!'

'Well, as you can see, in the end I had to go in after it. Settle it man to man.'

'I see.' She picked up the rod. What fly were you using?'

'Well . . .' began Slater, 'I . . .'

'Improvised,' Eve nodded, peering at the hook to which a segment or two of worm was still attached. 'And fell in, obviously.'

'Will you tell him?' asked Slater.

'What? That you fell in? I think that's going to be obvious!'

'No, that I bent the rules a bit.'

'What rules? I didn't hear anyone lay down any rules.'

'You know what I mean. The rules of sportsmanship. Gentlemanly conduct and all that.'

She smiled. 'Only the Colonel and his guests fish here.'

It wasn't until late that evening, when they had eaten the fish with butter and parsley and were ensconced in a corner of the Dunns Ford Inn with a pint glass in front of each of them, that professional matters were raised.

'Tell me,' Ridley said with deliberation, 'about Operation Greenfly. And your part in it.'

'How much do you know already?' asked Slater.

'As regards the planning side of it, quite a lot. As regards what happened on the ground, rather less.'

Slater nodded. 'Well, you'll remember that the operation was set up immediately after the murder of a part-time RUC officer called Frayn, who was shot in a drive-by outside a betting shop. Special Branch decided that it was time that three of their top operators were taken out, and handed the job to the Regiment. The targets were Henry O'Day, who shot the officer and was stupid enough to boast about it, a bomber called Frankie Coyle, and a shooter, name unknown. The operations were coded Mayfly, Cranefly and Greenfly.

'I was put on the Greenfly team that was tasked to take out the shooter. He was known to have killed at least two squaddies – a lance-corporal from the Cheshires, and a young signals guy who was fixing a mast on one of the OPs on the border – and the word that the undercover guys in the FRU were getting from their touts was that he was going to hit a checkpoint near Forkhill.

'Now I don't know who the FRU had on the inside – as you know the Regiment are basically just called in to do the chopping – but the data was very good. The weapon had been cached on a border farm about five miles from the checkpoint, and the shooter was due to collect it some .time after ten o'clock. It was December, a night with no moon, so it would be black as the ace of spades by that time. The hit on the checkpoint would probably take place within half an hour of the collection – Greenfly wouldn't want the weapon on him for a second longer than necessary; he'd want it fired, cleaned and back in the ground.

'We were desperate for Greenfly to be a success. These shooters go off to Texas or Louisiana to do a sniper's course and when they come back the word gets around. No one says anything, but everyone knows who they are, and they become like these legendary figures in the community. It was a propaganda thing as much as anything else. We wanted to whack him and score the Regiment a hatful of points with the powers that be. I'll not lie to you – we wanted a killing and we wanted it bloody.

'Well, everything seemed to bear out the accuracy of the intelligence. PIRA dickers with CB radios had been seen sniffing round the Forkhill checkpoint on the day in question, doing a last-minute target-area recon – there was one called Deathly Mary who always used to do a walk-by on foot; everyone knew her – and we were certain that the shooting would be going down as planned. Sean Delaney, the owner of the farm where the shooter's weapon was cached, was known to be an IRA sympathiser, if not an actual player. His wife had left him twelve months earlier and moved to Derry, and he was living with his brother Joey, a mentally retarded boy who helped him about the farm, and his unmarried sister Bridget. Like the dickers, we had done our own close-target recce. We knew where all the exits were and we knew to within a few yards where the cache was.

'The team went in at last light. We were dropped off from an unmarked vehicle a mile away and tabbed across country to the farm. In the surrounding lanes, mobile units moved into position. A helicopter waited on stand-by ten miles out at one of the camps, turning and burning. It was a very cold, very dark night . . .'

Slater had reached his firing position, a small rise beneath a stand of firs, within twenty minutes of the drop-off. Carefully, aware that the area might easily be under night-sight observation, he had manoeuvred into place, concealing himself beneath the spreading branches and covering his body with cam-netting and foliage. Soon he was satisfied that, to all intents and purposes, he was invisible. He was in a comfortable firing position, or as comfortable as he could expect to be given the situation, and his weapon – a Heckler and

Koch 53 sniper's rifle loaded with ten 7.62 armour-piercing rounds – was readied for action on its bipod. The HK's night sight had been zeroed for 120 yards, and the sight's miniature generator was emitting its faint characteristic whistle. It was a very cold night – by 7pm the ground was already stiffening with frost – but the adrenaline racing around Slater's system anaesthetised him to the cold, to the icy flint of the ground, to everything except his own intense concentration.

Through the night sight all that he saw was an undersea green. The farmhouse, a low, discoloured building with a slate roof, was about 120 metres in front of him. Amplified green light bled through the curtains; their edges blazed with it, as did the gap beneath the back door, which gave on to a flight of steps and a stone-flagged farmyard. As Slater watched, a fox slunk into the yard, nosed cautiously at the dustbins, climbed the frozen dung-heap to the wall and looked around him.

A hunter, thought Slater. A killer like myself. Good luck to you, brother. May you be spared the shotgun and the flick of the boot on to that same dung-heap.

Through a throat-mike and earpiece, Slater was in communication with the three other members of the SAS sniper team, now silently readying themselves, and with the outlying mobile units. As team leader he had the position covering the most probable killing-ground; the other snipers were invisibly disposed around the farm as back-up. Like him they were taut-wired with adrenaline. Like him they felt no cold, saw the night as green day. There will be a death tonight, thought Slater, and I have never felt more fully alive.

On the wall the fox stiffened, leapt to the ground and raced for cover. Soon Slater could hear the car too. And see it. A muddy Toyota hatchback, showing sidelights only, swinging carefully up the track.

'Vehicle approaching,' murmured Slater into his throat-mike.

It disappeared for a moment behind a rough coppice and was suddenly there in the farmyard, its sidelights two blinding swirls in the ghost-green landscape. In the yard, the car came to a greasy, shuddering stop. The driver stayed at the wheel, and a second figure wearing a heavy trenchcoat — looked like military surplus, thought Slater — ducked from the Toyota.

'Target exiting vehicle.'

It was the shooter.

He would identify himself to the occupants of the farmhouse, collect the weapon from the cache, and change into 'sterile' overalls, headgear, footwear and gloves. IRA shooters, Slater knew, favoured yellow Marigold gloves as the least likely to leave any trace of forensic. Afterwards these would be burnt at the farmhouse.

The greatcoated figure hurried to the door. As he got there he pulled a mobile telephone from his pocket, thumbed it briefly, and seemed to mouth a single word. The door opened — a blare of green-white light, swiftly extinguished — and he was inside. Get ready to die, motherfucker, thought Slater, his heart thumping hard at his ribs. Get ready to die.

'Target entering house. Back door.'

For ten minutes nothing happened. The driver lit a cigarette, smoked it, flipped the smoking butt from the car, waited. Then the door of the house opened, and the greatcoated figure exited, his breath smoking, his shoulders hunched against the cold. OK, thought Slater grimly. OK.

'Target in view.'

Through the night sight he saw the shooter cross the yard. He was carrying a gardening fork, and with this he carefully cleared an area of dung and straw at the base of the heap. Then, crouching, he lifted one of the heavy flag-stones.

'Target retrieving weapon.'

I'll take him when he straightens, Slater told himself. As soon as I can see that he is holding the weapon. Gently exhaling, he placed the inverted black V of the sight above the shoulders of the crouching man. Took up the play in the trigger. Inhaled.

The target rose, weapon in hand. Rose in profile into the clear line of Slater's zeroed sights, the inverted V meeting the perpendicular crossbar just forward of the target's ear.

Exhale to stillness. Squeeze. Muzzle-flash.

The lower half of the pale green face vaporised into black spray. The report splitting the night, punching the compound plastic stock of the HK against Slater's shoulder and cheek, dropping the target like rubbish to the dung-heap.

'Contact. Target down.'

Slater, dragging his ski-mask over his eyes with his free hand, all but gagging with the release of tension, was already half-way to the fallen man. Reaching him he whipped the HK to his shoulder to deliver the killing shot but at the last moment held his fire. The target was alive, although he no longer had a jaw, or a mouth, or indeed a lower half to his face. He still had his eyes, however, and the eyes were the terrified, incomprehending eyes of a child. They held Slater's for a moment, and it seemed as if – in a last desperate plea – they were trying to smile.

From 150 yards away, as Slater froze in horror, the sniper team's number two delivered the double tap. It was a flawless display of shooting, the twin reports sounding as one, and the fallen man – now almost headless – jerked spasmodically as his nervous system arrested. At his side lay a Match M16 rifle with a telescopic sight.

His hands slippery with brain-spray, Slater swung the HK towards the car, where the driver was sitting with his hands raised in terrified surrender, and the back door of the house.

The yard flooded with the noise of running soldiers as the rest of the team closed in. Over the radio Slater heard rapid-fire instructions as an outer cordon was set up.

A long stain of blood on the ground around the fallen figure, and beyond him a sprayed and scattered mess of tissue, bone-fragments and teeth.

And then a man in a muddy windcheater running from the house, and a wild-eyed woman in a leather jacket screaming behind him: '*You shot my little brother, you cunt! You SAS pigfucker! He was just a . . .*'

And the pair of them seized – the man speechless with shock, the woman still dementedly screaming – and plasticuffed.

And the words and the events finally making some sort of sense, and the icy cold kicking in, and Slater knowing for certain that he had shot the wrong man . . .

'Joey Delaney was twenty-four years old,' said Slater, lowering his glass, 'but his mental age was nine. The shooter had sent him out to retrieve the weapon and deliberately lent him the coat. Sent him out as a decoy in case there was an SAS hit team waiting out there. His brother Sean, who wasn't all that switched on, didn't realise what was going down – he just wanted to be a good volunteer, doing his bit – and he let the lad go out for the weapon.'

There was a long silence. Eve glanced at Slater but his face was blank.

'So what happened next?' asked Ridley.

'We plasticuffed Sean and Bridget Delaney and hit the farmhouse. And there was your man, cucumber-cool, in the kitchen, unzipping his overalls. He was a tallish guy, perhaps thirty, with receding hair. Distinguished looking, you might say. Certainly not your run-of-the-mill PIRA trigger-man.'

'And you arrested him?' asked Eve.

'We held him. I was for doing him there and then – I got as far as thumbing down the safety catch – and I know the lads would have backed me up if I'd said he'd reached for a weapon. But it would have got very complicated very quickly. I could hear the chopper landing outside – the police were on their way. And in truth no one would believe that he would have been carrying at that moment anyway. He wouldn't have been so stupid.'

'You knew that you were going to have to let him walk away?' asked Eve.

'I knew it, and he knew it. But the truth is that there was something else going on between me and this guy. Something personal. He knew what he'd made me do by sending that boy out in his place, and he knew just from looking at me in that kitchen that it was going to do me real damage. And that pleased him. I could see it in his eyes. "Shooting me won't bring him back," he said when I brought the HK up to my shoulder. "Shooting me would only make the whole thing worse. Don't you think?"

'His accent was – how can I describe it – a kind of Irish American. Something about it said money. Something said this was the sort of guy you'd normally see in a smart suit in an expensive restaurant, and I wondered who the hell he was. He certainly wasn't on the regular list of known players – he'd probably come over specially from the States. And he'd probably get straight on to a plane when the police released him, go back there, and disappear until the next hit.

'And then I thought: If I can't actually kill him, I can at least put him out of action as a shooter. Break a few fingers, perhaps, smash his hand up a bit. I was just wondering about the best way to do that, given that I still had the night sight attached and couldn't use the butt of the HK, when about five RUC guys came steaming in and took charge. A couple of minutes later we were pulled off the position and choppered back to the barracks.'

'And that was the beginning of the end as far as you and the Regiment were concerned,' said Ridley.

Slater nodded. 'It was. I went off my head, basically. Call it post-traumatic stress or whatever you like, but I hit the Darkland big-time. I became super-aggressive – always picking fights – I gave the Regiment guys under me a really bad time, I started drinking a lot, which I'd never done before . . . and became like a totally aggressive, violent loner.

'And I had these nightmares. Endlessly. In which I saw Joey Delaney. I saw him in crowds, I saw him in shops, I saw him in bars, I even saw him on television. Just standing there in that oversized coat with half his face shot away and those nine-year-old's eyes looking at me, not understanding what was happening to him, or why. And I'd try to run away but he'd always be there, following me, as if I was the only one who could help him rather than the one who was half-way through killing him. And I'd have my weapon with me – the HK53 – and I'd threaten him, tell him to leave me alone or I'd shoot him again, and eventually I would shoot him again, and I'd go on shooting him, endlessly, but . . .'

Slater fell silent. No one moved. Ridley studied his signet ring.

'And then I actually saw Joey Delaney in real life, when I was wide awake, walking down Bridge Street in Hereford. Same expression, same shot-away face, right there in front of me. I ended up running all the way back to the camp at Sterling Lines. Told the head-shed I was having hallucinations and flashbacks, that I couldn't carry on, and that I wanted an immediate discharge.'

Slater emptied his glass, and shook his head when Ridley mimed a refill.

'And they gave me one. They'd seen people in my condition too often to doubt that I meant what I said. First, though, they sent me to the psychiatric unit at the tri-service hospital. The shrinks did the usual stuff, got me to talk the incident through and so on – got me to put what I felt into words – and the nightmares started coming less often.'

'Do you still get them?' asked Eve sympathetically.

'Occasionally. They came back for a time after the incident at Bolingbroke's School. I know the signs and symptoms now, though, and I know that I just have to ride the whole thing out. That in the end it'll go away.'

'And after the hospital?'

'I did a coaching course – athletics and rugby. I'd got

it into my mind that school life might suit me. That I might be able to teach young lads something about themselves on the games field.'

'And did it? Suit you, I mean?'

'In the end, no. Or not life at that particular school, anyway. But I'm sure you know most of this already. You're not going to tell me you haven't vetted me pretty thoroughly.'

Ridley smiled. 'We would have been foolish not to, I think you'll agree.'

Slater turned to him. 'Can you fill in a historical detail for me?'

'I can try to.'

'The shooter at Forkhill. I know they had to release him, but did they ever find out anything about him? Was he an American, for example, as I thought?'

Ridley steepled his fingers. 'His name was John McGirk, and he had dual citizenship. He grew up in a Catholic family in Belfast and he and his parents moved to New York State in the mid-eighties. I seem to remember they were both research chemists; anyway, they ended up doing very well for themselves. The young McGirk enjoyed the best education that the city of Buffalo had to offer and studied . . . oh, literature I think. Something to do with James Joyce, or am I imagining that? Anyway, he chucked it in after a couple of years, dropped out of the University of Buffalo, and joined the Marine Corps.'

'Quite a jump,' said Slater.

'Indeed. He ended up going to Saudi with Desert Storm as a sniper, and after that we think he went back to Belfast to look up some of his old pals. Now up to that point, as far as anyone knows, he had no particular Republican sympathies. He was a Catholic, like I said, but the middle-class suburb he grew up in was a world away from the Falls Road.

'Somehow, though, he made PIRA connections. One theory is that one of his schoolfriends had become a member of the Army Council. And obviously it was felt that a man with his skills who was completely unknown to the security services was too good to waste. And unknown he remained – the PIRA made sure of that. Until Cropspray we didn't have a name or a face for him, just a reputation and a whole lot of conflicting rumours.

'When the RUC pulled him in they discovered he was in the Province on a false passport. The man he was claiming to be was a quadraplegic living on Rhode Island who hadn't left the States for fifteen years. And so all the agencies started digging.' Ridley spread his hands. 'And we identified Greenfly as McGirk. If Cropspray accomplished nothing else, it accomplished that. He hasn't been back since, and I'd guess that that means that lives have been saved.'

'So what's he up to now?' asked Slater.

'He's back in the States, where as far as we know he hasn't raised his head above the parapet. I'm sure we'll hear from him one of these days, though.'

'I'd very much like to,' said Slater with feeling.

Ridley smiled. 'I'll see what we can do to bring you together. I'm sorry you've had such a bad time — it's the occupational risk of our calling.'

'I'll survive,' said Slater, aware of Eve's thoughtful gaze.

'I'm sure you will. And I'd like to say how glad I am you're joining us. We're a small team, but the work we do is vitally important. As, right now, is refilling these glasses. Eve, would you be so good?'

He turned back to Slater. 'As I said before, that was a splendid fish you caught this afternoon. Very few of my guests have managed one of that size on their first visit. By, er, whatever method!'

Slater smiled in acceptance of the compliment.

'And without wishing to talk shop on such a beautiful evening, it looks as if we might be able to put your improvisational skills to work on behalf of the Cadre rather sooner than anticipated — assuming, that is, that you agree to join us.'

'Can you tell me in specific rather than general terms what it is that you do?' Slater asked. He wanted to hear it put into words.

Ridley smiled, a benign amusement lighting up every weathered crease of his features. He would make, thought Slater, a very good Father Christmas.

'We assassinate enemies of the State,' he twinkled.

Slater nodded slowly. He could hardly ask for plainer speaking than that. He realised that on some level he'd already known it. But was that really what he wanted to be — a political assassin? Did he, ultimately, have any choice? Wasn't he an assassin already?

'I'm informed,' said Ridley, taking Slater's silence for assent, 'that we have the beginnings of a situation.'

EIGHT

Over the course of the next week, things moved fast. Slater did not return to the Highbury flat – instead a van collected his furniture and possessions and he was re-installed in a similar-sized place in Primrose Place, hard by Waterloo Station.

The new flat, he discovered, had been vacated by his predecessor a fortnight before, and although nondescript-looking from the outside was fitted with state-of-the-art alarms and anti-intruder devices. There was also a scrambled landline phone to the office at Vauxhall Cross. The place was in good decorative order, and although he had nothing to hang on the walls, Slater soon had it looking cheerful enough. There was a market nearby, he discovered, where exotic fruit and vegetables could be bought, and he determined to expand his cooking repertoire to include a few curries.

Most days he walked along Lambeth Palace Road and Albert Embankment to Vauxhall Cross. Mainline trains from Waterloo stopped there, but the rail-journey took almost as long as travelling on foot. At the MI6 headquarters he had been provided with passes, entry codes and swipe-cards. He had also inherited a Liverpool FC coffee mug from his unknown predecessor, and had been formally introduced to Ray and Debbie, the Cadre's support team. For reasons of security, Slater discovered, Cadre members were only ever referred to by their first names. To keep things simple – especially vis-à-vis radio and communications procedures – they used the same names when operational, adding false surnames where necessary.

Ray and Debbie were both computer experts, and much of Slater's first week was spent learning secure communications procedures from one or other of them. Ray's passion, apart from obscure Arabic-language websites, was the cinema of the Cold War, and he wore heavy black-framed glasses and knitted silk ties in homage to Michael Caine in *The Ipcress File*. Being just over five feet feet tall and prematurely balding he resembled Michael Caine in no other respect, but this deterred him not one whit. His dream, he told Slater, was to wake up one morning and discover that henceforth life was to be lived in black and white.

Debbie was the spiky-haired young woman Slater had met on his first visit to the office. Like Ray she undercut the serious and stressful nature of her work by affecting to play the clown. Some days she would report for work wearing corpse-white make-up, on others she would remove her motorcycle helmet in the atrium to reveal purple gothic hair-extensions. Debbie had been recruited after hacking into the MI6 database while at university and planting a job application amongst the Balkan desk's top-secret files. Hearing about this audacious approach, and needing a replacement for her predecessor, who had left to marry a diplomat, the Cadre's director of operations had snapped her up immediately.

Like Ray, Debbie was a highly competent computer engineer, and the two of them ran a small repair workshop in an annexe of the office. As she explained to Slater, none of Nine's computers, once used, could ever be repaired, serviced or disposed of outside the department. Even a completely smashed-up terminal dumped on a skip could yield important information to a good forensic engineer. When Slater had ruefully confessed to her that computers made him nervous, Debbie had smiled. 'We'll get you up to speed,' she had promised him. 'And all you really have to remember is not to lose your fucking laptop!'

The director of operations was the smooth-jowled man Slater had encountered at his last interview with Lark. Named Manderson – as a regular, non-operational MI6 officer seconded to the Cadre, he kept his real surname – he was a clubbable old school type who at first sight looked the exact opposite of a switched-on intelligence operator. With his pink cheeks, raked-back hair and foxy smile, he looked like a wealthy stockbroker who had done a short-service commission in the guards. There was a hardness about his eyes, however, which belied this genial impression.

Slater met him on his second morning, when Manderson hurried into the office to collect some reconnaissance photographs. Introduced by Debbie, Manderson shook Slater's hand, held up the photographs – 'Ingushetiya. *Fucking* awful place!' – and raced out. He returned in time to take Slater out for a pint and a sandwich at a cheerless pub near the Oval cricket ground. He apologised for the fact that Slater had not yet been introduced to the rest of the Cadre, but explained that they had all been tied up with the aftermath of a long surveillance operation relating to Eastern European money-laundering. He should, however, be meeting them all in a day or two, as there was 'something biggish bumping down the pipeline'.

In the meanwhile, Manderson suggested, he should spend a day on the range and in the killing house down at Warlingham, in Surrey. When they were not operational he usually suggested that Cadre members spend at least a half-day a week at Warlingham working on their sniping and close-quarter battle skills.

Slater heard him out expressionlessly. He knew the smooth, power-hungry Manderson type only too well from the army. Secure in the knowledge that they would never have to face such horrors themselves, they invariably made liberal use of gung-ho phrases like 'hard contact' and 'close-quarter battle'. He was certainly a clever man – no fool could have advanced to Manderson's level of seniority – but Slater suspected that his greatest skills were those he deployed on behalf of his own career.

Returning to the office, and with a mixture of anticipation and apprehension, Slater booked himself in for a session at Warlingham the following morning.

He arrived on the range to find a face that he knew: a wiry old ex-Scots Guards armourer named Jock MacLennan who'd been seconded to the Regiment for several years. MacLennan watched in silence as Slater put himself through his paces on the range. He re-acclimatised himself with a variety of weapons, and discovered to his relief that he was not quite as rusty as he had feared he might be. With hand-arms, in particular, his accuracy and reaction times were pretty much as good as ever.

The two men had a bite of lunch at the South London Aero Club, and then returned to the killing house, where they were joined by a Cadre membre named Terry. Terry was a pale, doughy-featured Essex-boy with a straggly goatee, and to Slater's eye looked seriously unfit. For the purpose of the firearms exercise he was dressed in a pair of blue garage-worker's overalls.

MacLennan loaded up the Heckler and Koch MP5s and Slater set up the killing room. The weapons had been rigged to fire paint-rounds, but in every other respect behaved like normal MP5s. Slater and Terry stalked each other through various set-ups for a couple of hours, and Slater's fears were swiftly confirmed: the lad was no combat soldier. He was slow on his feet, and looked awkward behind a weapon. Slater, on the other hand, had not enjoyed himself so much for ages. The old instincts were still in place, and the blood sang in his veins as he went to work. Needless to say he splattered his overweight opponent every time.

'I'm sorry, guys,' Terry said eventually, his overalls dripping with yellow marker-paint. 'I'm crap with guns – they're just not my thing.' He turned exhaustedly to Slater. 'Any advice you can give us, mate . . .'

Slater nodded and smiled encouragingly. Inwardly he was wondering what the hell kind of outfit he'd committed himself to. This fat lad was a waste of space, for a kick-off.

At 7.30 on the fifth morning, Ray called Slater on the scrambled landline. There would be an important departmental briefing in one hour, and his presence was required.

It was a cold, overcast day – a promising May had become an indifferent June – and Slater made his way down Albert Embankment with a sharp prickle of anticipation.

He arrived in the office to find Eve in close conference with Andreas and a slightly built black man of about thirty in jeans and a leather jacket whom the others introduced as Leon. An air of urgency prevailed and for once even Debbie looked comparatively subdued. As the newest recruit to the outfit Slater decided to keep the lowest possible profile. Raising a quick hand in greeting to Ray and Terry he buried himself behind his terminal and went through the motions of checking for incoming messages. A new driving licence and European community passport, he saw, had been placed in his in-tray, as had a first-class Eurostar ticket. All were in the name of Neil Clissold.

Manderson arrived ten minutes later, murmured general greetings and disappeared into the briefing room with Debbie. He looked tired, strained and in no mood to suffer fools.

Eventually Debbie emerged and ushered the assembled company into the briefing room. They moved slowly – most were carrying styrofoam cups of hot tea or coffee. At the far end, trailing wires, a large, panoramic TV/DVD set stood on a wheeled stand.

Manderson raised his hands for silence and the faint murmur evaporated.

'Good morning, everyone. I hope I haven't interrupted too many breakfasts.'

Silence. A few taut smiles.

'Before this briefing gets under way I'd like to take this opportunity to welcome a new member to the department. Neil is already known to some if not most of you, and I'm sure you'll all, er, make him feel welcome and so on.'

Manderson gave Slater a peremptory nod. Around the table six faces directed polite smiles at the newcomer. Apart from Leon there was only one person present that Slater hadn't met – a nondescript dark-haired woman whom he guessed to be in her late twenties. Catching Slater's eye she leaned over the table with one hand extended. 'Hi,' she said. 'I'm Chris.'

From his place on Eve's left hand, Andreas raised his styrofoam cup an inch or two and gave Slater a stealthy wink.

Manderson turned to Ray, who was inserting a DVD into the player. 'When you're done, I'd like to lock down. No calls, no visitors, no interruptions. When was the place last swept for bugs?'

'An hour ago,' said Debbie. 'All clear.'

Manderson nodded, and Ray and Debbie withdrew from the briefing room, closing the soundproof glass door behind them.

'Right, ladies and gentlemen,' said Manderson, thumbing a button on the remote control, 'I'd like you to study these images.'

A photograph from – of all things – *Hello!* magazine. In the foreground the portly figure of the arms-dealer Adnan Khashoggi, canapé in hand, and a dark-haired woman in a cloth-of-gold dress. Others present, Champagne flutes in hand, all dressed in black and gold.

'This photograph is eight years old,' said Manderson. 'It was taken at the Hotel de Paris in Monte Carlo. Now the man I want to draw your attention to' – he took a laser-pointer from the table – 'is this one.'

The tiny arrow showed a smiling figure in a black dinner jacket, black tie, and gold cummerbund standing in a group behind Khashoggi. Slater guessed him to be in his mid-forties. He looked tanned and prosperous; his spectacles were gold-framed, his thinning hair expensively barbered.

'His name,' said Manderson, 'is Antoine Fanon-Khayat. He is an arms-dealer and fixer, Franco-Lebanese in origin, Christian by denomination, place of birth, Beirut, 1950. Educated at the French Lycée, South Kensington, and at the Sorbonne in Paris.'

Manderson flicked the remote again and a silent Super-8 home-movie played across the screen – a Middle-Eastern rooftop with parasols, sky-signs advertising BOAC, the sea blue in the distance, and a youthful Fanon-Khayat mugging for the camera in a white suit.

'A bright young man. Bit wild as a student – drugs, protest marches and so on – and in 1972 gets a French girl pregnant. Fellow student at the Sorbonne. She has a botched abortion and nearly dies, Antoine legs it back to Beirut. In '75 he inherits his father's import-export empire and becomes involved in the arms business when he allows one of the F-K companies to be used as a front for sanctions-busting operations in South Africa. We wait until we've got enough evidence to put him out of business and then suggest that there are ways in which he can help us.'

A brief colour-film sequence on the screen showed Geneva Airport, an anonymous office block, and a name-plate: Services F-K Commerciaux. This cut to a series of still photographs of Fanon-Khayat in a top-hat and morning-coat in the enclosure at Royal Ascot. Accompanying him was a chic, rather strained-looking blonde woman in an ostrich-feathered hat.

'Marries Solange de Cotigny June '75. Buys her a house in the sixteenth arrondissement of Paris. None of which inhibits him from undertaking a series of extramarital liaisons.'

A series of grab-shots, mostly black and white, of Fanon Khayat with other blonde women in hotel lobbies, outside night-clubs, and on resort beaches.

'Over the years, one way and another, Fanon-Khayat becomes a good friend to the British government, and a highly important source of non-attributable weaponry. We use him in Afghanistan, when he outfits a couple of our training teams with specially adapted SAMs to counter the Sovs' Hind assault helicopters. He equips our people in South America for the Gacha job, he arms the SAS Subversive Action Wing team for operation Waterline in Sri Lanka, and he is extremely helpful to the Firm when we need to place undercover operatives in Azerbaijan to keep an eye on developments regarding the pipeline. He has undertaken never, either directly or indirectly, to supply the IRA, and he has passed on marketplace intelligence to us concerning those who have. A useful asset, all in all.

'For our part, we have always paid him well and promptly, and avoided stepping on his toes overseas. As Terry and Chris in particular will remember, we fell over backwards ensuring that his name was never mentioned in connection with the Matrix-Churchill and Arms-to-Iraq affairs.'

Nods around the table.

'So far so cosy. Unfortunately all is not so lovey-dovey in our man's private life.'

A black and white image of Solange Fanon-Khayat, looking distraught, climbing into a white Mercedes outside the Paris house. Cut to an exterior shot of a Paris courtroom, with Fanon-Khayat hurrying up the steps.

'In 1992, Solange sues for divorce, citing her husband's physical abuse, mental cruelty and persistent adultery – which has apparently included unprotected sex with prostitutes and Brazilian transvestites in the Bois de Boulogne. She is awarded a huge settlement, which as it happens coincides with a falling off in her ex-husband's business activities.

'Shortly after the judgement is announced, Fanon-Khayat sets up a meet with his MI6 handler. He needs cash badly, he says, and in return claims that he can offer hard documentary evidence that President Slobodan Milosevic of Serbia is providing arms and support to Radovan Karadjic in the breakaway republic of Bosnian Serbia. He claims to have an inside track to the Serbian administration.

'Unfortunately for Fanon-Khayat, we already have all the evidence we need to that effect, and we turn the deal down. We cut him loose, basically. We distance ourselves from him. The general feeling is that he is becoming too flaky to do business with. And we're right. The next sighting of him is in – of all places – Serbia.'

A wedding scene. A small local church. Flower-petals in the air. A portrait of the bride – very blonde, very pretty, barely in her twenties.

'Within six months of talking to us, we learn, Antoine has remarried. Her name is Branca Nikolic, she is twenty-three, and she and her family are well-connected Serbs living in Belgrade. What the cash-strapped Fanon-Khayat is doing socialising with Serbs at that point in history I leave to your collective imagination. It is unlikely to be a coincidence, for example, that his new father-in-law Goran Nikolic is a senior officer of the RDB – the Serbian secret service. From this point onwards Fanon-Khayat's former contacts and handlers in London hear nothing from him.'

Removing his glasses, Manderson briefly polished them with a silk handkerchief from his breast pocket before once again thumbing the remote control.

Fanon-Khayat and an overweight man in a cowboy hat on a Sheraton-style hotel terrace. Palm trees and a swimming pool visible.

A low-ceilinged airport lounge, the crowd mostly African. Fanon-Khayat in profile at a car-hire desk.

A grainy, long-distance street shot. Three men in coats and fur hats leaving a marble-faced office-block. Snow on the steps.

Manderson replaced his glasses. 'Six weeks ago word reaches P4, the head of Balkan operations downstairs, that Fanon-Khayat is on the move again, re-activating his old networks. Ten days ago, for the first time in the best part of a decade, he gets back in touch with us.

Specifically, he couriers a compact disc to C/CEE, the controller of eastern European operations, who will be speaking to you later this morning. This is some of the photographic material from that disc.'

A jungle scene. Sunlight filtering through light scrub. A South East Asian youth with a red bandanna tied around his head crouching over a disassembled AK47 Kalashnikov rifle. The spare parts on a cloth on the jungle floor.

A younger man, also wearing a red bandanna, posing with a Dragunov sniper rifle armed with a telescopic sight. Next to him, his faded khaki jacket all but falling apart on his shoulders, a man who might have been his twin, grinning.

Six young men. And a pile of several dozen Claymore-style anti-personnel mines in satchels. In the background, slightly out of focus, a Westerner in a red bandanna carrying a steel ammunition box and a young Asian woman toting a Soviet RPG 7 grenade launcher.

The first young man again, gleefully indicating a wooden box stencilled 'GRENADES – W PHOS'. Two Western soldiers in tiger-stripe camouflage smoking roll-ups and laughing – something very familiar to Slater about both of them.

A dead woman in DPM camouflage trousers, South East Asian of origin, dragged to a sitting position by the hair by a pair of hands. The freckled forearms vanishing out of shot, but a Cross-of-St-George tattoo clearly visible. Severe burns to the dead woman's face and neck. High-velocity round entry wounds to her bared upper chest. A cooking-pot over a fire in the background.

A dozen dead soldiers, their uniforms caked with dried blood, in a pile in a clearing by a stream. Several with their ears cut off. Around the corpses, like hunters around a trophy display, a group of red bandanna-clad soldiers carrying AK47s. One wearing a necklace of ears. Crouching alongside them, a tall, Western soldier. Jungle smock, droopy moustache, scar on left cheek.

Three Western soldiers, all known to Slater, crouching outside the bleached stone ruins of an Asiatic temple. On the ground before them a row of sharpened bamboo stakes. Two of these hammered into the ground and topped with human heads. A red bandanna-wearing youth placing a cigarette between the lips of one of the severed heads.

Manderson turned to Andreas. 'Any doubt in your mind about the identity of any of these instructors?'

Andreas shook his head. 'No.'

'Neil?'

'I don't know all the names, but I recognise all the faces. They're Regiment guys.'

Manderson nodded. 'OK. The background to all of this is that during the eighties a rolling contingent of instructors from 22 SAS's Subversive Action Wing, usually referred to in this building as the Increment, were attached to "a non-communist wing of the Coalition for the Democratic Government of Kampuchea". In plain English, to the Khmer Rouge.

The idea – queasy though it sounds now – was that the struggle against communism could be effectively continued by supporting the Khmer Rouge's war of resistance against the North Vietnamese, who had ousted them in 1979. The US started the ball rolling, but the CIA contingent pulled out after Irangate in 1986. Basically Ronald Reagan left Mrs Thatcher holding their joint baby, if that's not too extreme an image to furnish you with at this time in the morning. The SAS team was based on the Thai-Cambodian border. They fed the Khmer Rouge with weapons – mostly non-attributable AKs and RPGs and white phosphorus grenades – and taught them how to use explosives, improvise and lay mines, and make booby traps.

'It's all old history now, of course, but the agent we employed to provide the bulk of that non-attributable weaponry was Antoine Fanon-Khayat. Unfortunately for us, sensibly for him, he kept detailed minutes of the affair. As well as the photographs you've just seen there are manifests, banking and shipping documentation – all manner of stuff. And the long and the short of it is that unless his conditions are met, all of this material will be made available to the press.

'What those conditions are, you've probably already guessed. Two months ago an SAS snatch team lifted Radovan Karadjic from Eastern Bosnia and conveyed him to custody on the British mainland, where he remains pending transportation to the Hague and trial for war crimes. Fanon-Khayat wants us to get the

Home Office to accede to Serbia's demands for his release on the grounds that the arrest was technically illegal. Now of course we don't accept that it was illegal and we're not about to give up Karadjic, but illustrated details of our close involvement with an overtly genocidal organisation like the Khmer Rouge would be very embarrassing indeed. A decade ago John Pilger made a TV programme accusing the British government of aiding and abetting the perpetrators of genocide in Cambodia – names were named, et cetera – but the government of the day denied its principal charges on the record and the whole thing faded. This will bring it all back with a vengeance. There's nothing like necklaces of human ears and severed heads on stakes to put the citizenry off their morning cornflakes, and the Serbian PR people would make sure that those pictures went round the world. You can imagine how weighty our accusations against Karadjic and his merry men would sound then.

'Unfortunately, the Cambodia pictures are not the limit of our problems concerning Antoine Fanon-Khayat. Our intelligence reports suggest that his recent world tour, which took in a number of weaponry fabrication sites and known middle-men, had a specific purpose. Namely, to set up a conduit to provide Serbian defence installations with a state-of-the-art surface-to-air missile capability. The system's called "Ondine", it's manufactured in France by Issy-Avionic, and the material we think will be going to Serbia is nominally destined for the "friendly-designated" Burkina Faso. We're not a hundred per cent certain that Belgrade's the real end user, but we're ninety-nine-point-nine per cent sure. We're also pretty sure that being the kind of operator that he is, Fanon-Khayat's kept both ends of the chain from meeting in the middle. The sellers won't know who they're selling to, the buyers won't know who they're buying from. Fanon-Khayat remains the vital link – the man that everyone needs.

'Basically, our man's decided to throw in his lot with Serbia. If he succeeds in securing them a high-end SAM capability as well as brokering the release of Karadjic, he can write his own ticket. Serbia would reinvade Kosovo on the back of a huge PR victory, and with the Ondine systems in place there's not a damn thing – short of a lethal, costly and quite possibly unsustainable ground war – that we or anyone else could do about it. The voting public simply wouldn't wear the sight of Nato fighter jets being blown out of the sky on television night after night, and Milosevic would win. In Serbia, Fanon-Khayat would be a national hero, with Branca Nikolic as his adoring mink-draped princess. And let's face it' – Manderson permitted himself a wintry smile as he re-projected the wedding photos – 'there are worse ways for a balding, overweight fifty-year-old to live out his days.

'However . . .' he looked at them all in turn. 'We do not intend any of this to happen. We intend – that is to say this department has been tasked – to assassinate Antoine Fanon-Khayat.'

A silence of some intensity followed this pronouncement. Slater flickered a glance around the room. Andreas appeared openly amused, Eve expressionless, Leon and Terry thoughtful, Chris almost absent-minded.

'At present,' Manderson continued, 'the target is in Paris, where he is expecting to conduct a meeting with one of MI6's Balkan desk officers. The subject is the handover of the Cambodia images against the release of Karadjic. For the sake of believability we've given Fanon-Khayat the impression that we may be prepared to negotiate some Pinochet-style deal – not mentally fit to stand trial, something like that – but that we draw the line at conceding any illegality in his arrest. Our best guess is that he will go for that.

'Now the reason that Fanon-Khayat's in Paris, and that we're seeing him in Paris, is that he's there for a series of meetings relating to the Ondine deal. As I said, he's handling the whole thing himself, so if we can eliminate him before the deal's done, there will be no deal, no Ondine system for Serbia. Our intelligence is that the whole thing is expected to be wrapped up by Monday – Tuesday at the latest – so we have two days in which to get the job done.'

Manderson leant back in his chair and spread his hands. 'So there you have it. Before I ask Eve to go through the operational details, has anyone got any questions? For example does anyone think that eliminating the target is morally or politically unjustified, given the circumstances?'

'Can we be sure that if Fanon-Khayat is taken out the Cambodia pictures won't resurface?' It was Chris who had spoken. She looked, thought Slater, like a *Guardian*-reading, left-leaning teacher from a Hackney comprehensive. He'd have to watch his p's and q's with her.

Manderson nodded and frowned. 'My guess is that he's flying solo on this, as he is on the Ondine deal. He may have married a Serb, but that doesn't mean he trusts them. Those pictures are his pension – he won't have handed copies around to his mates in Belgrade. My estimation, with which P4 concurs, is that he'll play it straight and give us all of the pictures in return for Karadjic. He knows us well enough to know that if we hear so much as a whisper that copies are still floating about after the deal's done, we'll come for him. Except, of course, the whole thing won't get that far.'

'Are we certain that he doesn't know that we know about the SAMs?' This time it was Leon, the black guy.

'If he thought we knew about them, he wouldn't be trying to negotiate with us about the pictures,' said Manderson. 'Experience would tell him that the scales were stacked up too high against him. Blackmailing he'd reckon we could accommodate. But re-arming Serbia at the same time? He'd know that was a bridge too far, that if we knew about the Ondine system we'd have to get rid of him. And if he suspected that's what we wanted to do, then he wouldn't see us. And he *is* seeing us.'

Leon nodded. 'And it wouldn't be possible to spike the Ondine deal by leaking it to the press?'

Manderson shook his head. 'Not without risking the lives of some of our most important agents-in-place, no. There must be no sign that we know about it.'

'Then what will those involved in the Ondine deal think that the motive was for killing Fanon-Khayat?' asked Leon.

'A couple of the least damaging of the Cambodia pictures will be found hidden in Fanon-Khayat's apartment. That'll send the right message to the right people.'

Leon nodded. His mind, Slater could see, was worrying away at every aspect of the case like a terrier. Terry, by contrast, presented a picture of almost Buddhist calm, and sat unmoving and without expression.

Slater found the atmosphere unsettling. He had been more shaken than he cared to admit to himself by the question of whether or not the hit was justified. He'd have preferred a direct order – waste the fucker and then get the hell out. The soldier was carrying enough of a load without having to consider the moral justification of his actions at every turn. But then, of course, he wasn't a soldier any more. He was a civil servant.

'Will this operation save lives?' he found himself blurting out.

That had always been the question he'd asked himself in Northern Ireland. Would his trigger-squeeze save some unsuspecting squaddie from a bullet between the shoulders, some housewife or child from dismemberment by a nail-bomb? The answer – apart from that terrible night near Forkhill – had been yes, every time. And even the killing of poor, simple Joey Delaney had flushed out McGirk, sent the bastard running from the hills of Armagh and back across the Atlantic.

'Yes it will,' said Manderson without hesitation, directing the full force of his gaze at Slater. 'This is not just a matter of political advantage; the target has to be eliminated to avert widescale bloodshed. Without his conduits and underground networks there is no way that a system as sophisticated as Ondine would get anywhere near Serbia. This would mean that as far as air defences are concerned, Milosevic would be stuck with his Russian-made SA7s, which frankly don't worry us too much. The Ondine system is something else, though, and would really frighten us. If Fanon-Khayat pushes this deal through the Serbs will know that they can re-annex Kosovo with impunity, and then, I promise you, there will be a bloodbath. A bloodbath we will be powerless to prevent. Does that answer your question?'

Slater nodded.

'Anyone got anything else before I hand over to Eve?'

Silence. A slow shaking of heads.

So, thought Slater. She's his deputy.

Eve straightened a sheaf of papers in front of her.

211

'Right. First things first. The name of the operation is "Firewall" and it is a sealed operation – no one outside this department is involved in any capacity. Nor can we reveal our hand to the French. At best we could expect non-cooperation, at worst – given the touchy-feely relationship between certain of their secret service people and Milosevic – active sabotage. The French, in short, are to be treated as hostiles. We will be on enemy territory.

'For the purposes of Firewall the team will divide into two groups. The forward team will consist of myself, Neil and Andreas; the back-up team will be Terry, Chris and Leon. Fanon-Khayat's apartment, which he's owned since his divorce from Solange, is in the Rue Molitor in the sixteenth arrondissement. This is a smart area, very *"bon chic, bon genre"* as the Parisians say – imagine Knightsbridge on the edge of Hampstead Heath. Big money, big houses, big privacy.

'So we're going to have to look and behave right. Debbie's done some research on this and is acting as our wardrobe expert – in fact she's buying the stuff as we speak. We're leaving this afternoon and we're booked into two hotels: the forward team are staying a kilometre to the north of Fanon-Khayat's apartment, at the Hotel Montmorency at Ranelagh; the back-up team on the Rue Molitor itself at the Hotel Grand Exelmans.

'The Grand Exelmans overlooks Fanon-Khayat's apartment,' Eve continued. 'And tomorrow morning Terry, Chris and Leon will set up an OP there. From

11.30 Andreas and myself will occupy a table at the Café Molitor, which is opposite the Grand Exelmans and next door to the block containing Fanon-Khayat's apartment. The apartment occupies the whole of the fourth floor. At midday Fanon-Khayat is expecting an MI6 representative to arrive there to discuss the Karadjic business and negotiate the handover of the pictures.'

To Slater, knowing what she was going to say next, the moment seemed to go into slow motion. The faces of his new colleagues, polite and solicitous, blurred. They were throwing him in at the deep end.

'That MI6 representative,' Eve continued, 'will in reality be Neil. Neil will enter the apartment, disable the two bodyguards, and take out Fanon-Khayat.'

NINE

Slater woke shortly before 7am, showered, dressed and left the Hotel Montmorency. The deserted streets shone with the night's rain, and the morning smell of the city – wet grass, fresh bread, petrol – rose from the pavement to meet him.

He walked for ten minutes through the streets before he found a café that was open, and installed himself at an outside table. Beside him, a woman was setting up a stall selling chrysanthemums, tulips and roses, and the scent of flowers drifted towards him on the damp air. Slater's French had never been up to much but he could manage *'café crème'*, and when the steaming tray was laid before him it occurred to him that he could not remember a more perfect beginning to a day.

A pity, really, that he had to spoil it.

The day before had been knackering. After the briefing, in the course of which he and the team had covered every possible eventuality and factored in every possible fuck-up, they had been dispatched to the Nine Elms safe house for outfitting. Slater had walked home with a battered Louis Vuitton suitcase containing several changes of clothes, all of them strictly conforming to the dictates of Paris weekend fashion. There was no question of his pretending to be French – merely of blending in, of looking unmemorably prosperous. In truth, he thought, as he raised his heavy coffee-cup and looked at his reflection in the café window, he had rarely felt more comfortable.

He and Andreas had travelled together on the Eurostar. Sitting in the first-class compartment with Andreas's laptop computer on the table between them, they had looked like a couple of well-off businessmen travelling to a weekend seminar. The train was crowded, and they had discussed neither the hit nor the department's business as a whole. Instead they reminisced about old times and Slater asked Andreas if he had a girlfriend.

Andreas looked uncomfortable, and then self-consciously admitted that he had been 'seeing' – as he put it – Debbie.

Slater absorbed this information. 'Do you know her name?'

'Debbie's her real name. I don't know the other. And I've never asked.'

'No envelopes around? No name on her flat?'

'Nope.'

'What about Eve? What do you know about her?'

'Nothing. Why, are you harbouring ambitions in that direction, by any chance?'

Slater pictured the wry smile, the sea-grey eyes and

the feminine curves that no amount of nondescript dressing could quite disguise. 'I'm not stupid,' he said.

'And what exactly does that mean?'

'It means that we've got to work together. Plus she's not my type. Plus she certainly doesn't fancy me. She's probably got some guy who works in the city and thinks she's got a job in PR. They probably go on holiday together in . . . where's that place all the Sloanes go?'

'Tuscany,' said Andreas morosely.

'That's right. Fucking Tuscany. And they probably go to that restaurant, what's it called?'

'River Café.'

'Right. River Fucking Café. And they probably go to the opera together, and shooting in Scotland with people called Piers and Annabel.'

'Well, look at us,' said Andreas. 'We're not doing so badly. We're going shooting in Paris with people called Terry and Chris.'

Slater ordered a second cup of the café's high-voltage coffee. The morning sunshine was lifting the moisture from the streets and pavements, patching them with paler grey. A faint haze still hung over the Bois de Boulogne.

He had been chosen as the trigger-man, Andreas had told him, because of his known expertise in CQB – close-quarter battle. Fanon-Khayat would almost certainly have his bodyguards around, and one way and another they would have to be dealt with.

Slater doubted the truth of this flattering analysis. They were sending him in because it was bloody dangerous, and as the newest member of the team he was the most expendable. He hoped he'd get the weapon he had asked for – a silenced Sig Sauer P239G.

Leon had been given the job of arming the team. In his twenties, according to Andreas, the Mauritian had spent five years as a Foreign Legion paratrooper and a further three in a French jail for acting as a driver in an armed robbery. Since that time he had made a point of retaining his contacts in the Paris underworld. All being well, he would be providing the team with a principal and a back-up weapon when they RVed at the Hotel Grand Exelmans at 9.30.

Under other circumstances the Cadre would have smuggled their own weapons into France with them. Eve had told them that she had considered driving them in. Given that Firewall was a sealed operation, however, and an operation to which elements of the French security forces might well be hostile, the very slight risk of detection had been thought too great. The advantage of a local weapon was that it might well confuse things, especially if it had been used before for criminal purposes. On the grounds that they were much cheaper than 'clean' firearms, Leon would be actively soliciting such weapons.

Regretfully savouring the last of his morning's solitude, Slater climbed to his feet and placed sixty francs in the saucer holding the bill. The pavements were no longer empty – the sixteenth arrondissement's dog-walkers seemed to have mobilised *en masse*, and large Citroëns and Peugeots were hissing past on the Boulevard Montmorency.

Slater found the other two in the dining room. Eve had hired a Peugeot 406 the day before in case a quick getaway was needed, and she and Andreas had just returned from a practice drive around the Bois de Boulogne.

'Are you hungry?' she asked Slater hesitantly.

'Starving,' he answered truthfully. He always ate well before an operation. The nerves would kick in soon, but for the time being he was content to fill his stomach.

After breakfast, they packed their bags, took the lift down to the underground car-park, and locked them in the boot of the car. They were booked into the Montmorency for the coming night, but were taking no chances – if something went wrong they might be unable to return.

In order to get the feel of the Peugeot, Slater took the car out of the park, tooled around the local streets for ten minutes, and then ran the other two south to the Rue Molitor. The car was a dream and the journey short – Slater had memorised the route from a Paris-Eclair guide-book the night before.

They parked in front of the hotel. Chris was in the lobby. Shaking hands with each of them as if this were a meeting of old friends, she led them to the lift. On the third floor she gave a light double knock at a door half-way along the corridor. 'Terry's room gives the best sight-line on the apartment,' she explained. 'But we've had all three made up already. We aren't going to be interrupted by any chambermaids.'

Leon and Terry were in their shirtsleeves, and welcomed the rest of the team with quick smiles. The room was a good size, with tall net-curtained windows, but felt crowded with all six of them in there.

'Did you get a car?' Eve asked Terry almost immediately.

He nodded. 'Silver Mercedes Cabriolet. I've got it at the side of the hotel.'

'Good. We're the Peugeot you can see down there.'

'Right. Are you ready to go through the rest of the kit?'

On the queen-size bed lay a combination-lock briefcase and six covert-fit Motorola transmitters and receivers.

'We've tested it,' said Terry. 'It all seems to be in working order. And we've got the briefcase Neil asked for. The combination is 1471 and it's a button-push electronic system – none of that old wheel-spinning. Do you want to give it a go?'

He handed the aluminium briefcase to Slater, who tapped in the code. The case sprung open – empty except for its foam lining.

Leon reached beneath the bed and pulled out a battered duffel-bag. From this he withdrew several heavy-looking bubble-wrapped objects which he placed on the bed. 'One Sig Sauer P239G plus silencer,

219

one Glock 17, two boxes nine-millimetre ammunition,' he announced. 'Both weapons almost certainly known to the police.'

Slater unwrapped the handguns and checked their actions. Both appeared to be in good working order. He attached the silencer to the Sig Sauer, then loaded the magazine and snapped it home.

'That's great,' he told Leon. 'Thanks.'

'No problem, man.'

The feel and smell of the weapons started Slater's heart pounding and he stood there motionless for a moment. He was aware, at the edges of his vision, of Eve and Chris watching him. The nerves would stay with him now – right up to the moment when he pressed the bell of Fanon-Khayat's apartment.

'Have you got a bathroom I can use?' he asked quietly.

Leon smiled and handed him a room-key.

When he returned, Chris called him to the window. 'The big gateway opposite,' she said, 'leads into a courtyard. You click open the gate by pressing that button on its right. There's no combination because it's right on the street and people are going in and out of the courtyard all day.'

Slater nodded. Even dressed by Yves St Laurent, he thought, she looked dowdy to the point of invisibility.

'Fanon-Khayat's instructions, as you know, are that the Firm's representative should enter the courtyard at midday and take the left-hand entrance. There you'll find a lift marked Ascenseur B – which you take to the fourth floor. Make sure you end up on the right floor because they number them differently from us. Our ground floor is their first floor, and so on.'

Slater nodded again. 'Into the courtyard, left-hand entrance, Ascenseur B, number four floor rather than English-style fourth floor. Do we know if the courtyard's monitored by CCTV?'

'No, but we have to assume that it is. If it was raining you could hold an umbrella in front of you, but looking at the sky I wouldn't say there's much chance of rain. A basic disguise like a wig and a fake moustache would do it as far as the CCTV is concerned, but then you'd look like a freak in the street and you'd certainly be remembered by anyone else in the courtyard or the lift. My thoughts are that you should wear a hat and dark glasses – it's just about bright enough – and that when you're crossing the courtyard you should appear to be lighting a cigarette. If you keep your head down and your hands in front of your face you should prove unrecognisable on the CCTV tape.' She pointed to the dressing table. 'Would you like to just try these?'

There were two hats – a trilby and a conservative number in dark brown straw – and three pairs of sunglasses. The straw hat and a pair of gold-framed, brown-lensed glasses made the most difference, and in conjunction with the clothes lent him a subtly Mediterranean appearence. Later, he would learn from Leon that Chris had been sent on a theatrical make-up and prosthetics course. Disguise was one of her specialities.

'That's good,' agreed Eve. 'It knocks out his most distinctive feature, which is those pale blue Anglo-Saxon eyes. I'd like to darken the skin tone a few shades too.'

'Hey!' said Leon. 'Why not just send me?'

They all laughed, and Chris handed Slater a tube of cosmetic cream. 'Face, neck, ears, chest, hands and forearms please. There should be enough in there.'

In the bathroom Slater stripped to the waist and rubbed in the cream as directed. 'Careful round the hair-line,' Chris called out.

The cream was greasy, and had a cloying, perfumed smell. Looking in the mirror as he rubbed it into his forehead, Slater saw that Eve was watching him through the open door. When he caught her eye she did not look away but continued to watch him with something that might have been amusement, might have been concern, might have been pure professional interest.

When he had finished, his appearance seemed unchanged. His blue Lanvin shirt felt tacky on his body.

'It takes an hour or so to take effect,' said Chris. 'But it should just make that difference. Your hair's perfect – half-way between dark blond and brown. Ask ten people what colour it is and they'll all come up with different answers.'

She pulled her cardigan-sleeves an inch or two up her arms and examined Slater critically.

'Two more accessories. Gloves, close-fitting,

leather, for inside the apartment. And I've got you a new belt. Something I had at home.'

He placed the gloves with the weapons and the aluminium briefcase, and stared doubtfully down at the belt. It was heavy, of plain brown leather and with a discreet silver buckle. Half-way along its length, on the inside, a narrow pocket had been let into the leather and from this Chris drew a flat, dagger-shaped sliver of transparent plastic compound. The knife was weightless and no more than five inches long, but its blade and point were sharp.

'Something you had at home?' said Slater, running his finger up a razor-toothed serrated edge.

'It'll do the business,' said Chris. 'Punch through steel if necessary. And it won't show up on any scanner.'

'Thanks,' said Slater appreciatively, slipping his St Laurent crocodile belt out of its loops and replacing it with Chris's. 'It's a nice piece of kit.'

'A present,' said Chris with an oblique smile. 'Welcome to the parallel universe.'

By 11am the tension was mounting. Slater's skin had browned to a pale cocoa colour, and the steady drip-feed of adrenaline was producing a familiar churning in his stomach.

'On the wire, mate?' Andreas had asked him sympathetically, and he had nodded. There were only so many times that plans and back-up plans could be mentally rehearsed. A decade earlier they had taken their places together in the belly of the helicopter which was to chopper them behind Iraqi lines, and the question in their minds had been the same: how does the story end? With cheers, laughter and backslapping in a bar? With discovery, terror and humiliation? With a bullet through the head? Each and every option was on the menu.

In the Regiment they'd crank themselves up with blokeish chat and a series of private rituals. Slater's included endless weapon-checking, and it irked him that he had not been able to test-fire the Sig Sauer. Although you never talked about fear the one thing you could be sure of was that everyone was feeling pretty much the same as you were. Here, though, in this overheated hotel bedroom, it was different. He had no idea what was going through Chris's mind, or Terry's, or Eve's.

Leon he found easier to read, as of course he did Andreas. Leon had started life like himself – as a good old green-eyed boy, hungry for trouble. Only a nutter would join the Legion, and only a maniacally switched-on nutter would make it into their para regiment, as Leon had. He'd been based in Corsica, he told Slater, and had done tours of duty in Africa, French Guyana and the Middle East.

When Slater had asked him how he came to be attached to the Department, however, he had clammed up. 'Later, man,' he'd said, and taken his place behind the binoculars focused on Fanon-Khayat's flat.

Although there was no confirmation that Fanon-Khayat was actually in the flat, the lights had been switched on at 6pm the evening before, then switched off shortly after 11pm, and no one approximating to Fanon-Khayat's description had left. An e-mail had also arrived from P4 at Vauxhall Cross confirming the rendezvous.

Fanon-Khayat would be expecting Neil Clissold at noon, local time.

At 11.20 Eve and Andreas fitted themselves up with their Motorola comms kits. These involved miniature throat mikes and earpieces with micro-antennae. A wire ran down one arm to a transmit-receive switch.

Slater watched them dubiously. Like many soldiers, he distrusted high-tech comms systems. They were great when they worked but they too often quite simply didn't. They weren't soldier-proof. You couldn't sit on them or drop them in a river.

Having checked each other, they departed for the Bar Michelange. Eve gave him a nod as she went, Andreas a quick thumbs-up. The other three continued their surveillance of the flat.

'I think the reason we're not seeing anyone is that the room facing us is unused,' Terry was saying, 'or a spare room, perhaps. That would be logical, given that it's the one overlooking the road.'

'Perhaps he's afraid of being sniped,' suggested Chris. 'We could get a fairly easy shot from here, wouldn't you say, Neil?'

'I guess you could,' said Slater. 'Although it would be pretty obvious where the shot had come from. And hotel staff often have good memories for faces.'

'Yes, but you wouldn't look at it like that if you were in his position . . . Hang on, isn't that someone now?'

Terry smoothly retracted the binoculars and their stand. 'Look, there's one of the bodyguards eyeballing us.'

Slater saw what Chris meant. A heavy-set type in a suit had parted the curtains opposite and was peering at the hotel.

'Yes,' Terry murmured into his mike. 'We see him. Over.'

He listened for a moment. 'Understood, you are in position, over.' He looked over his shoulder and raised one eyebrow.

Slater nodded, the anticipation was taut as a bowstring now.

'Yes, good to go. Repeat, Neil is good to go. Over.'

Slater flexed his fingers, put on the dark glasses and the hat, picked up the briefcase, checked himself in the bathroom mirror, allowed Chris to give him the once-over, and nodded to the others.

'Neil is go,' came Terry's calm report. 'Repeat. Neil is go.'

Slater took the stairs rather than the lift, and left the hotel by a side door. Turning away from the Rue Molitor, swinging the briefcase as if it contained nothing more than a mobile phone, a packet of

Gauloises and a copy of *Paris-Match*, he made his way up the Rue Chardon-Lagache. The impression he wanted to give was that of a man who had appointments to keep, but was in no great hurry to do so. It was Saturday, after all, and the sun was shining. He didn't want to radiate midweek city-centre strain.

Ten minutes later, and feeling a little less knotted-up for his walk, Slater found himself once more on the Rue Molitor. He wasn't being followed, of that he was certain. Nor, as far as he could see, did Fanon-Khayat have any kind of outlying security presence. If the French had a watcher team on him, then they were inside a building, and well concealed. The streets were residential, and all but empty. There were no roadworkers, no loitering telephone repair teams, no fat guys eating ham and cheese sandwiches in cars.

Outside the Café Michelange, their faces turned to the sunshine, Eve and Andreas stirred *demi-tasses* of hot chocolate. Eve was still wearing her watch, Slater saw – the signal that all was clear.

Slater's hands found the packet of Gauloises and the Dupont lighter in his jacket pocket. Taking advantage of a hiatus in the traffic to cross the road, he placed a cigarette in his mouth, and pressed the button beside the entry-gates to the courtyard with his lighter. The judas-gate clicked off the latch, and Slater ducked and entered. Keeping his head low, flicking the lighter in front of his mouth as he walked and with his other hand shielding the flame, he crossed the smooth cobbles to a shadowed doorway. Up three steps, past the CCTV camera, and past a row of locked postboxes. Pinching out the cigarette, he slipped it into his jacket pocket and pulled on the gloves Chris had brought for him. The sign in front of him read 'Ascenseur B'.

Cool it, Slater told himself. Breathe. You're meeting a professional colleague for lunch. You have much to discuss. You're looking forward to it. There will be BGs there but you will ignore them. You will submit politely – with an ironic smile, perhaps – to their search. You have nothing to hide.

You are expected, a Balkan desk-officer.

Your name is Neil Clissold.

The lift slow and grumbling, each floor sliding past. A lurch as it came to a halt. Six feet of polished parquet. A single large door. The bell sounding far inside, and with it Slater's nerves lifting away, and a frozen calm descending.

Beyond the door-chain, a bodyguard with a face like a dumpling. Fatty jowls, suspicious eyes, and a gone-to-seed body in a shiny Adidas tracksuit. Beneath the zipped top, the cross-strap of a shoulder holster. From the interior of the flat, melancholy piano music.

'Clissold,' said Slater, removing his hat and placing the dark glasses in the top pocket of his jacket. *Je m'appelle Neil Clissold.*'

The bodyguard nodded – maybe understanding him, maybe not – and unlatched the chain. Behind him, another suet-featured Balkan, this one toting a hand-gun, a heavy Tokarev 7.62 automatic. The weapon had a strip of Scotch tape across the end of the barrel – an old Soviet affectation intended to keep the weapon clean in wet weather. Blinking, and with all the confusion that he could manage, Slater placed the briefcase between his legs. Looking from man to man with a nervous smile, he half-raised his hands.

The first bodyguard indicated that he should turn and face the wall, and stand with hands braced against it. When Slater did so the bodyguard patted down his arms, chest and legs. Just as well, thought Slater, he wasn't wearing one of the comms sets. Finally the bodyguard was satisfied, and stepped back. 'Ouvre!' he ordered, pointing at the briefcase. 'Open!'

'Moi?' asked Slater idiotically, prompting a contemptuous exchange in Serbo-Croat between the guards.

'You!' said the guard with the Tokarev.

Slater pointed to a marble-topped sideboard, and the other man placed the briefcase on it. Sauntering up to it, Slater punched in the 1471 code. The briefcase sprang open. From the street below came the distant grumble of traffic.

The Sig Sauer was out of the briefcase and aimed at the first bodyguard's face before the Serb fully comprehended what he had seen.

'Drop it,' ordered Slater. 'Both of you. Guns on the floor.'

The bodyguard facing him slowly reached for his shoulder holster, a wary but professional acceptance of the situation showing in his eyes. Deliberately, Slater thumbed down the Sig Sauer's safety-catch. In the interior of the apartment, the music played sadly on.

'Any bollocks,' he said, 'and I'll fucking shoot you. *Comprenez*?'

The bodyguard nodded, began very slowly to lift a handgun from his shoulder holster – but with his thumb and index finger only, in order to emphasise his non-hostile intentions.

The other guard was still uncertainly holding the Tokarev – wondering, Slater was sure, if he could get a shot in without hitting his colleague. Taking a fast sidestep, Slater lowered the Sig Sauer and squeezed off a single silenced round. With the impact the Tokarev and the Serb's right thumb seemed to leap across the hallway to the carpet.

Hurriedly, the first bodyguard lowered his weapon to the floor. A Stechkin, Slater saw – another clunky Soviet relic. The second bodyguard was staring vacantly at his severed thumb. Blood from the trailing hand was pooling blackly among the carpet fibres beside his Nike cross-training shoe.

That knocked the fight out of the fucker, no error.

From the briefcase he took two pairs of plasticuffs, and handed them to the first – and now entirely compliant – bodyguard. With the Sig Sauer he gestured towards the bleeding man. 'Cuff him,' he said, pointing to his wrists and ankles. *'Quickly!'*

Carefully, as if providing him with medical care, the Serb helped his shocked colleague to the floor and handcuffed his hands and feet.

'Now yourself,' said Slater quietly, handing the Serb two more pairs of plasticuffs and waving the Sig Sauer in his face. 'Move it! *Vite!*' He was becoming increasingly anxious that Fanon-Khayat would appear before the guards were fully immobilised.

When both men were recumbent, he tightened the plasticuffs to their limit, took a roll of zinc-oxide tape from the briefcase, and wrapped it several times around their mouths. A blue cotton hood – originally a Church's shoe-bag – was then fastened over each man's head. Slater considered giving them a blast of Mace in the nose and eyes for good measure, but decided against it. They were adequately immobilised as things stood.

Two doors led off the hall. Carefully, Slater opened the left-hand one, which he calculated led to the room visible from the hotel opposite. The room was empty, and although fully decorated and well lit, appeared to be in use as a store-room. It held perhaps forty pieces of old furniture, all with labels attached. Moving a set of six upholstered chairs to one side, Slater returned to the hall, took the bodyguards by the collar and dragged them over the polished floor into the store-room. There, panting with the effort, he stowed them under a mahogany dining table. Noticing on the way out of the room that there was a key in the lock, he turned it and pocketed it.

Quickly, he straightened the hall.

Exhaling, Slater deliberately loosened his neck and shoulders. Keep switched on, he ordered himself as he

231

quickly attached the Motorola to his belt and fitted the throat-mike and earpiece. Keep it tight.

'Neil send. Do you read me? Over.'

Nothing.

'All stations, this is Neil. Do you read me? Over.'

Nothing again. Just hiss and blank air. The walls of the flat were too thick.

Taking the key from his pocket he let himself back into the store-room. This time the response was clear.

'Eve to Neil – all clear, repeat, all clear. What is your situation? Over.'

'Two hostiles immobilised. Now targeting Fanon-Khayat. Over and out.'

Move, he told himself. Get in, get the pictures, whack Fanon-Khayat, and get out. You're wasting time.

Gun in one hand, briefcase in the other, he pushed open the door from the hall to the interior of the apartment. The volume of the music rose. Was Fanon-Khayat a piano-player? For some obscure reason Slater hoped not.

To his left an unlit corridor lined with framed paintings led into darkness; to his right, illuminated by tall windows, the same corridor curved round the side of the building. In front of him was a half-open door.

Slater moved left-handed, along the unlit corridor. A worn but elegant Persian runner covered most of the floor, effectively muffling his footsteps. In his ear the miniature receiver had gone dead again.

Carefully, Slater tried the end door. It opened into

another store-room. Racks held several dozen dusty bottles of wine, and shelves held bound editions of periodicals, maps and books about antiques. A single unshaded bulb hung from the ceiling, and directly beneath it, on the uncarpeted parquet flooring, a foldaway canvas bed had been erected. An orange sleeping-bag lay half-unzipped on this, as did two overnight bags with crumpled clothing spilling out of them, a couple of German or possibly Dutch pornographic magazines, a gold-plated identity bracelet, a half-empty bottle of slivovitz, and an opened carton of Balkan cigarettes. Over all of this hung the odour of stale masculinity – of dirty socks, sealed windows, unwashed armpits and sperm.

Serbian bodyguard quarters, thought Slater, quickly slipping out again. Unappetising even by the generally low standards of Balkan paramilitary hygiene.

The next room held paintings – scores of them, stacked against the wall – and a few small furniture pieces. Chandeliers and stacks of china plates lay in open-topped cardboard boxes. They must be on their way to the auction-rooms, thought Slater. Fanon-Khayat must be realising his assets. Again, the floor was bare, but this time the room was untenanted, and the smell was the lavendered smell of old possessions – of furniture-polish, varnish and dust.

A spare bedroom next. Doubling, guessed Slater, as a dressing room for Branca Nikolic, Fanon-Khayat's twenty-something Serbian bride. A wardrobe stood half-open on a garish Mexican carpet and Slater caught a glimpse of cellophaned dry-cleaning and expensive-looking shoe-boxes. Tacked to the watered-silk wall were posters of Madonna, Geri Halliwell and a couple whom Slater recognised as the assassinated warlord Arkan Raznatovic and his pop-star wife Svetlana 'Ceca' Velickovic. Arkan and Ceca's magic-markered signatures had been scrawled across their portrait.

Exiting, Slater crept past the half-open door of the drawing-room, from which – to Slater's relief – the music still poured. That, certainly, was where Fanon-Khayat would be waiting. And waiting impatiently, if Slater didn't get a move on. He would know Slater was here, and he would expect the bodyguards' search to take a few minutes. The desire to appear in control of the situation would lead him to wait until the bodyguards showed him in, calculated Slater, but there were limits. Much longer and he'd come out and see what the hold-up was.

The first room in the right-hand corridor was the Fanon-Khayats' bedroom, decorated in orientalist style with hanging lamps and drapes. Hurrying in, quickly sweeping the place with the Sig Sauer, Slater checked the dressing area and the gold-accessorised en-suite bathroom. Empty.

A further spare bedroom. Empty.

A second bodyguard hutch. The magazines about martial arts and attack-dogs this time, as well as the inevitable wank-mags. A shell-suit on a wire hanger. The smell the same.

Slater and Fanon-Khayat, it seemed, were alone.

Placing the Sig Sauer out of sight behind the briefcase, Slater hurried back up the corridor and stepped into the drawing-room. It was vast, panelled and flooded with dusty light. Huge abstract canvases shared the walls with crumbling tapestries. Invisible fingers raced up and down the keyboard of an invisible Steinway grand piano. The source of the music was a quartet of loudspeakers shaped like nautilus shells.

Antoine Fanon-Khayat looked older than his half-century of years, and a Lacoste tennis shirt and Versace jeans did nothing to mitigate this impression. He was also balder than he had appeared in Manderson's presentation – his remaining locks combed with unconvincing bravado across a billiard-ball scalp.

Smiling, the arms-dealer had risen from an armchair and half-crossed the room by the time that he realised something was very wrong, that the man with the briefcase had not been shown in by the bodyguards – indeed, that there was no sign of the bodyguards.

'Mr Clissold . . .' he began uncertainly, his hand still outstretched.

Slater revealed the Sig Sauer. Seeing it, Fanon-Khayat seemed to crumple, to shrink inside his expensive leisurewear. His hand fell tiredly to his side.

'You know exactly what I want,' said Slater levelly. 'I want those pictures. This gun is silenced, I've already used it on those idle shitbags in the lobby, I'm happy to use it again. So get the pictures – the disc – now.'

'I thought we were . . . going to discuss a deal.' Fanon–Khayat looked sulky and disappointed, but not yet truly afraid.

'I'll give you a deal,' said Slater, casually bringing up the Sig Sauer, aiming, and reducing a portrait-bust on a plinth to a shower of shattered clay. 'Those pictures against your life.' He turned the Sig Sauer back towards his quarry.

Fanon–Khayat looked at the pottery shards dispassionately. His eyes flickered. 'You've come from Ridley?'

Mentally, Slater reeled. He knew Ridley's name? In that case he probably knew what Ridley's department did. And what Slater had come to do. What else did he know?

'I've come from London.'

'For the pictures.'

'Where are they?'

Fanon–Khayat tentatively ran his fingers through his thinning hair. 'Suppose they're not here?'

This was bad, thought Slater. This had to be turned around, and fast. He lowered the gun and took a step back.

'Look, Mr Fanon-Khayat, make it easy for yourself. You know who I am, you know where I come from, you know we don't fuck about. Just give us the disk and I'll be off.'

'And if I refuse?'

He knows, thought Slater. He knows what I'm here

to do. Knows he has nothing to lose by refusing to co-operate.

'Have you heard of the *Ustashe*, Mr . . . Clissold?'

Slater stared at him, not listening, wondering how to proceed. Shooting him in the hand or leg would probably put Fanon-Khayat into shock and accomplish nothing. Threatening to hit him might bring some focus to the situation – most people were frightened of being hit. He took a step forward, and Fanon-Khayat visibly cowered.

'The *Ustashe* were a Croatian army, Mr Clissold, who joined forces with the occupying Nazis during the last war, and turned on their neighbours, the Serbs. An army whose crimes equalled for sheer horror anything the Nazis themselves committed. They executed Serbs with knives, with saws, with—'

'History later,' said Slater, ignoring him. 'The disc now.'

'History cannot wait much longer, Mr Clissold. And there are many copies of the disc. Destroying this one would accomplish nothing.'

Slater was not going to be drawn into an argument. Besides, he was certain that Fanon-Khayat was bluffing – Manderson's calculation was that he would not have made copies for fear of devaluing his original.

'The disc now,' he repeated, raising his voice.

At that moment the door re-opened. His heart sinking, Slater recognised Branca Nikolic. From the duty-free bags in her hands he guessed that she had just come in from Charles de Gaulle airport. She was wearing an ankle-length pink chiffon coat and white trainers and her pretty, spoilt face looked tired.

Sprinting across the room, Slater grabbed her before her husband had a chance to speak. Gagging her with one hand and wrenching her head backwards, he held the Sig Sauer to her throat. She whimpered, began to shake in his arms.

'Please . . .' said Fanon-Khayat. 'She—'

'The disc now!' Slater shouted, jabbing the silencer up beneath her jaw. 'Or I'll shoot her in front of you. I'll blow her fucking throat out.'

Visibly distressed, Fanon-Khayat raised his hands, crossed the room to the massive fireplace and reached for a carved roundel on one of the side columns. The wooden disc, some nine inches in diameter, turned smoothly beneath his hands. Once removed, it revealed a small barrel-safe with a combination lock. A moment later the circular steel door swung open. From the interior of the safe Fanon-Khayat removed a CD in a flat plastic case. His hands were shaking badly now.

'Please, Mr Clissold,' he begged quietly. 'Please. Let her go. She doesn't know anything about—'

'Stay where you are,' said Slater. 'Tell the girl to bring the disc over here to me.'

Fanon-Khayat spoke to his wife in halting Serbian, and she nodded.

Slater released her, wiping her saliva from his hand on to his trousers. As she stepped backwards away from him her eyes widened. At the fireplace Fanon-Khayat froze. Slater had time to half-turn, to catch a blurred glimpse of a descending arm, and then – simultaneously – a sick crunch, a whipcrack of white light, and the enfolding bloom of darkness.

TEN

Slater woke in darkness. His hands were cuffed behind his back, there was blood in his mouth, and the pain in his head was so great that he retched. It was as if a spiked cannonball was rolling in his skull, crushing nerves and bone as it went. His eyes, too, were in agony – seared by the glare of that phosphorescent impact.

He gagged up an acid, throat-rasping gob of bile. It smeared sourly around his face, mingled with the metallic blood-smell. He was lying face-down, he realised. Was he in bed?

Reality came stamping home. He was in the boot of a car, the car was on the move, and his vomit-smeared head was rolling around inside a plastic carrier-bag.

There had been a third man.

He must have come with Branca. Stayed downstairs, perhaps, to pay a taxi-driver. Followed with baggage. And unlike Branca, he must have noticed that the bodyguards were not where they should have been, armed himself, summed up the situation at a glance.

Well, thought Slater wretchedly, this was certainly an impressive debut. Given a chance to distinguish himself he'd fucked up royally. It wasn't good enough

240

to blame the comms – in truth, he had barely been in control of the situation before Branca's arrival. He had had the gun, but Fanon-Khayat had had the psychological advantage. Guessing that Slater had been ordered not to leave the apartment without the disc, he had decided to call his bluff. And had Branca not shown up . . .

The floor bucked as the car went over the edge of a pavement, and Slater retched again. His eyes were burning as if rubbed raw with sandpaper and he realised that as well as coshing him they'd taken the Mace from his briefcase and given him a liberal blast of that too. Just after cutting themselves out of the plasticuffs, Slater guessed. The ones that were cutting into his wrists and ankles so painfully had come straight off Suet-Face and Potato-Head.

I should have shot Fanon-Khayat straight away, thought Slater miserably. I should have put one through his ear or taken off a finger or something to get him going, like I did with that Serb. And if he hadn't produced the disc after that, well, I should have just wasted him and got the fuck out.

The trouble was, he hadn't looked like the sort of guy you shot. In the past, all those against whom Slater had waged war had been young men – tough and motivated volunteers who knew the score and who could reasonably be expected to survive a bit of rough treatment. Torturing middle-aged art-collectors was very much a new departure for Slater, whatever their political sympathies, and he'd held back.

241

Even though they weren't expecting her to be arriving in Paris, both support teams would have identified Branca Nikolic on sight. They would have tried desperately to get through. If he could contact them, they would have reasoned, then they could contact him. And when they couldn't, they must have thought that he'd switched off – that he'd deliberately broken contact.

And now what? A deserted patch of woodland somewhere outside the city and a bullet through the head, probably. They would use his silenced Sig Sauer – a much sweeter and lighter piece of kit than that Cold War junk they all carried about. They were probably arguing right now about who got to keep it. And who got the Motorola.

Would Fanon-Khayat and the Serbs question him before killing him? Slater wondered. Unlikely – there were no useful answers he could give them. They knew where he came from, they knew what he wanted, they knew what he'd been trying to do. If they were not going to look like a bunch of complete pussies, they had to kill him. That would bring MI6 to the negotiating table fast enough.

They were in traffic now, Slater realised. And every jerked start and bad-tempered foot-brake stop was red-hot agony. Someone – probably the now single-thumbed Suet-Face – had given him the mother and father of kickings in the bollocks. Fuck, he was in a bad way.

Was there any hope of pulling out of this? Precious

little. Would the team have got on to him? Were they behind him now, tailing this very car? Unlikely. These people weren't stupid. They'd have known he had back-up and have taken evasive action.

So, what to do? Struggle, or go gently? Thrash pathetically around in his handcuffs and get another kicking for his pains? Or bow his head to the bullet, soldier to soldier?

Slater considered the quick 9mm round through the cerebellum. At that moment there seemed no point in continuing to fight. The vehicle swung through a pothole, sending red-hot needles coursing through his bruised neck and testicles.

Who would miss him or notice that he was gone? He couldn't come up with a single name. He struggled to remember his mother, but could barely recall the creased photographic image that he had carried around for so many years. She had been hit by a police-car in Hong Kong and had died the next day in the colony's military hospital. Slater had been five at the time – rising six – and hoping for a bicycle for his birthday.

His distraught father had remained in the army until his alcoholism became as apparent to his seniors as it was to his fellow-NCOs, and thereafter found employment as a nightwatchman in Aldershot. Bill Slater had died of pneumonia at sixty, while Slater was serving in Belize, but in truth Neil had started to lose his father on that never-to-be-forgotten day in Hong Kong. His sixth birthday had come and gone uncelebrated – the bicycle was not mentioned again –

and a year later Slater had been dispatched to a boarding school outside Trowbridge in Somerset. His classroom work had been undistinguished – mild dyslexia had seen to that – but on the rugby field he'd proved one of the best fly-halves the school had ever known. He'd enjoyed the place, all in all, with its friendships and conspiracies, and unlike the other pupils had never looked forward to the holidays, which had been spent with his mother's unmarried sister Amy near Bedford.

Amy was unlikely to have been impressed by the way he had turned out. She had taken him into her house out of a sense of family duty rather than any fondness for children, and her relief when term-time came round again had been obvious. Amy had notably lacked her younger sister's sense of fun and adventure, but she had taught him one invaluable skill: how to iron and fold a shirt to a professional laundry standard. This facility would earn Slater valuable beer-money in the five years that he spent with the Royal Engineers. The Engineers had been his father's regiment, and joining up – Slater had never seriously considered any other career – had been like coming home. He was flagged almost immediately as an exceptional soldier. Selection for the SAS had followed shortly after he was made up to corporal.

Schools and regiments were ultimately the same though, thought Slater. People came and people went. You were there for a time and then you moved on, and in personal terms you ceased to exist. Other boys, looking much like you, sat at the desk where you had sat. Other soldiers, looking much like you, trained where you had trained. No one was different enough to make a mark. Your name was typed on a list, pinned to a board, placed in a file, and forgotten.

It occurred to Slater as the vehicle plunged into yet another furrow – another red-hot knife in the neck and the balls – that he was about to die for his country, and for the first time since recovering consciousness the ghost of a smile touched his lips. Hooking the thumbs of his plasticuffed hands into the back of his belt, he attempted to brace himself against the jolting of the car, which was getting worse. They had been driving for over an hour, he guessed, and had moved from main roads to local lanes. They were probably in the countryside now – the going certainly felt uneven enough.

His thumbs found the knife Chris had given him. They had searched him, but they hadn't found it. He'd forgotten about it himself.

No, he begged the trained part of himself – the part that had been, and always would be, an SAS soldier. Please no. Don't order me to go on fighting.

You're not dead, a quiet voice whispered, until you're dead. This is what it's about. This is what separates the wolves from the sheep. This is the moment that your entire life has led up to. Fight.

Please. Let me close my eyes. Let me die.

Open your eyes. Whatever the odds, whatever the pain. Fight.

Another horrendous jolt, banging Slater's cheekbone hard into his own blood, tears and vomit.

Agonisedly, inch by inch, he fingered the sliver of compound plastic from his belt, pushed it down his left sleeve, fitted it under his watchstrap.

It was laughable, no defence against anything or any one, let alone a team of heavily armed and quite possibly sadistic RDB enforcers – but when all was said and done it was a weapon.

When daylight suddenly and violently flooded the car-boot, Slater guessed that they had covered about 100 miles. He had been unconscious, he guessed, for about twenty minutes. The bag was pulled from his face and he blinked painfully – his eyes and sinuses were still acutely tender from being blasted with Mace.

As his vision cleared he saw one of Fanon-Khayat's bodyguards – Potato-Head – reaching for him. Noted the gold-plated identity bracelet on the hairy wrist.

Distaste showed on the Serb's face at the vomit and blood-smeared features before him. Gripping Slater by the lapels of his jacket, he wrenched him from the car and pushed him to the ground.

They were in a farmyard, Slater saw blearily, and he was lying on a grass verge that had been churned up by cattle and had then dried hard and uneven. The land surrounding them was hilly and sparsely wooded, and there was no sign that they were overlooked from any direction. Certainly there was no other dwelling-place of any kind in sight. The car he had travelled in was a metallic olive Audi Quattro, new-looking. The day was hot and cloudless.

The farm itself was in a poor state of repair. Thistles and tall grass grew through the cracks in the yard's concrete floor, and the brick outbuildings were badly dilapidated. Beyond the yard several dozen young pigs intermittently squealed and jostled in a makeshift pen. On a rutted track beyond them a tractor and trailer were parked. Two cabbage white butterflies tumbled around each other in a looping aerial ballet. There was the hum of bees. It was a drowsy and peaceful scene.

Not for long. From the front seat of the Audi climbed Suet-Face, a bloody dressing round the stump of his thumb, and a third man, as pasty-faced and heavy-set as the first two. This, Slater guessed, was the guy who had bumped him in the apartment. The two spoke together, Suet-Face spat on the ground and took a half-bottle of spirits from his pocket, and they stared at him, amused.

Slater was not encouraged. None of the trio had the look of a man who intended to be merciful. With his bound hands he felt for the knife. It was still there.

'Music?' Suet-Face asked Slater, swigging from the bottle and reaching inside the car. 'You like?'

Without warning the quiet of the farmyard was shattered by the ear-splitting thump of a techno beat, on top of which a woman's voice began to screech a coarsely amplified ethnic folk-song. It was, thought Slater as he turned his head away, a truly hideous sound, and the Audi's top-of-the-range hi-fi did it full justice.

'You like?' shouted Suet-Face, tipping back the bottle again. 'Is Ceca Raznatovich.'

'Is shit,' Slater shouted back. 'Ceca fucks pigs. So does your mother.'

Best, he thought, to keep it simple.

But Suet-Face, despite being in what must have been considerable pain from his missing thumb, refused to be wound up. Instead, to Slater's staring disbelief, he started to dance – or at least to move his body in rough time to the music.

'You like pigs?' he said, still grinning. 'Is good you like pigs.'

The other two joined in, grinding their hips, punching the air and yelling the choruses with formless, incoherent abandon. The bottle passed hands. On Suet-Face's features a look of almost drooling anticipation had taken residence. They're cranking themselves up to kill me, thought Slater. This turbo-folk shit is the last music I'm going to hear.

The three men danced, drank and yelled for the twenty minutes that it took for the tape to play itself out, and then, sweating heavily, Suet-Face made for the barn which made up one side of the farmyard. From its shadowed interior Slater heard the faint grumble of a generator and then, above this, the heavy vibration of another, much larger piece of equipment. For some reason the sound seemed to excite the pigs, which scrabbled and fell over each other frenziedly.

Smiling, Potato-Head strode over to where Slater lay hunched on the verge.

'Pigs, English,' he grinned. 'Come!'

Between them he and the cosh-man dragged Slater to his feet and pulled him roughly into the entrance to the barn. With a surge of dread that almost caused him to give at the knees Slater saw the machine that had been vibrating with such menace – a heavy-duty industrial wood-chipper. It shuddered on its battered chassis on the hard earth floor as if ravenous for matter to consume.

Seeing Slater's white-faced horror, Suet-face gave him a thumbs-up with his good hand. He then repeated the gesture with his bad hand, shrugged, and smiled. The message was clear: I've lost my thumb, but you're about to lose your life.

He gave an order, and the cosh-man stepped outside, taking a pitchfork that was leaning against the barn-wall. From the yard came an agonised screaming, and when the cosh-man returned a small pig was writhing and keening on the pitchfork's upturned tines.

Shaking with the effort, the cosh-man unloaded the pig hind-legs first into the waiting maw of the shredder. The animal was still screaming when the churning started and the first bloody slush began volleying into the waiting bin. When the outflow had finally been reduced to a slow drip of pink fat, the cosh-man wiped his forehead and winked at Slater.

'Fuck you, fuck your mother, and fuck your country,' said Slater conversationally. Inside, he was almost deranged with fear. Do I keep the knife hidden and try to stick one of these fuckers, he wondered, or do I saw through my wrist right now and hope that I bleed to death before they can feed me into that machine?

Suet-Face issued another order and Slater was dragged back out to the yard. Potato-Face followed with the slop-bin, and poured the still-steaming contents over the fence into the pigs' enclosure. Grunting and squealing furiously the animals piled in, devouring every scrap of tissue and bone. After less than a minute there was nothing left except for a few bloody smears on snouts and cheeks.

'Recycle!' explained Suet-Face. 'Very . . . ecology, no?'

Slater, whose legs were threatening to fold beneath him, forced himself to remain standing. Not to vomit.

A rotten-toothed smile split the broad peasant face. 'And now, England, we recycle you!'

Taking his upper arms, the other two began once again to drag the hopelessly writhing Cadre member across the rough concrete of the yard to the barn. Conscious that terror and the anticipation of unspeakable pain was beginning to shut down his thought-processes altogether, Slater forced himself to act.

Twitching his head crazily and screaming the foulest obscenities he could think of in order to attract attention away from his hands, he palmed the knife.

In the dead centre of the yard he yanked his feet forward, braked himself, and swinging his cuffed fists backwards with all the force he could muster, drove the blade up to the hilt into Suet-Face's crotch.

Slowly, and in total silence, the Serb fell to his knees, but Slater did not see this. What he saw – incomprehendingly – was Eve rising into the double-handed firing position at the entrance to the yard.

The sound of her weapon – the multiple reports – travelled almost lazily over the hot air, and it seemed to Slater that he heard the bone-smashing impact of the rounds and felt the hot tissue-spray on his cheek first.

The Serbs at his sides pitched away from him, their heads bloodily open-ended, lifeless before they hit the ground.

'Move!' shouted Eve. 'Move left.'

Wonderingly, Slater threw himself to the concrete, heard the double crack and a thrilled screaming as the rear portion of Suet-Face's skull landed among the pigs.

Businesslike now, Eve raced forward, paused for a moment with weapon extended over each fallen man. The Serbs, however, were very dead indeed, and finally Eve returned the Glock to her shoulder-holster and rebuttoned her Levi jacket.

'So,' she said, and for a long moment they stared at each other.

Slater tried to think of something to say – some word of gratitude – but a paralysing weariness seemed to have overcome him, and he lowered his eyes. For the first time, he noticed the extreme tightness of the handcuffs.

She knelt down beside him. Her leopardskin velvet

trousers, he saw, were shredded at the knees. She was dressed for the sixteenth arrondissement, not for a life-or-death stalk across open ground in the countryside.

'Who had the cuff-key?' she asked.

'Don't know,' he answered numbly.

Quickly she searched the corpses, pulled the key from the cosh-man's pocket and, kneeling, sprung open the biting cuffs at Slater's wrists and ankles.

'Thanks!' he breathed, flexing his puffed and agonised fingers and gasping at the pain of the renewed circulation. Slowly he climbed to his feet, took a few tentative steps and turned to her. 'What can I say? Thank you again. I was . . .'

He nodded at the wood-chipping machine, still thrumming expectantly.

'How badly are you hurt?' asked Eve, walking into the barn and reaching for the generator button.

The machine grumbled to silence.

Slater felt for the back of his skull. There was a large and acutely tender lump there, but he was able to turn his head without the crunching agony that vertebral or skull-damage would have engendered. His sinuses were sore and his eyes were still very inflamed, his ribs were painfully bruised from a kicking that he suspected had been delivered to him when he was lying unconscious in the apartment, and his testicles were badly swollen.

'I'm . . . I'm pretty much OK. They gave me a good seeing-to in that flat, but I don't think they did any permanent . . .' Tears, Slater discovered, were streaming down his face. 'They Maced me, too,' he apologised. 'My eyes are a bit fucked. Sorry.'

She handed him a handkerchief, and he scrubbed the tears and the congealing blood and brain-matter from his face. Seeing a tap in the corner of the yard he limped over and held his head under it for half a minute.

'Tell me honestly how you are,' Eve said when he had finished.

'I'm still a bit concussed,' he admitted. 'Mentally the handbrake seems to be on and I'll probably get the shakes at some point, but basically I'm OK.'

She nodded. 'Right. Well I'll tell you what we're going to do. We'll bring each other up to speed about events in the car, but first we're going to do to our new friends what they were going to do to you. It'll be messy and unpleasant but it's got to be done.'

'But what is this place? Who owns it?'

'No idea. But this is quite a common Mafia set-up for body disposal. Very popular in Russia. Some hard-up pig-farmer gets paid a whack of cash to leave the premises for a few hours – the whole thing arranged over the phone – and when he gets back the place is neat and tidy and his animals have been fed.'

'So we're not going to have some irate bloke turning up with a shotgun?'

'I doubt it. And we'd see him a mile off, anyway. And he'd see us, and know to keep his distance.'

Slater nodded. 'Are you going to tell me what happened? How you got here?'

'Let's get shot of this trio first.'

'Where are the others?'

'Andreas followed Fanon-Khayat, who's holed up at a hotel near the airport outside Paris. Terry and Leon stayed at the OP to keep an eye on Branca, who's still in the Rue Molitor flat. I'll hear if there are any developments. Now do you think you can lift these guys?'

Slater was amazed at her composure. The entire operation had gone arse-up, she'd just had to shoot three men dead, and she was carrying on as coolly as if they were out on a shopping trip.

'Do you think the pigs will eat the clothes?'

'Not sure.' Eve frowned. 'Perhaps best to strip the bodies and drive the stuff away. Let's do it.'

They started. By unspoken agreement they worked as fast as they could, and in almost total silence. Soon a pile of clothes and shoes lay beside the three naked corpses. Eve went through the pockets, extracting several thousand francs in cash, the Tokarev and Stechkin handguns, the gold Dupont lighter, and the keys to the Audi Quattro. Slater removed his knife from Suet-Face's perineum, and washed it under the tap before returning it to his belt.

There was no question, he knew, of merely setting the car on fire with the bodies in it. There would be inquests and autopsies and the manner of death would swiftly come to light. Then there would be headlines.

No, there was no easy or pleasant way out. The dead men had to disappear completely.

'Pity we haven't got a bit more time,' observed Slater. 'In six hours they'd be nice and stiff.'

Eve nodded blankly.

In the barn, Slater found a square of plastic sheeting. One by one he rolled the dead men on to this, and dragged them, bumping, into the barn. Once there he covered the heads with fertiliser bags, to prevent any blood escaping on to the earth floor. When all three corpses were ready for destruction, he fetched the plastic bin from the enclosure, where Potato-Face had left it. Bluebottle flies were swarming in and around the bin, feasting on the congealed remains of the pig, and rose in a black fury as he lifted it.

With the bin positioned beneath the funnel, Slater and Eve looked at each other. Eve turned on the generator, and Slater knelt to hoist the first of the bodies in a fireman's lift.

The man was very heavy – dead weight – and blood and liquid matter dripped from the fertiliser-bag on to the shoulder and arm of Slater's jacket. Finally he had the body poised, and tipped it in head first. There was a terrible grinding and roaring from within the machine, and then an obscene pink soup whitened by bone-chips began to sluice into the plastic dustbin. The head disappeared comparatively fast but the shoulders took much longer. Slowly the body inched downwards until Slater signalled to Eve to shut the machine off.

'I don't want to carry so much that it spills or splashes,' he explained.

Carefully, averting his head from the stinking stew around which the flies were already circling in their hundreds, Slater manhandled the bin over to the pigs' enclosure.

Smelling the blood the pigs began to trample over each other to get close to him. With care, Slater poured the flyblown contents of the bin into the trough which ran the length of the enclosure. The pigs piled in, lapping and crunching uninhibitedly.

'You haven't by any chance still got those Gauloises?' asked Eve, when he returned to the wood-chipper. Slater had. The packet was a little battered but most of the cigarettes were in one piece.

'I always want to smoke if I miss lunch,' she explained with a quick smile.

'You're hungry?' asked Slater. A purple set of genitals and two fat, hairy legs were sticking bolt upright out of the woodchipper.

'Well, you know how pathetic French breakfasts are.'

'Do you want to hit that on-switch?' suggested Slater.

It took two more hours to process all of the bodies, and by the end both of them were bloodspattered, nauseated, and physically and emotionally drained. Slater was worried that the pigs would lose their appetites half-way through and leave the trough filled with shredded human tissue, but his final visit to the enclosure was greeted with all the squealing enthusiasm of the first.

When they had finally finished, Eve lit another cigarette and Slater attached a hose from the barn to the
courtyard tap. He sluiced down the bin, the pigs, the
trough, the plastic sheet, the inside and outside of the
woodchipper and the concrete surface of the yard. To
further clean out the machine, Slater fed a pile of logs
through it, pouring the resulting woodchips into the
pigs' enclosure. Microscopic forensic analysis might
have indicated the vestigial presence of human tissue
here and there, but why was anyone going to subject
this particular farmyard to that kind of scrutiny? Within
minutes all the hosed-down surfaces had dried in the
sun, leaving no sign of the horror that had unfolded
there. A blackbird sang on the baked tile roof of the
barn. There was a buzzing of grasshoppers.

'Where are we, anyway?' Slater asked. The pain in
his groin had subsided to a dull ache and the sunshine
was making him sleepy.

'Half-way between Chartres and Le Mans. Eighty
odd miles south-west of Paris. It's quite nice, isn't it?'

'Maybe we could retire here,' said Slater, yawning.
'And raise pigs.'

'We need to change our clothes,' said Eve, audibly
refocusing herself. She moved to the pile of discarded
clothing. 'What have we got here?'

Pulling off her short leather boots, she unzipped and
lowered her torn velvet jeans. Her legs, Slater couldn't
help noticing, were long and well-toned, with the
suggestion of a fading tan.

'Legs courtesy of the Vauxhall Cross gym,' she said

drily, intercepting Slater's covert glance. 'And knickers by La Perla. Anything else I can help you with?'

To replace the jeans, she took Potato-Head's shiny Adidas pants and belted them round the waist. With the Levi jacket the effect was a bit weird, but not so unusual as to attract attention.

As Slater stripped to his boxer-shorts and began pulling on the cosh-man's grey track-suit pants, Eve soberly examined the bruises on his upper body.

'They were really quite cross with you, weren't they?'

'I think it was the guy whose thumb I shot off that did most of the damage,' said Slater. 'To be honest I'd probably have a good go at anyone who did that to me.'

'But nothing broken? You're not pissing blood or anything?'

'I'll let you know,' said Slater, pocketing the Stechkin and the Tokarev. The weapons were so heavy that Slater had to tighten the draw-string at his waist to prevent the track-suit pants from being pulled down as he walked.

When they had taken the clothes they needed, the remainder went into the boot of the Audi. 'There was a place I passed about half an hour's drive back towards Paris,' said Eve. 'A kind of dump. We can get rid of these there. In the meanwhile' – she stabbed at the buttons of her mobile – 'we should get up to date. Andreas, yes, tell me.' She listened in silence for thirty seconds. 'Understood.'

Pressing the off-button she turned to Slater.

'Right. Here's the position. Andreas has Fanon-Khayat under surveillance. He's in a hotel called the Inter-Lux near Charles de Gaulle airport, and as far as Andreas can tell he's there alone. There's no sign that he's going anywhere – he's just holed up in his room. If he's got back-up there, he hasn't made face-to-face contact with them.'

'Fanon-Khayat's got a hard decision to make, presumably,' said Slater. 'Either to go for safety and run for Belgrade, or to go for profit and glory and tie up the Ondine deal. Am I right in thinking that he has to stay here to do that?'

'According to our assets, he'll want to do the deal here. If he goes back to Serbia and his contacts follow him there, then the RDB will find out straight away who they are and cut Fanon-Khayat out of the deal. By staying here and operating outside their orbit he can keep hold of all the strings, and come out of the whole thing looking like the single-handed saviour of Republica Srpska. This'll ensure him hero status in Belgrade – never underestimate the need of a middle-aged man to impress his baby-doll trophy wife – and a fat backhander from the supplier.'

'Which he's going to need when Branca hits the shops,' Slater added wryly.

'You better believe it! I only saw her for thirty seconds but she looked to me like a girl who knew how to give a gold Amex card a hard workout.'

'So we think he's going to lie low at the hotel, then?'

'That would be my calculation.'

Slater nodded. 'So we have to do him there.'

'That or persuade him to come away with us so that we can do him somewhere else.'

'And he's got the disc there? The Cambodia pictures?'

'He must have. He wouldn't leave them in the flat without the bodyguards there. And the bodyguards all went off with you.'

'So one way and another we've got a better than average chance of completing the operation as intended?'

'I think so, yes. But the first thing we've got to do is make this Audi disappear. You haven't seen a slurry-pond or anything like that?'

'I haven't seen anything. I was in the boot. But mightn't it be a better idea just to dump it? Somewhere it's absolutely bound to get nicked, replated and sold on. Do you know any really rough Parisian housing estates?'

'Yes, I do. And you're right, that would be the best way to get rid of it. We've got to go into Paris anyway.'

Slater looked around him, at the farm buildings bathed in afternoon sunshine, at the peace and quiet and solitude of the place.

'What's the plan?' he asked.

'Let's get rid of the clothes and the car,' said Eve. 'I'll

brief you on the way out to the airport.'

The dump was a vast, hellish smear of a place, covering several acres. Bulldozers shovelled mountains of refuse, seagulls wheeled overhead, and smoke rose from a score of fires. With the heat of the day the smell was unspeakable. Slater threw the armful of clothes and shoes over a stinking garbage cliff-face, hurried back to the Audi Quattro, and gunned the engine in pursuit of Eve's Peugeot.

An hour later he wiped the controls and steering-wheel clean of fingerprints and parked the car in the litter-strewn shadow of a high-rise public-housing block in Arcueil, two kilometres south of the Périphérique ring-road. With his hands inside the sleeves of his sweat-shirt to avoid leaving further prints he let himself out of the car and walked away, leaving the key swinging from the ignition.

Three streets away he eased himself into the passenger seat of the Peugeot, and he and Eve headed northwards for the Porte de Gentilly and the city of Paris. As she drove, he told her what had happened in Fanon-Khayat's apartment and at the farm. When he had finished she told him her version of events.

'We got your first transmission,' she told him, 'when you said that the two bodyguards were down. Then about ten minutes later we saw Branca arrive in the Quattro. We all spotted her – she's pretty unmistakable. She got out and started giving instructions to the driver and I called you on the

Motorola but got nothing. Walls of the building too thick, you'd switched off, whatever. The others all tried in turn but no one could raise you.

'The driver let Branca out and then drove round the back – presumably to some underground car-park entrance. At that point Andreas and I left the café, got into the two cars and waited. We had no way of knowing what was happening in the flat.

'Nothing for another fifteen minutes and then the Quattro re-appeared. Two passengers, same man driving.'

'The cosh-man,' said Slater, touching the back of his neck.

'Exactly. So I took off after them. No idea if you're in the car, Fanon-Khayat's in the car, what the hell's happening. Anyway they carry out a couple of rudimentary ploys to lose anyone who's following them – nothing I can't handle, though – and I tuck in half a dozen cars behind them.

'At that point Terry comes through on the mobile. Fanon-Khayat, carrying a case, has just walked straight past Andreas and picked up a taxi at the Porte Molitor. Andreas is following in the Mercedes and is pretty sure Fanon-Khayat isn't on to him. They're on the Périphérique, heading east.

'I tell him I'm heading at speed down the A10 away from the city. No idea if you're in the car. The others all reckon you probably are, because as far as they know Branca hasn't left the flat. Whether you're dead or alive, Fanon-Khayat's hardly going to leave her there with you. The consensus at that point is that you're dead, and that the bodyguards are taking your body out into the countryside to get rid of it.'

'Close enough to the truth,' said Slater grimly. 'I hope you were suitably upset!'

'Mad with grief,' Eve said with a faint smile. 'Anyway . . . I follow the Audi from the A10 on to the A11 and I assume we're going to Chartres, but we by-pass it and head on towards Le Mans. Then Terry comes on again. Fanon-Khayat's going towards Roissy and the airport. It looks like he's running for Belgrade.'

'Bad news.'

'The worst. It looks as if a hit's been botched, a sanctioned target's escaped, and a Cadre member's been killed.'

'Embarrassing.'

'Just a bit. So I just press on, and eventually the Audi pulls off the A11 on to a minor road and from there on to a series of farm tracks. I'm lying well back, like I told you, so I'm able to pull in and watch their car crossing the fields. After that, well, you can imagine. I work my way across the fields for a half-mile or so and lie up behind that farmyard wall. What's really lucky is that it's me that's got the Glock, not Andreas.'

'How long were you there?'

'Long enough,' said Eve. 'The main thing I wanted to discover was whether they were armed or not. As it was I never found out, and so as soon as you put one of them down I reckoned it was my best chance and . . . went in.'

Slater turned to her in his seat. 'You were brilliant. That was a great bit of shooting.'

Eve tried not to show her pleasure, but her eyes gave her away. 'I do like a Glock Seventeen,' she admitted.

'There is one question, though,' said Slater. 'Where's the Sig Sauer the bodyguards took off me?'

Eve considered. 'My guess is that Fanon-Khayat took it. It would have been the sensible step.'

'Which means,' said Slater, 'that Fanon-Khayat is armed . . . and Andreas isn't?'

'We have to assume that, yes.'

'So we should get up to that hotel as quickly as possible.'

'That's what's going to happen. Except that it's not going to be we. I'm dropping you off at the Montmorency and taking one of the others up there.'

'You're kidding!' Slater protested vehemently. 'I'm fine, I really am. Apart from anything else this whole situation's at least partly my fault. I was the one who let that bodyguard get the drop on me.'

'It's not a question of fault,' said Eve. 'It's a question of the team as a whole getting the job done, and I'd be completely irresponsible if I asked you to carry on at this stage. You had the hit on Fanon-Khayat to deal with this morning, for a start. Then you had a bad knock on the head, a severe beating and a hundred-mile journey in a car-boot, and to top it all off you were told you were about to be fed through a meat grinder. You're fucked, basically, and no bloody wonder.'

Slater was silent. As an SAS soldier he had been trained to keep going whatever his state of exhaustion. Exercises had often been designed to run for days without a break, and he was familiar with all the temptations that extreme tiredness brought in its wake: to cut corners and to skimp on detail. To mistake light-headedness for clear-headedness; to let the concentration wander; to make over-emotional decisions.

Like his colleagues, Slater had learnt to monitor his own condition and to compensate for these tendencies. But there was a point, he knew, beyond which the best soldier's efficiency was compromised. Today had not been an especially long day but heavy expenditures of adrenaline and terror had taken their toll, and the blazing relief of his deliverance had been replaced by the dull blur of emotional fatigue. Eve was right – he was running on empty.

She parked the Peugeot outside the Hotel Grand Exelmans, and they hurried in a side-door with the overnight bags they'd taken from the Montmorency that morning. In the room designated as the OP, Leon and Chris gave them a relieved welcome. The pair had barely left the room all day and their faces betrayed the strain they'd been under, listening to the day's events via radio links and mobile phones.

'Good to have you back, man!' said Leon quietly. 'Thought we'd lost you then.'

'So did I,' said Slater, clasping the other man's hand. 'Believe me, so did I.'

He turned to Chris. 'The knife,' he said. 'Thank you. It saved our . . .'

'Bacon?' asked Chris with a wry smile.

'I was trying to avoid using that word,' said Slater. 'But yes.'

'I don't want to spoil the party,' said Eve. 'But where's Terry?'

'Left to follow Branca five minutes ago,' said Chris. 'She came out of the apartment dressed up to the nines, and headed north on foot.'

'Terry followed her on foot?'

'No, he'd hired another car this afternoon. Said he'll call in as soon as he's got anything to report.'

Eve nodded and punched out a number on her mobile. 'Why don't you take a shower and change?' she suggested to Slater.

Slater agreed gratefully. The edges of the room were beginning to blur. Fishing the Stechkin and the Tokarev from his pockets he dropped them on the bed next to Leon. 'From Serbia, with love.'

Leon looked down at the heavy automatics. 'This is not fashionable weaponry,' he observed.

'These guys have fairly old-fashioned values,' said Slater.

For ten full minutes he stood beneath the power-shower in Leon's room, letting the hot water blast away the sweat and fear of the day.

He returned, smartly dressed, to find a pot of freshly brewed coffee waiting on a tray. Leon had disappeared.

'How are you feeling?' Eve asked, cautiously.

'Better,' said Slater.

'Up to keeping going?'

'Sure.'

Eve looked at Chris, and then back at Slater. 'The position is this. I've just been talking to Andreas at the Inter-Lux and he needs back-up for tomorrow morning. Two people. The problem is there's only one room free there – and that's a double. Now the ideal arrangement is that Chris or I go with Leon or Terry and let you recharge your batteries. The trouble is – we've lost Terry for the time being and we're pretty sure that a mixed-race or two-woman couple would stick out. The staff would remember us and it's very important that that doesn't happen. So, basically' – she folded her arms across her chest – 'it's you and me again. Up for it?'

'Sure,' said Slater.

ELEVEN

'So, where are we going for our week of passion?' Slater asked, pulling out into the fast lane to overtake a line of slow-moving trucks.

'Better make it somewhere boring,' said Eve. 'How about London?'

'Why not Venice?' suggested Slater. 'Lovers always go to Venice.'

'Maybe, but that wouldn't explain why we were taking an eleven-stone trunk with us. My suggestion is that Neil Clissold and Eve Benbow are two single English people, working in Paris, who have come together as a result of a shared love of old books. As we're going to spend a few days together in London, we're taking a trunkful of books back with us.'

'So where did we meet?'

'At the flea-market, let's say. At the Porte de Clignancourt.'

'So what were we buying?'

'You were buying, let's see, books about Indochina, perhaps – and the battle of Dien Bien Phu. I was after, um . . .'

'An illustrated guide to old rose varieties?' suggested Slater.

'That would be nice,' said Eve. 'What made you think of that?'

'I used to spend school holidays with my mother's sister. She had a big book, all in French, about roses.'

'OK. So what happened? How did we actually make contact?'

'You asked me in English to pass you a book from a pile. I asked how you knew I was English, you told me the French don't wear Clarks desert boots. We had dinner together that night at . . . Fuck off!'

'Excuse me?'

'No, not you. That guy flashing at me.'

'Well, cool it. We don't want anyone taking our number. Where were we?'

'Deciding where to have dinner.'

'We ate at a brasserie on the Ile St Louis. A place where all the rugby supporters go.'

'OK, and it was deafening. There had been an international, France had won, and we had to shout at each other. We drank too much Alsatian beer and ate too much pork.'

'Pig is definitely the theme of the day, isn't it?'

'It does seem to be,' Slater agreed. 'How much further, do you reckon?'

'Well, the last sign said Aéroport Charles de Gaulle ten kilometres, and according to Andreas the hotel itself is two kilometres from the airport, and signposted.'

Dusk was falling when they finally pulled up at the front entrance to the Inter-Lux. The hotel was vast, spotlit, and American-styled, and while two porters struggled inside with the heavy trunk a driver relieved Slater of the keys to the Peugeot. When men like Fanon-Khayat went to ground, he mused, they did so in comfort.

Arm in arm, he and Eve sauntered through the lavishly appointed hotel entrance and checked in under the names in their false passports. In an alcove, apparently reading a tourist brochure, sat Andreas, and when they had been given their room-key, their tour of the lobby's amenities and luxury concession-booths took them straight past him.

'Room nine thirty-three,' murmured Eve. 'Give it ten minutes.'

They made a leisurely progress to the lifts. The trunk reached their room before they did, and Slater handed the waiting porters a hundred francs each. Given the dead weight of the thing he reckoned they'd earned it.

Parting the curtains, Slater looked out over several smaller hotels, the still-busy motorway and the lights of the airport complex. He was no longer feeling tired, and in some curious way the day's events seemed to belong to another time-frame. He felt razor-sharp – as alert as he'd ever been. Part of him knew that this feeling was false and a symptom of stress-fatigue; part of him didn't care.

Andreas was business-like. 'Fanon-Khayat's in his room on the fourth floor. Room four-twenty-seven. Hasn't come out since he checked in this afternoon. Given that this is an airport hotel, though, I shouldn't think that anyone's surprised at guests keeping odd hours. How are we doing for weapons?'

'I've got the nine-mil Glock and ammunition,' said Eve. 'We thought it would lessen the risk of compromise if we didn't bring more than one firearm. What do you reckon the options are? Would he open the door if one of us knocked?'

'He doesn't know that I followed him here,' said Andreas, 'but I think we have to assume that an unexplained knock would spook him. He's got a "Do not Disturb" sign on his door, and it's a good bet that he's armed.'

'Can we pick his lock?' asked Slater.

'He's right in the middle of a corridor,' said Andreas. 'And the locks, as you've seen, are those plastic card-locks. We could get in if we had a programmer and a blank card, but . . .'

'The room-staff have master-keys, though,' Eve cut in. 'Could we steal one?'

'Possible,' agreed Andreas. 'But hard to do without the staff-member noticing. I've checked the cleaners out: they have the key-cards on little chains attached to their belt-loops or round their necks.'

'Fire-alarm?' suggested Eve. 'Let it off, rush in and take him out in all the confusion?'

'There'd be hotel-staff checking in all the rooms,' said Andreas. 'I thought of the fire-alarm, but we'd never be able to get rid of the body in time. It's a last resort, I agree, but—'

'As we said, there must be people checking in and out at all hours,' Slater said. 'So the rooms must need to be made up at all hours. So there must be cleaners here at all hours.'

'I've got an idea,' Eve said. 'I'm going straight down. Four-twenty-seven did you say?'

'That's right.'

When she had gone, Andreas turned to Slater. 'You look completely spaced out,' he grinned, shaking his head. 'I got the basic story from the OP team. How you were almost made into pork scratchings and how Eve blew the bad boys away with her little ceramic Glock.'

'I've never, ever been so glad to see anyone in my life,' said Slater. 'I was just about to cut my wrists with the knife Chris gave me. That farmyard was the most sinister place I've ever been, and that includes Iraq.'

'Eve's pretty resourceful,' Andreas agreed. 'I'd put money on her getting into that room within five minutes.'

It was closer to ten minutes, but eventually Eve rang Andreas's mobile. She was whispering.

'I'm in his bathroom. Fanon-Khayat's asleep. Can you guys come down? The door's on the latch.'

They took the lift down, and Andreas led Slater to Room 427. They could hear Fanon-Khayat's snores from the deserted corridor, and silently they let themselves in and relocked the door. On the bed, in a dressing gown, Fanon-Khayat lay open-mouthed. Pills strewed the bedside table and the curtains had been drawn on the gathering dusk. On the TV screen the porn channel was playing, and a woman in a St Trinian's style schoolgirl costume was being pensively buggered by a man in a cowboy hat. Something about the cowboy looked strangely familiar to Slater.

At the other end of the room, Eve stood by the open bathroom door.

'With the pillow?' Slater whispered.

She nodded.

It was over fast. Slater held Fanon-Khayat down, while Andreas stifled him with the down-filled pillow. As the Lebanese weakly kicked and bucked beneath him, Slater concentrated on trying to remember where he had seen the cowboy before. Concentrated on distancing himself from the present moment, the present killing.

But without success. He was unable to remember where he'd seen the cowboy before, and he was unable to escape the moment. Eventually Fanon-Khayat was still, and Andreas lifted the pillow.

'Thanks, guys,' Eve said, checking the dead man's wrist for a pulse as if she were a nurse, finding none, and replacing it on his chest. 'I was pretty sure bringing you in would be better than my shooting him and making a mess of the sheets and walls and so on.'

'We've got a bit of time,' Slater said. 'He won't have ordered any room-service if he was asleep. And the sign on the door will keep people away. How did you get in here, in the end?'

'Well,' she smiled. 'I found a nice Portuguese lady cleaning a room out in the next corridor, and asked her what time the shops in the lobby shut. Told her I'd seen a rather nice Bottega Veneta bag I fancied. She said she thought the boutiques were still open, and I nipped down and bought the bag.'

'That's it?' asked Andreas, indicating a smart creation in woven leather.

'That's it,' said Eve. 'A snip at £450, give or take a quid or twenty. I thought it might be nice for Debbie – a little something from Paris at the taxpayers' expense.'

'What about Ray?' asked Andreas. 'We can't not get him a present. That would be discriminatory.'

'Do you want to hear the rest?' asked Eve.

'Sorry,' said Andreas. 'Go on.'

'When I came back, I showed the housemaid the bag. She said it was terrible how expensive things were in the lobby – that they were a tenth of the price in the supermarkets, and so on. I then told her I'd done something really silly, that I'd left my key inside my room, and that my husband was asleep and I didn't want to wake him – he tended to be a bit grumpy first thing, you know how men are – so could she very sweetly let me in with her pass key? Well, she was fine about it – I could see her calculating that someone who'd just spent over four thousand francs on a handbag was pretty unlikely to be a sneak-thief – and old Fanon-Khayat here was snoring away so loud you could hear him half-way down the corridor. So she let me in with her key, and *voilà*, we parted the best of friends.'

'And she's not going to mention this to anyone?' asked Andreas.

'Why should she? Stuff like this must happen all the time – stupid rich people forgetting their keys. Just to prove how stupid and rich I was I gave her a five-hundred-franc note. She won't mention it. Anyway, there I was, there he was, and the rest you know. Firewall accomplished.'

The three of them set to work, collecting everything connected to the dead man and placing it on the bed. It didn't take long – he hadn't even brought a change of clothes. He had, however, brought his passport, driving licence, phone, credit cards and the silenced Sig Sauer, all of which Andreas now pocketed. For the next twenty-four hours he was going to occupy the hotel as Antoine Fanon-Khayat – it was for this reason that he had not booked himself into the hotel when he arrived.

The dead man had brought one other thing, which Slater found in the breast pocket of a jacket slung over a chair. A compact disc, which Eve immediately pocketed.

'Mission accomplished?' Slater asked her.

'Well, there's a bit of tidying up to do, but basically yes. As soon as we've packed this guy away we can go down to the restaurant and have a good meal. Would you two nip upstairs and get the trunk?'

Slater nodded, and he and Andreas took the lift to the ninth floor. Inside his and Eve's room, Slater unlocked the trunk. Inside were two sleeping bags and a large double duvet. From each of the sleeping bags he dragged a twenty-litre plastic jerrycan of water.

'Heavy in, heavy out, eh?' said Andreas.

'That's right,' said Slater, lugging the jerrycans towards the bath. 'It would look a bit odd if our trunk somehow put on eleven stones in weight overnight. If anyone asks me and Eve about it we're book collectors. Book collectors having a passionate sexual affair.'

'When did you last read a proper book?' smiled Andreas.

'I'm reading one by Salman Rushdie right now,' said Slater.

'Fuck off!' said Andreas.

The water gurgled from the jerrycans and splashed into the bath. 'Just check, would you, if Leon remembered to put in a knife,' said Slater. 'We'll need to hack these up to make room for Fanon-Khayat.'

'He remembered,' said Andreas, tossing a Stanley knife on to the bed. 'He's Mr Forward Planning, is Leon. He also knows Paris like the back of his hand, which is useful when you need trunks and jerrycans at six o'clock on a Saturday evening.'

Finally they were ready.

'You call the lift and hold it open,' said Slater. 'I'll get the trunk over there.'

They had to let three lifts go but eventually an

empty one arrived, and they got the trunk down to room 427 unobserved. Both Slater and Andreas were conscious that porters, rather than guests, hauled the luggage in five-star hotels.

As Eve and Andreas emptied the trunk, Slater started to manhandle the dead man into the smaller of the two sleeping-bags. With Andreas's help, he then manoeuvred the first sleeping-bag into the second, stuffed the hacked up pieces of plastic jerrycan in after it, and crammed the mummy-like result into the trunk. With the duvet tightly packed around the body so as to allow no shifting when the trunk was carried, the lid was then forced shut.

Experimentally, Slater and Andreas then lifted an end each. The trunk was heavy, but not noticeably heavier than when it had been carried into the hotel. In the unlikely event of the same porters carrying it out again, no difference would be detectable. Nor, even when they tilted the trunk sharply, did the body shift.

'I think,' said Andreas, 'we're cooking with gas.'

'Simon!' said Slater, remembering.

The others stared at him.

'Snaking the schoolgirl on the TV when we first came in. The guy in the cowboy hat. His name's Simon. He did the same to a woman I used to guard.'

'Not Grace Litvinoff, by any chance?' asked Eve drily. 'I believe she's quite keen on the odd bit of rough.'

It was Slater's turn to stare.

Eve smiled sweetly. 'If the cowboy hat fits,' she said, 'wear it!'

They made it back to the ninth floor room without incident. Leon had taken care to buy them a trunk with comfortable carrying handles, and Slater and Andreas were able to carry it to the lift as if it weighed much less than Fanon-Khayat's eleven and a half stone. In the event, no one took any notice of them, and the trunk was soon ritually laid on the floor at the end of the bed.

The atmosphere, Slater thought, was a weird one. In the Regiment, after a terrorist kill or a successful contact, they'd all pile into the bar and get hammered. Right now, however, the three of them were planning to celebrate a day of quite extreme violence with a quiet dinner.

Eve had called the back-up team to report that Fanon-Khayat was down and the disc recovered. Terry, she discovered from Chris, had followed Branca Fanon-Khayat.

Although Branca gave a convincing impression of being a shopaholic trophy wife, Leon and Chris had agreed that it was essential to keep tabs on her. How would she react when her husband's bodyguards failed to reappear? Would she seek the help of the French police or security services? Would she attempt to contact associates of her husband's? Anything was possible.

In fact, Terry had discovered, Branca had gone to a

house in the eleventh arrondissement, where a vast party was under way. The host was a Franco-Tunisian rap star called Gil Dazat, the music was loud, and the crowd – chic, louche and international – was spilling out into the street. Terry had simply climbed the stairs and joined in. Branca was there on the arm of an expensively dressed young man whom Terry quickly identified as the resident drug-dealer. Business was brisk and quite openly conducted, and from the way that the guests greeted them it was clear that the dealer and Branca were an established couple. Terry had reported his intention of staying at the party in order to ID the young man – it was the kind of information that could well come in useful.

What amazed Slater was Branca's sang-froid. On the evening of a day in which she and her husband had been held at gunpoint by the trigger-man of a hostile government – an event that had so traumatised her husband that he had gone into hiding – she had elected to dress up and go out on the town with her underworld boyfriend. In a way, he thought, you had to take off your hat to the girl. Having lived through the bombing of Belgrade, Branca Fanon-Khayat knew how to prioritise. Drink, dance, for tomorrow we die . . .

He said as much to Andreas and Eve over the langoustine and baby octopus salad at dinner. Andreas had checked Fanon-Khayat's phone and found no text or voice messages. Unless the arms-dealer had cleared his phone earlier, Branca hadn't attempted to ring him.

'I'd love to know what she's wearing tonight,' said Eve. 'That chiffon coat this morning was just too much.'

'Pity she had to wear all that stuff underneath,' said Andreas. 'Just the coat would have looked better.'

'You're a dinosaur, Andreas,' said Eve. 'A sexist dinosaur.'

'A dinosaur maybe, but no sexist!' insisted Andreas. He turned to Slater. 'Am I a sexist?'

'I wouldn't say so,' said Slater. 'I've never known you discriminate on grounds of race, gender, religion or sexual orientation. You've always been very much an equal opportunities guy – happy to kill anyone.'

Eve turned to Slater. Three glasses of Chablis had admitted a pale sparkle to her sea-grey eyes. 'What about you, Neil? Are you a new man?'

'Me? Sure, yeah! I've got my . . . What's that thing you're supposed to have?'

'Inner child?' suggested Andreas.

'Exactly. I've got one of those. And I can tell you, my inner child was crapping itself this afternoon before you turned up with your Glock and your velvet jeans.'

'My pleasure,' said Eve. 'It would have been very embarrassing to have gone back to London without you.'

'What happened to your predecessor?' asked Slater. 'They went back to London without her, I seem to remember you saying.'

'Ellis? Ellis was killed in a firefight here in Paris. She . . .'

'Yes?' said Slater.

'The truth is I never really knew Ellis. I'd seen her about the place, because I'd been on a kind of informal attachment to the Cadre, but I never got to know her.' She turned to Andreas. 'You did, though, didn't you?'

'Ellis was great. I only knew her for a few months, and I was very much the new boy then, but . . .' he shook his head.

'All the guys go very misty-eyed when they talk about Ellis,' said Eve.

'She was the total professional,' said Andreas to Slater. 'I doubled up with her a few times for live-firing CQB sessions at the killing house. I don't know if you've had the pleasure yet but we're supposed to do a minimum of four days a month there as well as practising on the range, and it's at least as dangerous as the stuff we used to do at Pontrilas. Like I said, I doubled up with Ellis a few times and she was very, very fast. They throw these horrible things at you – CS gas, white noise, guns that jam as soon as you try and fire them – and I never saw her lose it once. She was just . . . cool. Ellis was cool. And afterwards she was funny, and gorgeous, and fantastic company, and completely crazy, and . . .'

He shook his head and fell silent.

'Everyone talks about Ellis like this,' said Eve. 'As you can imagine she wasn't the easiest act to follow. It was impossible, in fact. Whenever I slipped up, which I did all the time, I'd know people were thinking: Ellis would never have done that. Ellis would have handled that better. Ellis would never have lost the surveillance target, missed the shot, made the bad decision . . . And of course she was killed in action, so she became a sort of departmental saint.'

'What exactly happened to her?' asked Slater.

Eve glanced briefly at Andreas. 'The truth is we're not sure, but we think it had something to do with Fanon-Khayat.'

'Fanon-Khayat? As in the guy upstairs?'

The waiter drew up, removed their plates, and filled their wine glasses. Eve waited until he was out of earshot.

'Ellis was in Paris as part of a . . . a check on Fanon-Khayat's reliability. Things were beginning to go belly-up for him financially, and London needed to know that he was still on-side, and wasn't going to use the information he had against us. His weakness was women, so Ellis mounted an old-fashioned honey-trap.'

'How did she do it?' asked Andreas. 'I never actually found out.'

'Quite straightforward,' said Eve. 'She drove into the back of his car when his driver was dropping him off at the apartment, and made like she was so upset by the whole thing that he invited her up. Things moved on pretty fast after that, and . . .'

'They had an affair?' asked Slater.

'My understanding is that they didn't. Ellis had definite theories about using sex to gain information, and her basic thing was that with sport-fuckers like

Fanon-Khayat – guys who were just in it for the chase and the conquest – you got what you wanted by withholding sex rather than granting it. Once you gave in to someone like that, she felt, you lost your power over them. So she flattered him. Played him along. She told him she was a political science graduate, and gave him the impression that she was turned on by his knowledge of covert activity. The more extreme stuff he told her, she implied, the likelier he was to get her into bed. According to the report, though, he didn't bite. He was crazy about Ellis – she could really get guys going if she wanted to – but he hardly told her anything. He mentioned as an aside that there had been a UK and US special forces presence in Cambodia, but then John Pilger had already made that pretty clear. He certainly didn't produce any pictures or anything like that, and all in all he seemed well disposed to us.

'The final decision at the time, based on Ellis's report, was that his knowledge of our dirty washing – such as it was – didn't represent any kind of security threat. We knew he had made some fairly dodgy friends in the Balkans, and that a watching brief had to be kept, but that was pretty much it.'

'Except that it wasn't,' suggested Slater.

'Except that it wasn't,' said Eve. 'On the morning of the day she was due to return to London for debriefing she went to the Science Park at La Villette in north-eastern Paris. We don't know why, and we don't know whether she went to meet someone or was following someone – all that we know is that she went alone and without back-up.

'At around 11.20am, according to a statement issued to the press by the French police, a firefight took place in the staff car-park area, resulting in the deaths of three men and one woman. The men had all been shot twice in the head and the woman, who appeared to have been unarmed, had been shot eleven times in the body. Their conclusion was that several people were involved on both sides and the whole thing was almost certainly drugs-related – rival gangs settling scores over territory, that sort of thing. Maybe an execution. By the time the incident was reported in the newspapers the drug-gang theory had hardened into certainty, and as everyone knows, gangland killings are never solved.

'The most interesting evidence, though, is buried in a later police report. The car-park at La Villette is huge, and the shooting took place in an area where there weren't many people around. The nearest person to the shooting was a maintenance guy from one of the display halls who was collecting equipment from a van. He didn't see what happened – he was a good hundred yards away – but he heard it. He said that to begin with there was a volley of shots in quick succession. Different sorts of bangs, perhaps fifteen or twenty in all, and at first he thought it was firecrackers – the fourteenth of July was coming up and the kids start letting them off as soon as they appear in the shops. But he'd done his Service Militaire and he soon realised that what he'd heard was gunfire.

'According to his statement this first volley was followed by silence for about twenty seconds, then three or four bursts of semi-automatic fire, and then, a half-minute or so later, three double-shots in fast succession followed by another extended volley. And then silence, and people running away.

'That statement, which we have no reason to doubt, suggests the following scenario: Ellis goes to the car-park for reasons unknown. She is carrying her personal weapon but has no reason to expect trouble. In the car-park she is ambushed by at least five people armed with a variety of weapons, all of whom open fire on her simultaneously and at short range.

'Ellis goes down wounded, but makes it to cover. The ambushers move up on her, not sure if she's dead, covering each other by cracking off the odd shot. Ellis, although badly and possibly critically hurt, realises that her only option is to seize the initiative, to move towards rather than away from the killing group. So, summoning whatever strength she's got left, she does just that – pulls out her Glock and goes in shooting. Three double taps in as many seconds, three ambushers dead on their feet, but there are five of them in total and this time she goes down for good.

'There's a picture of the scene an hour or so later which was taken by the police photographer. There are two lines of cars, and behind the first and hurled backwards against the second are three men who do in fact look very much like drug-gang enforcers. Each has two black holes between his eyes; none has much in the way of a back to his head. On the ground you can see a Skorpion machine-pistol and a couple of heavy automatics.

'Bundled up on the tarmac twenty feet away is Ellis. She's wearing the leather jacket she used to carry her weapon in – she just used to stick it in the inside pocket, she hated shoulder holsters – and a black T-shirt and jeans. And the strange thing is that although she's been literally shot to pieces – eleven short-range shots to the body – you can't actually see any of the wounds at all. Her face is untouched. She's just lying there with this blank stare in a shining pool of blood.'

Eve nodded pensively. 'When the picture came into the office the atmosphere got very strange. No one talked to each other – everyone sat alone in corners trying to figure the whole thing out. And trying to work out how to deal with their own reactions to it. Your predecessor' – she looked up at Slater – 'had worked with her a lot and I think was pretty upset. Leon disappeared to Paris that evening to see if he could get the inside story and came back a week later none the wiser. The dead men, as everyone had suspected, were basically hired triggers. And although Leon soon established the identity of the other two – the two who finished Ellis off and escaped – it quickly became clear that they'd vanished off the face of the earth. They'd been professionally "disappeared".

'Since then, our assumption has been that Ellis's killing was sanctioned by Fanon-Khayat, who then had the surviving shooters wiped out in their turn. We've never known why – six killings seems like a bit of an over-reaction to wounded sexual vanity – but then a lot of things that people like Fanon-Khayat do defy rational analysis.'

'So there's a revenge angle to this operation?' asked Slater.

'There's a tidying up of unfinished business,' said Eve. 'Yes. It's time Ellis's ghost was laid to rest.'

'I'd say you'd done bloody well,' said Andreas, picking his words with care.

Eve smiled at him gratefully. 'Thank you. If there's one thing I learned in the short time I knew her it's that there are no second prizes in a firefight.'

As the meal progressed, Slater considered their situation. The three of them had agreed with the back-up team that they should stay the night in the hotel rather than check out immediately and return to Paris. Leon was working on a plan for the disposal of Fanon-Khayat's body and until this was finalised, they had decided, the wisest course of action was to stay put. To drive the trunk around at night, when there were far fewer cars on the road than in the day, was to increase the risk of discovery significantly.

None of them needed reminding that they were on hostile territory. If the DGSE or any of the other French security services found out that an MI6 hit team was operating on its patch, the political repercussions would be appalling. There would be no quiet deal done – instead the French would scream the news to the world. They had never quite lived down the humiliation of the 1985 *Rainbow Warrior* affair, when Alain Mafart and Dominique Prieur – both DGSE agents – were convicted of manslaughter after the bombing and sinking of the Greenpeace ship in Auckland harbour. If any of the Cadre were arrested on French soil and convicted of murder or conspiracy to murder, they could expect to serve very long jail-terms indeed – no matter what the political justification.

Slater was also increasingly conscious of the fact that he was about to spend the night in a hotel bedroom with Eve. They had joked about the charade of their being a bookish couple, but not with quite as much hilarity as they might have done. Was it his imagination, or had there been a tiny edge of regret in her voice that life was as it was? That the whole thing was an act? That they were not players in some Tom Hanks and Meg Ryan-style romantic comedy, but in a grim game of death – of covert slaughter and counter-slaughter.

That they were able to relax and enjoy themselves after a day like today was extraordinary in itself, Slater thought, and showed perhaps just how deformed their sensibilities had become. Had his part in the death of Antoine Fanon-Khayat helped prevent another round of Balkan tortures and executions? Or had he merely contributed to a squalid murder whose principal motivation was the desire to save political face? Would the Serbs simply go to the next dealer for their anti-aircraft system?

Useless to wonder, he decided, watching the way that the light fell on Eve's hair and painted the soft line of her cheekbone. She was wearing a dove-coloured cashmere sweater and skirt, and the muted tones subtly highlighted the sea-grey of her eyes. There was nothing obvious about her appearance, he thought. Nothing that jumped out and grabbed you in the way that it did with, say, Grace Litvinoff.

But you wondered. You looked at her and you wondered if you'd ever quite get the measure of her, ever quite get the measure of that distant gaze. There was a self-discipline and a quiet symmetry there that was – he admitted to himself – very attractive indeed. What would it be like to disrupt that cool poise, to see that control thrown to the four winds, to hear her . . .

'You've gone very quiet,' said Eve.

Slater smiled. 'I'm just . . . enjoying myself,' he said.

She held his gaze for a moment, delivered her oblique smile, and looked away.

Afterwards they had drinks in the bar. At 11pm Eve was due to call Leon for his suggestions concerning the disposal of Fanon-Khayat. The original plan had simply been to leave him dead in the apartment and trust that the DGSE would clean up the mess. Despite the fact that it was self-evidently the case, the French Government were acutely sensitive to suggestions that their military establishment was overwhelmingly pro-Serbian and anti-Muslim. Any evidence that Issy-Avionic's Ondine system was heading for Belgrade would be covered up and deleted whatever the cost.

Nothing would have linked the Cadre to Fanon-Khayat's death.

But now the Cadre had a problem. Because Slater, Andreas and Eve had been seen in the same hotel as Fanon-Khayat, and Slater and Andreas had physically handled him before and after his death, Fanon-Khayat had to disappear completely. If his body was discovered and submitted to any kind of forensic examination, there was a risk – a slight risk, but a risk nevertheless – that the trail would lead back, sooner or later, to the three of them. The hotel guests and staff would be questioned, photofit portraits would be made, and a connection established. This must not happen.

The dead man, the Cadre members all agreed, had to vanish from the face of the earth. Leon had told Eve that he was going to ask Manderson to send a cleaner team to spirit the body back to England, but Eve doubted that Manderson would sanction such an exercise. Taking bodies over borders was risky, and he would almost certainly order them to take care of the disposal themselves. They were on the spot, after all, and they had the expertise.

Either way, the job had to be done fast: Branca would soon be asking questions about her husband's failure to contact her, and in this weather it wouldn't be long before the body began to smell.

Leon was working on a solution.

At five to eleven, Eve left the two men in the bar and took the lift up to the ninth floor.

'It must be hard for her,' Slater said, when she had disappeared.

'What must?' asked Andreas.

'Well, everything. Following on from Ellis, like she said. And being in charge of a bunch of head-bangers like us.'

'She didn't actually follow on from Ellis in quite the way she suggested,' said Andreas. 'Eve joined after Ellis was killed, but she didn't step into Ellis's shoes. Ellis was like us – a footsoldier, one of the lads – but Eve was fast-track from day one. She's been given more responsibility with each operation, and my guess is that if she can pull off Firewall and get us all back in one piece, Manderson will hand the Cadre over to her.'

'Tell me about the guy I replaced,' said Slater.

'Bernie?' said Andreas. 'He was SBS. A couple of their guys were pulled in about ten years ago for some very big, super-sensitive operation – presumably something at sea. One left before I joined – went off to live on some Pacific island, I think – and Bernie stuck around until a few months ago. He ended up going overseas too, bought into a boat-building firm in Norway. He was one of those mystical types – thousand-yard stare, dreams of the Far North and all that. A good guy to have at your side if things came on top, but serious, and played his hand very close to his chest. I can't say I ever got to know him very well. The only person who did, in fact, was Ellis, who used to take the piss out of him. If he got heavy, she just used to laugh at him – which I tell you is more than I would have dared do. But because she was Ellis, she got away with it.'

'What did she look like, Ellis?' Slater asked.

Andreas shrugged. 'Dark hair, prettyish, quite scruffy . . . Like Eve said, she always used to wear this old leather jacket with her handgun in one inside pocket and a couple of spare clips in the other. She always used a nine-mil Glock Seventeen, and I've noticed that Eve now carries exactly the same weapon.'

'She knows how to use it, too.'

'She does. And it meant a lot to her that you praised her for that, by the way. Stand you in good stead after lights out, I expect.'

'I'm not daft,' said Slater. 'I wouldn't try anything on with her.'

'You fucking are and you fucking would. I know you of old.'

'I've changed,' Slater protested. 'I've grown up.'

'The great cry of blokes down the centuries?' Andreas smiled. 'I've changed! I've grown up!'

At 11.30 the three of them met in Fanon-Khayat's room on the fourth floor. The plan was simple: Andreas was to wait until the reception was at its busiest, pay for his stay with one of the dead man's credit cards, take a taxi to the airport, and then double back to Central Paris and the OP on a shuttle bus. Neil and Eve, meanwhile, were to check out, load the trunk into the car, make as if they were heading for the airport, and then in their turn double back to the OP. There, Leon would take them through the body-disposal plan. This was not yet finalised in every detail, but the basic elements had been decided on. The body was to be rendered unrecognisable and then sunk in a lonely stretch of the river Seine, some distance outside Paris. The job would almost certainly be carried out under cover of darkness the following night.

In order to give Eve some privacy in the room, Slater said he would stay and have a last drink with Andreas. They raided the mini-bar, and had a malt whisky each. But they had run out of things to say, and in the end they sat in silence, staring out of the floor-to-ceiling window at the crawl of traffic on the motorway and the city of light that was Charles de Gaulle airport.

'I guess I should practise the signature on that credit card,' Andreas said eventually, and Slater nodded.

To his irritation, Slater discovered that his heart was pounding as the lift carried him up to the ninth floor. There would probably, he thought, be some slightly tense negotiation about who slept where. The simplest thing would be if he just crashed out on the floor. A sleeping-bag would come in handy – but would it be completely tasteless to borrow one of those presently enshrouding Antoine Fanon-Khayat?

The lift halted with a soft gasp and Slater felt for the key. Eve had it; was he going to have to knock like some old-fashioned corridor-creeping seducer?

He was. Sensibly, given that there was a dead man stuffed into a trunk at the foot of the bed, she had not left the door on the latch.

He knocked. She answered in French.

'Eve!' he said. 'It's me. Neil.'

The door opened on the chain and then – as soon as she had identified him – fully. She was wearing a pale blue T-shirt, and had a white hotel towel round her waist. She looked scrubbed, clean and younger than the twenty-nine years that her passport claimed for her. He looked at her for a moment and then came in.

Carefully, she doubled-locked the door behind him, then turned off the main light, leaving only a bedside lamp illuminated.

'You take the bed,' he said. 'I'll grab a couple of blankets and hit the floor.'

She nodded absently, staring beyond him as if not quite hearing what he was saying. He looked down at her short fair hair, the neat line of her shoulders, the fading brown of her arms. Then her gaze rose to meet his.

Impossible to say which of them reached for the other first, but they were suddenly and urgently devouring each other. He felt her hands in his hair and her mouth moving beneath his, and then his own hands found her waist and the warm sweep of her back. He kissed her mouth, her eyes, her neck, her hair, and as she buried her mouth in his shoulder felt the towel at her waist fall to the floor. Her hands scrabbled at his shirt-buttons and were then forced upwards as he pulled the T-shirt over her head.

'This isn't happening,' she gasped, pulling his shirt open and pressing her breasts against his chest. 'God, the *state* of you. You're one solid bruise.'

'Yeah,' murmured Slater. 'And still a bit tender in the bollock zone too.'

Her fingers found his belt. 'Help me,' she whispered. 'I can't get this . . .'

'Sorry, it's a bit stiff. A present from Debbie.'

They both laughed, and she gasped as he reached down, clasped her round the thighs, and lifted her up so that his tongue could scour her breasts. 'Oh, please!' she gasped, bracing her arms on his shoulders. 'Oh, yes!'

Slowly he returned her to her feet and they kissed again, more slowly this time. Pulling back from her he looked at her closely, examined her in a way that politeness and their respective situations had previously made impossible. She looked quite different from how he remembered her – it was as if he was seeing her for the first time. She, in her turn, looked back unflinchingly at him.

They were both naked now, and taking a couple of steps backwards he lowered himself to a sitting position on the trunk at the end of the bed. She sat facing him, her thighs straddling him, her nipples hard against his chest, the dark triangle of her pubic hair damp against his stomach.

'Just promise me,' she said, 'that this is happening to two different people. To Eve Benbow and Neil . . . what's your ID again?'

'Clissold,' whispered Slater into her ear. 'Not a name I'd have chosen, but . . .'

'Promise me that you'll never tell anyone. That this'll never be mentioned. Ever. Promise me and then fuck me.'

'I won't tell a soul,' said Slater, slipping his hand palm-upwards between her legs and parting her with his fingers. 'I've signed the Official Secrets Act, remember?'

She squirmed, and he felt his fingers slip inside. Steadily, gasping louder now, she began to move against the heel of his hand. Below them, the lock of the trunk set up a ticking squeak.

'It's Fanon-Khayat,' Slater couldn't resist murmuring. 'He wants to join in!'

Eve groaned. 'You really know how to sweet-talk a girl, don't you? Did you bring any condoms with you?'

Slater froze. Stared at her. She smiled wearily back.

'I was under the impression one could rely on the SAS to turn up with the right kit.'

He shook his head. 'I didn't know it was this sort of operation.'

'It isn't – none of this is actually happening, we've already established that. But why don't you search the bathroom? These swanky hotels often have them hidden away somewhere.'

Slater did as Eve suggested, wrapping the towel round himself and searching the drawers and shelves. In the end, though, he had to admit defeat. Eve checked the bedside tables, but with no more success. Self-conscious now that the mood had changed, she had pulled on one of the hotel dressing gowns. Frustrated, Slater saw the moment slipping away.

'I'll go downstairs. There should be a gents with a machine. Will you wait?'

'I'll come down with you.'

Quickly, they both dressed themselves.

There was indeed a machine in the gents toilet next to the bar, but a sticker announced it '*Hors Service*'. Slater exited shaking his head.

Eve laughed. 'I think next stop the airport.'

In the taxi they stared into each other's eyes and held each other like love-struck teenagers. The journey was over in less than ten minutes, and soon they were wandering arm in arm through the echoing and largely empty departure halls. Outside an arcade of locked shops they kissed each other, enjoying the extended anticipation of what was to come.

'You're beautiful,' Slater heard himself saying to her, and realised that he meant it.

'We could fly away,' she said. 'We could choose a name off that departure list over there and go. Live near a beach somewhere, work in a bar, go for walks along the seashore, make love all night.' She threw her arms round his neck. 'Would you like that? Would that make you happy?'

He touched her cheek. 'Yes. That would make me happy. I would be the finest barman on the Coast and you'd cook the best freshly caught snapper and we could have lots of illiterate children who could work as waiters and dream of life in London.'

'You spoil everything,' she reproved him. 'You're so unromantic!'

'I'm not unromantic,' he said, placing his hand inside her coat on her breast. 'I want you here and now and as you are. Right here and right now. Up against this partition if necessary.'

'Not before we've got what we came for. I don't want to start having those illiterate children quite yet.'

Finally, Slater found a vending machine that worked, and for which he had the correct change. He held up the packet and she applauded.

'Would you do that?' he asked her in the taxi back to the hotel. 'Seriously? Would you walk away from everything and come and live with me in the back of beyond?'

She closed her eyes and snuggled against him. 'Until you ask me properly,' she said demurely, 'you'll never know.'

In room 933, as Eve quickly undressed and climbed into bed, Slater examined the packaging of his purchase. 'My French isn't that brilliant,' he said, 'but these look as if they might be quite weird shapes and colours. Still, I guess they'll match my balls.'

'Don't worry,' said Eve gently. 'I'd say that one way and another we've pretty much broken the ice today, wouldn't you?'

TWELVE

Slater and Eve checked into the OP at the Hotel Grand Exelmans at 10.00am, after an extended breakfast in the sunny dining-room of the Inter-Lux. The Peugeot and the trunk, as Leon had suggested, went into the paying car-park on the Rue Jouvenet.

At the OP the mood was cautiously upbeat – Firewall's main objective was achieved; all that remained now was the disposal of the body. And in Leon's hands, that shouldn't be a problem. This was his turf, after all. If anyone could make a dead arms-dealer vanish in northern France, Leon could.

Terry, now sleeping off his night's work, had also had a good result. He had identified the drug-dealer from the party as one Miko Pasquale, and confirmed that Branca Nikolic – now unknowingly a widow – had spent the night at his apartment close to the Bastille. At 8.30 she had emerged from the building and taken a taxi back to her late husband's apartment. Right now she was less than 100 metres away.

At 10.30 Andreas joined them. To his relief his impersonation of Antoine Fanon-Khayat had been accepted without question. The check-out desk had been at its busiest in the mid-morning, as they had calculated, and the clerk had barely glanced at him as he had handed over the dead man's platinum Amex card. 'I might just go on a little shopping spree with that piece of plastic,' he suggested, and feigned indignation when Chris held out her hand for all the dead man's effects. 'I think these are being withdrawn from circulation,' she said firmly, taking the overnight bag from Andreas and stowing it next to the trunk.

Slater noticed that Chris was making a particular point of observing Eve and himself, and concentrated on giving the impression that a breezily normal professional relationship existed between them. The giveaway, he knew, was not too much closeness and eye contact but too little. People enjoying a passionate covert affair tended to avoid each other's gaze in case any lingering intensity communicated itself to others. And they never made jokes.

So he did all those things, even making a point of saying that next time he and Eve posed as lovers it would be her turn to roll up in the duvet on the floor.

Would the night ever be repeated? He doubted it. It had come about as a result of a unique and very extreme set of circumstances. In the course of the preceding day both of them had looked violent death in the face more than once, and the experience had isolated them. They had found themselves in a world without rules, a dark and surreal place to which no outsider was permitted access. Their coming together had been inevitable, and it had been highly charged. They had reached for each other several times in the course of the night and it had been as if they were making love in an electric storm, with the air smouldering and crackling around them. He smiled to himself as he remembered the feel and taste of her body, and how she had suddenly looked so different to the person he had known up that moment. Perhaps this was what Chris had meant when she welcomed him to the 'parallel universe'.

'You look pleased with yourself,' Andreas remarked.

'I was thinking of those poor hotel porters staggering out to the car with the trunk. I gave the poor buggers fifty francs each but it should really have been more: there was a notice in the room saying that there was a fifteen hundred franc surcharge for supplementary guests.'

'What did you say was in the trunk?' asked Chris.

'We didn't,' said Eve. 'But we were going to say it was books.'

'Holiday reading?'

'Second-hand books. Which we collected.'

'Cute,' said Chris drily. 'How many for coffee?'

Leon arrived ten minutes later, carrying maps, and congratulated the forward team on the success of the hit and of their smooth extraction from the hotel. 'Now,' he said briskly, pouring himself a cup from the steaming cafetière, 'this is the plan. Four of us will go – it's going to be heavy work so I'd suggest the four guys. Any objections to that idea?'

'I'll come,' said Eve.

Leon nodded expressionlessly. As the team leader she had final say.

'OK. Eve, Neil, Andreas and myself. Terry can grab a few more Zs, Chris'll stay and run the OP.'

Everyone nodded. Chris examined her nails.

Leon spread out one of the maps. 'The location is here – about seventy or eighty clicks outside Paris in a place called the Forêt de La Roche-Guyon. What we do is drive out of Paris at midday via the Porte d'Auteuil and then, keeping more or less parallel to the river, take the A13 motorway north-west to Bonnières-sur-Seine. We'll take both cars – if we take one and it blows up with that trunk in it we're in serious shit. At Bonnières we swing up northwards on this minor road via Freneuse, and then follow this . . . track, it must be, into the forest.

'Switching to the local map you can see that the track continues for five or six clicks past Joigny, which looks as if it consists of a few farm buildings and not much else, and then peters out in the middle of nowhere. The nearest place apart from Joigny is Thieux, which is a good two clicks away and served by a different track. Thieux's no Las Vegas, either.

'What I think we should do is park up at the end of the track so that we're in the empty countryside between between Joigny and Thieux. It looks as if you can get down to the river quite easily from there, and according to the map this is one of the widest and deepest parts for miles in either direction. There's also this jetty going out, perhaps for barges to tie up to, and for my money that's where we want to drop our friend off. It's the only way – short of stealing a boat with an outboard and waking everyone up within miles – of getting him out to deep water. I'd suggest swimming or rowing him out, but I know that area and it's one fat mother of a river up there. It's deep, it's dirty and the current is very strong.'

'What about weights and so on?' asked Andreas.

'I've got all the kit we'll need in the car.'

Item by item, he went through this with them until they were all certain that nothing had been overlooked. 'I've also bought four pairs of night-vision goggles. The moon's on the wane, but there should be some ambient light. The routine is going to have to be two of us on the dump-and-splash detail, two on stag. We're going to need the comms kits, warm clothing, sensible footwear, rations and a cover-story in case we're bumped by the local police. There's no reason to suppose that's going to happen, but just in case it does – if someone saw us, for example, and thought we were burglars – I think we should leave all the weapons here. Explaining away a midnight walk by the river is one thing, explaining away the fact that we're armed to the teeth is quite another.'

He looked around questioningly. The others nodded.

'Ideally we get to the place about three this afternoon, park up, and have a recce. Then we finalise details and wait till dark. I've included a couple of sleeping bags and bivvies in the kit so that if we're challenged we can say that we're looking for somewhere to camp. The first thing we've got to do though – and do fast – is buy ourselves some sensible outdoor clothing. It's Sunday, so it's going to have to be supermarket stuff. There's a place on the Périphérique about fifteen minutes away.'

On the journey, Slater made a point of sharing the lead car with Leon. Not to avoid Eve, but to try and get to know a fellow team-member with whom, indirectly, he felt he had much in common. Leon drove, having devised the route to the disposal location. He ran the Mercedes fast but with care, ensuring that the Peugeot was no more than a car or two behind them at any time.

At the same time both he and Slater scanned the traffic at intervals for signs that they were being followed. Their fear – expressed by neither of them but felt by both – was that the French DGSE might be on to them. Had the DGSE been watching Fanon-Khayat too? Was there an anti-Serbian element in the French secret services – there was certainly an anti-British element.

At this moment, carrying the body with them as they were, the team were acutely vulnerable, and they knew it. One nosy traffic-cop asking them to unlock the trunk and they were finished. To Slater even the flat suburban countryside was spooked territory. The sooner Fanon-Khayat's body was deep beneath the mud-brown surface of the Seine, the better.

To distract himself, and to pass the time, Slater asked Leon about his life.

Leon's story was an unusual one. After leaving school on the Indian Ocean island of Mauritius he had found himself in some sort of 'trouble' – upon which he chose not to elaborate – and had worked his passage to Europe in the kitchens of a cruise liner. Poorly paid domestic and 'protection' work had followed in France, and when the Marseilles pimp who had hired him was arrested and imprisoned on charges of corrupting minors Leon had hitchhiked to Castelnaudary and offered his services to the Foreign Legion. After a short, sharp initiation period at Aubagne which he described as 'interesting', Leon had been dispatched to Canjuers and Orange to undergo basic training and selection. Six months and several violent beatings later he had passed out top of his cadre, and had chosen to join the Legion's parachute regiment at Calvi in Corsica.

There, in counterpoint to the chronic drunkenness and whoring enjoyed by his fellow Legionaries, Leon studied contemporary European history by correspondence course. To make his studies more challenging, and to improve his English, he signed up with the Open University.

The Deuxième Régiment Etranger de Parachutistes did not discourage Leon in these academic activities. Within two years he had been promoted, and as a Junior NCO accompanied the 2nd REP to Rwanda where they were involved in the covert training of militia forces.

Repelled by the future implications of this policy Leon transferred to the Legion's 3rd Infantry Regiment in French Guyana, whose nominal task was to guard the Ariane Rocket launch site at Kourou. There, having qualified as a jungle warfare instructor, he earned French citizenship by serving out his five-year contract with the Legion. At about the same time he was awarded a BA by the Open University. His plan on leaving the Legion was to train as a schoolteacher, but things did not quite work out that way.

'I went back to France . . .' he began, but Slater silenced him with a gesture.

'I may just be paranoid,' he said, 'but I think we might have picked up a tail. There's a large grey or blue car I've just seen which I'm pretty sure was there about fifteen minutes back.'

'Well, this is a motorway,' said Leon. 'What kind of car?'

'Looks like some big German thing. An Opel or something – it was too far away to get a make on.'

'And it was . . .'

'It was just at the extreme of visibility. I might be imagining things, but it just seemed to me that it was tucked in perfectly for a long-range tail.' He shrugged.

'Let's pull off at the next exit,' said Leon. 'See if we can get a fix on it. Why don't you ring the others, warn them that's what we're going to do?'

Slater did so, and five minutes later they left the motorway by a slip-road. As they waited at traffic-lights on the exit roundabout. Slater watched the passing motorway traffic. There was no sign of the car he thought he had seen. The lights turned green and they progressed a kilometre up a country road to a lay-by, where they drew to a halt. Behind them the Peugeot did the same.

'Let's give it five minutes,' said Leon. 'After that I'm going to get nervous. The last thing we need is for some bored cop to drive past and start asking questions.'

The two cars sat motionless in the afternoon heat. Cars drove past at intervals, but none resembled a grey or blue Opel, and Slater began to wonder if his senses had been overtuned to danger. When on enemy territory, as they undoubtedly were now, the mind had a habit of conjuring up enemies. At the same time you disregarded your instincts at your peril. The line was a fine one.

'We should move,' said Leon eventually. 'We're beginning to push our luck.'

Slater agreed. They returned to the motorway and drove for five minutes in silence.

'So you decided to train as a teacher,' he began eventually, still watching the wing-mirror.

At the wheel Leon nodded. 'Yeah,' he said. 'That was the plan . . .'

Returning to France and hooking up with a former REP colleague in a bar in the Rue St Denis in Paris, Leon allowed himself to be talked into driving the getaway car for an armed robbery. The attempt to hijack a wages delivery-van went badly wrong, with a security guard and a gang-member both fatally wounded in the firefight which ensued. As the unarmed driver, Leon got off comparatively lightly, and ended up serving less than three years.

It seemed long enough at the time, however. The twenty-three-year-old ex-Legionary served his sentence at Clairvaux prison, some 250 kilometres east of Paris. The former monastery, a notorious dumping-ground for hard cases, is often described as the French Alcatraz, and the regime was brutal. To make matters worse Leon realised that with better planning – planning he himself would have been happy to undertake – the robbery attempt would have worked perfectly and no one would have got hurt.

In between reading books of political theory in his cell, Leon passed the time by planning – and mentally executing – increasingly complex and ingenious crimes. Or, as he himself prefered it, 'events'. Packed into the jail were experts in fraud, larceny, embezzlement, kidnapping, drug-smuggling and every other field of illegal activity. Leon consulted them all. He would submit imaginary scenarios to these criminal tutors – scenarios detailing companies to be defrauded, banks to be robbed, officials to be kidnapped, and rivals to be executed – and invite them to pick holes in his plans.

For the first six months the experts were able to suggest better solutions than Leon, but not thereafter. When interviewed by the prison rehabilitation board at the end of his second year, he informed his questioners that he intended to retrain as a risk assessor in the private security sector. One of the board must have had connections in the field, for a month later he was requested by the prison governor to undertake a voluntary 'exercise'. On the basis of given data, he was asked to assess the vulnerability to armed assault of a microprocessor fabrication plant in Bordeaux. He was given pencils, paper and the use of an office.

Within forty-eight hours he had produced a fully-budgeted plan which, if put into execution, would have seen the company in question relieved of 30 million francs' worth of stock for an outlay of less than FF750,000. Although he had not been asked to do so, Leon also produced a detailed proposal for the selling-on of the stolen microprocessors.

He was thanked for his efforts, and heard no more. A week later, however, he found himself on one of the prison's coveted computer-training courses, and on completion of his sentence was passed the name of a personnel officer employed by the Paris branch of a multinational security group named Nordstrom. A year's training in their offices at La Défense was followed by a two-year posting to London, where he was head-hunted.

Even by the standards of the Cadre it was a curious recruitment. Leon was walking home from the Nordstrom office in Sloane Street to his flat in Victoria. It was a five-minute journey by bus, but he liked to clear his head after the overheated fug of the office. It had been a long and dizzyingly dull day – he had been compiling a report on the security needs of a private hospital in Marylebone blessed with an 'upscale, high-profile clientele'.

A woman fell into step beside him – a dark-haired woman in a leather jacket, jeans and Doc Marten boots – and invited him to join her for a drink in the Grosvenor Hotel at Victoria Station. At first he assumed she was a prostitute, but when she asked after a couple of Nordstrom employees – former MI5 officers whose names were very far from being in the public domain – he started to pay attention.

'Ellis?' asked Slater.

'Ellis,' Leon confirmed. 'You've heard the stories, then?'

'I've heard how she died.'

Leon nodded, and was silent for a moment.

Ellis had led him to the hotel's Travellers Bar, ordered them a gin and tonic each without bothering to ask what he wanted, and set out her stall. She represented a co-ordinating wing of the Foreign Office, she told him in rapid and fluent French, and she had been empowered to offer him a job. Her department needed someone with specialist military skills, the ability to plan and execute covert operations overseas, and an intimate knowledge of the French underworld. The last was perhaps the most important – the service had assets on French soil, of course, but they were not . . .

Not *bien câblés*? Leon had suggested. Not . . . connected?

No, she had admitted. They weren't. The complex web that linked the French military, mercenary and criminal underworlds was not one that the service she represented had been able to negotiate with ease. They constantly found themselves beholden to the DGSE – the French secret service – for entrées to that world, and the way things were, frankly, they were increasingly reluctant to do so.

Ah, Slater said. Right.

In return for joining her department, Ellis had continued – peremptorily draining her gin and tonic – the Crown was offering him British citizenship, a substantial drop in salary, and the guarantee of acute stress and physical danger. And that was about it.

Leon had agreed almost immediately. At twenty-eight he was not ready to grow stale in an office – whatever the material benefits of his position. He wanted to deploy his old skills. He wanted the thudding excitements and terrors of operational life. The fact that he had not been born French and was free of conventional French loyalties and prejudices, he guessed, had probably encouraged them to approach him.

And so, for the second time in his life, he told Slater, he had assumed new citizenship. He had joined the Cadre seven years ago, become a British national, and never regretted his decision. He even liked British cooking – it was next to impossible, he claimed, to find a decent kebab or vindaloo in France.

Almost the deciding factor, however, had been the

charismatic personality of his recruiter. Something about the lean, leather-jacketed figure, some wild and fundamental nonconformity, had told him that this was the organisation he had been looking for all his life.

'Supposing you'd been approached by Eve?' Slater asked him. 'Or by Andreas or someone else? Would you still have joined?'

'It's academic, man. I did join – that's all that matters. As you'll have realised there are some very good sides to this job and some very weird and freaky ones. But I am what I am, just as you are what you are. If you're good enough to be offered the job and mad enough to accept it, then by definition, brother, you are right for it.'

Slater laughed. 'I guess so.'

A few minutes before two o'clock they swung northwards off the motorway towards Bonnières-sur-Seine, and Slater saw the river to their left – deep, grey and forbidding. At that point the Seine looked about a hundred metres across, and Slater understood instantly what Leon had meant when he said that swimming the corpse out was very much a last resort.

Pulling off the N13, the two cars followed the sign for Freneuse and Joigny. The minor road led them past a paper-mill and cement-works, both of them with gates padlocked for the weekend. Soon they were driving between stands of pine-forest, with the sun splashing the road only sporadically. Outside the car, after the background roar of the motorway, all was oppressively silent.

'The temperature's dropped,' said Leon. 'I'm glad we bought all that outdoor clothing. It could be a cold night.'

For the next fifteen minutes they barely saw another car. From time to time, parallel to the road, they caught sight of the steely, baleful glint of the river. Joigny, as Leon had suspected, proved to be little more than a collection of farm buildings. There was a church and a small village shop, but both appeared untenanted. The only sign of life was a new-looking Renault Espace parked outside one of the farmhouses.

'Paris plates,' said Leon. 'Well-off Parisians like their kids to watch TV and play computer games in the countryside at weekends. They'll assume we're scouting around for property too – that or we're a pair of antique dealers looking for agricultural scrap to flog to rural-theme restaurants.'

'A mixed-race gay couple, perhaps,' suggested Slater. 'Intent on perverting their children?'

Leon laughed. 'They'd probably rather the truth than that. Did you catch the National Front posters on that last motorway bridge?'

As the map had indicated, the track petered out a kilometre or so beyond the village. Leon and Andreas parked the cars, and the four of them climbed out and stretched. They were all wearing jeans, gumboots and hiking jackets. Leon was carrying a knapsack containing biscuits, a flask of coffee and other bits and pieces. Andreas was smoking. In a group, as Leon had intended, they looked like a bunch of middle-class Parisians intent on local exploration.

A damp path between saw-edged reeds continued ahead of them. Locking the cars, they followed Andreas and his cigarette. The path led down to a weeded towpath and the broad sweep of the river.

'We'll need a bit of weight,' observed Eve, eyeing the remorseless flow of the water and the distant bank.

'We've got a bit of weight,' said Leon. 'As we're going to discover tonight when we try and haul it all up here from the car.'

Six or seven minutes later the path led them away from the river, between two dark stands of trees, and back to the bank. Here the river widened on the bend to almost twice its normal breadth. There was a locked boat-house, with a peeling green-painted door, and beyond it, as the map had promised, a jetty extended a clear fifty metres into the bay. In the distance, a couple of kilometres away, the steeple of the church at Thieux was visible between the trees.

'It looks good,' breathed Eve. 'It looks very good.'

Several wooden and fibreglass boats were moored alongside the jetty, and deep grey water swirled around its heavy supporting piles.

'It looks deep,' said Andreas. 'That's the main thing.'

They spent an hour there, working out the final details. With a ball of fishing line and a lead plumb, Leon took a series of depth soundings along the length of the jetty. The deepest point, which he estimated at seven metres, was shortly before the end. The river was very full, but unlikely – they all agreed – to fall more than three metres in the near future. And that would be drastic.

'One more thing,' murmured Leon, and took a plastic bag and a knife from the knapsack.

'What now?' asked Andreas.

'Watch, little bro, and learn,' said Leon quietly, taking a slab of raw steak from the plastic bag. Carefully, he cut off a cube of meat and tied it to the end of his fishing line, then lowered it into the water, where the lead plumb took it straight to the bottom. After ten minutes he very slowly drew it back through the powerful current, and the others were amazed to see a small black freshwater crayfish clinging by one angry claw to the meat.

'I think we can count on our man being pretty unrecognisable pretty soon,' said Leon. 'There's nothing those little mothers like more than a side of meat.'

'Dental records?' asked Eve.

In reply, Leon wordlessly removed a pair of blunt-nosed pliers from his pocket.

'Oh Mama!' said Eve.

'You did say you wanted to come,' Leon said reasonably, tossing the remains of the steak into the river. 'Coffee and shortbread fingers, anyone?'

Back at the cars, once they had thoroughly rehearsed their movements for the night ahead, they discussed whether they would attract more attention by remaining in the vicinity or by pulling back into a local town and returning after dark.

The final decision was to pull back. Cars obviously came and went along the Joigny road, Leon argued, but few remained until dark. They would disappear until 11pm.

Returning to the cars, they made their way to Vernon, twenty-five kilometres away. According to Leon's research the town was always full of tourists at weekends due to the presence, at nearby Giverny, of the house and gardens of the impressionist artist Monet.

His research was accurate. The place was very busy, with American, British and Japanese accents much in evidence. At Eve's suggestion the four of them behaved like conventional tourists, booking themselves dinner at a small restaurant in town and attending a guided tour of the artist's house and gardens.

They stayed there until the house closed at 5.30. At the museum shop Eve bought two tea-towels showing details of Monet's famous Waterlily paintings, which Andreas described as 'a nice role-playing touch'.

'We need them for the office,' Eve said severely. 'That area round the kettle gets really disgusting at times.'

Returning to Vernon they walked idly through the town and alongside the river for a couple of kilometres. Returning as the light began to fade, they installed themselves in a café. The minutes crawled past. None of them was able to dispel fully the thought of the night's work lying ahead of them, and in consequence they found that they did not have a great deal to say to each other. Slater found that he was ravenous, and suspected that the others were too.

Finally it was nine o'clock and they presented themselves at the restaurant. They lingered over the meal, which featured local speciality dishes of freshwater crayfish and braised pork, and shared a large carafe of red wine. For four adults on holiday in the French countryside to have gone without alcohol altogether, they agreed, would only have drawn attention to themselves. As the designated non-drivers, Slater and Andreas also ordered Calvados to accompany their coffees.

'Right,' said Leon, as they stepped out into the night air. 'Let's do it.'

Climbing back into the cars, they drove back the way they had come. Once they were in the Roche-Guyon forest, Leon dipped the headlights of the Mercedes and dropped the speed to forty kilometres an hour, damping the engine-noise down to a faint hum. They proceeded in near-silence along the pine-needled track, and as they approached Joigny, Leon halved the speed again.

At the house with the Renault Espace outside, upstairs lights were showing. 'They might wonder who we are,' said Slater, 'but they won't come out and investigate. They'll just make sure the front door's double-locked.'

'You saying that because you think it's true?' asked Leon. 'Or because you want it to be true?'

'Bit of both,' admitted Slater. 'But what are they going to do? Ring the police and say two cars have driven past their house and could someone come and investigate?'

Soon they were at the end of the track. The temperature had dropped considerably in the course of the half-hour drive, and as they quietly climbed from the cars they were glad of the warm outdoor clothing they had brought. The interior lights of both cars had been switched off, so there were no sudden bursts of yellow light when the doors opened. Instead, a clear star-filled sky and a nail-paring moon provided a faint illumination of the desolate waterside scene.

Unhurriedly, taking it in turns to keep lookout through a pair of night-vision goggles, they fitted and tested the Motorola comms kits. Leon then filled a long zip-up holdall with the various items of kit they were going to need, and called them together. For the purposes of this particular exercise, Slater noted, he seemed to have taken charge.

'OK, listen in,' he whispered. 'I'll do the actual disposal with Neil, as we planned. Andreas, you go first and do a quick recce of the location – Neil and I will follow with the trunk on your all-clear. Eve, you stay here and watch our backs.'

Five minutes later, hearing Andreas's all-clear in their earpieces, Slater and Leon lifted the trunk. Neither was wearing the night-vision goggles;

although they were the best Leon had been able to find they were still fairly cumbersome. Instead they were trusting their night-vision. Slowly, they carried the heavy trunk along the mud path between walls of reeds which sighed in the faint night breeze. After a couple of minutes the carrying handle was biting painfully into Slater's fingers, but if the slighter-built Leon could manage it, then so could he. Eventually though, they lowered the trunk by mutual agreement and swapped places.

'Heavy fucker, isn't he?' Leon murmured, shaking out his fingers.

'Not for long,' answered Slater.

It took them more than ten minutes to reach the bay, where Andreas was waiting for them. Carefully, in a pre-agreed position among the trees and well back from the track, they lowered the trunk to the ground. From the cars, Eve reported the all-clear.

'Keep watching,' Leon ordered Andreas. 'Neil, you cut back to the Merc and get the other bag down here.'

Quickly, his senses alert and his night-vision at full aperture, Slater jogged back along the path. When he got to the cars he couldn't see Eve, but knew that she was lying up in the reeds, watching him. Unlocking the Mercedes he pulled out a heavy 1.5 metre zip-up bag, and swung the carrying strap over his shoulder. Steadying the bag at his side, he jogged back. As he rejoined Leon he felt sweat running down his back and fought to control the heavy rasp of his breathing.

Steadying himself, he put on his night-vision

goggles, heard the faint whir as they started up. Leon, he saw, had unlocked the trunk. He had removed the body and pulled off the two sleeping-bags, and was cutting off the clothes with a knife. As he hacked and sawed, a dank smell rose from beneath his hands.

Slater, who had had to undertake similarly unpleasant exercises in the past, unzipped the bag and removed a roll of wide-mesh chicken wire. When this was unrolled and flattened on the ground it made up a rectangle of one metre by five. When Leon had cut most of the clothing from the front of the body, the two men manhandled it on to the wire lengthways.

'Pliers,' murmured Leon.

Slater removed them from the bag. The former legionnaire, he mused, seemed as familiar as he himself was with the grim routine. To make the job easier he forced the dead man's jaws apart with his hands. Slowly, with a sighing exhalation, the mouth eased open.

'Thanks, man,' whispered Leon.

As Slater held the mouth open, Leon knelt behind the head, and with some difficulty extracted half a dozen teeth from the corpse's lower jaw with the pliers. Repositioning himself on the chest, quivering with the effort, he extracted half a dozen more from the upper.

Collecting the teeth, Slater hurled them as far as he could into the river – their entry into the water was barely audible. Taking the knife Slater then stabbed downwards into the guts and sawed a long transverse cut. There was a low belch of escaping gas, and a stench of such foulness that both men involuntarily jerked their heads away.

'Should save your crayfish a few days' work,' Slater explained.

'Thanks, brother,' said Leon, taking a three-metre chain and padlock from the bag. 'They'll be grateful.'

Wrapping the disembowelled and half-naked corpse and the cut-off clothes in chicken-wire, the two men quickly threaded the chain through the mesh until the corpse was completely contained by the chicken wire. Pulling the chain tight, Leon padlocked it to itself.

From the zip-bag, Slater then took a 10 kg grapnel anchor. Unwrapping it from its towel, he shackled it to the chain binding the chicken-wire, and laid it on the corpse's chest.

Leon thumbed the transmit button on his comms set. 'Are we all clear, Eve? Over.'

'All clear. Over.'

'Andreas? Over.'

'All clear here. Over.'

'Thanks. Over and out.'

'Right.' He turned to Slater. 'Let's go.'

Lifting the mummy-shaped remains, the two men moved at a crouch across the towpath and along the jetty. Near the end they lowered the body to the planking. Below them, Slater sensed the dark, rushing mass of the river.

'OK,' he whispered. 'On the count of three.'

Lifting the weighted bundle by the chains, they lowered the remains of Antoine Fanon-Khayat to the black surface of the water. There was no splash.

Leon thumbed his transmitter switch. 'Job done, people. Over and out.'

For a moment, exhausted, they sat there at the end of the jetty.

'I'm impressed,' said Slater. 'You thought of everything.'

'Thanks,' said Leon, throwing the knife, the pliers, and the plumb-line far out into the river. 'Now let's all get the fuck out of here.'

On the towpath, they reconnected with Andreas. The three of them were light-headed with relief now – whatever happened at least they didn't have a corpse in the back of the car.

Ducking under the trees, Andreas picked up one end of the trunk. Slater took the other. As it now contained only a duvet, two sleeping bags and the zip-up holdall the effort involved was not great. Andreas lit a cigarette, and the party moved jauntily back along the path. As they approached the parking place Eve stepped from the reeds, her night-vision goggles still in place.

'Talk about a herd of bloody elephants,' she said reprovingly. 'Honestly, guys!'

'We're tourists, lady,' said Andreas. 'What do we know?'

As they approached the Peugeot and the Mercedes, Eve and Leon pulled out their keys and activated the remote unlocking devices. Opening the Peugeot boot Slater and Andreas slung the trunk inside. Andreas flicked the stub of his cigarette to the ground and trod on it.

'See what I mean about this job?' he grinned. 'Piece of piss, isn't it?'

'I'm not sure I'd call it that,' said Slater. 'I hate these fucking disposals.'

'But you're glad you joined, aren't you? I mean, I was right to tell them that you were the guy for the job?'

Slater nodded. The other man was a dim outline beside him. 'Yeah. You were right. And I haven't really thanked you for that. When we get back to the land of proper beer I'll buy you a pint or ten.'

Andreas punched Slater's shoulder. 'It's a deal! And just in case you're wondering, Cadre operations aren't always as fucking seat-of-the-pants as this one has been. Usually we just whip it in, whip it out and wipe it.'

Slater shrugged. 'We've done what we came to do. That seems good enough to me.'

And they had. Fanon-Khayat had vanished from the face of the earth, and the disc was back at the OP under the watchful eye of Chris. To be precise, it was in the Bottega Veneta bag that Eve had bought for Debbie. It shouldn't have been beyond the capabilities of six resourceful agents to get an Italian handbag from Paris to London.

Slater exhaled. Fuck, but he was glad they'd got rid of that body.

Slater was just turning to find Eve, and perhaps to

323

squeeze her hand in the dark, when a torch shone directly and blindingly into his eyes. Several others flicked on around them until it became apparent that they were surrounded. Slater's first irritated assumption was that this was some kind of local posse suspicious of their night-time activities, but a second glance drained from him every last vestige of optimism. The torches, he saw, were attached to suppressed MP5 Heckler and Koch machine guns. One of the lights behind him illuminated the figure in whose unwavering sights he now stood. A figure he recognised immediately as Branca Nikolic.

'*Alors,*' she said. '*Monsieur Neil . . . Clissold.*'

This was a different Branca. Like her four companions she was was wearing a leaf-patterned windproof smock, combat trousers and hiking boots. No trace now of the fashion-victim or the party-girl. At a pinch, but for the MP5s and the unwavering stares, she and her team might have been returning from a weekend's birdwatching.

'Madame Fanon-Khayat!' said Slater, his heart lurching in his chest. 'How are you?'

In reply she raised her weapon to her shoulder. 'You have something belonging to my husband,' she said. Her voice was like gravel, and strongly French-accented. 'A compact disc. Where is it?'

Slater said nothing. He felt sick. Beside him, Eve, Andreas and Leon stood in expressionless silence.

'We know why you come here, Clissold, and we know you have just . . . sunk Antoine's body in this river. Of that *je m'en fous* – I'm not interested. He was a stupid and greedy man and you have saved us the trouble of getting rid of him ourselves. *Je vous remercie.*'

She spoke several words in a language Slater assumed to be Serbian, and the others smiled.

'Who are your friends?' Slater asked her.

'They are loyal soldiers of my country, and they are here to take what is theirs. The disc, Mr Clissold.'

'I don't know what you are talking about.'

'I'm talking about the disc you were in the process of stealing from my husband when I came into the flat, Mr Clissold. The disc you finally stole from him after you murdered him in the Hotel Inter-Lux at Roissy. Now you have a choice. You give me the disc right now – and we have brought the hardware to verify it – or you give us the woman and exchange her later for the disc.'

Could they take them out? Slater wondered fleetingly. If the four of them went in fast and hard and without concern for their own safety? Would there be a sufficient element of surprise? He dismissed the idea out of hand – this was obviously a highly trained, highly professional team. They had played it perfectly, with a silent and invisible approach and clever tactical positioning. As things stood, each of the Serbians had a clear field of fire on each of the Cadre members. Any attempt to rush them would lead instantly to fatalities.

'I told you, we don't have any disc,' said Slater. His voice was calm but inwardly he was screaming.

We're blown. They know fucking everything. They've followed us everywhere.

In response, Branca Nikolic flicked off the safety catch of her MP5, marched over to Eve, and jammed the muzzle of the weapon's silencer under the point of Eve's jaw. A second team-member joined her, pressing his weapon into Eve's back.

'OK,' said Branca. 'This is the deal. You have thirty-six hours to produce the disc, and as I said, we have the hardware for instant verification. If you do not hand over the disc to me in the bar of the Hotel Grand Exelmans at midday on Tuesday – time enough to get it back from London if necessary – this woman will be killed. Evidence also will be made available to the police implicating you, this gentleman here' – she nodded at Andreas – 'and the British Secret Intelligence Service in the murder of my husband. *Compris?*'

Slater shrugged. He caught Eve's eye. She looked angry but unafraid, and held his gaze even when Branca jabbed her painfully in the throat with her weapon.

'We'll be there,' he said, hoping that Eve understood that his words were intended for her. 'Don't you worry, we'll be there.'

'Good,' said Branca, and then spoke in Serbian again.

A member of the team accompanying her walked over to the Peugeot and the Mercedes. One by one, he let down all the tyres until both cars were flat on their wheelrims.

'We don't want to slow you down more than we have to,' Branca explained, 'but we do have to take this woman away with us. Professional to professional, I'm sure you'll understand. And understand one other thing, Mr Clissold, if that is your name. Understand that even after all that has happened my country has no wish for lasting enmity with yours. We have been allies before, we can be allies again.'

Surprised, Slater met her hard blue eyes and inclined his head wordlessly. This was a very different Branca to the one he had met in her husband's apartment. What the hell kind of game was she playing? She clearly occupied a position of some authority if she was in charge of a team as switched on as this one appeared to be.

They had to be Serbian RDB agents, thought Slater despondently. It must have been these jokers who had been tailing the Cadre cars up the motorway. The fact that his instincts had been proved right on that particular point gave him no pleasure at all.

Branca raised her hand in a quasi military salute. 'Until we meet again, gentlemen. Au revoir.'

And with that, accompanied by Eve, all of the team except one withdrew into the darkness. The remaining man kept Slater, Leon and Andreas covered with his MP5. After fifteen minutes, as the trio stood there in helpless, dazzled silence, they heard the faint, far-distant sound of a vehicle starting up. It came slowly closer, and then halted out of sight. The guard backed away, keeping his torch and weapon trained on the three men, and at the last moment turned and ran into the darkness, where none of the three was inclined to follow him. They heard a door open and close – the vehicle was showing no lights, either internally or externally – a crunching acceleration, and then silence.

'Fuck,' said Slater.

THIRTEEN

None of them enjoyed the night that followed. Leon called up Chris on his mobile, and outlining the position in a few terse sentences, gave her their map co-ordinates and asked her to arrange for a breakdown service to come out and inflate their tyres.

They had been waiting for twenty minutes when a man holding a torch arrived on foot. At his side, held on a short leash, was an agitated-sounding Dobermann Pinscher guard-dog.

Vandals had let down their tyres, Leon explained. They were waiting for assistance.

The word 'vandals' had the effect that he hoped: to distract attention from what they had been doing there in the first place. The man offered to ring the police – there had been other incidents, he said. Personally he suspected that drug users frequented the area. He had bought a property up the road a couple of years ago under the impression that he had found a tranquil corner for his family to enjoy at weekends, but it had not been long before they started discovering the condoms and the used syringes on the towpath. 'What do you say to your children,' he asked them, 'when they say, Papa, what's this?'

Leon admitted that he had no idea. The culprits, he said, were probably *zonards* – occupants of the public housing estates which ringed Paris. There were, he added mischievously, a lot of immigrants among them . . .

The householder agreed. Wherever immigrants established themselves, problems followed. He had nothing against them personally, but there were just too many of them. It was a cultural question – a question of standards.

Eventually, in a warm glow of nationalist outrage, and having failed to register that Leon himself was one of the 'problematic' immigrants in question, the man led his dog back to Joigny.

The breakdown service arrived twenty minutes later from Mantes-la-Jolie, and Leon settled their considerable bill with cash.

'They were RDB, for sure,' Leon told Chris an hour and a half later. 'My guess is that they were in Paris to find out who he was doing the Ondine business with, so that they could knock out the middle-man and take control. And he'd obviously boasted – perhaps to Branca – that he had a disc containg material so damaging to Britain that it could be used to negotiate the return of Karadzic.'

'So what do you reckon Branca's part is in all this?' asked Chris.

Leon shrugged. 'My guess is that the bimbo act was strictly for her husband's benefit. That was the real Branca we saw last night. She's an RDB agent like her father, and the whole marriage thing was a set-up to tie Fanon-Khayat to Serbia.'

Slater agreed. 'She certainly looked as switched-on as the rest of them this evening – I can't imagine Eve's that easy to creep up on. And she looked pretty familiar with that MP5.'

'Yes,' agreed Chris. 'I think we have to agree that you saw the real Branca Nikolic this evening. What she's doing with this Miko Pasquale guy – the dope dealer – I'm less sure of. That's where Terry is right now: watching Pasquale's flat.'

'Any joy?' asked Slater.

'No. There's no one there at the present minute. He's the only connection we've got to Branca, though. For obvious reasons she hasn't gone back to the apartment over the road. My guess is that the RDB team followed Fanon-Khayat to the hotel, bribed some staff-member to point him out, discovered that his place had been taken by Andreas and that Andreas was hanging out with a *Monsieur* Clissold and a *Mademoiselle* Benbow and . . .' She shrugged. 'They've been on to us ever since. From what you say they certainly know that we're based here at the Grand Exelmans.'

Leon nodded in agreement. 'I'm sure you're right. I also think we should look pretty closely at our own counter-surveillance efforts. We've been pretty badly shown up here. The only one of us who spotted anything was Neil.'

There was silence. Leon had said what everyone else had been thinking – that they all shared the responsibility for Eve's capture.

'So what do you propose?' asked Slater. 'They've probably got us staked out right now.'

'There's a good chance they don't know about Terry – he's only been in and out once since they've been on to us – and I'm almost certain that they don't know about me, because I haven't left the room. For the moment all they know is that you, Andreas and Eve use the place. It won't take them long to figure out that there are more of us here, though, because if they know the names that you checked into the Inter-Lux with – Clissold, Benbow, et cetera – and have found out that there's no one of that name registered here . . .'

'And they might have gone to work on Eve, too,' said Slater grimly.

'That is a possibility, yes. I've spoken to Manderson and agreed that we'll leave here tomorrow morning, get the hire company to pick up the cars, and regroup later in the day – this time, hopefully, without being followed. Meanwhile, Terry keeps watch for Pasquale, and as soon as he finds him a couple of you guys go in and force him to make a meet with Branca. We're watching the RV, and we'll follow Branca back to wherever she's holed up with her RDB mates – and Eve. Then we go in and extract Eve.'

'And all this in twenty-four hours?' asked Andreas dubiously.

'We have no choice,' said Chris. 'Manderson says there's no question of handing over that disc on Tuesday. Even in return for Eve.'

'That's fucking outrageous!' Slater exploded. 'They could kill her. They probably *will* kill her.' Grabbing the room-service menu from a table, he hurled it against the wall.

The others regarded him in silence.

'Look,' Slater continued angrily, 'I may be just a thick ex-squaddie, but are the pictures on that disc really such a big fucking deal? I mean I know chopped-off ears and heads don't look good, but that Cambodia stuff is old history. Nobody's admitted that guys from the Regiment were training the Khmer Rouge, but nobody's exactly denied it either. It's certainly not going to come as a shock to anyone in the know.'

One by one the others turned away. Only Christ met his eyes. 'I'm afraid it's a question of "ours is not to reason why",' she said quietly. 'For whatever reason we have to hold on to the disc and get it to Manderson. That's non-negotiable.'

Slowly, and with an effort, Slater brought himself under control. 'So how do we play it?' he asked.

'Leon gets on the phone to suppliers – we're going to need some automatic weaponry in case it comes to an assault. You and Andreas sleep. If anything comes in from Terry, I'll wake you. There's nothing else we can do.'

Slater nodded. Chris was right. He glanced at her. Even close up there was a kind of deliberately cultivated ordinariness about her. But Chris was not, Slater knew, an ordinary person. She could hardly have slept over the last couple of days, but continued to dispense good sense and cool judgement. When they had returned, stunned by their reversal from the forest of La Roche-Guyon, it had been to find that the wheels had continued to turn, that contingency plans had been made. Every group, Slater had learnt, needed a figure like this – a co-ordinator who held things together by attending to the details that fell outside the remit of the specialists.

Her early career, Leon had told him, had been spent in MI5, as had Terry's. Their shared speciality had been the tracking of terrorists in mainland Britain, and their surveillance skills had been legendary, as more than one PIRA active service unit had discovered to its cost. Their great gift was for self-effacement – for making themselves invisible. You could probably spend an hour with them in a station waiting-room, Slater mused, and then climb on to your train convinced that you'd been alone all along. It was a rare skill.

Slater took Terry's room. For a long while he lay awake, thinking of Eve and how different she had looked and sounded the night before.

'Sometimes I just need to escape and be human again,' she had whispered as she settled herself against him. 'Will you be my escape route?'

'I will,' he promised her. 'I'll be anything you want me to be. But what about our working together? Isn't that going to be a problem?'

'Not if we don't make it one. We're just going to have to be very cool about it all. Keep all . . . all of this outside of the Cadre. Because if it touches on the way we work, people won't like it. It'll unbalance the team. So we don't let it touch on the way we work. The moment we walk out this door tomorrow morning the whole thing snap-freezes.'

'And how will I know when you next . . . need to escape?' he asked.

'You'll know,' she answered, her voice a dreamy smile. 'I promise you, you'll know.'

He woke to Andreas's urgent shaking of his shoulder. For a moment he had no idea where he was, and then the room took shape around him. He glanced at his watch; it was 4am.

'The drug-guy's turned up,' said Andreas, stuffing Eve's Glock 9mm into the waistband of his trousers and handing Slater the silenced Sig Sauer rescued from the Hotel Inter-Lux. 'We're going to go and shake him down.'

Slater was still wearing his outdoor clothes from the day before, and quickly pulled on the walking boots he had bought in the Mammouth supermarket. They weren't ideal, but if there was going to be a fight he didn't want to be caught in a pair of thin-soled loafers. The Sig Sauer went into a pocket of the hiking jacket.

'We'll take the Peugeot,' said Leon. 'I'll drive.'

They exited by the hotel's side-entrance, knowing that they were being watched by RDB agents and quite possibly by the French DGSE too, and made their way to the car.

Leon drove slowly at first – sedately almost, as if unaware he was being observed. Andreas and Slater quickly identified the twin black Citroëns that were following them – no great achievement given the sparseness of the traffic at that time of night.

From the Boulevard Exelmans Leon swung south-east on to the Avenue de Versailles, and from there, still maintaining a decorous speed, turned right across the Pont Mirabeau. Once across the bridge, however, he put his foot down hard. They screamed up the Rue de la Convention, swung hard left, and entered a warren of tiny interconnecting streets, at which point Leon turned off the headlights. After throwing the Peugeot down a dozen streets so narrow that Slater would have reckoned them non-negotiable, Leon swung the passenger side of the car up on to the pavement and came to an abrupt halt. They were in a small, unlit square, one of several cars grouped around an equestrian statue.

'Down!' hissed Leon.

The three of them crouched on the floor of the car for fifteen minutes, during which time no other cars entered the square. Eventually, cautiously, Leon restarted the Peugeot and they made their way to the broad and still comparatively busy Boulevard St

Germain. Five minutes later, certain that they had lost their earlier pursuers, they recrossed the river by the Pont de Sully. Soon they were in the eleventh arrondissement, parking a couple of hundred metres down the street and round the corner from the building containing Miko Pasquale's apartment.

Materialising from the shadows, Terry climbed into the back seat, carrying a crumpled salami sandwich and an open bottle of wine in a paper bag. He looked vaguely disreputable – a borderline alcoholic, perhaps, who had taken to drinking in the streets.

'Pasquale came back in about half an hour ago, alone. The lights went on in the second-floor flat for about ten minutes and then went out. I think we can assume he's asleep. I've watched half a dozen people going in and out of the place, and I've got the keypad code for the gate . . .'

'Have you tested it?' asked Andreas.

'No, but from where I was on the bench back there I was able to see people punching it in. I couldn't see the actual numbers, but I could see that the code went top row, bottom row, and then middle row twice. When I walked past you could see the finger marks around the one, the nine, the four and the five. So it's either 1945 or 1954.'

Quickly he fitted on one of the Motorola comms kits. Leon put on the other.

'OK, give me five minutes to get back in place, and I'll give you the go-ahead. You all three going in?'

Leon nodded. 'Yes we are. And we're going to need

you to stay out here in case we have any visitors. It's not impossible Branca might show up.'

'OK. Wait for my word.'

Slater checked the Sig Sauer, ensured that he had a spare clip of ammunition.

'Clear to go,' came Terry's message. 'Over.'

The three men climbed from the car and sauntered unhurriedly up the street, as if returning home from a long weekend. When they got to the gate they pulled on gloves and Slater punched 1954 into the keypad. Nothing. He keyed in 1945, and with a muted click the gate unlocked and the three pushed their way into the small courtyard.

Pasquale's name and flat number were on one of the letter-boxes. Slater led up the stairs and waited outside the second-floor flat. The bell-push was grimy; drug-dealers, Slater thought, must get quite used to late-night visitors. Even so, 4.30 in the morning was stretching a point.

'Why don't you ring the bell?' Andreas suggested to Leon. 'You look the druggiest of all of us.'

'You mean the blackest?' whispered Leon. 'Thanks a lot!'

'White boys in hiking jackets don't buy smack at 4.30 in the morning,' hissed Andreas.

'And black ones do? Man, just where have you been hiding your sweet ass?'

'Guys,' intervened Slater. 'Wind your necks in, OK?'

Leaning forward, he pressed the bell. From within,

they heard slowly approaching footfalls and a protesting mutter. To conceal themselves, Leon and Andreas took a couple of steps up the staircase.

The spyhole briefly went dark, and the door opened a couple of inches on a brass chain.

'*Oui?*'

As the door opened a couple of inches, Slater slammed his heel against it, hard. The chain snapped off and the door flew backwards into the face of the man opening it, who sank to his knees with a groan, head in hands.

The three men barged in, kicking the door shut behind them, and Pasquale raised his head. Blood was pouring from his nose. He was a tall man, not unhandsome, with pale scars showing in his cropped hair. His night-time attire was a Paris St Germain football strip. He looked more puzzled than afraid.

'What do you need?' he asked in heavily accented French, pulling a handkerchief from his pocket and holding it to his nose. 'Smack? Crack? Ecstasy?'

'We need to talk,' Leon answered in English, quickly frisking him. 'Let's go inside and sit down. Any fucking around and these two men will shoot you.'

The drug-dealer looked at the faces of the three men standing in front of him, and then led them through to a spacious lounge containing an acre of white carpet, a giant widescreen TV and several tons of furniture upholstered in black leather.

'OK,' he said, indicating the sofas and armchairs. 'Tell me what is it you want.'

Slater positioned himself so that he could cover both Pasquale and the door.

'We want Branca,' said Leon simply.

'So you are who, police?'

'Why should we be police?'

Pasquale shrugged. 'Because of the Branca business.'

'Which is?'

Pasquale shrugged again.

'She deals drugs?' asked Leon.

Pasquale smiled and said nothing.

Slater strode over. Grabbing Pasquale's left hand, he wrenched the little finger back until there was a snap of breaking bone. Pasquale screamed – a long, high keen of terror and shock, and fell white-faced to the carpet. For a moment he lay there, gasping.

'Tell us,' Slater ordered him. 'Does Branca deal drugs?'

And still Pasquale hesitated. Casually, Slater stamped down hard on the dealer's wounded hand. For a full minute, blank-faced, he watched the other man's agonised writhings on the carpet.

'Does Branca deal drugs?' he repeated.

Pasquale's face was grey with pain. Still disbelieving, he stared at his broken hand.

'She buy into my operation,' he managed eventually. 'We partners.'

'How did that work out? Take your time. We've got several hours.'

'Several hours? What you mean several hours?'

'We're going to be here until tomorrow morning.'

'Fuck, man! Please. I need a doctor.'

Slater aimed the Sig Sauer at the dealer's face.

'You'll need a fucking undertaker if you don't answer my questions!'

'OK,' Pasquale gasped. 'She pay me cash. Five hundred thousand francs. In return she get fifty per cent share of profits for one year. And contact list.'

Slater frowned at Andreas. Why were the Serbian secret service buying into the Parisian drugs trade? It didn't make sense.

'How did you meet her?' asked Leon.

'She was at all the parties. The music parties, the fashion parties, the film parties, the TV parties, the porno parties – all the parties where my clients go.'

'And she became your lover.'

'Me and some others, I think. I was not . . . in exclusivity.'

'Did you meet her husband?'

'Yes.'

'And was he involved in this . . . deal?'

'*Non*, shit, *pas du tout*. He was not into all that scene.'

'So tell me about your clientele.'

'The usual. Models, designers, actors, business . . .'

'Politicians? Journalists?'

Pasquale regarded Leon warily. 'A few.'

'Give me names.'

Silence.

Stepping briskly forward, aiming with care, Slater shot Pasquale through the top of the arch of his right foot. The pain, he knew, would be extreme – all those tiny bones smashing through sensitive tissue – and the shock would be sufficient to break any resistance immediately.

The effect was the intended one. Arching his back in agony, the drug-dealer began to shake and babble as if electrified. His eyes rolled back and his tongue danced crazily in his mouth.

'The names,' said Slater, jamming the muzzle of the silenced Sig Sauer into Pasquale's eye. '*Comprenez*?'

Pasquale understood. It took him a little time to form the words, but he understood.

There were the inevitable socialites, footballers and models, but there was also a prominent female broadcaster on current affairs, a columnist on *Le Monde*, the wife of the *chef de protocole* at the Elysée Palace, and a Nato liaison officer from the defence ministry.

Leon looked at Slater and Andreas. The RDB's interest in Miko Pasquale was suddenly very easy to understand. Five hundred thousand francs had been a very small price to pay for access to this kind of influence, and probably an excellent investment as well, given the scale of Pasquale's business.

'Why did you agree to Branca's terms?' asked Leon. 'Half a million wasn't much to pay for half your profits.'

Pasquale took a deep breath, struggled to control himself. Tears streaked his face now. 'Branca is very *chouette* – very sweet – but many of her friends are not so *chouette*.'

'They're like us?'

'*C'est ça.* They're like you. Can I get something to put on this . . . my foot?'

'No,' said Slater. 'Bleed. I don't like drug-dealers.'

'What time do you guys think we should wake Branca?' mused Leon.

'Early,' said Slater. 'Get her when she's not thinking too clearly.'

'But not too early,' Andreas intervened. 'She'll just get pissed off and tell Smacko Jacko here to ring her later. And then we'll be stuck here for fucking ages.'

'Seven o'clock?' ventured Leon.

'I agree with seven,' said Slater. 'We're just going to have to inject a little urgency into the phone call.'

'Agreed?' Leon asked Andreas.

'Agreed.'

For clarity's sake, Leon explained the plan in French. At seven o'clock, Leon told the dealer, he – Pasquale – was going to ring Branca on her mobile. He was going to say that something of vital importance had come up, that someone had just given him a message which had to be passed on to her in person, and that he had to see her within the hour. He was to divulge no more than this, and he was not to take no for an answer.

'Just this?' asked Pasquale, pathetically grateful. 'This is all you want from me? You don't want some shit? Some Es?'

'For the moment,' said Leon ominously, 'this is all that we want. But be sure of one thing: if you try and

343

communicate anything else to Branca, we will shoot you in the face. Now where does she stay?'

'Rue Exelmans,' said Pasquale. 'In the *seizième*. With her husband.'

'And where else?'

'I don't know about anywhere else. I promise you.'

Slater pressed the muzzle of his silencer against the side of Pasquale's temple, and thumbed down the safety catch.

'*Non!*' screamed the dealer, his eyes bulging with fear. '*Je vous prie – non . . . Attendez . . .* I tell you' – his voice was shaking now – 'There is another place that she goes, but I never go there with her. I think it's somewhere in Barbès – in the *dix-huitième*.'

'What makes you think that if you haven't been there?' asked Slater.

'I hear her talking with one of . . . the others. She was speaking some East Europe language, I think, but I hear her say *"Eau de Javel"* and *"Prisunic"* and *"Boulevard Barbès"*. She was speaking in a low voice so I am not supposed to hear her, but I have good ears.'

'What's—' began Andreas.

'Prisunic's a cut-price supermarket chain,' replied Leon. 'And Eau de Javel is Jeyes fluid. Barbès is in north Paris, just east of the mainline railway track from the Gare du Nord, where you come in on Eurostar. It used to be very run-down, with a lot of immigrants' hostels and so on, but recently it's become quite hip. It's where middle-class white kids go to get their fix of black African culture. There's still a lot of crime there, though, and it's still one of the easiest places to buy weapons – especially since the Eastern European influx.'

'You're sure she said Barbès?' he asked.

Pasquale shrugged. 'That's what I heard.'

To Slater, his jaw clenched with the effort not to yawn, the affair was taking on an air of profound unreality. First light was beginning to stain the sky beyond the floor-to-ceiling windows, and he wondered if Eve was awake, or if she had managed to sleep. How were they treating her? While he knew from experience that she was more than capable of looking after herself, he still revolted from the idea of her being afraid, or confused, or hurt. More than anything he wanted to save her, as she – with such despatch and skill – had saved him.

They waited for two hours. Leon went out into the corridor in order to make a report to Chris and Terry. After a time, so pliant seemed Pasquale, they turned on the giant TV and watched the rerun of a football game in which Marseilles managed to snatch victory from Liverpool.

As the players exchanged shirts, Andreas turned to Leon. 'Why don't we make that call now?'

Leon looked at his watch, and nodded. For ten minutes he rehearsed Pasquale, taking him through every contingency, every possible variation on the conversation. 'Tell her,' he kept repeating, 'that you can come to her. That it's urgent. That it's political. That you can't discuss it on an open line.'

Finally Leon was content, or as content as he was ever likely to be. 'Just remember,' he told Pasquale. 'I'm going to understand every word you say. One nuance, one *inflexion* that you are being coerced, and my colleague here will blow your brains through that window into the Rue de Lappe. So don't get clever.'

Pasquale hesitated for a moment, and then used his good hand to dial a seven-figure number, which Slater memorised.

The phone rang for thirty seconds.

'Branca? *Chérie? Oui, c'est moi, Miko* . . .'

Branca Nikolic was clearly very pissed off indeed at being woken before 7am, and in no mood to listen to the rantings of Miko Pasquale. Finally, however, the drug-dealer's urgency and fear communicated itself, and she listened. Thirty seconds later he clicked off the phone.

'She wouldn't let me come to her. She said to be at the Café Metz just outside Strasbourg St Denis metro station in half an hour.'

Leon nodded. Slater pulled out a metro map. 'What's the nearest station to here?' he asked Pasquale.

'Bastille.'

'Look,' Slater said to Leon. 'You can get to Strasbourg St Denis station direct from Bastille. No changes. And it's exactly the same—'

'. . . from Barbès,' Leon nodded. 'I know. I noticed that too. So, here's what we're going to do.'

Two minutes later Leon had gone, leaving Slater and

Andreas to guard Pasquale. The plan, Leon had decided, was that Terry should go ahead to Strasbourg St Denis by metro, locate Branca at the café, and be ready to follow her back to wherever she was staying. Given that it was approaching rush hour, and that Branca had nominated a café next to a metro station, it was reasonable to assume that she would be arriving and departing by metro.

Given also that there were reasonable grounds for supposing that Branca was staying in Barbès, Leon would go straight to Barbès-Rochechouart metro station. If their calculations were correct, Branca would return from the Strasbourg St Denis rendezvous to Barbès, a journey of only four stops, and lead Leon and Terry to wherever she was staying. Of the three of them bumped by Branca and her RDB team in the Roche-Guyon forest, Leon insisted, he was the least likely to be recognised. There were always a handful of black guys in and around Barbès station handing out cards advertising the local *marabouts*, or West African witch-doctors. He wouldn't stick out. In case Branca arrived by car, Chris would be standing by in the Peugeot.

Slater and Andreas stayed with Pasquale. The smell of freshly baked bread and freshly ground coffee was rising up enticingly from the Rue de Lappe below, but the two ex-SAS men dared not allow Pasquale to make them all breakfast, as he had offered to do. The shaven-headed dealer had not got to carve out an important slice of the Parisian hard drugs market by being amenable, Slater reflected. Only abject fear would keep him in line, and then not for long.

At eight o'clock precisely, Slater recocked the Sig Sauer and Pasquale dialled Branca's number and said what Leon had earlier ordered him to say. He had been sick since speaking to her, the dealer complained. He was feeling terrible. He could no longer make it to the rendezvous. Would she forgive him?

Slater and Andreas smiled at each other. They couldn't understand all the French, but Pasquale's Nokia was practically jumping out of his hands, so violent was Branca's fury at having been woken up and had her time wasted.

'The problem?' Pasquale mumbled in response to a particularly vitriolic squawk. 'The problem's to do with one of the English models. The UK press are on to her habit and there's a danger that names are going to be named . . . Yes I *did* ask you to get out of bed to hear that, damn right . . . Well, it's important to me, and . . . No, you can't just pay off British tabloid journalists, no. But . . . Of course I'll deal with it, but you should be aware that . . .'

He held the phone away from his ear, shaking his head. He had clearly been cut off mid-sentence. Andreas reached over to confirm that the mobile was switched off and then nodded to Pasquale.

'That was good, man. I have to say that you were good there.'

What he did not say was that neither his nor Slater's French was good enough for them to have known if he had attempted to warn Branca. Luckily, this possibility did not seem to have occurred to Pasquale.

'How about a drink, Miko?' Slater asked.

Pasquale stared at him. 'A drink? You mean . . .'

'A whisky, yeah. Or a vodka. What've you got?'

'I have whisky,' Pasquale gasped, screwing up his eyes as a wave of pain overtook him.

'Where?' asked Slater.

Pasquale pointed feebly to a cabinet, from which Slater took out a sealed bottle of twelve-year-old Islay and a glass.

Half-filling the glass, he placed it in front of Pasquale. 'Cheers!'

The dealer stared from Slater to Andreas and back again. '*Non*', he said, disbelievingly.

'*Oui!*' smiled Slater and Andreas together.

Slowly, hesitantly, Pasquale sipped at the drink, his face creasing as the alcohol reached his throat.

'Come on, mate, drink up,' said Andreas. 'You've got a whole bottle to go.'

Still Pasquale hesitated. Pensively, Slater levelled the Sig Sauer and blew the screen out of the television. The gesture had the required effect. With a shaking hand, Pasquale lifted the glass and took a deep swallow.

'There's a boy!' said Andreas. 'That wasn't so bad, was it?'

Five minutes later half the bottle was gone. Pasquale was muttering to himself, his words slurring into incomprehensibility.

'Come on, mate, down the hatch!' said Andreas

encouragingly, pinching the drunk man's nose, pulling back his head, and pouring in another neat glassful.

'Empty stomach,' said Slater. 'Always speeds it up. He isn't half going to feel like shit when he comes around. Not that it'll be anything to compare with what he puts smack and crack addicts through.' He looked at the dealer contemptuously. 'Will it? Eh, fuckface?'

Pasquale groaned and closed his eyes. Two thirds of the bottle was now washing around in his stomach.

'See if you can find a funnel in the kitchen,' Slater suggested to Andreas.

Ten minutes later the bottle lay empty on the floor. Laying him on a carpet, Slater and Andreas dragged the by now helpless Pasquale into the furthest bedroom, hauled him on to the bed, plasticuffed him with his arms behind his back, and pulled a duvet over him. He started to snore almost immediately. In order to be forewarned if Branca attempted to make contact, Slater also pocketed the dealer's mobile phone.

'How long's he going to be under for, do you reckon?' asked Andreas.

'At a guess, until this evening,' replied Slater. 'We'll probably have to make a return visit at some point and top him up.'

'Well I looked in the cupboard and there's another five bottles of this stuff, so he can carry on his bender without switching brands.'

'He'll be glad of that,' said Slater.

They closed the bedroom door on the unconscious

Pasquale and placed the empty whisky bottle inside the shattered television, as if it had been hurled there in a fit of drunken rage. Anyone searching further – for the next few hours at least – would find the sleeping figure beneath the duvet. Should the searcher go further still, discover the plasticuffs and attempt to wake him, it was unlikely that a coherent explanation of his condition would be forthcoming. The rapid consumption of high-proof alcohol induces short-term memory loss, and it would be some days before Pasquale would be able to piece together what had happened to him.

But just to be on the safe side, Slater and Andreas locked themselves into the flat. 'How about some breakfast?' asked Andreas. 'The kitchen's pretty well stocked and I'm bloody starving.'

'Full English, then,' said Slater.

Slater's mobile rang shortly after 8am. It was Chris. 'Is your man immobilised?' she asked.

'He's down,' Slater answered.

'Get back here ASAP. Terry and Leon have a result.'

Slater punched the air. 'That's brilliant!'

'Fingers crossed. See you soonest.'

At the hotel, the mood was optimistic. Terry had stayed to stake out the location, so Leon told them what had happened since the two of them left Pasquale's flat an hour and a half earlier.

'When Pasquale rang to say he wasn't coming to the RV at the Café Metz, Branca got seriously, *seriously* pissed off. She shouted at the waiter, banged down

351

some change, and headed straight back to the Strasbourg St Denis metro. Four stops up the line to Barbès and she charges out again with Terry in tow. I'm hanging out at the station exit with the Africans when she comes screaming through – still far too angry to think about counter-surveillance – and starts moving up the Boulevard Barbès at high speed. I lock on behind Terry and we tail her up the boulevard and into the Rue de la Goutte d'Or. A few more twists and turns through the *souk* and she goes into this narrow little place called the Rue de Coude.

'Terry and I wait until she's inside, make a couple of passes past the building, and then pull back. The place is a brick-built warehouse block, previously containing garment-industry sweatshops. Most of the units now look vacant, but the security's recently been reinforced on the top-floor windows – and I mean very recently, because the wood shavings, iron-filings and spare bolts are still lying out on the roadside beneath the windows – so our best guess is that that's where they've got her. Terry's still over there, anyway, so he'll let us know as soon as he's got confirmation.'

'Did you get a look at the roof?' asked Slater.

'I knew you were going to ask that!' said Leon. 'And the answer is not really. Terry'll certainly give it a good recce, but I didn't have time. All I can tell you is that it's tiled, and not flat.'

'Our main advantage,' said Chris, 'seems to be that they don't know that we've sussed the place. They're not going to be expecting any kind of assault.'

'I agree with that,' said Leon. 'My guess is that the bars on the windows were put there specifically to keep Eve in. They're not anticipating having to keep us or anyone else out.'

'So how do we play it?' asked Slater. 'If we go in mob-handed with automatic weapons and try and shoot it out, we'll have the place crawling with armed police within minutes. Can we do it on an official level, get the Regiment in, or at a pinch the French GIGN?'

'I've had a word with the boss,' said Chris. 'And we're on our own. No Regiment, no GIGN, nothing – not even the police. Politically the whole thing's just too touchy. The basic message is that Eve's ours, we've got to extract her on our own, and if anyone gets nicked they can expect no help from HMG. Hostile territory, remember?'

'Brilliant,' said Slater.

The others looked at him. 'That's how it usually is, mate,' said Andreas. 'That's the price we pay for our no-questions-asked status.'

Slater nodded. He didn't want the others to think that he had an emotional involvement in the situation – an involvement that might compromise his operational efficiency. If Leon or Chris suspected that there was something between him and Eve, they'd relegate him to the background immediately. He was the most recent recruit to the Cadre, he reminded himself, and as such the most disposable.

'It's when situations like this come up,' Andreas continued, 'that you realise how dependent you were in the Regiment. On the MOD, the police, the Home Office, whoever. If you wanted something – kit, money, back-up, firepower – you just had to ask and it was there.' He hooked his thumbs fatalistically into the belt-loops of his jeans. 'Here it's different. Here it's just us.'

Slater nodded. 'The RDB aren't going to want to attract the police's attention either, though, are they?'

'If there's unsilenced shooting, the police will be there within five minutes,' said Leon. 'Ten, max.'

'Look,' said Chris. 'Until Terry makes his report, we can't make any plans. Why don't you guys go and get some sleep? Whatever's going to happen is going to happen tonight, so you're going to need to be sharp. Paris has bad associations for us, we don't want to lose anyone else here.'

She turned to Leon. 'What arrangements did you make about weapons?'

'The best I could manage for definite was three ex-military FAMAS rifles with silencers. They're quite reliable, in fact – we had them in the Legion.'

'Ammunition?'

'Comes with. The guy's waiting for my call to arrange an exchange. The price is thirty thousand francs, cash.'

'Why don't you make the call now?' Chris suggested. 'Arrange the pick-up for tonight, so you don't have to bring them back here. Do you trust this guy?'

'I've done business with him before,' said Leon. 'That's where I got the Glock and the Sig Sauer. And FAMAS rifles are never a problem – all the French armed services have them.'

Chris nodded. 'OK. Get some sleep.'

At 1 pm, showered and changed, Slater rejoined the others. He had not slept well; fractured images of Fanon-Khayat's disembowelled body slipping into the rushing darkness of the Seine had alternated with the sensation that he himself was drowning. And Eve. What was happening to her, locked up with Branca Nikolic and her RDB footsoldiers? They would have questioned her, at the very least, about the Fanon-Khayat assassination. They would have wanted to find out if MI6 knew about the Ondine deal, or whether they just wanted to recover the disc.

Tactical questioning, as the Regiment had called it, was a refined science. Eve was trained to resist interrogation and would hold out for as long as she could, but everyone broke sooner or later. Training exercises at Pontrilas or Imber, however harsh, came to an end. Fingernails were not ripped out with pliers, electrodes were not taped to the genitals, prisoners were not anally raped with cattle-prods. In the field, however, it was a different story. In the field it went on and on, and got worse and worse, until you fell – or were pulled – apart.

If the disc was not delivered intact, that would certainly be Eve's fate. Slater had no illusions about that. She would be tortured until she had given up all that she knew, and then killed and disposed of.

But the orders from Manderson were that the disc was not to be sacrificed for Eve. They would have to go in and pull her out: to assault what would probably turn out to be a near-impregnable position defended by a numerically superior, better-armed force. Tactically, it made no sense at all.

But then, Slater had mused as he drifted into sleep, what the fuck did?

In the room that had been the OP he found Terry, who had handed over watcher duties to Chris. Slater congratulated him on the success of his knackering surveillance marathon.

'Well, you know what they say,' said Terry, swigging on a can of Fanta from the minibar. 'When all else fails, bring in a fat lad from Essex!'

'I'll remember that,' smiled Slater, buoyed up by Terry's cheerful manner.

A large steak and French fries was waiting for him on a trolley, and he devoured it at the glass-topped dressing-table. Around him the others were making similar arrangements. Slater watched them covertly. Basically the unit divided into the brains, the eyes and the muscle. Eve and Leon were the brains, the planners; Chris and Terry were the eyes, and he and Andreas were the muscle. But it was more complex than that, because according to Eve the others were all pretty good with firearms, too – excepting Terry, of course. Terry's job, like Chris's, was to bind the team together. The two of them seemed to have almost limitless patience and steady good humour. Of course all of these roles overlapped – at a pinch they could all do each other's jobs. He himself, Slater reckoned, was no bad planner, and there wasn't much Andreas didn't know about surveillance, and so on.

They were a good team, Slater concluded. He'd had his doubts to begin with, but having seen them in operation he wouldn't have changed any of them. And now the team was to be put to the ultimate test – an urban hostage-rescue.

With coffee poured, cigarettes lit, and the loaded trolley returned to the corridor, Terry belched meaningfully into a paper tissue. 'All right lads, listen in. The position, as far as we can calculate, is that Eve is being held on the fifth floor of a warehouse in the Rue de Coude. We have no hard proof of that, but I found this' – he held up a scrap of paper – 'just outside. As you can see it's a receipt for a cappuccino from the Bar Mocha at the Waterloo Eurostar terminus. The date is last Friday, the day we came over. Like I said it doesn't prove anything, but if this wasn't Eve trying to leave us a sign, then it's one hell of a coincidence.'

The others nodded. 'It would have been dark when they brought her in,' said Andreas. 'She'd have been able to drop it without being spotted.'

'Now I've had a close look at the building through these' – Terry held up a small pair of Zeiss binoculars – 'and I've done a few drawings.'

From the pocket of his coat, which was lying on the

bed next to him, he took out a French schoolboy's notebook.

'This is of the front, which is in glazed brick, and this is of the back, which is the same. The roof is the mansard type. It's steeply pitched and covered in very old, very insecure-looking slates. The roofs to either side are the same. The only way up there that I could see is through the building itself and out through a skylight. There's a fire escape, but it's very old and narrow, and I doubt whether it would take the weight of an armed man. And even if it did you'd be spotted the moment you left the ground. They've got a pretty effective security rota going, with at least one guy patrolling the area at all times. As we already know, these guys aren't the usual brandy-swigging, shell-suit-wearing Serbian paramilitary bullies, they're well-trained RDB agents. They're going to notice if a mountaineering team armed with assault rifles starts making its way up the front of their building.

'A more sensible option, in my opinion, would be to pick the lock of one of the buildings next door, which are both five-storey warehouse blocks, and take armed possession of the top-floor. Once up there you could remove some brickwork and go in through the partition wall.'

'Too noisy without special equipment,' said Slater immediately. 'And takes for ever. I've been involved in jobs like that – you need fibre-optic lenses and all sorts if it's going to work. Even with the right kit it would take all night to pick our way through. There is another way, though. And that's straight in through the front door.'

The others fell silent.

'The main trouble with an assault through a partition or roof is that it's a kill-em-all option. The only way to get Eve out if we assault the place is to kill or disable all of them. Whatever happened there'd be a bloodbath, and it's a probability that a fair amount of that blood would be ours. Plus there's a good chance Eve wouldn't survive anyway.'

'We've got to give it a go,' said Andreas, although Slater could tell from the tone of his voice that he had the same misgivings. 'We can't just leave her there.'

'I'm not suggesting we leave her there,' said Slater. 'What I think we ought to do is snatch Branca, and then arrange an exchange of hostages. My suggestion is that someone from the RDB rings Branca, asks for a private meet, and we jump her.'

The others stared at him.

'Someone from the RDB?' said Leon, incredulous. 'How do we arrange that?'

'Ring Ridley,' said Slater. 'Tell him to get on to the Balkan desk and find a native Serbian speaker and to go through the files for the names of a couple of senior RDB officers. At a given time, the Serbian guy rings Branca's mobile from London – I got the number when Pasquale rang her this morning – and says he's been ordered to contact her. He drops a couple of classified names, just to show he is who he says he is. One of the men with her, he says, is working undercover for the Americans, or the Albanians, or whoever. She must come alone and in secret to such-and-such a place, where she will be told what to do.'

'And once she arrives we grab her, drag her back to where she's got Eve, and arrange an exchange,' said Leon. 'I like it!'

'It avoids a shoot-out.' Slater shrugged. 'A shoot-out that we might well lose, as things stand.'

Terry, who had been listening in silence, helped himself to one of Andreas's cigarettes. 'Why don't we go through it point by point?' he said.

FOURTEEN

At 7.30pm Slater went with Leon to pick up the weapons. Chris had spoken to Manderson several times in the course of the afternoon, and the Cadre chief had approved the plan to kidnap Branca and exchange her for Eve. P4, the head of Balkan operations, had agreed to help Manderson out without insisting on knowing the precise circumstances. This was unconventional, but as Manderson had gently pointed out, it was at P4's request that the Cadre had become involved in the first place. It had been the Balkan desk, not to put too fine a point on it, who had wanted Fanon-Khayat dead.

The time agreed for the fake call from Belgrade was midnight French time – any earlier and there would still be people on the streets, any later and there was concern that Branca's mobile might be switched off.

A decision had been made in London that a twenty-seven-year-old Serbian-speaking MI6 agent was to make the call. Until recently Pavel Djukic had been a BBC World Service employee, and had only joined MI6's Balkan desk six weeks earlier. His time behind a sound-studio microphone had given him a vocal

authority beyond his years, however, and he was
confident of his ability to bamboozle Branca Nikolic.
The service had amassed a fair volume of information
on the Serbian secret service, and Djukic was swotting
up the files on individual RDB officers in preparation
for a heavy bout of name-dropping.

Once again, Leon and Slater swiftly threw off their
Serbian tails. The weapons contact was an Algerian
named Schafa, who fronted a business in used small
arms with a bicycle repair shop in Belleville in the
twentieth arrondissement. Leon and Schafa had done
hard time together at Clairvaux prison, and since
joining the Cadre Leon had brought a fair amount of
business the Algerian's way.

On their arrival in Belleville, Schafa insisted that
they join him in a glass of mint tea. The tiny grease-
stained office attached to his workshop smelt pleasantly
of cycle oil and tyre-rubber, and Slater resolved to buy
a bicycle when – and if – he got back to London. He
had never owned one as a child; now was the time to
put that right.

As he looked round, fingering chains, wingnuts,
spokes and drop-handlebars, Schafa and Leon
chattered away in rapid-fire French. As most of the
language that they used was underworld slang, Slater
could barely understand a word of it but he gathered
from their expressions that Schafa had managed to pull
something special out of the hat for his old Clairvaux
cellmate.

Eventually the Algerian led them through the

workshop and up a grimed and narrow flight of stairs to his stockroom. At the end, beyond a plastic-strip curtain, was the locked entrance to the next-door unit. This, Leon murmured to Slater, was also owned by Schafa, but under the front of a mail-order company selling DIY tools.

The door swung open to reveal ceiling-to-floor stacks of cheaply finished tyre-jacks, pipe-cutters, screwdriver and spanner sets and adjustable monkey wrenches. The casing indicated that these goods originated in a variety of countries, including China, Slovakia, Romania, Israel and Byelorussia.

From beneath a bench Schafa slid a metal case with Chinese characters sprayed on to it. Opened, a tray containing a display set of variously sized Maglite-style torches was revealed. Beneath this, however, nestling in a dense black bed of foam-rubber, was a 9mm Uzi submachine gun, and three twenty-five-round magazines. Reaching down, Schafa pulled the weapon out, ran an affectionate hand over its square, riveted, steel-pressed outline, and handed it to Leon.

'*Douce!*' said Leon.

'I thought you said he had FAMAS rifles,' murmured Slater.

'They've gone,' said Leon. 'Probably Corsican terrorists – apparently they're quite good customers.'

From the fatter-than-normal barrel Slater could tell that the Uzi was one of the suppressed models built for covert and urban use. You could cheerfully blast off 5000 rounds outside a police station with one of these and no one would hear a thing. Given a close-quarters firefight Slater would have preferred the MP5s that the RDB carried, but the Israeli-designed Uzis were an acceptable alternative.

'I've got three of these altogether,' said Schafa reverently. 'Licence-built by FN in Belgium. They came up from Marseilles this afternoon.'

Leon nodded and translated for Slater.

'These would be great,' Slater agreed. 'Apart from anything else they're small, which will help when we're carrying them in the streets. Has he got the subsonic ammunition to go with them?'

Schafa nodded. 'I have nine-mil subsonic. I also have this – *la pièce de résistance*.' Ducking down, he reached another flat steel case from below the bench, opened it, and removed a layer of plug-spanner sets. Beneath, embedded as the Uzi had been, was a black matt-finished rifle, luminated sniper-scope, compensator, magazine and cleaning kit.

'A Dragunov sniper rifle,' said Leon thoughtfully. 'Not bad. Not bad at all.'

'A Romak-3,' said Schafa. 'Takes ten rounds of 7.62.'

'And if you need all of those,' added Slater, 'then you're well and truly fucked. This is the Romanian-made model, isn't it?'

Schafa nodded.

Slater drew Leon aside. 'This could be useful. Who's the best shot out of the four of us?'

'Hard to say. What about you?'

'Well, I led an SAS sniper team a couple of years ago, but I'm probably the rustiest in terms of recent range-hours. How are Chris and Terry?'

'As good as any of us.'

'Because whatever happens we're going to need to set up an OP or possibly two OPs on the rooftops. If someone could get this Dragunov up there and establish a clear line of fire it could just swing things if it all comes on top.'

'In that case, I should go,' Leon said. 'I'm not a better shot than Chris and Terry but I'm pretty sure that I'm a better climber. Anyone firing an unsilenced weapon from the roofs around there is going to have to disappear very fast indeed.'

'So how do you think the rest of us should deploy?'

'Let's hash that one out later. But we're agreed we want the three Uzis and the Dragunov?'

'I think so, aren't we?'

'I also have body-armour,' said Schafa.

'What do you think?' Leon asked Slater.

'Nothing bulky,' said Slater. 'It'll show in the street and tell the RDB that we're ready for trouble. It'll just escalate things.'

In the end they settled for 'second chance' vests. These, much less bulky and heavy than conventional flak-jackets, incorporated a layer of Kevlar-over-Perspex 'trauma-packs'. The Kevlar slowed the bullets down, while the Perspex panels dispersed their impact. You'd go down, but with any luck you wouldn't die.

Schafa had half a dozen of these in a packing-case.

None showed signs of having taken bullets, but all were sweat-marked and had the sour smell of fear and stress about them.

'We'll take three,' said Leon.

On the way back to the hotel, he dropped Slater off at the Rue de Lappe. Pulling on his gloves and undoing Pasquale's front door with keys stolen from the apartment earlier, Slater checked the drug-dealer's condition.

Pasquale was half-awake, and feeling very sorry for himself indeed. His wrists were badly chafed from the plasticuffs and a strong smell of urine rose from his bed. Seeing Slater he narrowed his eyes, as if struggling to remember in what context he had met the former SAS man.

'English, yes?'

Slater nodded.

'Please, English. Taking off the handcuffs. *Je vais* . . . I want to vomit, please.'

'Wait,' said Slater, leaving the room.

When he returned it was with a tumbler, a carafe of water, and a fresh bottle of malt whisky. Pasquale, who had thrown up on his pillow while Slater was out of the room, groaned at the sight of them.

'It's called the hair of the dog that bit,' said Slater, his eyes watering at the ammoniac stench.

'Please,' said Pasquale. 'I piss, OK? *Toilette?*'

'I'm sure you piss OK,' said Slater grimly. 'But first you drink OK. It'll make you feel better.'

Ignoring Pasquale's groans, he mixed a half-pint of Islay whisky and water. Casually, he unholstered and checked the Sig Sauer. 'Drink,' he ordered.

Hesitantly, Pasquale drank.

Watching him, Slater saw the alcohol take immediate effect. Colour returned to the sallow cheeks and the nauseated look was replaced by an expression of tired relief.

'It's better,' admitted Pasquale, struggling to a sitting position. 'Please, English. I need to piss.'

'Another glass,' ordered Slater.

'Why you do this?' asked Pasquale miserably.

'Because I don't like people who sell drugs,' said Slater. '*Comprenez?*'

Pasquale shrugged. Ten minutes and a half-bottle later, he slumped into unconsciousness again. As Slater watched, his bladder voided itself copiously into the bed. Short of shooting him, Slater thought, which would lead to more complications than the man was worth, he couldn't do much more to shut him up.

Outside, with 40,000 francs' worth of unlicensed weaponry in the back of the car, Leon was glad to get moving again. Pointing the nose of the Mercedes northwards, he joined the traffic on the Boulevard Beaumarchais, and twenty-five minutes later pulled up in the Rue de la Goutte d'Or in Barbès.

The area was unlike anywhere else in the city. As the long-time home of Paris's immigrant community – Arabs and West Africans for the most part – it offered a heady mixture of the tawdry and the exotic.

Marabouts, or West African ju-ju men, handed out cards advertising their services. Overfilled immigrant hostels spilled their robed *Togolais* and *Béninois* occupants on to garish, neon-lit pavements. Hairdressers' shops offering elaborate braided coiffures stood cheek by jowl with halal butchers, cous-cous joints and small mosques. From the cafés came the click of dominoes. There was the murmur of many languages.

Leaving Slater in charge of the car, Leon set off on foot to find a hotel in which the team could base itself.

A quarter of an hour later he was back. 'I've booked three twin rooms in the Hotel Aissa, a couple of streets away,' he told Slater. 'It's not the Ritz but it's out of the way and no one's likely to be asking questions. I played the heavy, paying up front with a fat wad of cash, so they'll almost certainly assume we're here on drug-business.'

When they arrived, Slater saw what Leon had meant. The Aissa was an unprepossessing one-star flop-joint, and as they watched from the car a fat, middle-aged Arab in a leather-jacket stepped on to the pavement, adjusted his trousers, scratched his balls, hoisted himself into the driver's seat of the taxi parked at the kerb, and drove off. A minute later a bored-looking prostitute strolled out, checked her watch, and took her place on the corner.

Parking where the taxi had been, the two men made their way into the hotel foyer carrying the anonymously cased weapons, their hiking jackets, and their overnight bags. Of the four men drinking minted tea and playing dominoes behind the counter none looked up, but the oldest slid three keys towards Leon and pointed at the worn and narrow staircase.

The rooms were small, smelt of spiced food, and were grouped together on the first floor. Slater and Leon moved their kit into the middle of the three. The walls and ceilings were not thick, and from above them came a muffled groaning and the creaking of bedsprings.

'Classy place!' remarked Slater, lowering the case containing the Dragunov to the greasy carpet and pulling the thin curtains closed.

Leon laughed. 'You said you wanted to see the real Paris! Why don't you get the rest of the Uzis in from the car while I call the others?'

By 11pm the whole team was assembled except Terry, who was watching the front of the building in the Rue de Coude from a nearby bar. Leon, it had been decided, armed with the Dragunov, would watch the back of the building – there were more windows at the back than at the front. The kidnap and hostage-swap would be carried out by Slater, Andreas and Chris.

While Slater and Leon had been buying weapons and pacifying Miko Pasquale, Andreas had been carrying out a discreet recce of the Rue de Coude. Slater and Chris had not yet seen the place, and after changing into old clothes they set out with Leon.

The latest intelligence from Terry was that though

Branca had left the building earlier for a couple of hours, she had now returned. Terry's guess, having followed her as she trailed round the streets, dropped in and out of cafés and newsagents, smoked cigarettes and drank coffee, was that she had wanted a break from her RDB colleagues.

As they approached the Rue de Coude, Leon left Chris and Slater to recce the target area together and hurried ahead to search for an effective OP and lying-up position. The three agreed to meet thirty minutes later.

As Leon slipped into the shadows, Chris slipped her arm through Slater's. She was wearing a polo shirt, jeans and plimsolls, had a sweater knotted round her shoulders, and looked subtly, indefinably French.

'You look as if you were born here,' he told her. 'And I look like some dodgy geezer from Catford.'

Chris smiled. She had, Slater noticed, a really very attractive smile when she cared to deploy it. 'Disguise is in the mind,' she said, 'not in the trousers. Although you might pull your sleeves up your arms a bit, like these funky Frenchy loverboys do. And stick your cigarettes in your shirt-pocket – this is a country with a soft-pack culture. And put your left hand in your pocket rather than letting it swing.'

'Like an ape.'

'You said it, not me. And for heaven's sake put your arm round me properly – you're not my father leading me up to the altar.'

Obediently, Slater hitched up his sleeves, pushed his left hand into his pocket, and slipped his arm around her slight, steely body. Beneath her cheap sweater he could feel the stomach muscles working as she sauntered slowly along the pavement.

'Now, having put your arm possessively around me to warn anyone else off, you curl your lip and ignore me altogether – yeah! That's the way! Now we're a French couple!'

'It was never this complicated in the Regiment,' Slater observed wryly.

'No snogging during recon exercises, you mean?'

'Very little.'

They walked in silence for a couple of minutes. The warmth of the day had all but gone.

'We'll get her out,' said Chris, reading Slater's thoughts. 'One way and another we'll get her out.'

'It could get very nasty,' Slater said. 'Those RDB guys had an all-the-way-to-hell look about them.'

She nodded. 'I know. But we're not exactly pussycats either. This is the place, isn't it?'

The Rue de Coude was a narrow street with four- and five-storey warehousing on one side and a series of garment-industry showrooms, all apparently vacant, on the other. The only sign of life among these blank frontages was the dimly lit portal of Chez Fatima, which is where Slater guessed that Terry had established himself. Loitering on the corner for a moment he and Chris scoped out the entrance to the building, some fifty metres away, where they suspected Eve was being held. As the others had reported, a fat little devil with horns and a forked tail had been stencilled in red spray-paint on to the front of the walk-up to the entrance. The door was new, and steel-framed. Slater flicked his eye upwards but the glance told him nothing; the roof was invisible from the corner of the street and the top floor almost invisible.

'Bad guy,' murmured Chris.

A distant figure was making its way down the pavement towards them from the direction of the warehouse building. Something about the man's bearing – some tension or alertness atypical of the time of night – indicated that this was a patrolling RDB man. Casually, Slater swung Chris round to face him and lowered his mouth to hers. As their lips touched he felt her flinch, and clamp her mouth shut. Slater had not intended anything except to hide their faces from the passing RDB man but it was immediately clear to him that Chris was not enjoying herself. As the Serb disappeared and he lifted his face from hers, she gasped for breath and dragged her sleeve across her mouth.

'Sorry,' said Slater. 'It wasn't that bad, was it?'

She avoided his gaze. 'No, sorry, I . . . I just wasn't expecting it. I know you weren't, um . . .' She shrugged, embarrassed. 'Did he stop and look at us?'

'I don't think so,' said Slater. 'No.'

Two streets further down Leon stepped from the shadows. He too had identified the patrolling Serb. He had also identified a potential OP and lying-up position.

'It's a long shot,' he told them, indicating the multi-storey car-park on his right, 'but it's easy to access, easy to escape and evade from, and I couldn't ask for a clearer field of fire. I'm going to take the Romak up there in the Mercedes.'

'What about Terry?' asked Slater. 'Where's he going to go at chucking out time?'

'Oh, he picked the lock into one of those showrooms opposite that building with the devil-stencil where they've got Eve. Did it this morning – so he just has to slip in and go upstairs.'

Slater nodded. He was beginning to get nervous about the part he himself was expected to play. The first traces of adrenaline were beginning to seep into his bloodstream. 'Shall we get back?' he asked. 'We must be coming up to the moment when Branca gets an unexpected phone-call.'

'We've got time yet,' said Leon grimly, glancing at his watch. 'Let's go into the car-park and see if we can see into that flat. I've brought the binoculars.'

Five minutes later, concealed behind the parapet, they were looking across at the rear of the Rue de Coude. They were on the almost empty fifth level of the car-park, and the top-floor flat was a little over 100 metres away. Chris held the binoculars, and together they identified the half-dozen windows of the flat, most of which were illuminated but hung with industrial blinds. As they watched, a small frosted window lit up, the upper half of a torso showed for a minute, and then the light went out again.

'That's the toilet,' said Chris. 'And that was an adult male. My guess would be that the other rooms are just open warehouse space. If those old seventies blinds are still up there, the interior won't have been converted.'

Slater nodded. 'The RDB guys probably doss down on the floor in gonk-bags.'

Leon took the binoculars from Chris and searched the windows. 'If you have any problems,' he said, 'try and get the blinds open.'

He turned to Chris. 'No disrespect, but now that there's no heavy roof-climbing involved on this side, would you rather lie up here and let me go in with Neil and Andreas?'

Chris considered. 'I thought about that, and my feeling is that when we go in with Branca, the fact that there's another woman there might defuse things a little. We want them to feel that they've been outmanoeuvred, not challenged.'

Leon frowned.

'And the other thing,' Chris continued, 'is that you're certainly a faster runner than me. If you fire that unsilenced Dragunov you're going to have to move very quickly indeed.'

He nodded. 'I suppose so. I guess we should get back and get ready.'

They returned to the hotel as they had come: Leon alone, Slater and Chris arm in arm.

As they walked, Slater thought how differently this

operation would have been carried out by the Regiment. The police would have been on-side, for one thing, and fibre-optic surveillance would have been under way for twelve hours. The building's architectural specifications would have been consulted, there would have been rehearsals in a mock-up of the warehouse, and an assault-team in gasmasks and full protective gear would be standing by with stun-grenades ready to blow the entrances and storm the place. Every detail, every eventuality, every possible outcome would have been considered and evaluated.

Instead, it was just the five of them and a stash of untried and quite possibly dodgy gear. Planning had been done on the run and the arrangements were – to say the least – sketchy. Everything was reactive, last-minute and makeshift.

But perhaps, Slater mused, he had simply been spoilt during his years with the SAS. Makeshift arrangements or no, the Cadre had done pretty well so far, and created an impressive amount of havoc for its size. Allowing the Serbian bodyguard to get the jump on him in Fanon-Khayat's apartment had been a bad mistake, and being bumped by the RDB in the forest had been another, but one way and another they had managed to keep going.

And several things greatly impressed him. Their streetcraft and surveillance skills – in particular those of Chris and Terry – were superior to any he had ever encountered. Their professional discipline was watertight, and perhaps because there was nowhere for them to be promoted to, there was none of the competitiveness, jockeying for position and general macho bollocks that had been such a prominent feature of Regimental life. In MI9, whoever was best situated to take charge of a particular task at a particular time did so, and everyone else fell into line. They were good people, he decided, and there was much to be learnt from the way they operated.

By 11.30 Slater, Leon, Andreas and Chris were reassembled at the Hotel Aissa. Terry had just called in to say that he had counted five males out of number 30 Rue de Coude at various times during the evening, and that all had now returned. Branca Nikolic was also on the premises.

A call to Manderson had confirmed that the call would be going through to Branca's phone in thirty minutes. Its content would be that one of the RDB men with her was an MI6 spy, and planned to steal the disc as soon as it was in her hands. She was to find an excuse to leave the flat immediately and make her way to the all-night Bar Suez in Rue de Laghouat, where she would be briefed by a controller from Belgrade.

Outside, the nearby church of St Bernard de la Chapelle struck the half hour.

On the bed, cigarette in hand, Andreas stretched and grinned.

At the table, Leon stared with unseeing eyes at an old copy of *Pariscope*.

At the window, his heart pounding at his chest, Slater forced himself to breathe normally.

Against the wall, Chris uncoiled herself from the lotus position in which, motionless, she had spent the last ten minutes.

It was time to stand by.

FIFTEEN

The plan was to allow Branca to get well clear of the Passage de Coude and any patrolling RDB sentries, and take her a couple of streets away on the corner of the Rue de Laghouat and the Passage des Ouled-Nail.

From where he and Chris lounged in an unlit doorway, Slater looked across towards Andreas, invisible in a covered entrance-way where vegetables were sold during the day. There were street lights and a waning moon, but neither reached the Passage des Ouled-Nail. A Moorish archway marked the entrance to the alleyway, and the star-shaped windows of a mosque showed half-way down its length. From some nearby source came the muted rise and fall of North African *rai* music played on a transistor. There was a smell of cloves, cardamom, trodden vegetables and fried *merguez* sausages. They could have been in the outskirts of a city in Morocco or Tunisia rather than in Paris.

Slater was wearing hiking boots, jeans and a loose green windshirt over his flak-vest. His Uzi and two spare clips of ammunition were slung in a black nylon satchel over his shoulder and the Sig Sauer was stuck into the waistband of his trousers. Next to him Chris was in black, with her weapon and ammunition similarly stowed. As far as Slater could tell, they were the only people on the street.

Slater checked his watch. It was midnight, and the call should be coming through right now. All being well, they could expect her within three or four minutes.

'All stations. Stand-by . . . Go!'

Without anything being said, it had been agreed that Slater should lead the operation. In part this was because of his extensive CQB experience with the SAS, but in part, Slater sensed, it was because Eve was the hostage.

When Andreas had questioned him about the night in the Inter-Lux, Slater had shrugged his shoulders and grumbled about sleeping the night wrapped in a duvet on the floor. He doubted that Andreas completely believed him, though, because in the short time that he had been with the department he had clearly hit it off with Eve in a way that the others hadn't. The fact that she had saved his life was part of it, but there was something else too. An affinity. An unlikely affinity given their very different backgrounds, but an affinity no less.

Chris sensed it, he knew, and so almost certainly did Leon. A group as tightly interdependent as theirs could not fail to be aware of the subtle dynamic shifts that took place within it. Did it lock him into the group, Slater wondered, or did it serve to distance him from the others? Time would tell.

'Terry to all players. Target has left the building. ETA you one minute, repeat one minute. Over.'

'Neil to Terry. Understood. Over.'

As he pulled the Uzi from its satchel, Slater felt the familiar adrenaline rush that preceded action. At his side he felt Chris tauten. The seconds thudded past, and then Slater heard the fast clip of heels on the pavement.

Branca Nikolic would have walked straight past them had not Slater reached out and grabbed her. She half-gasped in shock, and in less than a second Slater's hand was clamped tight across her mouth. Branca writhed furiously and tried to bite, but with a hissed 'Shut up, cunt!' Chris drew back the heavy butt of her Uzi and slammed it into the other woman's ribs.

Dragging the groaning Branca into the doorway where Andreas was waiting, Chris grabbed her hard by the windpipe. Branca's face contorted in agony as she struggled to breathe – the writhing defiance continued for a few more seconds, and then sensing the racing approach of death, she went limp.

Quickly, Chris released the Serbian to the ground and felt inside her shirt for a wire or throat mike. There was none, but she was carrying a Mini-Glock 26 in the inside pocket of her jacket, which Chris pushed into her own waistband.

As Chris backed away, Slater took over. Defeated but furious tear-streaked eyes looked up at him. Next to him, Andreas levelled his Uzi at Branca's face.

'No noise,' Slater whispered. '*Silence*. OK?'

Branca nodded sullenly. Fear, pain and fury at having been deceived battled it out behind her eyes.

'We want the woman. You understand?'

She nodded again.

'Any noise,' Slater continued, 'and we . . .' Taking the Uzi from Andreas, he mimed bringing it down hard on her face.

Again, closing her eyes, Branca nodded.

'How many men have you got there?'

She held up the fingers of one hand.

'And where is the woman?'

They questioned her intensively for five minutes, until all of them were certain that they were familiar with the layout of number 30 Rue de Coude. From her satchel, when they had finished, Chris took a pre-cut section of zinc-oxide tape and pressed it over Branca's mouth. Over her face, so that they would look like party-goers if they encountered anyone on their return journey, she slipped a child's elasticated rabbit mask. Re-packing their weapons, the three of them then turned Branca around, linked arms so that the two men were on either side of her, and marched her back in the direction she had come.

As they approached the Rue de Coude, Chris darted ahead to recce. A minute later she returned. The RDB sentry was in front of the building.

Slater nodded to Andreas, who quietly detached himself. As he did so, Slater and Chris sat Branca down on a flight of steps.

Andreas returned five minutes later and they

continued on their way. When they passed the sentry he was barely visible, lying in a shadowed entranceway as if drunk. To hide the zinc-oxide tape over his mouth, Andreas had pulled the man's leather jacket around his head, as tramps often did to provide themselves with a makeshift pillow.

'Alive?' whispered Slater.

'Yeah, but shouldn't wake for half an hour or so,' replied Andreas. 'And I took his keys in case he does. He had a comms-set but it was switched to receive when I bumped him – from the fat grin on his face I think one of his mates was telling him a dirty joke.'

'Does that mean to say they're expecting an answer from him?'

'Well, I switched it on and off a couple of times after I whacked him and then left it on transmit. Hopefully they'll just think he's fucked up his procedure.'

'OK. We'd better move it though, in case they send someone down to check.'

Andreas nodded, and all but lifting Branca off her feet, he and Slater ran her to the walk-up entrance above the stencilled red demon. Chris had Branca's keys ready, and a moment later the four of them were inside the small foyer.

Quickly, Slater plasticuffed Branca and they prepared their weapons, extending the Uzis' telescopic butts. 'Neil to players, we have our bunny and are entering building. Over.'

'Understood, Neil. Over.'

'Terry, do you copy? Over.'

'Seen and copied. Over.'

The building was probably built in the late forties. There was a lift, but it looked old and wheezy and Slater did not want to risk the advantage that surprise would give them. Instead, they went up on foot. A steel-banistered staircase climbed between walls of yellowing marble composite, with warehouse units extending to right and left at each level. From the street no lights had been visible in any of these units, and judging by the rubbish accumulated outside them, most were untenanted.

'Neil to players, we are entering hostage-location with Flopsy. Starting ten-second countdown now. Over.'

Andreas pulled off Branca's rabbit-mask but left the zinc-oxide tape in place.

Chris unlocked the heavy armour-plated door.

Slater and Andreas marched Branca into the unit, each with an Uzi to her head.

They were in a long, low loft-unit containing three steel desks, a couple of battered filing cabinets, and a half-dozen stackable chairs. There were three RDB men visible.

Two of these were lounging twenty feet away on the threadbare carpet with an ashtray and a bottle of Orangina between them and their MP5 submachine guns at their sides, and a third sat a little further away with his feet on one of the desks and his weapon in his lap, suspended in the act of paging through a copy of *Gros Lolos*. They were fit-looking military types with cropped hair and hard, watchful faces. For a moment all three remained frozen in shock.

Slater digested the scene at a glance, noting the state-of-the-art laptops, cyber-phones and zip-files which lay around on the desk. Where was Eve? According to Branca, she was in a 'sleeping-room' at the far end of the unit.

There was the sound of a flushing toilet, and a fourth RDB man entered the tableau, wiping his hands on his trousers. After two paces he stopped dead, looking from his colleagues to Branca and her escorts. In his mind, Slater knew, was the knowledge that he had committed the special forces operative's cardinal sin: he had separated himself from his personal weapon. It was lying half a dozen paces away in the middle of the carpet, next to a smoking ashtray, a packet of Bastos, and a bottle of Chimay beer.

Slater shook his head and the standing RDB man froze like his colleagues.

Stepping forward, Chris ripped the tape from Branca's face.

'Tell them what I said,' he ordered her. 'Tell them that if any of them makes a move for his weapon, he will be shot. And so will you.' The adrenaline had fully kicked in now, and he felt the familiar light-headedness and slow-motion clarity.

Branca spoke in Serbian. The men didn't move but Slater saw that the shock in their faces had been replaced by alertness. He would have liked to have ordered them to hand the weapons over, but he didn't want them even touching them. The Cadre team had had the advantage of surprise, but that advantage was fading with every moment. Beside him, he was aware of Chris thumbing the selector of her Uzi to single-shot.

'Tell them to get their fucking hands up,' Slater snapped.

Branca spoke, and the RDB men slowly obeyed. Looking from face to face, however, Slater saw only wariness and battle-readiness. Beyond them, less than twenty yards away, was Eve. His heart pounded against his chest.

'Do you want one of them to get the woman?' Branca asked.

'No, one of us will go. Is she still where you said?'

Branca nodded.

At that moment, to his left, Chris threw her Uzi to her shoulder and fired a fast double-tap. On the other side of the room the head of the man at the desk seemed to twitch before exploding in a spray of scarlet. A wet blast of brain and bone spattered the vertical blinds, and the MP5 that the dead man was about to fire hit the threadbare carpet with a thump.

As Slater kicked down the desk in front of him and dragged Branca to the floor, he saw a flurry of movement as the RDB team scrambled for their weapons. He just made it behind the cover of the desk when, with a rapid-fire staccato coughing, three silenced MP5s opened up straight at them.

From a crouching position Andreas snapped off a pair of fast shots with his Uzi and then crammed in behind the desk next to Slater. To his left Chris acted identically, but finding Branca there bundled the handcuffed woman out into the open where a fast-reaction shot from one of the Serbs smacked into her thigh, tumbled through six inches of gym-toned tissue, and exited gapingly and bloodily beside the copper buttons of her Levi 501 jeans. Gasping in disbelief, shaking as if electrocuted, Branca Nikolic went into immediate and massive shock.

Another volley of rounds hammered into the steel desk. For the three of them to stay there, Slater knew, would be suicide. They had to split up and divide the RDB fire.

It was clear that the Cadre had lost the initiative but it would have been a miracle if things had turned out any other way. From the moment that Manderson – fuck him – had refused to let them buy Eve's safety with the tape, a shoot-out had been a dangerous probability. Grabbing Branca had been their best chance of avoiding a blood-bath, but the gamble had failed.

A half-second glance confirmed the general picture for Slater. Ahead of them, some fifteen metres away, was a concrete roof-support pillar. Ten metres to its right was its twin. Two steel desks and a steel filing cabinet were grouped around the right-hand pillar, and these were providing cover for the three Serbs. The fourth, dead, lay between one of the desks and the right-hand window.

386

If Slater could get behind the left-hand pillar he could draw the enemy fire and perhaps snipe at the RDB team from the side.

'Swap places,' he whispered to Chris, and she clambered over him so that she was next to Andreas.

'OK, cover me.'

Jumping over the still-shaking form of Branca he sprinted for the pillar, wrenching down the blinds from the window as he went. Behind him he heard the double-cough of aimed shots from Andreas and Chris and longer bursts from the Serbs. With all of the weapons silenced the smack of impact and the scream of ricochet was made hideously evident. Brick and plaster chips careened from the walls and pattered to the carpet. The air was thick with dust.

Slater made the pillar. As he ran he got a brief impression of the arena of battle: one Serb behind a desk, one behind a filing cabinet, the third behind the opposite pillar to his own.

Silence.

A bluish smoke hovering at shoulder-height.

The soft click as one of the Serbs unlocked his empty magazine.

Now, thought Slater. The plastic shroud that provided the Uzi's foregrip was still cool in his hand. Stepping sideways from behind the pillar he fired a pair of aimed shots at the filing cabinet at head height. The response was a volley of rounds cutting the air past his face – one of them so close that he felt the wind of its spinning flight.

As Slater swung back behind the pillar the RDB man who had fired at him raced towards the desk covering Andreas and Chris. Standing, leaning hard into the submachine gun as if he was on the range at Pontrilas, Andreas took off the top of his attacker's head like a boiled egg. Cartwheeling to the floor with his finger on the trigger and his selector on automatic, the RDB man fully and lengthily discharged his magazine. Four of the 9mm rounds punched through, respectively, Andreas's carotid artery, windpipe and second and third cervical vertebrae – snapping back his head and flipping him, all but decapitated, against the back wall.

Not yet dead, Andreas's RDB attacker kicked lazily on the carpet. Behind the desk, her movements icily controlled, Chris fired a double-tap through the open top of his skull into his exposed brain. The kicking stopped.

As the dead body of his friend slid bloodily down the wall, Slater forced himself to remain in control. No one, it was clear, was going to come out with their hands up. The Department's single bargaining card – Branca – was bleeding to death, and thus no longer negotiable against Eve.

As he considered his options, he saw Chris lean round the end of the upturned desk and fire a long, exploratory burst with her Uzi in the direction of the remaining two RDB men. Slater couldn't see them, but he heard their grunts as the rounds screamed and ricocheted around them.

The two exchanged breathless comments in

Serbian, and an MP5 magazine slid across the carpet between them. Then one of them gave a hoarse and urgent shout and an instant later a door opened at the far end of the warehouse.

Another RDB man came out – a man they hadn't seen. In front of him, still dressed as she had been in the forest, was Eve, gagged. The man had the fingers of one hand knotted in her hair and with the other was holding to her throat a small rubber-handled automatic that some card-index in Slater's brain recognised as a NAA Black Widow. The man was short and broad, and his head and body were almost entirely concealed by Eve's.

'Come out, please, or I shoot your woman.' The voice was nervous – dangerously so – but undoubtedly sincere. 'I count to three, OK, then I'm killing her. Yes?'

Slater said nothing. He was in plain sight of the man holding Eve. If he tried to move out of the RDB man's firing line he would become visible to one of the others.

'*One!*'

No one moved. Chris waited behind the desk, taking her lead from Slater.

'*Two!*'

Slater bent down, placed his Uzi on the floor. Let go, he told himself. Let go of reason, let go of fear, let go of everything. Enter the zone.

The man holding Eve nodded, waiting for Slater to straighten and walk out unarmed.

Enter the zone. Access the physical memory of those hundreds of hours in the killing-house. Let the body do the thinking, not the brain. Let go of everything but instinct. Become that instinct. Let the body speak.

Slater straightened. But his hands were no longer empty – they held the Sig Sauer, which had somehow become part of his body, a taut and deadly extension of his gaze.

Chris, describing the events to Ray and Debbie a fortnight later, would say that things seemed to freeze at that moment – that there was an instant of pure motionlessness. And in that split-second, she would tell them, there was time for certain details to strike her – the painful-looking twist of Eve's neck, for example, and the way that the RDB man had to twist his stubby fingers in her hair to retain a grip of her, and even the entirely irrelevant fact that he was carrying the Black Widow in his left fist.

And then the Sig Sauer swinging upwards, stretching the moment to unbearable length. Time hurtling on.

'Three!'

Slater's first shot – double-handed, arms at full reach – smashed through his target's left elbow, reducing the joint to a shattered hinge of bone, cartilage and synovial ligament. As the RDB man's forearm twitched spastically, fingers fanning into a last fluttering dance, the Black Widow spun off behind him. He seemed to half-turn after it, and then the air briefly reddened as Slater's second and third shots drove through his right temple. Dying, his hand involuntarily clenching in her hair, the RDB man dragged Eve down to the carpet.

One of the remaining Serbs screamed to the other, and poured a volley of fire towards Chris. Grabbing his Uzi, Slater leaned round the pillar and fired a burst at her attacker. The RDB man fell sideways, hit in the upper body, and Chris finished him off with a double-tap from behind the desk.

The last man charged at Slater, firing as he came.

Slater swung sideways to evade, but felt the rounds slam into him. *Fuck*, he thought, more in irritation than fear. I've been hit. Adrenaline kept him on his feet for a moment, but then another jackhammer blow dropped him to the carpet. His body stopped responding to his will.

So this was how it was. No pain, no fear, just the red card. Just disappointment at not being allowed to continue.

Your time's up, whispered a voice he almost recognised. And I'm coming to get you, like I always promised I would. Above Slater, an RDB man who bore a curious resemblance to his father was preparing to shoot him in the face. Time had jammed again.

He heard the tiny plink of window-glass an instant before the damped crack of the distant Dragunov. Leon, ever the conservative, had opted for the chest shot, and the heavy 7.62 round drilled neatly through the Serb's sternum before exiting his back in a grapefruit-sized wad of loose tissue, bone and lung.

Dead on his feet, the RDB man hit the floor like a ton of condemned beef.

Silence, except for Branca's shivering gasps. Five men dead and the place a blood-hosed slaughterhouse, dense with smoke, rank with death. Everywhere on the carpet – now a sodden red-black – the yellow-metal casings of expended nine-mm ammunition.

Slater on his back, helpless, the black wetness spreading beneath him, the carpet a warm marsh, feeling nothing.

Eve face-down twenty feet away, waiting for the next exchange of fire, with a dead man's fist stiffening in her hair.

Andreas motionless against the wall in a clotted puddle, his eyes sightless, his neck bonelessly and horribly twisted.

And finally movement. Quiet footfalls as Chris runs through the blood-stink and the brick-dust from Serb to Serb, levels her Uzi at each man, delivers the formal double-tap where necessary – a quick tubercular cough – and hurries on.

Finally she makes her way to Eve, briefly squeezes the other woman's shoulder and whispers her name, works the dead man's hand from her hair, finds the keys for the plasticuffs in his pocket.

Eve, looking up with stunned eyes, clambering stiffly to her feet.

Chris moving on to Slater. Touching his neck for the pulse. Exhaling.

'Chris to all stations. Come in. Over.'

Her voice shaky, but procedure holding her together.

Eve seeing Andreas's body, noting Branca Nikolic bleeding to death beside the desk, falling to her knees beside Slater. The sight of the blood coursing from his shoulder returning a sense of purpose to her movements.

'Hold this,' she ordered him, pressing a crumpled handkerchief to the wound.

He winced, but managed it, and she began to unbutton his shirt.

When she got to the protective vest, her eyes widened. Three subsonic 9mm rounds had penetrated the vest's Kevlar outer skin and flattened themselves against the perspex trauma-shield. Only the fourth round had actually penetrated Slater, and this had passed straight through the muscle overlying his collar-bone.

Painful, but not fatal. Loosening the Velcro shoulder-straps, Eve removed the combat-vest and ripped open his T-shirt.

Slater's chest looked as if a sledge-hammer had been taken to it. Where the rounds had struck the trauma-shield three mauve compact-disc-sized whorls covered broken ribs. Even as Eve watched the bruises were darkening and expanding – within hours they would be the lurid purple of rotten plums.

She shook her head in disbelief. 'Well, it looks as if you've got that second chance you paid for. You're not actually going to die.'

'No?'

'No. And don't sound so disappointed. You look as if you've been kicked by a carthorse and there's a neat nine-millimetre hole straight through your right shoulder – but no, basically you're going to make it.'

'Andreas?' Slater asked, although he already knew the answer, and she shook her head.

'Branca?'

'I doubt it. She's taken a round in the groin.'

He shook his head, and then winced, closing his eyes.

'You saved my life,' said Eve. 'Or something very like that. I felt those rounds go past me.'

'I honestly don't know how I made that shot. I think it was something to do with seeing Andreas killed. I just . . .' He shrugged, helpless, and winced again.

'I'm sorry,' said Eve. 'You were old friends, weren't you?'

'We went back a few years,' said Slater, his mouth twitching at a dim memory of Trooper van Rijn, as he had then been, baring his buttocks at a party of outraged Kuwaitis from the back of a commandeered Chevrolet during the aftermath of Desert Storm.

'Well, we liked him too,' said Eve, folding her arms tightly across her chest as her eyes filled with tears. 'And I just can't believe he's dead. I mean it's pretty pointless, isn't it – his life for my life?'

'You can't think like that,' said Slater. 'It doesn't take you anywhere.'

She nodded and stared at the floor. 'So what happened to the disc?' she asked eventually. 'Did you bring it with you just in case?'

'I sent it back to London,' Slater said, avoiding her gaze. 'Stuck it in a postbox at the Bastille in the early hours of this morning.'

She looked at him quizzically and then nodded. 'Good idea. The sooner it's processed and destroyed the better.'

Chris joined them, the Glock 26 hanging from her hand. 'So,' she said wearily.

She and Eve made their way downstairs to let in Leon and Terry. The priority now was to report to Manderson and get the hell out of France. When they had closed the door behind them, Slater attempted to get to his feet. The attempt was agonising – his broken ribs sent waves of white-hot pain lancing across his chest – but he made it to his knees.

A few metres away, Branca lay on the carpet, her lips moving uncertainly as if singing along to a song she only half-knew. Bright red arterial blood flooded the carpet beneath her.

Slowly, painfully, Slater made his way over to her. 'I'm sorry, Branca,' he said quietly. Reaching for a copy of *Paris-Match* which lay among the detritus of the upturned desk, he slipped it as gently as he could between her head and the carpet, and shrugging off his ripped T-shirt he pressed it to the bloody well at her groin.

She flinched, but her eyes thanked him. 'We should not be enemies,' she whispered, and Slater shook his head.

'You're a good soldier,' he told her. 'You played it well.'

She managed the shadow of a smile.

'What is your true name?' she asked him.

'Neil.'

'I think I'm dying, Neil. Yes?'

He nodded gently and took her hand.

'No doctor coming?'

He met her fearful gaze. 'No doctor, Branca. I'm sorry.'

She closed her eyes as a wave of pain overtook her. 'Will you stay with me?' she gasped, eventually. 'I'm frightened to . . . to go alone.'

'I'll stay with you,' he promised, moving the damp strands of blonde hair from her eyes. 'Don't be frightened.'

Her skin was very pale and very cold. As he watched, she lost focus for a moment as the pain returned and then she seemed to gather herself, to draw down a last brief lease of life.

'Please, Neil, do something for me.'

Her gaze was steady now. She knew she had very little time.

'Tell me,' he said.

SIXTEEN

Slater decided to take the slow road to Brighton, across the Downs. It was a warm day – alternatively bright and overcast as the clouds scudded across the sun.

No one, he thought – no one in the world – knows that I'm here. It was a pleasurable thought. Reaching up he pressed the sun-roof button, and the wind streamed easily into the car.

His shoulder hurt less now. There had been two bad days, but now the wound had subsided to a dull ache. His ribs, on the other hand, were worse. The service doctor who strapped him up in Paris had worked at Aintree for several years and treated the jockeys who fell and broke bones in the Grand National. So he had been less than impressed by Slater's attempts at stoicism. 'You'll be back on the rugby pitch within the week,' he'd said cheerfully, briskly turning down Slater's request for pain-killers. 'It might tickle a bit, but nothing that'll worry a tough lad like you.'

Despite himself, and despite his screaming ribs, Slater had smiled.

They'd been back in England for ten days. After the

firefight at the Rue de Coude, Eve had spent an hour on the mobile to Manderson, explaining the situation. Terry and Leon had kept watch, but the street remained deserted. The shots fired on the top-floor had all been silenced, and no trace of the mayhem had been discernible outside.

Manderson had ordered them to stay put, and after alerting the Paris station chief had flown in an MI6 cleaning team.

The cleaning team had worked all night, subtly rearranging the bloody tableau and planting certain artefacts and substances. By dawn they had vanished, leaving behind them clear evidence of a lethal firefight between members of an East European heroin importation ring.

The cleaners had thought it best to remove a coded notebook containing contact numbers for Branca's various clients and lovers. Evidence that a number of prominent Parisians were being blackmailed by the RDB was felt to be safest in British hands. That their number included a French NATO official was considered of particular interest.

Andreas's body was spirited away from the Rue de Coude in a sealed van, along with the rest of the team. They had raced out of Paris, and shortly before dawn, in a field near Cap Gris-Nez, a Puma helicopter had swung out of the mist and taken them on board.

The extraction was carried out by a special team seconded from the RAF. The flight had not been cleared with the French authorities, but then neither had Operation Firewall – hardly surprising given that it had cost the French arms industry many billions of francs in lost business.

By midday Andreas's body had been cremated and a certificate issued to the effect that he had died of heart failure. His ashes were returned to an address in South London, from where they were collected by Debbie. In common with the other members of the Cadre, he had no immediate family.

Slater had been dropped off by the van at a small flat behind the British Embassy in the Rue du Faubourg St Honoré, where a service doctor had dressed his wound and strapped his broken ribs, administered a single dose of Volterol, and put him to bed.

Two days later he had been pronounced fit and driven to the Gare du Nord, where with the compliments of the MI6 station chief he had been handed a first-class Eurostar ticket and – with the compliments of the doctor – a half bottle of Laphroaig whisky 'to help him sleep'.

He had been met at Waterloo by Eve, who drove him back to his flat. They barely spoke during the two-minute drive, but as soon as they were behind closed doors he dropped the bags and reached for her. She had responded hungrily for a moment but then had gently disengaged herself.

'Ten days,' she told him, placing a finger on his mouth. 'For the next ten days it's going to be all work. After that, though, there's going to be a week's leave. And then we can . . . escape. How would that be?'

A little unwillingly, Slater had agreed that it would be fine. He wanted her with every nerve and sinew in his body, but he also knew that she was right – that the only way things would work between them was if their relationship remained deep-frozen while they worked together. Any other arrangement would be destructive of the subtle dynamics of the team. They could not allow themselves to be more concerned for each other than for their colleagues, and they could not allow their colleagues to think that this was a possibility. There would be leave-periods, and there would be the odd night at weekends, but for the time being that would be the limit of it.

Slater agreed. Having thought that he had lost her altogether, he was prepared to wait for her.

'It'll be special,' she'd promised him with a small smile. 'But for the next ten days I'm not even going to think about it. And you mustn't either.'

'That's a bit of a tall order,' Slater had said.

'Well, I expect you've taken a few of those in your time. And let's face it, a covert relationship has definitely got its sexy side. Neither of us would be in this line of work if we weren't at least a little bit addicted to secrecy, would we?'

Slater had laughed, then winced and touched his ribs. 'I'm not telling you,' he said.

At Vauxhall Cross, the team had been debriefed both individually and as a whole by Manderson. The general feeling, apart from regret at Andreas's death, was that Operation Firewall had proved a great success.

The Balkan desk were beside themselves with joy. Antoine Fanon-Khayat was dead, as was the Ondine deal. Any chance of its resurrection by Belgrade had been scuppered by the elimination of the entire RDB unit tasked with identifying Fanon-Khayat's contacts.

With the potential embarrassment of the Cambodia pictures eliminated, what was more, Radovan Karadjic could now be tried for war crimes at the Hague in the full glare of publicity. It would look good, it would feel good, and mainland Europe – with the possible exception of France – would be properly grateful to Britain.

When, Manderson had politely enquired of Slater on his return from Paris, did he think that the disc might be reaching them? Slater had shrugged. He told Manderson that he had taken a stamp and a small padded envelope from Miko Pasquale's desk – not hard to guess what those pocket-size envelopes were usually used for, given Pasquale's profession – stuck the CD inside, addressed it, and slung it into a postbox on the way back to the car. That had been on the Monday evening, after picking up the Uzis with Leon, and now it was Thursday. The European post was generally pretty slow – chances were it wouldn't arrive until after the weekend.

Manderson had nodded, supposing that Slater was right. Typical French, of course. Quick enough to criticise 'slow' British trains, but when it came to delivering a letter within seven days . . .

Just as a matter of interest, Manderson had

continued, why had Slater gone to the trouble of posting the CD? Why hadn't he just pocketed it with a view to carrying it back to London?

Slater had shrugged. 'At that stage,' he'd explained, 'the RDB had Eve, and we knew that they weren't going to give her up lightly. If we had come off worst in that firefight, and I hadn't survived, the CD would have been in Belgrade by now. It seemed safer to trust it to the post.'

Manderson had nodded slowly. 'You did well, Neil,' he said, extending a congratulatory hand. '*Bloody* well.'

On the Friday night, fully debriefed, the Paris team plus Debbie and Ray had gone out to celebrate and, in their own way, to bid goodbye to Andreas. By tradition, each member of the Cadre kept a 'stag night' account in which a few hundred pounds was permanently invested. Should he or she die in the field, this money was used by the others for a giant piss-up.

These memorial evenings, Slater discovered, invariably took place in a private room in a pub in Waterloo. Only Guinness and champagne were drunk. The room was booked for a stag night, in order that the ensuing drunkenness, singing, fighting, shouting and tears should come as no surprise to the landlord.

They had arrived at the Green Man early, stayed late, and drunk a very great deal. In retrospect the details of the evening were a little blurred, but it was generally agreed that Andreas's send-off had been every bit as spectacular as Ellis's. Afterwards – again in accordance with Cadre tradition – Debbie had poured Andreas's ashes into the river from Waterloo Bridge, and they had wished him safe journey.

It was the time he had spent with the dying Branca that had confirmed Slater's suspicions that the disc contained more volatile material than they had been shown. Embarrassing though the Cambodia pictures were – and one of Slater's early instructors who had taken part in the operation had once let slip that 'some of those Khmer lads could get a bit excitable when prisoners came their way' – the limited damage that they could do to British interests could not begin to be balanced against the political advantage of having 'fast-balled' Radovan Karadjic to the Hague. No, there had to be more on the disc than that, and given that Slater had seen his own and his colleagues' lives placed on the line, he was buggered if he was going to be lied to about it.

He had decided on a course of action which, if discovered, would have seen him expelled from the service. As he had told Manderson, he had indeed taken a padded postbag and a postage stamp from Miko Pasquale's desk, and he had indeed sealed, stamped and addressed the envelope with the CD inside it. But he hadn't posted the package at the Bastille, as he'd told Manderson – instead he had stuffed it into the side-pocket of his combat-pants. If it looked like Eve was going to be killed as a result of the Cadre's refusal to hand the disc over to the RDB, Slater had resolved to hand it over to them himself, and bollocks to the consequences.

But they had rescued her, and so he had posted the CD shortly before leaving Paris. Not to the Cadre's office at Vauxhall Cross, however, but to an accommodation address in Kingsway, a short walk from Holborn underground station. In return for a modest monthly charge paid to a newsagent, and anticipating frequent changes of address, Slater had used the service since his departure from the Regiment.

On the Saturday following his return to London he had collected the package – which had in fact arrived a mere two days after posting – taken it back to his flat, and run it through the laptop. It was password-protected, but some thoughtful soul – Fanon-Khayat at a guess – had slipped a piece of paper bearing an 8-letter place-name inside the CD case. Armed with the means of entry, Slater had accessed the images inside.

There were six of them, and as he had suspected they were nothing whatever to do with SAS activity on the Thailand-Cambodia border. The images were much older than the ones that had been projected at the Firewall briefing, and while obviously historically interesting had meant nothing to Slater.

He sincerely hoped that they would mean more to Aleksandra Marcovic – whoever she was. Branca had told him nothing about the woman except her name and the fact that she lived near Brighton. There hadn't been time for more, but before Branca died Slater had made a solemn promise that he would find Aleksandra Marcovic and show her the photographs on the disc.

At a randomly chosen data service centre in Victoria he had had a copy made of the CD. He had then returned the original to the envelope with the Paris post-mark. He had previously sealed it with a single staple, but now he peeled away the protective strip, stuck the flap down in the normal way, and restapled it at the same point.

He had disguised the detour that the package had taken by removing the label with the Kingsway address on it. Beneath it he had written the Vauxhall Cross address, and with nothing to indicate that it had not come straight from Paris the envelope was now ready for adding to the next morning's mail-drop.

This was not difficult – shortly after each delivery came into the building the Cadre's letters were placed in a locked box outside the office. Making sure that he arrived before the first delivery, Slater had slipped the package into the box, and when Ray emptied it half an hour later, the package was among a sheaf of other mail.

Shortly afterwards Manderson had emerged from his office waving the CD. '*Bloody* French!' he mouthed cheerfully to Slater, who was sitting at his terminal slowly and dyslexically bashing out a report. To Slater's considerable relief he then dropped the envelope into a shredder without checking the date it had left Paris.

It had been a long week. Detailed report-writing was not Slater's forte, and his slowly healing ribs and shoulder had not made the task any more enjoyable. But the report-writing had to be done if anything was to be learnt from the operation, and each of them was engaged in a similar task. The consoling factor was that the promised week's leave awaited them – on Friday evening they would be going their separate ways.

Slater had resolved to visit Aleksandra Marcovic on the Saturday morning.

Slater knew he shouldn't really have been driving – a breathalyser test would probably have shown a unit or two of alcohol in his blood from an end-of-week drink hosted by Manderson the night before. On the other hand he had never felt more alert, more alive. A post-traumatic stress reaction would be stalking him in the wake of the slaughter in Paris – and there was no chance of escaping the Darklands after a bloody fiesta like that – but it hadn't yet declared itself. Even the pain lancing through his ribs and shoulder served merely to remind him that he was alive – that he had stood eyeball to eyeball with death and walked away.

He was on the crest of the Downs now, and the grass, defiant of the wind, was flattening itself against the chalky hillside. Far below him was the long sprawl of Brighton and its satellites – Portslade, Hove, Kemp Town, Rottingdean.

Aleksandra Marcovic lived between the two easterly suburbs of Rottingdean and Saltdean. She was not on the telephone but it turned out that she was one of the hundreds of thousands of British citizens known to the security services, having been settled in the UK as a refugee after the Second World War.

Slater had been given a number of tutorials by Debbie in the use of the ATHS desktop network used to access MI6's computerised archive, and had found Marcovic without difficulty in the course of an after-hours data-surfing session. Her file, which was marked UK EYES ALPHA and so cleared for all security service personnel, indicated that she had been born in 1933/4 to a Serbian family near Kutina, Yugoslavia. At the time of her registration as a refugee in 1946 her parents and two sisters were believed dead as a result of inter-factional strife following the 1941 German invasion, and the subsequent creation of the Independent State of Croatia (ISC). Settled post-war with a family in Croydon, Marcovic had married one Vernon Smedley, a solicitor, in 1953. Widowed in 1986, she had moved to Saltdean, where she had become an active member of the Anglo-Serbian Friendship Society, a cultural and travel organisation. In April 1996 she had applied for a tourist visa to visit Belgrade, where she had spent several weeks.

Nothing very contentious in any of it. A not especially happy-sounding life, but then how many people could lay claim to a life which looked happy on paper?

Bypassing Brighton, which he calculated would be choked with visitors on a warm summer's day, Slater drove past Kemp Town racecourse and cut southwards towards Saltdean. Soon he was driving past caravan parks and rows of identically gabled 1930s villas, and could smell the sea and the salt on the air.

Philomena Avenue was the easternmost of several roads flanking a line of seafront shops. Number 54, a small, pebbledashed villa fronted by a spray of Pampas-grass, was the end house in the row. Climbing from the car, bracing himself against a sharp wind which worried its way between the net-curtained villas, Slater rang the bell.

The door was answered by a tall, gaunt-faced woman in a candlewick dressing gown, who regarded him for a long moment in silence.

'Aleksandra Marcovic?' he asked her.

She said nothing, and Slater noticed that beneath the bluish perm her ears were curiously deformed — little more than stumps. Perhaps, he thought, she was deaf.

'I've come on a rather unusual errand,' he continued uncertainly. 'My name—'

'I know who you are,' she said flatly. 'You're a man of death. I've known people like you all my life. Does your name matter?'

Slater stared at her, stunned. There was, as she had said, a kind of recognition in her eyes. Did a familiarity with violent death truly mark you in some way?

'My name doesn't matter. I was given your name by Branca Nikolic.'

The woman looked at him, looked down at the briefcase in his hand. 'You had better come in.'

Slater followed her into the pastel-coloured lounge and she indicated an armchair covered in a crocheted shawl. In the other chair an obscenely large cat snored on a newspaper.

'Tea?' she asked him severely.

'Please.'

He sat down and she disappeared through a curtain of plastic strips into the kitchen. Opposite him, net curtains framed a blue-brown expanse of wind-whipped sea. On the horizon he could make out the vague form of a container ship. It barely seemed to be moving.

'So,' said Aleksandra Marcovic, placing a loaded tray on a small dining table. 'You know Branca.'

This lack of curiosity about my name, thought Slater. It's almost as if she knows that she would never be told the truth, so she's not going to bother asking.

'I know Branca,' he nodded, 'and she asked me to come and show you some pictures.'

Her eyes narrowed. 'What pictures?'

'Can I show you? And then ask you to tell me who the people in them are?'

She shrugged. 'If that's what Branca suggested, then I guess that's OK.'

Slater was longing to ask her how she knew Branca but held back, knowing that he would never be able to explain how he knew her himself. Was this woman perhaps connected to the RDB in some way?

He took the laptop out of his briefcase and carried it over to the table. The machine, no larger or heavier than a London A to Z, had been assigned to him for report-writing and communications purposes, and had a specially protected hard disk. Powering it up, he slipped the copy of the Fanon-Khayat CD into the drive. The dark blue screen lit up with the words RENAISSANCE 1945 and a password dialogue box, into which Slater typed ISERLOHN. The title page dissolved, to be replaced with a half-dozen tiny thumbnail photographs.

'Sugar and milk?' asked Aleksandra Marcovic.

'Thanks.'

'A biscuit?'

'Please.'

With these rituals observed, she seated herself at the chair next to him, and took a pair of plastic-framed spectacles from a case. Glancing at her, he could see curiosity on the broad features. Positioning the cursor over the first thumbnail, he clicked.

A black and white image resolved itself.

Next to him, Marcovic froze. 'Oh my God,' he heard her whisper. 'Oh my God, no.'

On the screen was a portrait of a young, fair-haired man in his early twenties, standing smartly to attention and holding a card marked 'WEGNER, Dietrich, HAUPTMANN'. A smudged date-stamp read 28 November 1945. Despite his military stance and fixed gaze, the young man was not in uniform, but wearing a tightly buttoned jacket of tweed or wool. He was unshaven. One cheek appeared to be badly bruised.

Next to Slater, Marcovic was gasping in disbelief. Her hand was across her mouth and she was shaking her head as if in shocked denial of the image before her. For several minutes she said nothing, but simply stared at the laptop screen.

Chris Ryan

'You know this man?' asked Slater eventually, conscious as he spoke of the inadequacy of the question.

'I last saw that face nearly sixty years ago,' said Marcovic, her chest rising and falling as she caught her breath. 'But I've seen it every night and every day since then. We called him *Guja*, which means the Snake.' She turned to him urgently. 'Why are you showing me this? Is he dead?'

'I don't know anything about him,' said Slater. 'He seems to be in some kind of custody, though, in this picture. Either British or American from the English date-stamp. Was that his name, Dietrich Wegner?'

'We never knew his name. To us he was just *Guja*.'

'And it was during the German occupation of Croatia, that you . . . knew this man?'

She shook her head, as if to re-establish some connection with the present. 'First, show me the other pictures.'

A broad desk, a conference room with pillars, an iron-jawed man in a grey suit surrounded by black-uniformed SS officers. Hauptmann Dietrich Wegner just recognisable on the outskirts of the group, smiling politely.

A handsome young man, brown-haired, on a white horse. Beneath his hands, folded on the pommel of his saddle, a coiled whip and a sub-machine gun. At his side, holding the horse's bridle and smiling, Wegner again. Both men's uniforms impeccable.

The balcony of a stone-built house. Several men and

women in hiking clothes drinking and smoking cigarettes. A uniformed man lifting black bread to his mouth. Wegner, wearing a patterned sweater, pointing down to the valley below.

A badly blurred image. A man in a black apron hurrying past a low shed, carrying a knife and apparently wearing some kind of necklace. To one side of him, preoccupied, Wegner.

Four men standing beneath leafless trees by a river, talking. Snow falling. One of the men wearing the robes of a monk. Another recognisable as Wegner.

As each image appeared, something in Aleksandra Marcovic seemed to die. She started mumbling to herself in Serbo-Croat, shaking her head, endlessly repeating the same few phrases. Finally she stood up and walked several times around the small room. She was very pale.

'Where did you get these pictures?' she asked him. 'From Branca?'

Slater nodded.

'It's unbelievable,' she said. 'It's just unbelievable. After so long to see the faces of these men . . .'

Slater was silent. He reached for his tea, which had cooled and was too sweet. He crunched a biscuit between his teeth.

Aleksandra Markovic closed her eyes. Reached into the past.

'I was born in a small town – not much more than a village, really – called Dusovac, on the Toplica River in Croatia. My parents were Serbian, and had a small farm. I had two sisters, Milla and Drina.

'In the spring of 1941, when the Germans partitioned Yugoslavia and set up the Independent State of Croatia – the ISC – I was seven. One morning that summer German troops came in a lorry and took away my father. The lorry was full of other men from the area – we knew most of them – and they waved to me and my sisters as the lorry drove away. At midday, we heard later, ten lorries full of men had arrived in the market place in Kutina. They were unloaded, lined up against a wall, and machine-gunned. Afterwards an announcement was made that they had been executed in reprisal for a German patrol which had been ambushed by partisans. The rule was that for every German wounded, fifty Yugoslavian men would be shot, and for every German killed, a hundred would be shot.

'In fact, most of those executed that day were Serbs. Although there were Croatians who resisted, there were many who were desperate to collaborate, and proved their loyalty to the Third Reich by turning against the Serbs who lived among them. They burnt and looted our schools and churches, banned our Cyrillic script, and forced us to wear patches saying who we were. And that was just the beginning of it – the early days.

'The man set up by the Nazis as the head of the ISC government was one of the most evil, degenerate creatures who ever lived – a monster called Ante Pavelic. If you go to the second picture – there – that's him with the SS officers.

'Pavelic styled himself the *Poglavnik*, or Führer, and his followers called themselves the *Ustashe*. A policy was decided on – probably at that desk there, in the photograph – whereby a third of Serbs would be forcibly converted to Catholicism, a third would be expelled, and the rest quite simply killed. Permission was given, in effect, for Serb men, women and children to be murdered at will. And hell came to Yugoslavia.

'That summer, after my father was taken away, terrible stories began to reach us. Orthodox priests were being murdered – often tortured to death – Serbian mothers and their children had been thrown over the cliffs at Jadovno, Serbian corpses were hanging from scaffolds all the way from Kutina to Banja Luca. We were petrified – frightened beyond belief – but we didn't know what to do. We had nowhere to go; to take to the roads would have been suicide. So we stayed where we were, and mourned my father, and lived on the food we grew, and hoped that people would forget we were there.

'Then one afternoon in August we saw smoke coming from one of the fields, and heard strange sounds. My sister Drina and I went out to see what was happening, and from the smell we thought someone was cooking beef. But when we got near we saw . . . something I cannot describe. It was a naked man, tied to pegs in the ground, and a fire had been lit on his chest. He was still alive.

'We ran away. We didn't dare go near. But when

414

we got near the house we saw that we had been followed by six men in uniform. They caught up with us, told us to stay where we were, and went inside.

'It took them two hours to finish with my mother and my oldest sister Milla, and then there were shots. The men walked me and Drina to a truck. We were told we were going somewhere we would be looked after. A camp – not far away – where we would be safe. There would be other children there. It was called Jasenovac.

'If Yugoslavia under the black legions of the *Ustashe* was hell, Jasenovac was the inmost circle of that hell. The cruelty there was bestial, unspeakable, far beyond anything you would think human beings were capable of. They burnt prisoners alive, they cut their heads off with saws . . . There were children there – thousands of children – but they received no mercy either. The opposite, in fact.'

Slater stole a glance at Aleksandra Marcovic. Any trace of emotion or expression had been ruthlessly wiped from her face.

'The camp was in the south Croatian marshlands where the Una and Sava rivers join. We were put in wooden shacks without even straw to sleep on, fed on potatoes, and put to work building the guards' quarters. The wire had gone up at Jasenovac a fortnight before, but by 1945 there would be a whole network of camps from Krapje in the west to Stara Gradiska in the east. About six hundred thousand Serbs, Jews and gypsies would be killed there, one way or another, and the deepest hatred and the worst torture was reserved for the Serbs.

'If I just tell you what I saw with my own eyes . . . Exactly a year after I came to Jasenovac, a competition was organised to see which of the *Ustashe* men could kill the most prisoners with his own hands. The winner – a young Catholic lawyer, I think he was – managed to cut the throats of thirteen hundred people in one night with a specially sharpened butcher's knife. He won a gold watch and the title "King of the Killers".'

Slater, speechless, shook his head.

'Even the Nazis protested at this kind of behaviour, but then the *Ustashe* were animals, not humans. How can you regard as human people who feed children caustic soda, or beat them to death with hammers and axes, as happened to my sister Drina? I saw all of these things at Jasenovac.'

She was silent for a moment. The wind pressed at the double-glazing. Beyond the net curtains the sea was the colour of galvanised steel.

'But you asked about the pictures, so let me tell you about this . . .' she smiled bleakly, '. . . this handsome young *Ustashe* knight on his horse. His name is Dinko Sakic, and at age twenty-one he was made commandant of Jasenovac. They said – although I never saw it – that his favourite weapon was a welder's torch. When I saw him he was always carrying this whip and a pistol. As the photo shows he was a great friend of the *Guja*, the snake. They used to walk around the camp together as if they were in the grounds of some beautiful mansion, admiring the lawns and the statues and the views. People said that they were . . . you know.'

Slater nodded.

'At the same time there were women prisoners – I can't expect you to understand this – who thought that they were in love with one or other of them. Dinko and the *Guja* knew this too, and I think it amused them.'

Seeing Slater's disbelieving face, Marcovic smiled faintly. 'You have to understand that this was a world without rules, sense or logic. A world of blood, butchery and chaos. The *Guja* was a German SS officer, as you can tell from the uniform, and usually when there were German or Italian officers around the *Ustashe* made an effort to behave like human beings. Believe me, we welcomed the sight of a Nazi uniform – even an SS uniform.

'But no one bothered to moderate their behaviour when the *Guja* was around – quite the opposite, in fact, because they knew that he liked what he saw. He came to the camp so often I think he must have been stationed somewhere very close, perhaps at Kostajnica. He couldn't keep away, and though I never saw him so much as touch a prisoner I think he was in some way . . . addicted to what he witnessed here.'

Slater pulled down the next image. The hiking party.

'Right. The man eating the bread is Andrija Artukovich, the *Poglavnik*'s minister of the interior.

Artukovich was also responsible for the *Ustashe* – he was a kind of Croatian Himmler. And there again is the *Guja* in the foreground. Could you go to the last picture?'

Slater nodded.

'I don't know where this is. It could be Jasenovac, or Stara Gradiska or one of the smaller camps, but I think the point of this picture is the necklace worn by the man in the apron. I heard about this, but I never saw it.'

'What is the necklace?' asked Slater.

'Human eyes,' said Marcovic flatly. 'The *Ustashe* were always gouging out eyes. I heard years later that the *Poglavnik* liked to have baskets of Serbian eyes delivered to his desk. If you were an ambitious young *Ustashe* knight it was a good way to get ahead.'

Slater slowly shook his head, appalled. 'I had no idea about any of this.'

'Well, perhaps it's time that your eyes were opened. Next picture.'

The snow-scene by the river.

'This is definitely in Jasenovac, at the south end of the camp by the river. This is the *Guja*, clearly, but I don't know who these two are. This man, however' – she took a deep breath and pointed to the robed monk – 'this man I do know. This man I will remember for all eternity. Can I get you some more tea?'

'Thank you, said Slater. 'That would be kind.' He didn't want the tea, but he sensed that Aleksandra Marcovic needed a break, a chance to rally herself. For five minutes, as she busied herself, he stared out of the window, trying to make sense of the horrors she was recounting. When she came back her voice was quieter than it had been before. At times it was almost inaudible.

'We called him *Fra Sotona* – Brother Satan. I think his real name was Filipovic. He had joined the *Ustashe* from a monastery at Banja Luca, and was promoted to commandant of Jasenovac around the time of the killing competition in the Autumn of 1942. He was a brutal-looking man with a lisping, almost feminine voice, and of all those *Ustashe* monsters I would say that he was the most terrifying. He was only commandant for four months – Dinko Sakic rode in on his white horse at the end of the year – but the ferry across the river to the execution place at Gradina was busy for all of that time.'

'And this SS officer Wegner was a friend of his too?'

'Wegner came to the camp when *Fra Sotona* was there, yes. But I'm not sure if they were friends. *Sotona* was a very coarse man, and I remember him as being much older than the *Guja*. Sakic and the *Guja* – I can't call him by that other name – must have been about the same age.'

Out of politeness, Slater addressed his tea. Outside, the brightness had gone from the sky, and the first flicks of rain were spattering the window. 'So what do you think these pictures prove?' he asked Marcovic. 'Why do you think they have been assembled?'

She frowned. 'These people like Sakic, Artukovic

and the priest – other pictures exist. To those who need to know them, they are known. But I have never seen a photograph of the *Guja* before, and these pictures link him to all these men. Perhaps their purpose is to disprove SS and *Wehrmacht* claims that they did not realise the full horrors of the *Ustashe* camps – after all, here is a uniformed SS Hauptmann looking very much at home at the heart of Jasenovac. Anyone who was there could identify the place from these pictures. Otherwise' – she shrugged – 'I don't know.'

Slater nodded. Privately he considered that there had to be more to it than that.

'Why did you call Wegner by that name – the Snake?'

Aleksandra Marcovic folded her hands tightly on the table in front of her. So tightly, Slater noticed, that the knuckles showed white. 'Let me . . . paint you a picture. Imagine a line of children sitting on a bench outside a shed. A shed like the one in that picture there, of the man with the knife. One by one the children are being taken into the shed, and their ears are being cut off. The children waiting outside on the bench can hear everything that is going on inside the shed. They can hear the screams and they can hear the smooth, silky voice of *Fra Sotona*. The last two children waiting in the line are called Goran Nikolic and Aleksandra Marcovic. Watching these two children as they wait is a German officer in a black uniform – a young man, not more than twenty years old. His cap badge, however, is the death's head insignia of the SS. He is a connoisseur of terror, and as the children wait, listening to the screams coming from the shed, and the sudden silences as the victims faint, he moves his face close to theirs. He looks into their eyes and he smiles, a broad almost rapturous smile, and his head seems to sway from side to side like a snake.

'And I, Aleksandra Marcovic, am hypnotised with fear. I cannot move, I cannot speak, I cannot think. But beside me Goran Nikolic is not hypnotised. Even though he is only eight or nine years old he sees the *Guja* for what he is – a man. And in that moment he makes himself a sacred vow. That he will live, and he will fight, and that his children and his children's children will avenge this day.'

Urgently, she leaned forward towards him.

'I have not asked who you are – I have been a British citizen for almost half a century now, so it is best, I think, if you do not tell me – but if you are a friend of Branca, I can guess easily enough. As I said, you have the look of death about you.'

Slater said nothing.

'If you see Goran, will you tell him that I have thought about him often over the last few years. He wanted many sons to avenge those children who never returned, whose bones lie beneath the execution fields of Gradina, and God sent him a single daughter. How is Branca?'

'A brave soldier,' replied Slater gently. 'Her father has every reason to be proud of her.'

421

And it was at that point that Aleksandra Marcovic finally broke down.

When Slater finally drove away from Philomena Avenue it was late afternoon, the rain had cleared and the sun was making fitful attempts to redeem the day. Rather than returning to London, he drove into Brighton. After the horrors of Marcovic's story he felt the need to surround himself with people – with noise and laughter and bustle.

Buying a copy of the *Sun*, he took a seat in a striplit fish and chip shop – he had had nothing except tea and biscuits all day – and quite deliberately emptied his mind of all that Marcovic had told him. When he had finished his meal, read up on the latest immigrant scare-stories, absorbed the facts concerning the Awayday Bonking Vicar, and dwelt at some length on the silicone-free charms of Bethany from Hunstanton, Slater wandered out into the Lanes – an attractive tangle of antique shops near the city centre. In one of these he discovered a small cloth-bound volume entitled *The Gentlewoman's Guide to Old Rose Varieties*, which he bought as a present for Eve and slipped in his pocket.

Driving back to London, his mind whirling, Slater attempted to make sense of what he had learned from Aleksandra Marcovic. Why were those half-dozen photographs, taken over sixty years ago, so important? The purpose of collecting them together was clearly to incriminate Wegner, but why had so much effort been made to prove his association with *Ustashe* murderers? Why had it been Branca Nikolic's dying wish that he make this connection? If Wegner was still alive, surely the fact of his former SS membership would be sufficient to disgrace him in the eyes of the world.

The point about these pictures must be that they incriminated Wegner both as a Nazi and as a friend of the *Ustashe*, and that was why the Serbs wanted them so badly. But who was Wegner – assuming that he was still alive, sixty years after these pictures were taken? Some pillar of the European community – a business leader perhaps? If the Serbs could prove that a former Nazi and *Ustashe* supporter was growing old in Germany it would represent a huge propaganda coup for Belgrade. Any linkage between their bombing by Nazis in 1941 and by Nato in 1999 would be immediately exploited. Was that what MI6 was so keen to prevent? And if so, why had they lied to Slater and his colleagues?

Was it, he wondered, because they wanted to use the photographs for some purpose so disreputable that it had to be kept secret even from insiders? Were they to be used to blackmail or apply leverage to some 'friendly' power? Certainly the fact that Manderson had wanted the CD returned rather than destroyed on the spot in Paris suggested something of the sort. But if so, why had they gone to such trouble to weave this elaborate deception about the Khmer Rouge training teams? Why had they bothered to tell Slater and his fellow operatives anything at all? Why hadn't they just handed them their Eurostar tickets and their expenses float and told them to get on with it?

Eventually, his head spinning, Slater gave up. Whatever the truth behind Operation Firewall, and whatever the purpose of the photographs of Hauptmann Wegner, he had proved to his own satisfaction that his new employers had lied to him – and worse, had used his loyalty to his former Regiment to underpin the lie. Well, he thought dispiritedly, at least he knew how it was going to be.

He was at his lowest ebb as he drove through Croydon, the sad lace-curtained suburb in which it appeared that Aleksandra Marcovic had spent most of her adult life. The roadside villas, grimly individualised with their concrete statues and their privet hedges, seemed to go on for ever. And then the phone on the passenger seat rang, and it was Eve, and the sound of her voice and the anticipation of the week that lay before them drove everything else from his mind.

SEVENTEEN

Eve owned a flat in a pretty Georgian square off Kennington Lane. It suited her, and it struck Slater as they drank Guinness and picked at a packet of crisps at a table outside the pub, that the other residents all looked as if their parents might be friends of Eve's parents.

'The men have all got that Rupert look,' he explained to her. 'That weekdays in the City, weekends in the Cotswolds look. And the women all have hair like you and borrow the men's Jermyn Street shirts and turn the collars up.'

She nearly hit him for that. 'When have you ever, *ever* seen me in a man's City shirt?' she demanded, aiming a swipe at his head.

'I'm sure you've got some upstairs,' he replied, ducking. 'I'm sure a quick check of your wardrobe would throw up a striped shirt or two.'

'Well, you'll never find out. Because if you think you're climbing the stairs to my flat after making suggestions like that you can think again. I didn't save your life just to be accused of turning my shirt-collars up, you big ape!'

'Well, just to prove me wrong, tell me that your father didn't work in the City.'

'He did work in the City, as it happens, but not in the way you think. He was a gunsmith, and worked in the back room of a shop near the Monument. He could mend anything – shotguns, stalking rifles, handguns – and if he couldn't get the parts from the manufacturers he'd make them himself. He travelled to the shop every day by bus from Dalston, which is where I grew up and went to school. So you see I'm not posh in the least.'

'But you do give that impression.'

'Oh, I certainly know how to play the games that posh people play. I worked in the shop in the school holidays, and later, while I was at university I had a job with a firm that did shooting lunches. I kept my eyes and ears open, sure, and when I came to join the civil service I was glad that I had. It's still a pretty old-school organisation.'

'That's true enough,' said Slater.

She shrugged. 'If I'd gone into night-club management I expect I'd have played my hand differently. The point is that these days we can all reinvent ourselves. If we don't like the hand we were dealt we can discard it and pick up another. That's what I've done. That's what everyone does.'

'Everyone except me,' smiled Slater.

'Yes, you're pretty unreconstructed,' Eve agreed, tucking herself comfortably under his good shoulder.

A moment later the phone rang in her bag.

'That was Ridley,' she said when the brief conversation was finished. 'All Cadre members invited to lunch at River House tomorrow. Apologies for short notice. No three-line-whip but he'd like to see us if we're free.'

Within minutes, Slater's phone rang with the same message. They agreed that they might as well drive up together – if the others were still in London they would probably be doubling up too.

In Eve's flat, later that evening, Slater noticed the details that bore out the truth of what she had told him about her background. She owned very few clothes, and very little furniture, but what she had was of a very good quality. She had decorated the flat herself – not a huge job, given its size – and most of her salary still went towards her mortgage. On the mantelpiece was a photograph of her, aged about nine, posing like Annie Oakley with a pair of long-barrelled Colts. Next to her was a man of about forty in a brown coat.

'That's me and Dad. You can't see it there, but I'm standing on the counter of the shop. And the revolvers are the real thing, too.'

'Gals and guns,' murmured Slater, burying his face in her hair. 'Works every time. What do you keep here in the flat? A cupboard full of Claymore mines?'

'Just my Glock. Nothing serious. What exactly are you doing?'

'Just kissing your neck and unbuttoning you. Nothing serious.'

Eyes closed, she allowed him to undress her. 'You

427

know something,' she said, her back arching as his mouth found her breasts. 'We still haven't decided . . .'

His mouth moved downwards. 'Decided what?'

'What we're going to call each other,' she whispered. 'Let's get your clothes off.'

Gently, she helped him pull his T-shirt from the hectic shoulder-wound, the cracked ribs, and the fading but still lurid bruises.

'Perhaps I should do most of the work this time. In Paris you were slightly less damaged.'

'At least it's just you and me. No corpse making up a *ménage à trois*.'

She smiled, the smile became a gasp, and she began to move against him.

Afterwards, quite a long time later, he came to a decision.

'You know that CD,' he said. 'The one we took from Fanon-Khayat. The one that the RDB wanted to swap you for?'

'Mmmm.' Her face was buried in the pillow.

'I looked at it.'

She half-rose, frowning at him through sleepy eyes. 'You *what*?' When?'

'The other day. When it arrived in London.'

'And?'

'And it was nothing to do with Cambodia or the Regiment at all. The pictures were of an SS officer visiting a concentration camp in Yugoslavia during the war.'

'Well maybe we got the wrong tape. Maybe there

was something they couldn't tell us. Maybe there are several tapes. Is that all there was on it? Just some SS officer?'

'His name was Dietrich Wegner. He was a nineteen-year-old captain. In the concentration camp they called him "the Snake". He was a sadistic voyeur – he got excited by other people's suffering.'

She rubbed her eyes. 'How do you know this?'

He took a deep breath and told her.

She heard him out.

When he had finished she pressed the pillow to her face and shook her head. 'Will you swear to me you will never again do anything so *stupid*, so *reckless*, so . . .' She dropped the pillow. 'I just can't *believe* you've—'

'They lied to us. They looked us in the eye and fucking lied to us!'

'So maybe they lied, and maybe they made a mistake. Who gives a shit? People do both the whole time. Our job was to take out Fanon-Khayat and retrieve that CD, and we did both – end of story.'

'So why feed us all that Khmer Rouge crap?'

'I don't have the first idea,' said Eve. 'And do you know what? Right now I don't care. The point is that your little jaunt to Brighton could have cost people their lives. That Marcovic woman's a fucking Serb, for God's sake! Her friends are officers in the Serbian secret service – the same people who kidnapped me at gunpoint a fortnight ago, killed Andreas, and were pretty keen to stuff you into a wood-chipper.'

They stared at each other, both of them speechless with anger.

'I'm sorry,' she said eventually, her voice muted. 'I shouldn't have said that, but I just don't want you to get into trouble, and I mean *serious* trouble. Please, promise me you'll never do anything like that again. Please.'

He nodded. 'OK. I guess it was a bit on the daft side.'

She placed her arms gently round his neck. 'Look, I'm sure no one will ever find out. Can we just forget about the whole thing – the pictures, the woman in Brighton, everything?' She kissed him softly on the mouth. 'After all, we're supposed to be escaping from all that, aren't we?'

'That we are,' said Slater.

'So please, let's escape and put it behind us. I wouldn't say this to anyone except you, but when those RDB people took me away I was really, really scared. They were bloody rough – not least your little friend Branca, who I promise you is pretty handy with the butt of an MP5.'

Slater held her.

'Please,' she whispered. 'For the time we've got together, just take me to a place where things like that don't happen.'

'I will,' murmured Slater, stroking her hair. 'I promise you.'

With Eve, for the first time in his life, he could see the possibility of a shared future. In the past his relationships had foundered because no woman had ever come close to understanding the life that he lived, with its wild terrors and fierce triumphs. But here at last was one who would understand – and more than understand. She would share the terrors and share the triumphs and at the end of the day she would still be a woman.

The next morning he woke before she did. The sun was pouring through the curtains, and he gently drew back the sheet and lay for a while admiring her. As always when she was asleep she looked lost, almost childlike, and it occurred to Slater that every time he saw her he discovered that he knew less about her. How much more unlearning would he have to do, he wondered, before he could start to understand her?

Gently, he started to kiss her, beginning with the dark triangle of her pubic hair and working his way upwards towards her mouth. At the end of his travels he discovered two sea-blue eyes regarding him through half-closed lids.

'That was nice.' She smiled drowsily. 'What time is it?'

Whatever time it was, it was two hours before they were both dressed. Slater wondered if he should go home and change into smarter clothes than he'd arrived in the night before but Eve assured him that wasn't necessary. 'Go as you are. Ridley doesn't like to be made to feel he's someone who has to be given special treatment.'

They made it to the M3 by 11am. Slater drove the BMW and Eve tilted back the passenger seat at his side. When they had driven to Hampshire a month earlier the countryside had still held the green expectancy of spring – now it was full-blown summer and a lazy heat overlaid the fields and the winding roads.

Never in his life had Slater felt as happy or as at ease with a woman as he did with Eve. The week's leave would come to an end and they would have to distance themselves from each other and there would be new assignments and dangers, but for the moment she was his and he was hers.

Wanting to express something of this he pulled the car over under the spreading branches of an oak tree. Switched off the engine. Turned to her in the sudden silence.

She held his gaze. Reached out and touched his cheek. And he knew that there was nothing to say, that the moment said it for them more perfectly than he ever could.

Slowly, they drove on through the warm countryside. 'I guess we should try not to look too . . . together,' said Slater.

'Perhaps if I get into the driving seat that might be a bit more believable,' said Eve. 'And if, when we get there, you thank me for the lift . . .'

'I was going to suggest that perhaps you should give one of the others a lift back,' said Slater. 'I could go back with Leon or someone and then we could meet up back in London.'

Unwillingly, she conceded that this was a good idea. 'You're not going back with Chris, though. My spies tell me that you and she made a very convincing couple in Paris – snogging on street corners and all sorts.'

'Snogging's a bit of an exaggeration,' Slater protested. 'She was just showing me how to be convincingly French.'

'Oh well,' said Eve, 'that makes all the difference. The next time you catch someone with his hand up my jumper and my tongue down his throat I'll remind you of it. Don't make such a fuss, I'll say, he was just showing me—'

'I didn't have my hand up Chris's jumper,' said Slater. 'And she didn't have her tongue—'

'I know,' said Eve. 'I was just teasing you. As you've probably guessed, Chris is more of a girl's girl.'

'Really!' said Slater, interested.

Eve rolled her eyes heavenwards. 'Just why is it that you men find all that so *endlessly* fascinating? I wish I hadn't told you now.'

'But you have told me,' said Slater. 'And it's going to make my French lessons even more exciting.'

'Shut up and swap places. We're going to be there any minute.'

Ridley met them at the door in a cricket shirt and an ancient pair of grey flannels. Shaking Slater's hand and throwing an avuncular arm around Eve's shoulder, he led them into the cool, stone-flagged hall, where Leon and Terry were drinking beer from pewter tankards.

'I was just saying to the others,' Ridley began, 'that if this service gave medals to agents in the field you'd all be in line for one. It was a particularly nasty job, and I understand from Manderson that you handled it with great courage. Jolly well done. Drink?'

'Thanks,' said Eve. 'I'll have a glass of that Pimm's.'

Slater accepted a beer.

'Something of a baptism of fire for you, Neil.'

'It went a bit pear-shaped towards the end. We lost a good man.'

Ridley nodded. 'Andreas, yes. He'll be a great loss. We'll have to think about who's going to take his place. Perhaps you might have some recommendations – we always ask existing members of the Cadre whom they suggest before casting our net wider.' He smiled and turned to Slater. 'Talking of which, you must come fishing again. There are some very wily old trout hiding in that river.'

'If you can't lure them out, sir, I'm sure I wouldn't be able to.'

'Don't be too sure, Neil. Your lateral approach may succeed where my more traditional tactics have failed. I've always thought that espionage and fishing go hand in hand. Both are essentially concerned with what happens beneath the surface, with what happens in the . . . let's call it the realm of the invisible.'

'Well, I'd be happy to give it a go,' smiled Slater. He turned to Terry and Leon. 'Do you lads fish?'

'I used to do a bit of match angling,' said Terry. 'Hours and hours on end sitting at the side of a canal smoking roll-ups. Then I found I was doing pretty much the same thing at work on surveillance details. It made for a bit of a sedentary lifestyle, so' – he indicated the back of his voluminous bowling shirt, which had the words 'Bali-Hai Casuals, Romford' on it – 'I took up darts instead.'

They all laughed, and Leon explained that he had been something of a fast bowler in his youth. Cricket, however, had not been one of the sports practised by the second parachute regiment of the Foreign Legion, and his skills had rusted. Now he was a member of an Aikido Club, and practised the art of combat with Samurai swords.

'Real Samurai swords?' asked Slater.

'Wooden ones,' said Leon. 'And you know something? I'm crap!'

A popping of gravel announced Chris's arrival. Like Terry she drove a neutral-toned Honda Accord – the classically invisible, reliable surveillance vehicle. She looked jazzier than usual, however, in an Ellis-style leather jacket and with her hair slicked back.

'Stop *staring*!' Eve hissed, kicking Slater smartly in the shins. '*Honestly*, you're like a sixteen-year-old!'

'Would you like a drink?' Ridley politely asked Chris. 'Or to employ the most depressing words in the English language, shall we go straight through?'

Lunch – a cold salmon – was served by Ridley himself,

so that they could all speak freely. And they did, recounting to Ridley the bizarre, horrifying and occasionally hilarious details of the operation. The Miko Pasquale sequence, in particular, seemed to amuse the old spymaster.

'Malt whisky at gunpoint,' he smiled. 'I can think of several colleagues from the old days who could have downed a bottle of twelve-year-old Islay for breakfast and not noticed the difference.'

Slater enjoyed himself, and enjoyed the company of the others. He felt that he had been accepted as a full member of the Cadre, rather than a probationer. They were a very mixed bunch, who under any other circumstances would probably never have met, but the surreal nature of their professional lives bound them together.

After lunch, which the housekeeper arrived to clear, they walked in the watermeadows by the river. The sun shone drowsily down, bees hummed around the thistles, the river-weed shone emerald green in the shadow of the bankside willows and poplars.

There were long periods of silence; while appreciating the beauty of the afternoon, Slater guessed, his colleagues were already wondering what dangers and terrors the future might hold. It was this that hooked you, he reflected – the anticipation of the next operation. And then, of course, once the operation was under way, the only thought was for its successful completion. And so you went on, drawn constantly forward to the next operation, the next adrenaline fix, the next desperate call on your resourcefulness.

'So,' said Chris, beside him. 'How are you feeling?'

'It's all healing,' said Slater. 'The shoulder's a bit stiff and the ribs aren't brilliant when I laugh, but apart from that . . .'

'How about the rest, though?' asked Chris. 'Are you sleeping all right?'

'For the moment, yeah, the nightmares seem to be on hold. Only a question of time, though – they always come sooner or later. Along with the rest of the post-traumatic package. How about you?'

Chris shrugged. 'OK so far, but as you say . . .' She stood still and turned to him. 'When it happens, talk about it, OK? To me, or Leon, or whoever. We're all in the same boat, and we all go off our heads from time to time.'

Slater nodded appreciatively. 'Thanks. I'll do that. And likewise if you're . . .'

'OK.'

They walked for a moment in silence.

'What are you doing for the week off?' Slater asked eventually.

'Oh, this and that,' said Chris. 'Nothing special. You?'

'Same,' said Slater. 'This and that.'

They both smiled. Looking around them, they saw that the dark shadow of a cloud was spreading across the water-meadow. Soon, taking their pace from Ridley, they were moving purposefully back towards the village. They just made it back to River House before the first heavy drops of rain began to fall. The arrival of the rain was taken as a signal that the afternoon was at an end, and one by one the Cadre members departed.

'As a cricketer – or at least an ex-cricketer – I want to show you something,' Ridley told Leon before he left, leading him to a photograph by the side of the large fireplace. 'This is the service's cricket team in 1949. We called ourselves the Carlton House Eleven. I made a rather useful opening batsman, as I remember – managed fifty once against the Ministry of Supply, including two sixes!'

'I'm impressed,' Leon smiled, shaking Ridley's hand and waving a general goodbye.

Soon only Eve and Slater remained. Eve requested a word with Ridley in private, and disappearing into his office left Slater in the hall. The sudden silence amplified the insistent beat of the rain on the leaded windows.

His mind on his conversation with Chris, Slater wandered around the room, examining the various books, photographs and stuffed animal trophies. Something nagged at him, some curious un-accountable absence that he couldn't quite put his finger on. He paused for a moment in front of a nineteenth-century photograph, presumably taken in India, in which a dozen languid young officers in pith helmets lounged with polo-sticks on the steps of some official building. The legend 'Walter Ridley, Lieut.'

was legible among the others in faded sepia ink. Next to it an equally browned but slightly more recent photograph showed a man in a Norfolk jacket and breeches landing a salmon with the help of a ghillie. Clearly the father had been something of a sportsman too.

Conscious of the baleful eye of the stuffed pike, Slater approached the mantelpiece to take a closer look at the 1949 Carlton House cricket-team. A dozen men in their late twenties and early thirties, their attitudes not dissimilar to those of the Indian Army officers, disported themselves on the steps of a suburban pavilion. Their caps were various and unmatching – Eton, Harrow, and Winchester predominant among them, Slater guessed – and their wide-cut white trousers were held up in several cases by ties rather than belts.

So which was Ridley? Which was the demon opener who had thrashed the Ministry of Supply's bowling all round the ground? Taking a large magnifying-glass from the mantelpiece he ran it down the line of good-humoured faces. There was a man with a bat over his shoulder, a man touching his cap to the photographer, and a man striking a vaudeville pose in a pair of wicket-keeping gloves. Next to the wicket-keeper, sardonic beneath a floppy sun-hat, was Hauptmann Dietrich Wegner.

Lowering the magnifying glass, Slater took an involuntary step back. He was mistaken. It was impossible.

Slowly, he readdressed the photograph. The face was Ridley's. A younger Ridley, a Ridley without the moustache, a Ridley he would not have recognised if he hadn't been looking for him – but the face was also Dietrich Wegner's.

His heart pounding, Slater went from wall to wall, examining the photographs. He found three more of Ridley as an adult – among a group in evening dress at a reception, standing with several other men in tweeds on a grouse-moor, sharing a picnic from the boot of a Range Rover at a race meeting – but as he had subconsciously noted earlier, none of Ridley as a child or teenager. No family groups. No tottering first steps across a lawn, no buckets and spades on the beach, no sports days or tree-climbing or messing about in boats.

Lifting the framed photograph of the cricket team from the wall, unwilling to believe the evidence of his eyes but knowing deep down that he was right, Slater carried it to the window. No wonder Ridley – or should he say Wegner – had wanted the disc returned. No wonder it been so imperative that it be kept from the hands of the Serbs. Did the Ondine system even exist, or had the sole purpose of Firewall been to suppress the truth about the old spymaster's identity?

When Ridley came out of his office Slater was staring out of the window with the framed photograph in his lap.

Looking the younger man in the eye, Ridley smiled philosophically and slowly nodded. Behind him was Eve, expressionless.

'You're a good man, Neil. A clever man. We're lucky to have you.'

Slater placed the photograph and the magnifying glass on the side table.

'Where did you go to school, Mr Ridley?'

Ridley laughed. 'Dogs sniff each other's bottoms. Englishmen ask each other where they went to school. Congratulations, Neil.'

Slater nodded at Eve. 'She told you I saw the pictures?'

'She told me.'

'And you admit that you're Dietrich Wegner?'

'I concede that many lifetimes ago I was a man named Dietrich Wegner. But we reinvent ourselves, Neil. We reinvent ourselves.'

'So everyone keeps telling me. Yesterday I was talking to a woman who said that when she was a seven-year-old concentration camp prisoner your *Ustashe* friends cut her ears off. Not much chance of her reinventing herself, I'd have said.'

'Needs must, Neil. There is reason and logic to the life I have led.'

Slater felt a cold rage expanding within him. 'Forgetting for the moment that the five of us who were here today have risked our lives for a lie, and that a fortnight ago a brave soldier died for that lie, can you give me one good reason why I shouldn't go straight to the newspapers and tell them that there is an ex-Nazi at the heart of British Intelligence?'

Ridley looked him straight in the eye. 'Yes. The

short answer is that I can. Give me an hour, and if at the end of that I haven't convinced you then you are welcome to walk out of here and tell whomsoever you please. If you want money, you can go to Max Clifford. If you want revenge, I'd recommend Alan Rusbridger of the *Guardian*. I've got both of their home numbers.'

Slater stared back at him, speechless at the man's nerve.

'Well, what about it?'

Slowly, Slater nodded. 'OK, you're on. Sixty minutes.' Undoing his watch, he placed it on the table next to the photograph.

'Eve, my dear,' said Ridley, his eyes still on Slater. 'Would it be very un-PC to ask you to go into the kitchen and make us all a pot of tea? The Lapsang would be nice.'

'I joined the SS in 1939 when I was eighteen. I came from Gotha, in the Thüringer Wald. And believe me, Neil, if you had been that age, and in that place at that time, you would have done the same. What did Wordsworth say? "Bliss was it in that dawn to be alive, But to be young was very heaven"!

'At the time of the invasion of France I was attached to an SS Panzer division in the Ardennes – the *Totenkopf*. Real soldiering, Neil, against a determined and honourable enemy – I remember an engagement against the Algerian Dismounted Light Cavalry which . . . Anyway, having been wounded in the arm and briefly hospitalised – my left arm, you'll be glad to hear, rather than my fly-casting arm – I was recalled to Berlin late in 1940 and sent on an intelligence course. Speaking good French as I did, I had had some success with the interrogation of prisoners – a complicit smile, I found, tended to accomplish more than a Schmeisser butt to the base of the skull – and the fact had been noticed.

'In the summer of the next year I was reassigned to Army Group E, stationed in the Balkans. My task, I was told, was to secure intelligence concerning the activities of partisans.

'The counter-partisan system I found in place was draconian. Reprisals for attacks on German troops and property were immediate, with a hundred Yugoslav males rounded up and machine-gunned for every German killed.

'Up to a point this policy was working. The main thorns in our side were a Serbian royalist named Dreza Mihailovic, whose followers were called Chetniks, and a half-Slovene, half-Croatian communist called Josip Broz. Mihailovic, who realised that public opinion would turn against him if his Chetniks' exploits caused the execution of thousands of civilians, decided to wind down his resistance activities and wait for the Allies to invade. Effectively, he was brought to heel by the reprisals policy, and by 1943 many of his Chetniks were openly collaborating with their German hosts.

'Broz, who used the alias Tito, was a different proposition altogether. Rightly or wrongly he considered that the reprisals policy would simply make loyal Yugoslavs hate the Germans even more. He resisted, and resisted hard. His orders came from Stalin, and his followers – quarter of a million strong by the end – came from all sections of Yugoslav society. He was a much tougher nut than Mihailovic, and ultimately we never cracked him.

'But we tried. We tried very hard indeed. I was attached to a unit simply known as 1c, based at a place named Kostajnica, and my brief ultimately contracted to one essential task: I had to insert Yugoslavian informers into Tito's partisan army. We had to know what his intentions were because, to be frank, he was getting the better of us. By 1942 it was clear that the reprisals policy, while discouraging Mihailovic, had failed. We were imprisoning the partisans, we were shooting them, there were corpses hanging at every roadside . . . It was a nightmare, frankly, and a very unpleasant atmosphere in which to work. Ah, this looks like our tea. And crumpets! Eve, you're a miracle-worker. Shall I be mother?'

'Now, where was I?' he asked two minutes later. 'Yes, in Kostajnica, where I had an inspired idea. An idea which became Operation *Senfsamen*, or Mustard-Seed. A few miles down the road was the *Ustashe*-run concentration camp of Jasenovac. It was a disgrace, frankly – a complete butcher's shop – and we and the Italians complained about it constantly. Having said that, there was an element of *real-politik*. The *Ustashe* were animals, but they were *our* animals, and we couldn't afford to be too choosy about whom we used.

'I took to visiting Jasenovac, ostensibly for observation purposes. The place was run by a series of maniacal sadists and psychopaths – the most extreme being a Catholic priest named Filipovic. Now I . . . "befriended" is not the right word, but I made a point of getting to know Filipovic and his successor, whose name was Sakic. They were both terrifyingly unbalanced and clearly took a deep pleasure in the pain and suffering that they caused, but for my plan to work I had to have them on my side.

'I got them there, basically, by pretending to be like them. I visited that hell-on-earth with a regularity that implied I couldn't keep away. And after a time no one took any notice of me.

'Now the camp was on a river – the Sava river – and opposite was a place called Gradina. Gradina was where the executions were carried out. Not the random killings that were a feature of everyday life at Jasenovac but the planned, systematic shootings and throat-cuttings which were carried out in groups.

'What I used to do was to monitor the execution parties when they were led off the ferry that had brought them over the river to Gradina. If I thought that any of the condemned men might pass muster as a soldier and a partisan – and not many did, most had the dull-eyed look of men who have given up all hope – I had him unchained and brought over to me. Was he prepared to spit on the face of Tito, I asked him? Was he, in return for his life, prepared to throw in his lot with the conquering armies of the Fatherland?

'Well, sometimes he was and sometimes he wasn't, and to this day I am amazed by the courage shown by those who refused. They knew why they had been brought across the river and as often as not they could hear the shots from the execution field. But still they said no, and I informed them that I considered them to be brave men and returned them to the guards.

'Others, for a combination of reasons, said yes. They were Chetniks, they hated Tito, they hated communists, they thought that Germany would win the war – I heard every possible reason. But mostly they were frightened for their lives and would have said anything to be allowed to leave that grim procession.

'I took them back to Kostajnica, trained them in espionage procedures and fieldcraft, and turned them loose. Some of my mustard-seeds fell on stony ground, and I never heard from them again. Some were identified as spies by the partisans and killed. But others had their cover-stories accepted and were integrated into Tito's organisation – they took root, you might say – and slowly the network grew to the point where an entire 1c department was devoted to the collating and assessment of "Mustard-Seed" data. It was, if I say so myself, an operation of some elegance.

'Unfortunately, despite some spectacular intelligence coups, it did not win us the battle for Yugoslavia, let alone the war, but by 1945 the ground was already being cleared for a much more important struggle – the struggle of the free world against communism.

'By the end of the war I was no longer the idealistic young SS lieutenant who had marched into France with the *Totenkopf* division. I was twenty-four years old, but I felt twice that age. For more than three years I had quite literally walked in the Valley of Death, and I had played a key role in one of the most savage and brutal guerrilla campaigns ever waged. When Army Group E was finally forced to retreat from Yugoslavia – the alternative being to surrender to the communists – a colleague and I were sent to contact the British Army, which was on the outskirts of Trieste. We both spoke reasonable Serbo-Croat, so it was thought that we had a good chance of getting through.

'I got through. It was a nightmare journey, and I was almost starving by the time I reached the British lines. My colleague didn't make it, and ended up in Klagenfurt in southern Austria, which by then had been appropriated by Tito.

'At Trieste, after being badly beaten by the patrol to which I had given myself up, I had the great good fortune to be interrogated by a British Field Security officer who immediately saw the value of the names and the knowledge that I carried in my head, and sent me on to the Intelligence Corps HQ at Bad Sulzuflen, outside Iserlohn. There, I met the man who was to be the instrument of my renaissance. His name was Captain Robert Maxwell, MC.

'Maxwell, who was born in Czechoslovakia and

spoke perfect German as well as Russian and half a dozen other languages, debriefed me over the course of several days in November 1945. In May, six months earlier, the CROWCASS list had been published. This was the Central Registry of War Crimes and Security Suspects – and I, along with several of my colleagues from 1c, was on it. My crime, or my so-called crime, was murder of partisans – an accusation relating to my having ordered the execution of Yugoslavian citizens. This was not in fact strictly accurate. My responsibility as an intelligence officer had been to identify and arrest partisans, and it fell to others to process those found guilty. That said, of course, history is always written by the victors, and the victors in this case were Tito's communists.

'Maxwell and I spent several days together, and without naming names I told him about Operation Mustard-Seed. I had a dozen agents within Tito's organisation, I told him, and a couple in his inner circle. These agents, I continued, could be persuaded into providing information on the regime almost indefinitely by the threat of exposure as former Nazi informers.

'Like all sensible men at that time, Maxwell was looking forwards rather than backwards. In common with the rest of his colleagues in the intelligence services, he was convinced that Europe should be bracing itself against communist invasion, and that Yugoslavia was Stalin's probable launch-pad into Europe. The offer of raw intelligence from a source as sensitive as the "Mustard-Seed" network was too good to pass up.

'And of course he was also looking forwards at his own future. He was already planning the publishing empire that would make him a vast fortune, but he needed a helping hand, both financially and in terms of contacts. A major catch such as I represented at the time would strongly predispose MI6 to come to his aid. As indeed they did. And I . . . let's just say that I was in a position to point him towards some sources of funds too.

'Robert and I understood each other perfectly. By the end of that week there was an unspoken agreement between us that we would, let us say, *keep an eye* on each other's careers.'

'And you did,' said Slater.

'And we did,' agreed Ridley. 'Although it would be some years before we saw each other again. I was officially arrested as a CROWCASS suspect, then sent to a military hospital at Magdeburg, where I was admitted as an isolation patient before "dying" of tuberculosis. I was certified dead, carried out feet first beneath a sheet, and driven to Berlin, from where I was flown to Croydon Airport.

'The rest, if you like, is history. I spent nine months being debriefed at a service safe-house in Hertfordshire, where a "legend" was prepared for me and I assumed my new identity as John Ridley. I have the advantage of a near-perfect photographic memory, and was able to reproduce intact every detail of the

"Mustard-Seed" files I kept at Kostajnica. The information was relayed to the MI6 station in Vienna, and used to mount a major intelligence operation against Tito. It was superbly effective. MI6 was warned in advance about Tito's break from Stalin, and was able to take advantage of this knowledge to help lever Austria into declaring its support for the West.'

Ridley smiled. 'And that's about it, really. The rest of my career is a matter of service record. The bare bones of it are that I served in Hong Kong, Oslo, Sofia and Moscow, came home to the Russia desk, and set up the Cadre. Rather than marry – a security risk I could not afford – I have dedicated my life to the service. In short, I have been a loyal and tireless servant of my adopted country.'

He spread his hands and reached for Slater's wristwatch. 'And that's about it. I've been talking to you for forty-five minutes. Do I have a stay of execution?'

Slowly, a little uncomfortably, Slater nodded.

'As I said, Neil, you are an intelligent man, and intelligent men ask searching questions. I would expect no less of you.'

Standing, Slater returned the photograph of the cricket team to its place beside the fire.

'I know that there are questions that I haven't answered,' said Ridley. 'Might I suggest that I do so while we enjoy the last of this sunshine?'

The rain, Slater saw, had stopped.

The landscape shone.

'Wellingtons, if you need them, by the front door,' said Ridley.

'Maxwell and I met from time to time over the years,' he continued, as they crossed the field to the river, leaving dark tracks behind them in the wet grass. 'Lunch at the Travellers' Club, the odd Foreign Office dinner, that sort of thing. There were small favours I was able to do for him and for his newspapers, and vice-versa. We were both, in different ways, aliens at the heart of the British establishment, and the fact amused us.

'By the end of the eighties, however, we had more or less lost contact. I had officially retired, while he had been swallowed up with the day-to-day concerns of the Mirror Group. I was aware, however – as most of us in the intelligence community were – that things were not well in his world, and by 1991 it was obvious that his empire was unravelling in front of his eyes. In October of that year he played one last desperate card. He contacted an associate of his whom he knew the service did business with – an arms-dealer and general fixer named Antoine Fanon-Khayat.

'A Serbian pressure group, he said, had contacted him with a view to publicising *Ustashe* atrocities committed during World War Two. They had photographs showing murders of civilians and Orthodox priests and scenes from Jasenovac, Stara Gradiska, Jadovna and other sites. He had viewed the material and noted that half a dozen of the photographs showed the man whom he had helped to become a British citizen, namely myself.

'In the first instance, I think, his motives in buying up the pictures were purely those of hiding his own part in my rebirth. If it was discovered that he had facilitated the integration of an ex-Nazi into the British civil service his rivals would have slaughtered him. But buy them up he did – every print, every negative. It probably cost the Mirror Group a hundred thousand pounds, for which I'm sure Serbia was duly grateful.

'I honestly believe that it was only when he was really on the skids that he decided to try and blackmail MI6 into bailing him out, and by then his judgement was all over the place. He basically paid Fanon-Khayat to broker the deal. In return for the pictures incriminating me and tarring MI6 with the Nazi brush, he wanted to be paid tens of millions of dollars in cash, bonds and bullion. Really crazy stuff.

'Fanon-Khayat, at that time very much MI6's man, presented Maxwell's case to Manderson, who handled him at the time, and then immediately disassociated himself from it. He claimed he merely wanted to warn the service of the existence of the pictures, and handed over the photocopies, which Manderson destroyed.

'So what still existed, Manderson asked? What did Fanon-Khayat still have?

'One set of prints, said Fanon-Khayat. The negatives had long since disappeared. The prints travelled with Maxwell, from safe to safe.

'Well, Manderson thanked Fanon-Khayat, paid him

for his trouble, and called me and a couple of other people in. It was clear that Maxwell was a very loose cannon indeed. We could raid his safe and take the pictures, but that would probably just force his hand. We had to go all the way.'

'The SBS guys,' whispered Slater, amazed. 'You mounted a hit using the SBS guys. My predecessor – what was his name, Bernie – was one of the pair who took out Robert Maxwell. That's unbelievable.'

'Believable or not, we did it. We eliminated Maxwell, removed the material from the safe, and covered our tracks. A classic Cadre operation.'

'And let me guess,' said Slater. 'Fanon-Khayat made a copy. A few years later he's in trouble and decides to throw in his hand with the RDB. Doesn't hand the pictures over, just tells them he's got them, suggests they can use them to negotiate with MI6 . . .'

'Exactly,' said Ridley. 'And the rest you know. I'm sorry we used your loyalty to the SAS to persuade you into action, but at that stage you were still . . .' He smiled. 'Let's just say that at that stage we didn't know you as well as we know you now.'

Slater shook his head, trying to absorb all that he had been told. They had reached a stile between two of the rain-sodden fields, and he came to a halt. 'There's something I still don't understand.'

'Go on,' said Ridley.

'Four years ago, or was it five, you sent Ellis out to investigate Fanon-Khayat and she reported that he was clean, that things weren't going so well for him but he was still our man. So why did Fanon-Khayat have Ellis killed? And how was Ellis – a highly switched-on agent, by all accounts – lured into a car-park and whacked by a bunch of hired Parisian thugs? What happened?'

There was silence. Ridley glanced at Eve.

Slater looked from one to the other of them – from the visibly frail figure of Ridley to Eve, who was staring regretfully and without focus over the brimming river – and a cold certainty gripped his heart. 'You set her up, didn't you? She thought she was coming to that car-park to meet a friend – to make a report or to be pulled out – and instead . . . No wonder they got the jump on her. And no wonder her killers were all taken out afterwards.'

Slater's head swam, and he reached for the wet timbers of the stile. 'I'm right, aren't I?' he said. 'You had Ellis killed.'

Eve said nothing.

Ridley frowned. 'Fanon-Khayat told Ellis about my former life – trying to impress her, I suppose – and she just couldn't deal with it. She met Manderson in Paris and told him she wanted to leave, that it had all become too much for her. She could no longer handle life in the Cadre, she said, and she intended to go public with the reasons why. In many ways, for all her professionalism, she was a very naive woman.'

Slater stared at him, incredulous. 'Just where do you people draw the line, for fuck's sake? Ellis was a Cadre member. She was one of your own.'

'Oh, please!' said Eve irritably, forcing her hands into the cartridge-pockets of her Barbour coat. 'Let's get real. We had no choice in the matter. We were at war. We *are* at war, and anyone who threatens our survival is the enemy.'

'Manderson will be retiring shortly,' Ridley continued, 'and Eve will be taking over the Cadre.' He placed a hand lightly on her shoulder. 'I suspect she would be very glad to have you at her side.'

'I would,' she said.

'You killed Ellis,' said Slater quietly. 'When would you kill me?'

'Neil,' she said gently. 'You are one of us – a soldier and a true believer. You made your choice long ago – long before I met you – and you confirmed that choice the night you rang me. "I am what I am", you told me.'

Neil Slater looked around him. Swallows dipped and swooped at the flies that danced over the river's surface. A faint vapour hung over the rain-heavy fields. Beyond them, he knew, waited only the Darklands and the crowding ghosts of the men he had killed. Was that Joey Delaney there, with his child's eyes and half his head shot away?

He was who he was.

'Let's talk about replacing Andreas,' he began.

THE POWER OF READING

Visit the Random House website and get connected with information on all our books and authors

EXTRACTS from our recently published books and selected backlist titles

COMPETITIONS AND PRIZE DRAWS Win signed books, audiobooks and more

AUTHOR EVENTS Find out which of our authors are on tour and where you can meet them

LATEST NEWS on bestsellers, awards and new publications

MINISITES with exclusive special features dedicated to our authors and their titles

READING GROUPS Reading guides, special features and all the information you need for your reading group

LISTEN to extracts from the latest audiobook publications

WATCH video clips of interviews and readings with our authors

RANDOM HOUSE INFORMATION including advice for writers, job vacancies and all your general queries answered

Come home to Random House
www.rbooks.co.uk